Meet Me
at Sunset

Carol Kirkwood is one of our most loved TV personalities. Millions of viewers and listeners know her for her weather reports on *BBC Breakfast* and Wimbledon fortnight, and for waltzing into our hearts on *Strictly Come Dancing*. Carol was inspired to write her first book by her passion for travel and her love of Hollywood glamour. Her novels *Under a Greek Moon*, *The Hotel on the Riviera* and *Secrets of the Villa Amore* all reached the *Sunday Times* bestseller list. Off-screen, Carol loves walking with her husband in the countryside near their home and planning their next holiday to somewhere exciting.

To find out more about Carol Kirkwood:

f OfficialCarolKirkwood

X @carolkirkwood

Also by Carol Kirkwood

Under a Greek Moon
The Hotel on the Riviera
Secrets of the Villa Amore
Once Upon a Time in Venice

Carol Kirkwood

Meet Me *at* Sunset

HarperCollins*Publishers*

HarperCollins*Publishers* Ltd
1 London Bridge Street,
London SE1 9GF

www.harpercollins.co.uk

HarperCollins*Publishers*
Macken House, 39/40 Mayor Street Upper
Dublin 1, D01 C9W8, Ireland

First published by HarperCollins*Publishers* Ltd 2025
1

Copyright © Carol Kirkwood 2025

Carol Kirkwood asserts the moral right to
be identified as the author of this work

A catalogue record for this book is available from the British Library

ISBN: 978-0-00-871583-0 (HB)
ISBN: 978-0-00-871584-7 (TPB)

This novel is a work of fiction.
References to real people, events, establishments, organizations, or locales
are intended only to provide a sense of authenticity, and are used fictitiously.
All other characters, and all incidents and dialogue, are drawn from the
author's imagination and are not to be construed as real.

Set in Meridien by Palimpsest Book Production Limited, Falkirk, Stirlingshire

Printed and bound in the UK using 100% Renewable Electricity by
CPI Group (UK) Ltd

All rights reserved. No part of this publication may be
reproduced, stored in a retrieval system, or transmitted,
in any form or by any means, electronic, mechanical,
photocopying, recording or otherwise, without the prior written
permission of the publishers.

Without limiting the exclusive rights of any author, contributor or the
publisher of this publication, any unauthorised use of this publication to
train generative artificial intelligence (AI) technologies is expressly prohibited.
HarperCollins also exercise their rights under Article 4(3) of the Digital Single
Market Directive 2019/790 and expressly reserve this publication from the
text and data mining exception.

This book contains FSC™ certified paper and other controlled sources
to ensure responsible forest management.

For more information visit: www.harpercollins.co.uk/green

I dedicate this book to everyone who has helped and supported me on this wonderful literary adventure.

Prologue

When Andre Fontaine had taken the wheel of his car earlier, just as the daylight was fading, full of champagne and post-lunch bonhomie, he'd felt like he had the world at his feet, he was expecting to head back to his chalet in Switzerland to carry on his birthday celebration. It wasn't every day you turned forty-nine, or had so much to celebrate.

His fashion brand with his wife Camille had been the talk of the catwalk that spring, their most recent collection had been worn by some of the most famous fashion icons around the world. Andre could buy whatever he wanted and go wherever suited him; he had a talented, dynamic wife and a son who was growing into a fine man – a son he adored. Life couldn't be better.

Perhaps he and Camille argued more these days than they used to when they were first married, when their passionate disagreements were quickly forgotten in the heat of their equally fervent lovemaking. Andre knew he could be difficult, mercurial some said, and maybe not the faithful husband he should be. It was all part of the image, the legend of the Camille Andre fashion brand. Extraordinary people do extraordinary things, he would have said in return – we don't live by conventional rules.

But Andre could neither speak nor move now. He lay shattered by the side of his treasured Ferrari sports car, and his flickering thoughts were of his only son Lucas, who had been sitting next to him in the car, and who Andre could distantly perceive was still caught in his seat. Trapped. Possibly dead.

If only Andre had listened to Camille. *You indulge him too much, Andre . . .*

Andre's broken body and mind clung to what life was left to him in the silence of the empty mountain road, but he could feel that life slipping away and now Andre was starting to drift far above the scene. He felt detached from his body, as light as air, able to see big things and little things; the snow-covered tops of the Swiss mountains; a swift darting through the pine trees, its black and white wings flickering like quicksilver; the melting teardrops of crystal-clear icicles falling from the branch of a tree.

He could also see the approach of a car, hear a voice he recognized speak to Lucas. Angry voices.

Please don't let my son die.

If only he'd listened. If only he could tell Camille and Lucas how much he loved them both.

But it was too late for words. It was too late for anything now.

Part 1

Chapter 1

Paris, June 2001

Camille Fontaine sashayed through Charles de Gaulle Airport and heads turned. She wasn't a movie star, or a model, but she had a timeless French beauty, and she carried herself with an air of confidence that made people pay attention.

Camille was fifty-one years old but looked a decade younger. She was chic and elegant, in wide-leg linen trousers with a cream silk vest, and her make-up was light, her dark hair pulled back in a smooth chignon. Over one arm she carried a 'Camille' handbag made from the softest lambskin in a classic shade of olive green. The coveted bag was every wealthy woman's must-have – but the difference in this case was that Camille Fontaine owned the company and had named the bag after herself.

'Gate Twenty-Seven, so we're almost there,' said René, Camille's assistant. Exceptionally tall and slim, with angular features and a sweep of blond hair, he hurried along beside her. He was holding a briefcase full of the latest designs she was working on, which were too precious to go in the hold, and a garment bag containing a couture dress from her own label. 'I don't know why you didn't want to fly private – you could have gone direct.'

Camille shook her head. She'd spent the last few days in New York and was now jetting out to the Spanish island of Mallorca to launch her latest collection, making her connecting flight in Paris. 'I don't mind. Besides, first class with Air France is hardly slumming it.'

The airport was busy. Around them business travellers and tourists swarmed and hurried, but a path seemed to magically open up for Camille, allowing her to pass through with ease.

'You must be looking forward to seeing Lucas again,' René commented.

'I am,' Camille agreed, a smile crossing her face at the thought of reuniting with her son. Mallorca was like a second home to Camille – so much so that her son Lucas, a talented chef, had established a restaurant in the beautiful north-west of the island. It had been almost six months since she'd last seen him – he'd spent Christmas with her in Chamonix – and she couldn't wait to catch up on all his news. Since Andre's death, mother and son had grown closer than ever, bound by loss and all too aware of the fragility of life, wanting to make the most of the moments they had together.

Camille and René arrived at the gate and were whisked straight through, past the lines of frazzled holidaymakers and fractious toddlers. Moments later, Camille was sitting in her seat next to René, as an attentive stewardess fussed around them.

'Would you like a glass of champagne, *madame*?'

'Thank you,' Camille accepted graciously. She would have just one glass, then stick to water for the rest of the short flight.

'And may I just say how much I love your bag.' The stewardess was staring at it with unconcealed admiration. 'I've never seen a "Camille" in that colour before. It's so chic.'

'That's very sweet of you, thank you.' Camille was too modest to admit that she was the famous designer behind the brand, but she never grew tired of hearing people say that they loved her products.

A short time later, the captain came over the tannoy to announce their imminent departure, and then they were in the air, bound for sun-drenched Mallorca. Camille gazed out of her window as they flew over the suburbs of Paris, the city where it had all begun for her. It felt like such a long time ago now. Astonishingly, it was over thirty years since she, Andre and Nicolas had all graduated from their respective schools.

Whilst Camille and Andre had fallen in love and founded their fashion label, Camille Andre, their friend Nicolas had taken a different route. He'd always been more interested in the manufacturing side of the fashion business, and now headed up American Athletics, a global, high-street label, insisting on ethical suppliers and revolutionizing the supply chain.

For Camille and Andre, it had taken years of hard work, of blood, sweat and tears, to go from unknown designers with dreams of making it big, to their breakout moment which catapulted them to fame and fortune. The 'Camille' handbag had captured the world's attention and become an instant bestseller, pictured on the arm of everyone who was anyone – from Princess Diana to Naomi Campbell to Julia Roberts. Socialites, singers and starlets all wanted their piece of the Camille magic.

Business had exploded, and the brand was soon in demand on every continent, as they opened shops in every major city across the world. But Camille's life hadn't magically become perfect overnight as she'd imagined it might. Not even vast wealth and international success could shield her from heartbreak and regret . . .

'Is Nicolas flying out to join you?' René asked, his voice neutral. 'I'll add his flights to your diary if so.'

Camille took a fortifying sip of champagne before she answered. 'I don't know what his plans are yet.'

'But he's not going to miss the launch, surely?'

Camille hesitated. 'You know, René, I'm rather tired after that long flight from New York. I'm going to rest for a while.'

'Of course,' René replied smoothly, but Camille knew he understood that she didn't want to talk about it.

She pulled down her sunglasses and leaned back against her seat, letting her head roll to the side, taking in the view from the window. They were over central France now, and below lay a patchwork of fields, dotted with medieval towns and sprawling chateaux.

What Camille had said to René was true – she *was* tired. She had barely slept the previous night, going over and over the conversation she'd had with Nicolas before she left New York.

Meet Me at Sunset

Nicolas Martin had been part of Camille's life for more than thirty years now. He was one of her closest friends, her trusted confidant, and the person she'd turned to after the death of her husband, a shoulder to lean on following the accident that had claimed Andre's life.

How has it come to this?

Camille exhaled sadly, closing her eyes as she recalled every word Nicolas had said to her barely twenty-four hours ago . . .

The two of them were having a late dinner in Nicolas's New York apartment, where Camille had been countless times before. It was a sleek, modern bachelor pad, a penthouse apartment on Fifth Avenue, with a stunning view over the treetops of Central Park to the Upper West Side beyond. Earlier, they'd sat out on Nicolas's glass-walled terrace and watched as the sun set over the Hudson, lighting up the sky in vibrant shades of purple and orange as the rolling clouds streaked away towards New Jersey. Now, the city lights blazed below them, the familiar skyline illuminated against the blackness, with a crescent moon hanging high above. Looking out at that view, it felt to Camille as though they were on top of the world – that they'd achieved everything it was possible to achieve in life.

Nicolas had ordered takeout from Mr Chow, and they were sharing a very expensive bottle of Montrachet. Sade was playing on the state-of-the-art Bang & Olufsen stereo system, and the dimmed lighting flattered Nicolas's features. He was tall and well built, with light brown hair peppered with the odd grey, and deep green eyes the colour of fir trees. Despite his corporate lifestyle, Nicolas's body was in excellent shape, and he was undoubtedly an attractive man, with a steely determination and quiet confidence that Camille had always found seductive.

They'd been discussing the upcoming collaboration between Camille Andre and the American Athletics brand, which would launch in Mallorca the following week. It would be the first time Camille Andre had ever undertaken a venture like this, working with a high-street line to offer a diffusion range, and Camille was nervous about the new direction. Nicolas had been encouraging and reassuring, as always, assuring her that companies had to move forward and take risks, or else they would stagnate. She trusted his instincts – his business acumen was second to none and had made him a very rich man over the years, with shrewd investments and perfectly timed exits. His words chimed with something more fundamental within her too – that *she* needed to move forward and take risks.

Since her husband's death, Camille had closed herself off, unwilling or unable to commit herself fully to anyone else. Nicolas had stepped into the void left by Andre's departure – he'd become her best friend, her confidant, her lover – but although she knew he adored her, something held her back from giving her whole heart to him. In recent months, she'd sensed his frustration with the situation, and she could feel his emotions had been rising to the surface in recent weeks. Now, as they finished their meal and drained their wine glasses, Camille sensed a shift in the air that she couldn't quite put her finger on. Nicolas looked at her for a long moment, before standing up from the black lacquer dining table and pushing back his chair.

Camille's pulse began to race, her sixth sense telling

her that something significant was happening, as he walked over to the high gloss cabinet and slid open the top drawer, taking out a small box.

Time seemed to speed up as the next moment Nicolas was on one knee in front of her, an antique ring with an enormous diamond winking at her from where it sat nestled on a bed of black velvet.

'Camille . . .' Nicolas began, gazing at her intently. Camille found she could hardly bear to look in his deep green eyes, at the hope and trepidation and love contained within them.

'Nicolas—'

'Marry me,' he said, his words spilling out in a rush. 'You know I adore you, and—'

'Nicolas, please get up,' Camille murmured.

'Just listen to me,' he insisted, his face resolute with intention. 'You know there's never been anyone else but you. I love you, Camille. I'm crazy about you. It should always have been us, and you know it.'

'Please . . .' Camille closed her eyes and pressed a hand to her forehead. *This can't be happening.* She would have given anything to rewind time by five minutes and put a stop to this passionate declaration. But Nicolas was still speaking.

'I've asked you before, but I'm deadly serious this time. I know you love me too.'

Camille opened her eyes and looked down at him, a stricken expression on her face. She loved him, undoubtedly, but *marriage?* She'd known deep inside her she'd have to make this decision one day, that Nicolas would want to seal the deal and put their relationship on a permanent footing. But she had always pushed away the notion, preferring to exist in the moment and continue as they were.

'But aren't we happy as we are?' she pleaded. 'Why do we need to change things? Who cares about a piece of paper?'

'*I* care. I want the world to see us together – I don't want to be kept in the background like some dirty little secret.'

'Nicolas—'

'I've loved you for thirty years, Camille. We should never have waited so long. This is our moment. Let's seize it.'

Camille swallowed. She didn't want to do this; he was putting her in an impossible position. 'You're right,' she said quietly, her voice thick with emotion. 'We *have* waited too long . . . And now it's too late. Our time has passed.'

'What are you saying?'

'I can't marry you. It's impossible. Please, Nicolas, for Christ's sake, get up.'

Nicolas stood slowly, confusion and hurt written across his handsome face. He closed the box and placed it on the table beside their empty plates. Now his shock had hardened into something else.

'This is the last time I'm going to ask you, Camille. I mean it. If you say no, then it's over between us.'

'Don't make me do this . . .' Camille was angry, the fight-or-flight instinct kicking in as she jumped to her feet, longing to run out of his apartment and never look back. She felt as though Nicolas had backed her into a corner. Too much had happened between them over the years for her to hide her feelings from him. Nicolas deserved the truth. 'Why can't things just stay as they are?'

'Because I can't live like this!' he roared, dragging his hands through his hair in despair. 'I love you. I want to be with you. Please, Camille.' His tone had changed now, and there was an undertone of anguish in his voice. 'Marry me.'

Camille shook her head, angry tears coursing down her cheeks, agonized that it had come to this, but furious with Nicolas for ruining the relationship they'd enjoyed for the past three decades. 'I'm sorry, Nicolas, but I can't marry you . . .'

'We're beginning our descent into Palma, where the temperature is a very pleasant 26 degrees, and the captain has now switched on the seatbelt sign . . .'

The announcement cut into Camille's thoughts, jolting her back to the present. She realized she was clutching the strap of her handbag so tightly that her knuckles had turned white, as though her life depended on not letting go. Perhaps her life *did* depend on it. This bag, and everything it represented – her business, her achievements, her life's work – needed to be her priority right now. Whatever else was going on in her life, Camille could always come back to her designs. It was her true passion, the one thing – aside from her son – that gave her unbridled joy, and it was where she needed to direct her focus.

She'd done the right thing by saying no to Nicolas, Camille reassured herself. Yes, she might be hurt and in pain now, uncertain of what the future would bring, but the sadness would pass, and Camille knew it. She'd been through misery and grief and come out the other side – battle-scarred but stronger than ever.

She had been alone before, Camille reminded herself, as the plane touched down on the runway at Palma de Mallorca Airport. She had survived, and she would do it again.

Chapter 2

Mallorca, June 2001

The journey from Palma Airport to Cala de la Belleza, in the north-west of the island, took less than forty-five minutes. Isobel and Stuart MacFarlane were travelling in style, in a luxurious black Mercedes provided by their hotel, the Palacio del Sol Radiante.

'Makes a change from back home, doesn't it, darling?' Stuart said, in his rich Scottish burr, reaching across to place a hand on Isobel's knee.

'It's beautiful.' She gazed out of the window as the two of them were transported through the spectacular scenery, with rugged, sun-bleached mountains soaring around them and warm, golden light slicing through the Aleppo pine trees. It had been drizzling when they had left Edinburgh Airport that morning, and although Isobel loved Scotland, the weather sometimes left a lot to be desired.

'*You're* beautiful,' Stuart replied, and Isobel couldn't

help but smile at her husband's sweet words. At forty-two, Stuart was a decade older than her, but as far as Isobel was concerned, he was in his prime. His sandy-coloured hair had yet to see its first strands of grey, and the fine lines around his eyes merely served to give him character. Regular gym workouts ensured he stayed in buff shape.

Isobel turned back to the view as the winding road continued through idyllic villages, with green-shuttered, honey-coloured houses swathed in a profusion of bright pink bougainvillea, church bells chiming midday. The air was delicately scented with a heady mix of the herbs and plants that flourished on the rocky slopes: rosemary, lavender, thyme and sweet genista.

Isobel could feel her shoulders beginning to drop, her whole body starting to relax. She and Stuart led busy lives back in Edinburgh. He was an extremely well-regarded and successful plastic surgeon, who owned thriving practices in both London and Edinburgh. He regularly travelled between the two, though his consulting work took him all over the world.

'And I love your dress,' Stuart continued. 'Is it one of your own?'

'Yes, it is one of my designs,' Isobel smiled, pleased with the compliment. The dress was bias-cut and clung to her figure, with fluted sleeves and a sweetheart neckline. The buttercup yellow colour complemented her fair complexion, and she'd left her long, thick, honey-blonde hair loose, to tumble in soft waves down her back.

'You're so talented, darling. I've always said it.'

'Thank you,' Isobel replied quietly. She knew that Stuart had nothing but the best of intentions with his praise, but his words touched a nerve. She, too, considered herself a talented designer, but her career had never taken off in the way that she would have liked.

At least he was being less insensitive than he had been the previous evening. He'd arrived home late, quickly taking a shower, while she'd been making sure they were packed and ready for travel the next day. In the bespoke, Shaker-style kitchen, the fridge was almost empty ahead of their holiday, but Isobel had nipped to M&S that morning, and quickly rustled up the grilled salmon and a fresh green salad she'd bought. Mindful of her last-minute holiday diet, she served herself a small plate with no dressing, and she was pouring two perfectly chilled glasses of Chablis when Stuart walked in. His hair was still damp, and he looked relaxed in chinos and a polo shirt.

'Thank you, darling, this is perfect,' he smiled, helping her to carry the plates through to their elegant dining room. 'Only a small portion for you?' he added, raising an eyebrow.

'A last-minute attempt to shift a few pounds,' Isobel said ruefully.

'Oh, you don't need to do that. I mean, I know all those models look great, but it's not what men really want. Anyway, I like you with a bit more meat on your bones,' Stuart laughed, as he squeezed the soft flesh above her hips.

Isobel had wriggled out of his reach, irritated by his flippant comments. 'Well, it's not up to you,' she told him, as she sat down and defiantly speared a forkful of lettuce. 'It's about how I feel. And if I want to lose weight, I'll do it for myself.'

'Of course, darling,' he said, as he reached over and patted her hand. 'Whatever you want.'

Isobel's irritation simmered to the surface again, though Stuart always seemed oblivious. *Drop it, Isobel*, she told herself, not wanting anything to ruin their holiday.

Despite training at the prestigious Central St Martins in London, followed by internships with high fashion brands in Milan, Madrid and Paris, Isobel's career had faltered. She'd had to cut short her time in France and return to Edinburgh, to take care of her mother, Sheena, when her father died unexpectedly. Despite Sheena's insistence that she would be OK alone, Isobel hadn't wanted to leave her, imagining that she could pick up her career at a later stage. One year off turned into two, and by the time Isobel met Stuart in the hospitality lounge at Murrayfield, her ambitions had taken a back seat. Marriage and a settled life in Edinburgh had been the final nail in the coffin of her dreams of a high-flying, high-profile career in international fashion, and Stuart had been quite happy to have a wife with more modest aspirations.

She was lucky that they enjoyed a great lifestyle – a beautiful home, enough money not to have to worry about bills, able to enjoy luxury holidays and top-of-the-range cars. But if Isobel was being honest with herself, she knew that it was largely provided by Stuart.

After their wedding, Isobel had soon grown restless, finding herself sketching and designing once again, dusting off her sewing machine to bring her creations to life. Seeing how happy it made her, Stuart had suggested she should source a manufacturer, and offered to invest in his wife's fledgling business, allowing her to rent a small boutique on George Street, in an affluent area of Edinburgh, and produce her first collection.

To supplement her own designs, Isobel sold pieces from other independent labels, and one of her favourite parts of the job was discovering and nurturing new, undiscovered talent. She adored owning the boutique – she'd built a wonderful team, and the women were like family to her. Business was thriving, though at times Isobel had the nagging feeling that it was a long way from the ambition she'd had as a child of building a fashion empire like Coco Chanel or Diane von Furstenberg. And there was another unfulfilled dream that had been on her mind a lot recently . . .

'I've been thinking . . .' she said quietly, as the landscape flitted past them. 'While we're away, it might be the perfect time to . . .' Isobel hesitated, suddenly feeling nervous, then pressed on, 'Start trying for a baby.'

Panic passed fleetingly across Stuart's face, and Isobel felt a stab of annoyance and disappointment. Why was he always so resistant? She'd thought they were on the same page about having children, but whenever she raised the subject, he insisted it wasn't the right time.

'Maybe . . .' he said slowly.

'But our lives couldn't be more perfect – we're financially secure, we have established careers and a beautiful home . . . We have so much to offer a child.'

Stuart stared out of the window, but didn't say anything.

'Just imagine,' Isobel continued, leaning across and taking his hand. 'A little girl, a daughter who's as pretty as a picture and adores her daddy. Or perhaps a son, a little boy who looks just like you. You can teach him to play rugby. Maybe one day he'll play for Scotland, and you can—'

'Oh look, here we are already,' Stuart interrupted, as they drove beneath a whitewashed stone archway that read Palacio del Sol Radiante – Palace of the Radiant Sun – and bumped down a long, stony driveway surrounded by glorious gardens.

The palacio was a five-star boutique hotel, a converted finca built from traditional stone, but now completely modernized and catering to an upmarket, jet-setting clientele. From the hotel's location high on the clifftop, it was a short, steep walk down rugged steps carved into the headland to reach the most perfect sandy cove with a sweeping crescent of soft golden sand. From there, guests could dive from rocky outcrops into the dazzling turquoise of the Mediterranean, where white yachts dazzled on the water, dropping anchor a short distance from the shore.

Alternatively, there was a coastal path flanked by palm trees that led directly from the hotel into the small town of Cala de la Belleza, a bustling hub of beachfront bars and restaurants serving delicious food and refreshing cocktails. It was the perfect place to watch the array of water sports taking place out in the gentle waves, whilst locals and holidaymakers relaxed on loungers beneath colourful beach umbrellas.

It was idyllic, Isobel thought with a sigh, leaning forwards to stare out of the window, drinking it all in. She would put the conversation with Stuart out of her mind for now. They had two weeks here together – that was plenty of time to bring him round to the idea of a baby. If everything went according to Isobel's plan, it would be an unforgettable holiday.

'Señora Fontaine, we are so pleased to welcome you back to the palacio. It's been too long.' Roberto Garcia Pérez, the general manager of the Palacio del Sol Radiante, came out to greet Camille as she arrived at the hotel with René. Roberto was in his fifties, a similar age to Camille, with tanned skin and sparkling dark eyes and greying hair which he wore swept back to give him a distinguished air. Despite the heat, he wore dark trousers and a crisp white shirt, with a matching waistcoat and jacket.

'Oh, Roberto, how many years have we known one another? It's Camille, please. And yes, it's been too long since my last visit. I'm delighted to be back.'

Camille glanced around from behind her oversized tortoiseshell sunglasses, taking in the ivy-covered façade, the shuttered windows and Juliet balconies of the guest rooms, and the wide, worn stone steps leading up to the entrance. The hotel was stunning, but the island was full of ghosts, and she briefly wondered whether it had been a mistake to hold the show here.

Camille's mother-in-law, Margarita, was Mallorcan, though she had moved to Paris when she'd met her French husband, Yves, and a few years later they had had Andre. When Yves died, Margarita had moved back to her childhood home, which she'd inherited from her parents, living full-time in the sprawling villa. Camille and Andre had spent long, lazy vacations in Mallorca when Lucas was small; he was practically an islander himself, and often came to stay with his grandmother in the school holidays whilst his parents were busy with work. Lucas loved it so much that he'd made his home here too, establishing a restaurant in Cala de la Belleza, along with his business partner, Paulo, who he'd known since they were children.

Camille adored her only child, but her visits to the island in recent years had been tinged with sadness. She couldn't help but think of Andre, of all the wonderful times they'd spent together in Mallorca, and how much she still missed him. He'd been her partner, in business and in life, for three decades. They'd had ups and downs – what couple hadn't? – but they'd weathered the storms until the terrible accident that had cruelly taken him away from her . . .

'Is everything OK, Camille?' René asked.

'Yes, of course,' she brushed him off.

'Let me take you to your room,' Roberto offered. 'Unless you'd like to view the preparations for your handbag launch?'

'No, I'll freshen up first.' Camille had been travelling for almost twenty-four hours, and longed to cleanse the memories of New York from her skin.

'Very good.' Roberto inclined his head. 'We have your regular suite ready for you. We've made a few changes, but I'm sure it's very much as you remember it.'

'Thank you, Roberto. Oh, and my son will be joining me for lunch at one. We'd like to take it on the terrace.'

'Of course. I'll oversee the preparations myself and ensure everything is perfect. Now, if you would please follow me . . .'

One hour later, Camille had showered and changed into a vibrantly coloured maxi dress, before applying suncream and a slick of lip gloss. Her shoulder-length, glossy, chocolate-brown hair, hung straight and loose, and she still wore her gold wedding band – she hadn't taken it off since Andre's death.

Now Camille was standing in the Sunset Room, a large, west-facing space with floor-to-ceiling glass windows, which was where the launch of the Camille Andre and American Athletics diffusion line would be held. She was running through a list of tasks with René – 'Have all the bags cleared Customs? Tell the florist we *must* have white roses. Ensure the gift bags are prepped. And we've had some last-minute guest requests – yes to Sarah Jessica Parker, no to Paris Hilton' – when she heard a familiar voice say, '*Salut, Maman.*'

'Lucas!' Camille turned round in delight to see her son strolling into the room. He was tall and muscular, physically imposing, but she knew that his nature was soft and gentle, and he had a heart of gold. At twenty-seven years old, he'd grown into a handsome young man, with brown, wavy hair, a broad smile, and the same mesmerizing hazel eyes as his mother. He was dressed in stone-coloured shorts and a white T-shirt, which emphasized his deep tan, and he wore battered espadrilles on his feet.

'*Ça va, mon chouchou?*' Camille asked, as she embraced him, and they kissed on both cheeks.

'I'm well,' Lucas smiled, and she believed him. He looked healthy and happy. 'And you?'

'Oh, you know. Busy as usual,' Camille said lightly. 'Making sure everything goes perfectly for the launch.'

'I know it will,' Lucas reassured her. 'You're a perfectionist.'

'That's very sweet of you, darling.' Camille turned to her assistant. 'Thank you, René. That will be all for now. I'll let you know when I need you.'

'Of course. Enjoy your lunch. Good to see you again Lucas.' He nodded.

Camille linked her arm through her son's and steered him towards the terrace. 'I reserved a table for us,' she explained, as they left the Sunset Room and meandered through the expansive gardens, crossing a small, cobbled courtyard with a stone fountain, where dragonflies dipped to drink, and large white butterflies fluttered around the dusty lilac hortensia bushes.

They were shown to a pretty stone table, dressed in white linen, beneath a wooden pergola draped with greenery to create welcome shade. Both declined the wine list and stuck to sparkling water; Lucas was working later, and Camille wanted to stay sharp in case she was needed for further launch preparations that afternoon.

'So, *Maman*, how was the flight?'

'Fine, though I'm feeling rather tired with all the travelling.'

'Did you come straight from New York?'

'Yes, I did . . .' There was hesitation in Camille's voice.

'With Nicolas? How is he?'

'Oh, he's . . . the same old Nicolas, you know.'

'I'm looking forward to seeing him at the launch.'

Camille sipped her ice-cold drink, glad that she was wearing sunglasses so Lucas couldn't read her expression. 'I'm not sure whether he's coming. He might have to stay in the States for work.'

Lucas frowned, sensing that something wasn't right. 'You two haven't had an argument, have you? Not about business? Nicolas always goes along with whatever you say,' he laughed.

Camille smiled ruefully. 'Perhaps a few creative differences,' she conceded. 'But nothing for you to worry about.' She knew how much Lucas liked Nicolas and looked up to him. After Andre's death, Nicolas had become a father figure to Lucas, and the two men respected one another enormously. To her relief, her son had accepted her relationship with Nicolas, mature enough to see the happiness and stability it brought her. But today, she didn't want to talk about him . . . *couldn't* talk about him.

'Let's change the subject – I want to have a relaxing day today. I plan to spend the afternoon round the pool doing nothing more taxing than reading a Jackie Collins novel. This coming week will be so hectic. Did I tell you I'm meeting Catherine tomorrow to talk about designing a gown for her?'

'Catherine—?'

'Zeta-Jones,' Camille clarified, as Lucas raised his eyebrows, clearly impressed. 'Her people got in touch with my people – she likes what I do,' Camille elaborated, with a small shrug, but a look of excitement in her eyes. 'I've wanted to dress her for years – though, of course, she's so beautiful she could make a garbage bag look incredible. You know that she and Michael have a villa along the coast? The S'Estaca estate?'

'Yes, they're regulars at Il Paradiso whenever they're on the island,' Lucas nodded, naming his restaurant.

'Well, that's perfect,' Camille smiled. 'How is everything going with the business? And are you still dating Elle? I want to know all your news . . .'

A waitress arrived to take their food order, and mother and son settled down for a leisurely lunch and a long overdue catch-up.

'Oh, Stuart, this is exactly what I needed,' Isobel sighed, as the two of them left their hotel room and headed for the main pool. She'd changed into a pale gold bikini with a coordinating silk kaftan thrown over the top and a Hermès scarf tied around her head to keep off the sun. With her vintage cat-eye sunglasses, Isobel hoped she was channelling a Grace Kelly vibe.

'I'm glad you're happy,' Stuart smiled, as they headed for two empty loungers and sank down on the thick blue-and-white cushions.

Isobel removed her kaftan and settled back for a spot of people-watching. The Spanish heat on her bare skin felt delicious, the familiar scent of sun lotion and coconut oil in the air. The sky above was a perfect shade of blue and completely cloudless, only the occasional aeroplane flying high overhead.

Around the large, rectangular swimming pool, everyone looked so glamorous, the women slender and toned, the men muscled and bronzed, some in European-style tiny trunks that left little to the imagination. Isobel watched admiringly as one guy pulled himself out of the pool with ease, his muscles flexing, water racing down his broad torso, discreet designer logos peppering his swimwear and sunglasses.

Beside Isobel, Stuart leaned across, his fingertips tracing a line up and down her arm as he softly stroked her skin. 'Mmm, this is the life, isn't it? We should do this more often. I tell you what, why don't we relax here for a while, have a couple of cocktails, then head back to our room for a siesta?' He narrowed his eyes wolfishly.

But Isobel was no longer listening. Her attention had been taken by a woman standing on the other side of the pool. She was wearing a glamorous red swimming costume teamed with an enormous sunhat, its wide brim covering most of her face.

Who needs a parasol? Isobel thought with a smile.

The woman looked wealthy, in that indefinable way – though that was hardly unusual at the Palacio del Sol Radiante. She was older than Isobel, perhaps in her early fifties, but she was in great shape, with long, lean muscles that came from a dedicated regime of yoga and Pilates. She had a glowing tan that clearly wasn't from a bottle, but spoke of holidays in exotic destinations and winters spent on ski slopes at the most exclusive resorts. Her expensively coloured hair swished out below her straw hat, and her gold jewellery was timeless and elegant.

It seemed that Isobel wasn't the only one taken by the mysterious stranger; heads swivelled in the woman's direction, and she was attracting a lot of attention. Then she turned, and as Isobel caught a glimpse of the woman's face, she gasped.

It's her!

'What is it?' Stuart asked in alarm.

Isobel sat up, her face alight with excitement. 'You see the woman in red across the pool,' she nodded discreetly.

Stuart followed her gaze, immediately finding the woman Isobel was referring to. 'Yes. What about her?'

'It's Camille Fontaine!' Isobel exclaimed gleefully. Seeing Stuart's blank expression, she explained, 'You know – the designer. I have all of her "Camille" bags.

You bought me the limited-edition red python-skin last Valentine's Day.'

Stuart frowned. 'Are you sure? Why would she be here?'

'Of course I'm sure,' Isobel replied, annoyed by his question. Then her mood swung back to excitement. 'Oh, I can't believe it's really her.'

'Well don't make a fool of yourself,' Stuart retorted, unhappy with the way Isobel had spoken to him, and by the fact that his wife seemed more interested in some fashion designer than in going for a siesta with him. 'The woman has a right to privacy. She's on holiday.'

'I know that, Stuart,' Isobel shot back. 'What do you think I'm going to do? Run over and greet her like a long-lost relative? Don't be so ridiculous.'

Isobel snatched up her book and lay back on her lounger, pretending to read. But she was silently seething at her husband's comments, and didn't take in a single word of her Jilly Cooper novel. Instead, she gazed over the top of the pages, watching Camille Fontaine as she sashayed around the pool, greeting admirers and graciously accepting a drink from a waiter.

Isobel *would* make herself known to Camille, there was no doubt about that. But she would bide her time and do it her way.

Chapter 3

Stephanie Moon finished her gruelling workout with a series of yoga stretches, feeling the muscles in her body lengthen and relax, her breathing slow and deep.

Inhale . . . exhale . . .

As she leaned into warrior pose, she focused on the stunning view through the gym's floor-to-ceiling windows, where dappled morning light pooled through the citrus trees in the courtyard area at the rear of the striking villa. A Mediterranean garden stretched away into the distance, bursting with brightly coloured flowers, sprawling shrubs and prickly succulents, as water trickled over a stone fountain and cicadas hummed their incessant tune. Beyond lay a tantalizing glimpse of the Balearic Sea, a wide strip of ever-changing shades of blue, dazzling in the sunshine like a diamond reflecting light. It was hard *not* to feel motivated when you had such an incredible location to inspire you, Stephanie reflected.

She'd come so far in the last few months, and was still

acclimatizing to the glamour and grandeur of her new life. It was a complete contrast with everything she'd known growing up in Brighton.

Following a final sun salutation, Stephanie brought her hands together in the prayer position. Opening her eyes, she caught a glimpse of herself in the full-length mirrors on the opposite wall and couldn't resist checking out her reflection. All her hard work was paying off, she thought happily, and she was more than satisfied with what she saw. In black Lycra shorts and a minuscule crop-top, her body was slim yet strong, slender yet toned. Her new training regime had whittled her into the best shape of her life – her waist was tiny, her bottom high and toned, her small breasts perfectly proportioned. Her shining copper-coloured hair was pulled up in a high ponytail, highlighting her dewy skin and deep blue eyes that were framed by pale lashes.

Her agent kept impressing on her how important it was to be on top form, how she was hot property right now and they needed to capitalize on that. Stephanie was ready. The buzz around her next movie, *Fields of Barley*, was intense, and she was already being tipped for Oscar success – an idea which seemed crazy for a twenty-two-year-old from East Sussex who'd been practically unknown this time last year.

Stephanie felt the familiar crunch of anxiety in her stomach when she thought about the current situation.

Frowning, she forced herself to make a final, deep exhalation, then picked up her water bottle and walked out of the gym, contemplating whether to shower first or make herself a smoothie to quell the rumbling in her stomach. She decided on the former, and was about to head to her room when she heard female voices coming from one of the reception rooms at the front of the house. They were speaking in Spanish, and she could identify one as the housekeeper, Maria, but not the second woman.

Curious, Stephanie moved closer, her feet quiet on the tiled floor. There was no door on this room – just a double-width, open archway that led directly from the expansive entrance hall to the immaculately decorated lounge – and Stephanie peered in. Sitting elegantly on one of the pale blue damask sofas was a woman in her fifties, with a sleek, long bob in a deep shade of chestnut brown. Her posture was excellent, her back straight and her chin tilted slightly upwards, and she was immaculately dressed in a crisp white T-shirt and slim-fit navy trousers.

'*Sí, claro,*' the housekeeper was saying, as the woman replied, '*Gracias,*' and Maria walked away, acknowledging Stephanie as she passed. 'Oh, señora, you have a telephone call, I was just coming to tell you.'

'Oh,' Stephanie said, her voice wary, 'who is it?'

'The same woman who called before . . . Her name is Victoria Hyde-Williams, you will take the call?'

Stephanie blanched, her heart fluttering at the sound of her agent's name. 'Please tell her I'll call her back, thank you.'

Maria hesitated for a moment then shrugged and said, 'OK, *bien.*'

Stephanie glanced towards the elegant woman on the sofa, who glanced up, her almond eyes following Maria out of the room. In that instant, Stephanie realized who she was.

'Oh!' she burst out, before she could stop herself. 'Camille Fontaine! Oh my God, I love your bags! And your dresses!'

Camille smiled at Stephanie's enthusiasm, seeming genuinely pleased with the compliment. 'Thank you,' she replied in English, with a French accent.

'I'm Stephanie Moon, by the way,' she said, stepping forwards and offering her hand. 'I'm . . . staying here with Catherine for a couple of weeks.'

'Lucky you,' Camille laughed, as they shook hands. 'It's wonderful to meet you, Stephanie. If you don't mind me asking, your face is familiar – would I recognize you from somewhere?'

'Maybe . . .' Stephanie said, a soft blush stealing across her face. This was happening more and more recently, and she was still getting used to it. 'I'm an actress.'

'*Mon dieu*, yes of course, I saw you on stage last year when I was in London, in *The Tempest* at the National Theatre. You were Ariel. You were electric, and you're even more beautiful in the flesh.'

'That's very kind of you. It's been a crazy year and everything is so intense.'

'Didn't I read that your new film is in production in England somewhere?'

Stephanie paused, unsure what to say. 'Yes, I'm in *Fields of Barley* with Colin Firth and Jude Law. I've been . . . taking a break from it for a short while . . .' She quickly ploughed on before Camille could ask her anything awkward about why she was in Mallorca in her yoga pants and not being shouted at by an angry director on a cold and grey Yorkshire film set. She set her face in a winning smile. 'Catherine's been so wonderful letting me stay here, to give myself a moment to recharge. She's been like my fairy godmother.'

'She's fabulous, isn't she? I've been longing to dress her for years, and now I finally have the opportunity. That's why I'm here,' Camille explained. 'Michael is receiving a Lifetime Achievement Award in Hollywood this autumn, and Catherine wants to wear something truly special. Today, we have our first meeting.'

'That sounds incredible. I honestly do love your dresses,' Stephanie gushed, genuinely, remembering as a teenager seeing footage of her idol Kate Moss sashaying down the catwalk in a flowing Camille white tuxedo suit. That was when life was very different, before everything changed.

'Well perhaps we could work together too?' Camille suggested. 'You have a premiere coming up, *non* . . .?'

Stephanie let out a gasp. 'Do you mean it?'

'*Absolument.* The pleasure would be all mine.'

The two women beamed at one another as Maria re-entered the room, carrying a tray with traditional Mallorcan pastries, a large silver pot and two cups, which she placed down on the marble coffee table in front of them.

'The lady said please call her back urgently.' Maria said. 'She sounded very . . . *tensa.*'

Tense? Hardly surprising, Stephanie thought to herself. 'Thank you, Maria.' She quickly changed the subject. 'So how did you end up being a fashion designer?' Stephanie asked Camille, as she sat down in the adjacent armchair. 'I can't imagine what it must be like to have an idea in your head, and then see women all around the world wearing the clothes you've envisioned.'

'It *is* rather surreal sometimes,' Camille agreed, pouring them both a coffee. 'But wonderful too. People tend to think that fashion is frivolous, but the right clothes can change your life. They can give you confidence, boost your mood, and make you feel a hundred times better about yourself. When you're wearing something beautiful, you can't help but feel beautiful too.'

Stephanie nodded. 'I did a photo shoot recently for *Vogue*, wearing vintage couture gowns. The hours of work that had gone into them . . . They were like works of art.'

Camille nodded in agreement. 'It's true, that's exactly what they are. It's how I started, you know – in couture. I trained at the most prestigious institute in Paris. It seems like such a long time ago now,' Camille continued, her eyes misting over with memories. Then she shook herself. 'I'm sorry, you don't want to listen to me droning on about the past. My goodness, I founded my company before you were even born!'

'No, I'd love to hear all about it.' Stephanie slipped off her trainers and curled her legs up on the armchair. 'Tell me all about how you started Camille Andre.'

Camille smiled sadly. 'Andre, my husband, founded the business with me. We met at the Chambre Syndicale and we were instantly inseparable. We were very much in love. When we left the school, it was only natural that we would set up a business together. And get married, and have a child . . .'

'That's so romantic,' Stephanie sighed.

'Don't misunderstand me – it wasn't all moonlight and roses. It took a long time for us to be successful, and that meant many years where money was tight, where we worked what felt like twenty-four hours a day, seven days a week, all whilst trying to raise our son and keep our marriage strong. We could have cut corners and aimed for mass-market appeal with a lower price tag, but we didn't want to. Andre insisted on quality,' Camille smiled. 'He always wanted the best, but success didn't come immediately.'

'What changed?'

'This,' Camille said simply, indicating the iconic red calfskin handbag nestled on the sofa beside her. 'We knew we had something special, but we didn't understand the impact it would have. *Everyone* was carrying it, *everyone* wanted it. It changed our lives.'

'Wow,' Stephanie said softly. 'Wait? Is Andre in Majorca with you? I'd love to meet him.'

Camille swallowed, her expression faltering. 'He . . . he died,' she explained quietly. 'Just over four years ago now.'

'I'm so sorry,' Stephanie burst out, feeling terrible. 'I didn't know.'

'That's all right,' Camille insisted. 'He was in a car accident. It was the most devastating time of my life. My son was also in the car and he was almost killed. I don't know what I'd have done if I'd lost them both . . .'

She trailed off, and Stephanie leaned across, taking Camille's hands in hers. She didn't speak, just squeezed them reassuringly. Words weren't needed. Camille squeezed back and Stephanie knew she'd appreciated the gesture. Even though she barely knew this woman, and their lives were very different, she felt a connection to her. Stephanie liked her immediately.

Camille sat up, extracting her hands to wipe away a

stray tear. 'Andre used to love Mallorca,' she explained. 'His mother was from the island, and we had so many happy times here. That's why I've come back to launch the new Camille Andre collection. But it's bittersweet. I'm seeing him everywhere, remembering everything we used to do – our favourite bar where we'd drink a *palo con sifón*; the little bakery where we'd buy fresh *ensaïmada* every morning; even the doorway by the monastery where we sheltered once during a summer rainstorm . . .'

'I'm sure he'd be so proud of you, continuing his legacy like this,' Stephanie murmured. She could see that Camille still carried a lot of pain, but imagined that she'd had no choice but to carry on. It was something that Stephanie understood well; she'd endured struggles in her own life too . . . but things had changed now. *You can still lose it all, Stephanie*, she heard a little voice in her ear say. She ignored it and tried to focus on Camille.

'I hope so. My son, Lucas, lives on the island now.' She smiled gently. 'He owns a restaurant, Il Paradiso.'

Stephanie tilted her head to one side, the name stirring a memory. 'I'm sure Catherine said that's where we were going for dinner tonight.'

'Of course! I invited her and Michael for dinner, and she asked to bring another guest, so that's perfect! They are both so welcoming, you can see how much friends and family mean to them. I can't wait for you to meet Lucas.'

'I'd love to.'

Camille sat back in her seat and beamed at Stephanie. 'I can see that you're a wonderful person. So talented and charming. You deserve all the success that's coming your way—'

'Camille, darling!'

Camille broke off as a throaty Welsh voice called her name, and she turned to see the beauty that was Catherine Zeta-Jones walking across the room towards them. She was wearing golf attire, but still looked utterly stunning in pristine white trousers and a pink polo shirt, her raven hair pulled up in a topknot with a white visor perched on her head, as she surveyed them with her mesmerizing feline eyes.

'I'm sorry I'm late,' she purred. 'Michael and I completely lost track of time.'

'Don't worry at all,' Camille reassured her, standing up as the two women air-kissed. 'Stephanie and I have been having a lovely chat.'

'Isn't she a doll?' Catherine beamed, turning to Stephanie who couldn't help but smile back. 'She's going to be the biggest star.'

'I can tell,' Camille agreed. 'I look forward to seeing you at Il Paradiso, Stephanie. It was so nice to meet you.'

'And you. See you later,' Stephanie smiled, as Catherine and Camille left the room, already talking about their ideas for Catherine's gown. Stephanie felt awestruck – she'd met the legendary Camille Fontaine! Stephanie had hugely enjoyed speaking to Camille, full of admiration for everything she'd achieved. Camille had clearly been through a lot, but she was a fighter, and Stephanie could relate to that. And now Camille had offered to dress her for her film premiere! She could almost explode with excitement.

A couple of years ago, she wouldn't have dreamed of seeing a Camille dress in real life, but she'd been forced to up her game recently, poring over glossy magazines and becoming familiar with the most on-trend designers. Her agent had even put her in touch with a stylist who'd taken her shopping on Bond Street, to ensure she looked every inch the sophisticated, upcoming starlet. Her agent . . . Stephanie let out a small groan, thinking of Victoria's call and imagining her steely, no-nonsense agent tapping her perfectly manicured nails on her desk and weighing up her next move.

'You can't avoid her for ever,' Catherine had told Stephanie, and she was right, she couldn't, but she hoped she could avoid her for a bit longer. For now, the Mallorcan sun was shining, and it was time for a refreshing dip in the Douglases' amazing pool. Fame would have to wait.

Chapter 4

Lucas Fontaine was in the kitchen of Il Paradiso, prepping food for that evening's service. His fingers were flying, the sharp blade so fast it was almost a blur as he made light work of a whole bag of fat, juicy tomatoes which he would use for his famous gazpacho. Of course, he had a sous-chef for work like this, but today Lucas wanted to get an early start. The restaurant was fully booked, and one of the diners would be his mother, along with her VIP guests. Besides, he liked doing the work himself; its repetitive nature lulled him into an almost trance-like state as he sliced and diced, and the end result was immensely satisfying.

Il Paradiso was Lucas's baby. It had been established almost two years ago, and his ambitions for its future were sky-high. Lucas wanted a Michelin star, no less. The food was elevated Catalan, with specialities including duck breast braised with pear, meatballs with cuttlefish, and his renowned lobster with chocolate sauce. Lucas liked the fact that he'd discovered his talent, and no one could take his achievements away from him. Finding success in a field completely unrelated to his parents meant that no one could accuse him of nepotism – he'd been successful through his skills alone.

It was true that his mother, Camille, had invested in his business, allowing him to buy the restaurant, but she was a silent partner. Everything that he'd accomplished since then had been down to him. Lucas dipped a teaspoon in the *sofregit* he was making, the traditional sauce made from tomatoes and onions, and tasted it thoughtfully. Almost there. It just needed a little more time to caramelize and then it would be perfect.

'Hey man, you're here early!'

Lucas looked up to see his best friend and business partner, Paulo Torres, stroll into the restaurant. Paulo was mid-height and stocky, with dark hair and a deep tan that spoke of a life spent on the island. He wore cargo shorts and a short-sleeved shirt that was open low enough to show a considerable amount of chest hair. The two had known each other since they were children, when Lucas used to stay with his grandparents in their villa. Paulo had grown up on a farm down the road, and was always delighted when the holidays rolled around and Lucas came to visit. The two boys were only a year apart, with Paulo being the elder, and they'd get up to all kinds of mischief whilst roaming the island on those long, hot summer days. They'd disappear from dawn until dusk, cycling deserted trails, and taking rowing boats out to sea, where they'd cast lines for fish and discover hidden coves. As they grew older, their interests shifted, and they spent their days hanging around the sandy beaches where they practised their rudimentary flirting skills on the local girls.

Their friendship had spanned almost two decades, and Paulo had been there for Lucas when his father had died, supporting him through that nightmarish time when Lucas had almost lost his life as well. Prior to the accident, Lucas had led a spoiled, playboy lifestyle, rolling from continent to continent, party to party, woman to woman. A more sombre, sober Lucas emerged from the aftermath, one who was ready to put down roots and work for a living, instead of having his every whim indulged by his parents. And whilst Paulo's parents were no longer farmers – with the increase in tourism to the island, they now ran a successful boat hire company – their son was always eager to make his fortune. It was a natural fit that the two men would go into business together, and so Lucas ran the kitchen whilst Paulo – a born hustler – handled everything else.

'So are you,' Lucas shot back with a grin, high-fiving Paulo as he entered the kitchen, before opening the fridge and helping himself to a *botifarra* sausage. 'Hey, they're for later,' Lucas protested.

'I'm doing quality checks,' Paulo countered, demolishing it in two bites. 'And they've passed with flying colours.'

'Naturally,' Lucas laughed. 'So why *are* you here?'

'Same as you. It's a big night tonight, right? I wanted to check that everything was flawless, and that front of house looks spectacular . . .' Paulo turned around, his practised gaze sweeping over everything. The space was open plan, with the kitchen visible from the main restaurant so that the diners could watch the chefs at work and inhale the delicious smells as the food was cooked.

The restaurant itself was smart and modern, airy and

light, with clean lines and cream walls accentuated by touches of red and yellow to evoke the Catalan flag. It was decorated in a simple, homely style. Lucas wanted his dishes to be the focus, not the décor, and for diners to feel comfortable, not intimidated.

'I've been thinking,' Paulo continued. 'Of the best way we can leverage tonight. I've got a photographer friend, Carlos Garcia – you know him, right? He usually does the clubs in Palma. I'll ask him to swing by. We'll get a great shot of Catherine and Michael, along with you, the chef extraordinaire – and me, of course.'

Lucas pulled a face. 'Carlos? I'm not so sure . . .' Catherine Zeta-Jones and Michael Douglas were to be guests of his mother, and she wanted the occasion to be extra special. Lucas was thrilled with their patronage, and he didn't want to take advantage of what should have been a private occasion by selling photos to the world's press.

'That's why you deal with the food, and I deal with the PR,' Paulo quipped. 'You've got to capitalize on every opportunity. Do you want that Michelin star or not?'

'Is that even a question?' Lucas laughed. Paulo knew his weak spot.

'Michael's a pro, he gets how it works. Of course we're going to want a photograph of him and his beautiful wife. We'll throw in a good bottle of champagne, and in return we get the kind of publicity that most restaurants could only dream of. It's win-win for everyone.'

'I guess,' Lucas said uncertainly, as he began grinding almonds for the *picada*. He suspected that his friend was right. After all, Paulo *was* better at that side of the business. That had always been the deal – whilst Lucas would concentrate on the food, Paulo would take care of the rest.

Despite their friendship, the two men were very different. Lucas was uncomfortably aware that he'd been something of a brat in his youth; with wealthy, high-flying parents, he'd never had to worry about money. He'd had a bohemian kind of upbringing, travelling the world with his parents, but everything had changed in his late teens when his mother had designed a bag that was crowned that season's 'It' bag.

Suddenly the Fontaines were playing in a different league – one that involved private jets and chartered yachts and VIP access to whatever their hearts desired. The influx of money meant that Lucas could live the life of a louche playboy; by his own admission, he'd been an arrogant bastard. Paulo had been his friend since they were kids – and he had stuck by him, despite all this.

Then everything changed, once again, with Andre's death. Lucas's carefree existence was shattered, but his father's death gave him a reality check and a renewed sense of purpose, a desire to achieve something for himself. He'd almost lost his life too, but he'd been given a second chance and was determined not to waste it. The scar across his cheek was a permanent reminder of everything Lucas had been through – he couldn't escape it, forced to confront his past every time he looked in the mirror. It had altered his pretty-boy looks, too. Lucas was self-conscious about the change in his appearance, but Paulo kept telling him women found it sexy as it gave him an edge of danger. But Lucas's outlook had changed anyway; no longer interested in one-night stands and playboy antics, he was determined to work hard in his career. Any serious relationship would have to be with the right woman, one who understood that the restaurant meant everything to him.

Paulo hadn't come from money, so always had his eye on a deal or a get-rich-quick scheme, and he was an instinctive hustler when it came to both women and business. That was how it worked with the restaurant – Paulo's extrovert, cheeky side was perfect for the front of house and working the PR channels, charming the critics and reviewers. He had a little black book stuffed full of contacts, but he was less concerned about always taking the legitimate route. If a plan required a backhander, or was of dubious legality, Paulo had no scruples in pressing ahead regardless and kept the details sketchy for Lucas, who would undoubtedly disapprove.

'Just leave it all to me,' Paulo insisted. 'All you need to do is smile and look pretty in the photo. Speaking of which,' he added, under his breath.

'There you are!'

A familiar voice, speaking in French, made Lucas turn sharply. The woman striding across his restaurant was a vision – long, slim legs in tiny denim shorts; a cropped white T-shirt that showed off acres of toned, tanned stomach; long, blonde hair that fell almost to her waist – and an angry expression on her beautiful face. It was his girlfriend, Elle Mettier.

'Why aren't you answering your phone?' she demanded, planting her hands on her hips, her gold bracelets jangling.

Lucas slapped the pocket of his chef's whites, a guilty expression on his face. 'I must have left it in my bag.'

'I've been trying to call you all day. I guessed you'd

be here,' Elle said with a sniff, as she glanced disdainfully around the kitchen.

'Hi Elle,' Paulo said deliberately, clearly annoyed that she hadn't acknowledged him.

'Oh, Paulo, I didn't notice you there,' Elle replied dismissively, walking straight past him and planting a kiss on Lucas's mouth. 'Why are you working so hard, baby?' she pouted, wrapping herself around him like a python.

'I told you. We're hosting a dinner for Michael Douglas and Catherine Zeta-Jones tonight.'

Elle's eyes lit up. 'Of course! Oh, I can't wait. I've always wanted to meet them.'

'I don't think you're invited,' Paulo told her gleefully.

'Well, I might *just happen* to be in the restaurant supporting my boyfriend,' she replied sweetly, though her eyes were narrowed as she shot daggers at Paulo.

'I don't want her in the photo,' Paulo said instantly to Lucas.

'What photo?' Elle demanded.

'Nothing for you to worry about,' Paulo retorted. 'By the way, Lucas, has Camille arrived yet?'

'Yes, she flew in yesterday. We met for lunch.'

'Oh, I can't wait to see your mother again,' Elle squealed in excitement. 'Is she coming tonight?'

'Yes, she's hosting the dinner. She's designing a dress for Catherine.'

'This is perfect,' Elle gushed. 'And did you speak to her about what we discussed?'

Lucas screwed up his face. 'Remind me, what did we discuss?'

'Me being the new face of Camille Andre, of course!' Elle playfully tapped his chest. 'You didn't *really* forget!'

'We didn't *really* get the chance to talk about it yesterday. We were catching up, discussing family matters . . .'

He trailed off as Camille's expression turned into a pout. She stretched out her long, slender left arm and gazed at it sadly. 'My arm looks so bare,' she sighed. 'What it really needs is a Camille bag and a huge diamond engagement ring.'

Paulo made a spluttering noise that sounded as though he was choking. Lucas's eyes widened, as he and Paulo exchanged looks of alarm.

Lucas and Elle had been dating since the previous summer. They'd met in Les Caves du Roy, the famous St Tropez nightclub, and though she was drop-dead gorgeous and they'd had a lot of fun, spending the evening flirting and kissing, Lucas hadn't asked for her number. When they had bumped into each other the next day over lunch at Le Club 55, Elle insisted it was fate.

One year later, she'd somehow charmed her way into Lucas's life, and now they were in a serious relationship. She had a sweet side, but she was demanding, and she'd recently started dropping hints about getting married. As with everything Elle wanted, she wasn't subtle about trying to get it . . .

'I . . . um . . .' Lucas began, his gold-flecked eyes flashing a signal to Paulo for help, but he was saved by a sharp knock on the external kitchen door. Lucas hastily extracted himself from Elle's penetrating gaze, only for the door to swing open sharply and reveal Diego, the seafood supplier to Il Paradiso. He was gnarled and weather-beaten, with grey hair and a thick moustache.

'*Hola*, Diego,' Lucas greeted him, then his face turned

to confusion. 'I don't think we ordered anything today; we have plenty in stock.'

Diego looked furious. 'I know you do – and I haven't been paid for it. So maybe I should take it all back, huh?' He strode over to one of the industrial walk-in fridges and wrenched at the handle.

'Woah, I'm sure there's just been a misunderstanding?' Lucas darted across and tried to placate him. He glanced over at Paulo questioningly.

'Just a misunderstanding,' Paulo agreed easily. 'Diego, listen, you know we are good for the money, I don't have any cash on me right now. I'll drop it in to you tomorrow morning, OK?'

'That's what you said last week,' Diego fumed. 'And the week before that. I'm tired of waiting. I don't know what game you're playing, but I'm not giving you lobster for free so you can sell it for a fortune to your fancy customers.'

'Hold on, Diego,' Lucas intervened, concern clouding his features. 'I don't know what's happened here, but just give me a moment.' He headed over to the cubbyhole where he'd left his rucksack. Opening it, he pulled out his phone – noting the seventeen missed calls from Elle – and took out a stash of notes. 'This should cover it, OK?' Lucas added, as Diego snatched it from him. He quickly riffled through, counting out the notes, then grunted, satisfied.

'Thank you, Lucas. *You*, at least, are an honourable man.' Diego shot Paulo a dirty look and walked out.

'What was all that about?' Lucas demanded, turning to Paulo once Diego was out of earshot.

'Nothing, man, nothing. Just a little cashflow issue,

that's all. But nothing for you to worry about. Everything's cool.'

'Are you sure?' Lucas pressed.

'Of course. Would I lie to you?' Paulo winked, back to his familiar, cocksure self. 'Now, I'll catch you later, OK? I've got a little business to sort out. *À plus tard*, Elle.'

She shot him a fake smile as he sauntered out of the door, then turned back to Lucas.

'What do you think that was all about?' Lucas wondered, a thoughtful expression on his face.

Elle shrugged her slender shoulders. 'I don't know. I mean, I know he's your best friend, but I wouldn't trust him with my car keys.'

Lucas's face fell, and Elle sighed, wrapping her arms around him and pressing her body against his in an attempt to cheer him up. 'Forget about him, he's not important,' she insisted, as she began nuzzling his neck with soft butterfly kisses. 'Now, *chéri*, let's talk about me being the next face of Camille Andre . . .'

Chapter 5

'Darling, you look sensational.' Stuart's eyes raked over his wife, as Isobel spritzed herself with perfume before slipping on a pair of cream high heels. She was wearing a silk form-fitting dress of her own creation, and the material flowed over her body like water. It had a high scoop neckline, and sat just above the knee, but despite not having acres of bare skin on show, it was still incredibly sexy.

'Thank you, darling. You're looking rather handsome yourself,' Isobel replied, kissing him. Stuart was wearing sharply tailored trousers and a short-sleeved shirt undone at the neck, paired with Gucci loafers. He'd caught the sun already, with a light tan on his face, and he looked confident and relaxed. 'Where are you taking me?'

'The restaurant's called Il Paradiso, specializing in Catalan food. It comes highly recommended.'

'It sounds delicious.'

'I had to pull a few strings to get a table at short notice.'

'Oh really?' Isobel looked at him admiringly. 'I didn't know you had contacts in Majorca.'

'The owner of the restaurant, in fact. He was in a car accident a few years ago. I was consulted on his reconstructive surgery.'

'Impressive stuff. But all this talk of food is making me hungry.' She patted her flat stomach and picked up her bag, opting for a Fendi Baguette, not a Camille. 'Let's get going.'

'Welcome to Il Paradiso. It's wonderful to see you again,' Lucas smiled, warmly greeting Michael Douglas and Catherine Zeta-Jones, and kissing his mother on the cheek.

'And this is Stephanie Moon,' Camille explained, introducing them. 'She's an actress who's staying at S'Estaca. If you haven't heard of her yet, you soon will do.'

'Pleased to meet you,' Stephanie grinned, as Lucas said, 'Likewise.'

It might have been Camille's imagination, but she thought she saw a ripple of interest between the two and was gratified. She liked Stephanie, and felt she'd be a much better match for her son than that stroppy gold-digger Elle.

Then Camille's face hardened as Paulo came swaggering out from the back, making a beeline for Catherine and Michael. He stopped as he saw Stephanie, making a show of kissing her hand as his gaze drifted over her with obvious interest.

'And who's this? I don't think we've been introduced,' he smiled charmingly.

'I'm Stephanie. It's good to meet you.'

'The pleasure is all mine, Stephanie, believe me,' he purred. 'I'm Paulo Torres, co-owner of Il Paradiso.'

'Oh, I didn't realize . . .' Stephanie faltered, glancing at Lucas.

'He just does the cooking, but I'm the genius behind it all,' Paulo grinned, as Camille's lips tightened into a moue.

'Now, Paulo, haven't you got something you should be doing, apart from bothering my guests? It sounds as though this place will collapse without you if you take your eye off the ball for two minutes.'

Her comment wiped the smile from Paulo's face, and he was about to respond when the door opened and another couple walked in.

'Lucas,' the man said, stepping forward to shake his hand. 'Great to see you again. You're looking extremely well. And thank you so much for fitting us in. I've been telling my wife all about your restaurant. The place looks fantastic.'

'I'm delighted to have you here. Actually, it's fortunate that you've arrived now, there's someone I'd like to introduce you to. *Maman* . . .' Lucas called, and Camille turned from where she'd been chatting to Catherine. '*Maman*, this is Stuart MacFarlane, one of the doctors involved in my surgery, after the accident. I don't think you ever met him.'

'Oh,' Camille exclaimed. 'Monsieur MacFarlane, *enchantée*. You simply must join us for dinner, I insist. I'm so grateful for everything you've done for my son. You don't mind, do you?' she asked, turning to her other guests.

'The more the merrier,' Catherine laughed.

'Well,' Paulo beamed. 'Isn't this a happy reunion,

Camille? You'll be able to spend the evening reminiscing about the accident.'

Lucas frowned, and Camille could tell he was wondering what on earth had got into his friend. She was about to reply when Lucas intervened, expertly smoothing over any awkwardness.

'It's wonderful to see you again, Señor MacFarlane. I'll get a waitress to set two extra places, and your table is right over here,' he said, leading them to a discreet corner of the restaurant. 'Now, I'd better get back to the kitchen or there'll be nothing for you to eat. Have a wonderful evening, everyone, and don't hesitate to let my staff know if there's anything they can do for you.' With a final glance at Stephanie, he was gone.

'*Bon appétit*, Camille,' Paulo added with a tight smile, as he turned to follow Lucas.

The restaurant was buzzing, the drinks were flowing, and everyone was having a wonderful time. Il Paradiso was at capacity, but it was cleverly arranged so that it never felt overcrowded, yet the atmosphere was bustling with conversation and laughter. The food was excellent, as the guests finished their main courses of salted cod with black rice, and *fricandó*, a traditional slow-cooked beef stew with tender meat and locally sourced mushrooms marinated in dry sherry. Camille beamed with pride as everyone effusively praised the chef.

Stuart was seated beside her, and was enjoying talking to the elegant Frenchwoman as they discussed their respective businesses. She'd led a fascinating life, and the conversation flowed easily.

'My wife is a huge fan of your bags,' Stuart told her.

'I must have spent a small fortune on them over the years.'

'Then it's the least I can do to buy you dinner,' Camille laughed good-naturedly.

Across the table, Isobel was trying to listen to their conversation, but could only make out the occasional word over the hubbub. She could read their body language, though. Stuart was clearly trying to impress the famous designer, whilst Camille appeared laidback and relaxed. Isobel couldn't tell if she was genuinely interested in talking to Stuart, or whether she was merely being polite.

'Where's it from?'

Isobel turned, realizing that the young woman beside her was trying to speak to her. She looked vaguely familiar, though she must have been better known than Isobel realized if she was friends with Michael Douglas and Catherine Zeta-Jones. Isobel was wild with excitement at the fact she was having dinner with them – she couldn't wait to tell all the girls back in the boutique – but so far she'd barely managed to speak to them.

'Sorry, what did you say?' Isobel turned back to Stephanie with a smile.

'I said, I love your dress, where's it from?'

'I designed it,' Isobel said proudly.

'Oh wow, it's gorgeous! Everyone here is so talented.'

Isobel smiled tightly, taking a slug of her wine.

'Are you a designer?' Stephanie continued.

Isobel nodded. 'I own a boutique in Edinburgh. We stock a mixture of young, up-and-coming designers, and my own creations too.'

'That's amazing. It's such a tough industry, isn't it?'

Isobel took another long drink of wine before she replied. 'It certainly is. I guess some people get lucky breaks, and others don't,' she added, her gaze finding Camille across the table.

Stephanie looked sympathetic. 'Maybe you should speak to Camille, see if she can help out.'

Isobel laughed lightly, a strange expression crossing her face. 'Yes, perhaps I should.'

'After all, it's all about connections. Who you know, and all of that . . .'

'Mmm,' Isobel nodded. Suddenly she had an idea, her eyes alight as she turned to Stephanie. 'Won't you have a big premiere coming up for your next movie? Perhaps I could design something for you?'

Stephanie looked apologetic, and Isobel instantly felt like a fool for asking. She was an unknown designer from Edinburgh – of course Stephanie wouldn't want to work with her. 'Forget I even asked,' Isobel insisted.

'It's just that Camille's already offered to dress me for my next premiere, and I said yes. She's designing something for Catherine, you see – Michael has a big event in Los Angeles later this year – and we got talking when she came round to the house . . .'

'I completely understand,' Isobel insisted, trying to hide the disappointment in her voice. 'Of course you'd want a big name for your premiere, not some unknown—'

'I honestly do love your dress,' Stephanie rushed to reassure her. 'And there'll be loads of events, and press conferences, and overseas premieres. Oh, you could design something for the UK premiere, in London. That would be incredible, and it's the one I'm most excited about. It'll be like a homecoming.'

'Really? I'd love to.' Isobel was genuinely thrilled, feeling a rush of warmth towards Stephanie. This could be her big break; her dress could be on the front page of the world's press, and the exposure would be priceless. 'You'd look incredible in cream or pale gold with your colouring. I can just imagine you in something chiffon and strapless, with a fitted bodice and full skirt . . .'

'What's this, darling?' Stuart leaned across, picking up on the tail end of their conversation.

'I offered to design a dress for Stephanie,' Isobel explained excitedly, noticing that Camille was now speaking to Catherine and Michael. To her surprise, Stuart pulled a face, apparently not sharing her enthusiasm.

'Oh, Isobel, would you leave the poor woman alone?' he said, with an apologetic glance at Stephanie. 'Don't be so bloody desperate. She's probably got famous designers falling over themselves to dress her, why would she want something of yours?'

Isobel felt as though she'd been slapped. She felt her cheeks flame, humiliation burning through her.

'No, it's fine,' Stephanie insisted, coming to her rescue. 'I'd love Isobel to design something for me. I adore what she's wearing tonight.'

'That's very sweet of you, but you don't have to pretend,' Stuart continued. He was slurring his words a little, and Isobel realized he was drunk – though that didn't excuse the unpleasant way he was behaving. 'I'm sure you'd much rather wear Gucci or something, and I don't blame you for that. Honestly, Isobel, you're embarrassing yourself.'

'No, *you're* embarrassing me,' she hissed back, feeling close to tears. She snatched up her bag, on the verge of walking out, when dessert arrived at the table – a traditional *crema catalana*, flavoured with lemon zest and topped with candied walnuts. It gave Isobel a moment to compose herself, and the conversation moved on, with Stephanie tactfully changing the subject as Isobel ignored Stuart.

After everyone had finished eating, Camille rose to her feet. 'Thank you all so much for coming. I've had a wonderful evening, and I hope you have too, but unfortunately I have a lot of work still to do this evening and an early start tomorrow, so I'm going to bid you all *adieu*. Please, stay as long as you like. I'm sure my son will make you feel welcome.'

Camille made her way around the table, saying goodbye to each of her guests, smiling and air-kissing. The restaurant was beginning to quieten down as she picked up her bag and went outside to find her driver, blissfully unaware of the way Isobel's eyes followed her as she left.

Chapter 6

Stephanie was thoroughly enjoying herself, carried through the evening on a bubble of happiness. It had been so nice of Camille to invite her to the dinner, and she'd had a fabulous time chatting with Isobel – until her husband had made his nasty intervention.

Stephanie's gaze drifted across the restaurant to where Lucas was tidying up. He was joking around with his staff; the team clearly got on well, and he was obviously well liked. He was speaking in Spanish, so Stephanie didn't understand what he was saying, but they didn't need to speak the same language for her to appreciate his smouldering hazel eyes and gym-honed physique. She watched the way he moved, biceps rippling beneath his chef's whites, in awe of the way he was so dominant in the kitchen. She found herself wondering whether he was dominant in the bedroom too . . .

Stephanie finished her glass of *ratafia* – Lucas had brought out a bottle of the traditional Catalan digestif and encouraged them to help themselves – and realized she felt a little drunk. Isobel was now chatting to Stuart, whilst Michael and Catherine shared a private joke, and before she had time to talk herself out of it, Stephanie got up and walked towards the kitchen. She stopped at the entrance and locked eyes with Lucas.

'Do you need a waiter?' he asked, moving towards her. He spoke English with a French accent, and she found it incredibly sexy. She loved that he was fluent in multiple languages; he seemed different from all the men she'd dated in Brighton, or the vacuous airheads of the acting world, who only cared about their 'profile' and who was getting what parts.

She grinned cheekily at Lucas. 'I was just checking out your equipment.'

Lucas raised his eyebrows.

'It's all working nicely, thank you.'

She laughed. 'In the kitchen!'

'Really? Why's that?'

'My dad ran a chippy in Brighton.'

Lucas's forehead furrowed in momentary confusion, either misunderstanding her English or not getting the joke. But then he broke into a smile, his full lips widening, his dark-fringed eyes crinkling into laughter lines. 'Ah! But fish and chips is an art form, *non?*'

'Of course. It's not easy to fry the perfect chip – crispy on the outside, fluffy in the middle . . .'

'For me it's all about the seasoning. A pinch of salt and a drizzle of vinegar – *parfait*,' Lucas finished seriously, before the two of them burst into laughter, an undeniable chemistry sparking between them.

Stephanie felt delighted to have broken through his

serious façade. Emboldened, she strolled into the kitchen and hopped up on one of the stainless-steel countertops that Lucas had been cleaning only moments earlier. She crossed her legs, showing off her slim, tanned legs, knowing that her body looked knock-out in the halter-neck mini dress she was wearing. Lucas watched her, intrigued. The rest of the staff were gathered at the other side of the kitchen, seemingly engrossed in their work, but Stephanie could tell they were casting surreptitious glances at the two of them.

'How did you get that scar?' she asked softly, her eyes fluttering over him.

Lucas's hand reached instinctively to his cheek, tracing the jagged line that ran from the top of his ear down to the corner of his mouth. His jaw tightened, and for a moment his face darkened. Stephanie wondered if she'd gone too far with the question, but then Lucas took a deep breath and looked her straight in the eye. 'I was in a car accident.'

Stephanie remembered what Camille had told her, and her eyes held his. 'Oh yes, I'm so sorry . . . Your father . . .'

Lucas inhaled, his broad shoulders rising as he gathered himself. 'It was a little over four years ago now. I'm mostly healed – physically . . .' Once again, he traced the jagged line across his cheek, and Stephanie had the crazy idea that she wanted to do the same. 'But I think this makes me more interesting, don't you?'

Stephanie hesitated, trying to read him.

'I was far too good-looking before. This gives me character,' Lucas grinned, breaking the tension, and Stephanie laughed.

'It really does,' she said with a soft smile. 'I shouldn't

have brought it up. My mouth didn't engage my brain first, as usual.'

'It's all right,' he said, with a Gallic shrug. 'I don't remember very much about it – it's all a blur. We had been at my dad's birthday party in Switzerland. My father and I were driving home, weaving down the mountain, and then . . . nothing. I woke up in hospital three weeks later.'

Sadness and uncertainty passed over his face, and Stephanie was overwhelmed with an urge to hold him in her arms. But she stayed where she was. 'I can't imagine what it must have been like . . . What you've been through . . .'

'Everyone has stuff to deal with, right?' Lucas replied, looking at her meaningfully, and Stephanie felt a jolt of recognition shudder through her body. It was as though he could see inside her, as though he knew what she'd been through.

'Yeah,' she answered. She felt oblivious to the busy restaurant outside, or the other chefs bustling round the kitchen, as though it was just the two of them in their own private world, and she sensed that Lucas felt the same.

'Except sometimes, recently . . .' he hesitated, rubbing his forehead. 'I've started to have flashbacks. Nothing I can really piece together. Just moments, snatches of memory, and a feeling that—'

'Stephanie, we meet again.' Paulo strode into the kitchen with a roguish grin, breaking the moment.

'Hi Paulo,' Stephanie replied, as she jumped down from the counter, amused by the way he was blatantly checking her out.

'I'm afraid I'm going to have to enforce the rule of no diners in the kitchen when the restaurant's open,' he said with a charming smile, placing a hand on Stephanie's lower back and steering her towards the archway. 'You can't disturb the chef when he's working. Besides, his girlfriend wouldn't like it.'

Stephanie's gaze flicked to Lucas, whose eyes narrowed almost imperceptibly.

'Oh, did he not mention Elle?' Paulo could barely hide the note of glee in his voice. 'Yeah, she's a model. What was it she said this morning, Lucas? That she was hoping for a ring on her finger very soon . . .'

Stephanie let herself be guided back to her table, as she took in Paulo's words. Typical. She'd thought Lucas seemed like a nice guy, and imagined they'd made a connection, but it turned out she'd completely misread the situation. She felt like an idiot.

'How long are you staying on the island?'

Paulo's question cut into her thoughts, and she forced herself to focus. 'A couple of weeks. I'm staying at Catherine and Michael's villa,' she explained, noticing how Paulo's face lit up as he realized who she was referring to.

'Nice. Well, can I get your number, Stephanie Moon? I'd love to take you out sometime.'

Paulo was staring at her expectantly, with an air of self-confidence, as though he didn't expect to be refused. They didn't share the same kind of spark that she'd felt with Lucas, but he seemed fun, he was good-looking, and she liked his boldness. Why not enjoy herself during her stay? A no-strings holiday romance could be just what she needed.

'OK,' Stephanie agreed, as he pulled his mobile out from his jeans pocket, and she dictated her number.

'I'll be in touch,' Paulo winked.

When she glanced back towards the kitchen, Lucas was still staring at her, but she quickly looked away.

Camille returned to the hotel, her mind racing. The night had gone exceptionally well, but she didn't feel as though she'd had a moment to herself since she'd arrived in Mallorca. Seeing Lucas and meeting that plastic surgeon had inevitably brought up memories of the accident, and everything that had happened that night . . .

'Señora Fontaine?' The receptionist called out to her, and Camille stopped abruptly as she crossed the chic stone lobby.

'Yes?'

'A package arrived for you earlier this evening, shortly after you left for dinner.'

'Thank you.' Camille smiled as she took the A4-sized brown manila envelope, her name marked in black capitals on the front. She hurried back to her suite, taking in the paperwork and sketches and fabric samples piled on the desk. She still had a lot of work to do before she could go to sleep, she thought with a sigh, as she opened the balcony doors, letting in the warm night air, the voile curtain gently fluttering in the breeze.

Distractedly, Camille began to open the envelope. Her memories of Andre felt fresh and painful this evening, his ghost a constant presence on the island. She thought enough time had passed since the accident, but it seemed she'd been wrong. What had happened that fateful night still haunted her – perhaps it always would.

Camille slid the thin pile of papers out of the envelope. It took a moment for her to realize what she was seeing and then she gasped. The package didn't contain a fabric sample, or a copy of a contract, or any of the documents she had been expecting. Instead, she was holding a grainy black-and-white photograph, a copy of the accident report from the Swiss canton police, and a newspaper article with the headline: **Fashion Mogul Killed in Horror Crash**. The items were fastened together with a paperclip, a note attached to the top with four chilling words:

I know you lied.

Camille felt sick.

Another one . . .

She glanced around her, suddenly imagining she could feel someone watching her. She strode over to the balcony doors and closed them quickly, shivering despite the heat as she pulled the curtains shut.

Camille poured herself a glass of water with shaking hands and tried to think logically. The papers were still laid on the desk where she'd thrown them, and she hastily gathered them up, shoving them back inside the envelope. Then she picked up her lockable attaché case, entering the code and undoing the clips, sliding the envelope between a sheaf of sketches before firmly slamming the case shut and locking it once again.

She sank down on the desk chair, taking another sip of water as she caught sight of her reflection in the mirror. She looked as though she'd seen a ghost. Her face was pale, her eyes wide and startled.

This wasn't the first time she'd received a note like that. *Someone* knew what had happened that fateful night. But who?

She turned the piece of paper over to read it. It was just an amount, €10,000, and an offshore bank account number – untraceable, her accountant had explained, when she had asked him to send the money there before.

The world felt as though it was spinning, and Camille sensed panic rising in her chest, her breath coming fast, as though she were about to have a panic attack. She reached for the phone on the desk and started to punch in the number that she knew so well. It came automatically to her fingers; she didn't even need to think about it.

Nicolas.

But halfway through, Camille stopped. Taking a deep breath, she replaced the receiver with a click. She should have told Nicolas about this ages ago, rather than panicked and sent the money, three or four times now. It *was* a lot of money, but also, she could afford it. Some couture houses spent that every week on flowers for the lobby. This was a drop in the ocean in some ways.

However badly she needed him, she couldn't call him. Not after all the hurtful things she had said to him. Nicolas had been adamant; if she turned him down, it was over.

She would call her accountant as soon as he was at his desk.

Camille was on her own now. She had to deal with this herself.

Chapter 7

Stephanie Moon's long copper hair shimmered like gold in the sunlight, whipping around her face as the white speedboat bounced over the Mediterranean waves. The sun was high overhead but the wind was deliciously cooling as they sped along, so fast they skated over the water's surface.

Standing at the prow, with flecks of saltwater beading her skin, Stephanie felt a burst of adrenaline. She turned to look at Paulo who was driving the boat; it was hard to hear anything over the noise of the engine, and the roar of the wind and the waves, and he had to shout to be heard.

'Scream if you want to go faster,' he yelled, and Stephanie threw back her head and whooped with joy. In that moment, she felt wild and free, as though she was truly living. Until recently, she'd felt as if she was still waiting for her life to start. But now it felt sped up, as Paulo pushed the throttle and the boat skipped through the deep blue of the Balearic Sea. To her left, she could see the coastline in the distance, a wild tangle of rocky cliffs and hidden coves, with sprawling villas high on the bluffs. To the right, nothing but the distant horizon.

'Do you want to drive?' Paulo suggested.

Stephanie didn't need to be asked twice. She eagerly left her spot at the front of the boat and scrambled over to the helm, taking over from Paulo, feeling the power of the boat and how it responded to the slightest touch.

Paulo grinned at her, and Stephanie smiled back happily. She was dressed in a casual strappy sundress and leather sandals from the market. She wasn't trying to impress Paulo – she still didn't know if she was interested in him, but she sensed he could be a lot of fun. And he was attractive, dressed in shorts and a polo shirt teamed with designer sunglasses.

He caught her looking at him and moved closer. Standing behind her, he put his hand over hers as she steered; his was large and tanned, a contrast with her slender fingers and her hot pink manicure. Slowly, he pulled on the throttle and slowed the boat down. His body was almost touching hers, and Stephanie felt a frisson of excitement and uncertainty – she barely knew this guy, and now they were all alone, in the middle of the Mediterranean.

Paulo killed the engine. The silence was stark, only the gentle lapping of the waves against the hull, as they drifted beneath an endless expanse of sky that mirrored the perfect sapphire blue of the water.

'That was quite a thrill,' Stephanie commented with a raised eyebrow.

'I knew you'd enjoy it. You look like someone who goes looking for thrills. I read in one of the papers yesterday that you are difficult, fiery. I heard they threw you off the set of your movie? Is that true?'

Stephanie bristled, and was also alarmed that there was industry talk about what had happened on set, and it was leaking out to the press. Her stomach tightened. 'You can't believe everything you read in the papers.'

'What are you doing in Mallorca, then? Not that I'm complaining. I like a woman with fire in her belly.' Was it fire in her belly, or something darker? Stephanie was still discovering who she was, but she was sure Paulo was too self-absorbed to be truly interested in her, so she pushed down her anxiety.

'So what now? Do we swim to shore?' she teased, turning to look at Mallorca in the distance. It had to be at least a kilometre away.

Paulo laughed easily. 'No. Unless you want to escape from me?'

Stephanie smiled slowly. 'Not yet.'

'In that case . . .' Paulo crouched down and pulled a cool box from the small storage area inside the boat. 'Lunch,' he announced with a flourish, taking off the lid and bringing out half a dozen plates with delicious-looking food: fresh bread with olive oil and tomatoes, slices of cured ham and chorizo, three different kinds of salad, Padrón peppers laced with salt, and thick slices of cold tortilla.

'This looks amazing,' Stephanie exclaimed. But there was something about it that seemed familiar. 'Wait, is this—?'

'Il Paradiso's finest. Hand-prepared by my head chef this morning.'

'You had Lucas prepare a picnic for us?'

'Yeah,' Paulo smirked. He watched her face as he picked up a juicy, garlicky prawn and bit into it. 'Is that a problem?'

There was something challenging in his tone. She remembered the connection she'd had with Lucas, and how much she'd enjoyed talking to him. She realized she didn't want him to think that she and Paulo were seeing one another, let alone be forced into doing the catering for their date. But Paulo had said that Lucas had a serious girlfriend, and Lucas hadn't denied it, so Stephanie should probably put him out of her mind.

'No,' she replied evenly. 'Why would it be?'

Paulo shrugged. 'I figure I'm the one busting my ass to make the restaurant a success. Lucas needs to pull his weight too.'

Stephanie mulled on his words as she speared a forkful of tuna salad, thinking that Lucas definitely looked to her like he was working his butt off in the kitchen. The food was delicious. 'So how do you two know one another?'

'We've been friends since we were kids,' Paulo explained. 'He used to come and stay on the island in the summer. Because his parents were always away, always hustling to build their precious business, so he used to spend the school holidays with his grandmother in her villa. I was the poor kid down the road. You know, things like that don't matter when you're young – you just want to play, you don't care about how much money someone has. It's only as you grow up that you notice the difference.'

'But you're doing OK for yourself now,' Stephanie said,

noticing the Rolex on his wrist, the designer labels on his clothes.

'I worked hard to make something of myself. I didn't have anything handed to me on a plate,' Paulo said, unable to hide the trace of bitterness in his voice.

'Lucas has had a hard time too,' Stephanie said, as she took a bottle opener and flipped the lid off a bottle of Mahou beer. It was ice cold and perfect. She noticed that Paulo – or perhaps Lucas – had packed a bottle of cava too. 'The accident,' she clarified, opening a beer for Paulo too.

Paulo's face changed imperceptibly, a muscle in his jaw twitching. 'Yeah . . . The *accident*.' The word seemed loaded, but Stephanie couldn't read his meaning. 'He's certainly done well since. *Maman* felt so guilty about everything that she bought him a restaurant.'

'Camille paid for Il Paradiso?' Stephanie was surprised.

'Yeah. She set him up with everything, paid the first year's rent on the building . . . She's supposed to be a silent partner – not silent enough for my liking. Why are you so surprised? Like I said, Lucas gets everything he wants handed to him on a silver platter.'

Stephanie fell quiet, taking another sip of beer. It was obvious that Paulo was jealous of Lucas, for the advantages he'd had in life, and she was intrigued by their relationship. She knew she had to tread carefully, but if she was clever she could flatter him into revealing more.

'So what's your role in the business? I mean, if Lucas is doing the cooking, then—'

'Everything else,' Paulo interrupted. 'You name it, I do it. The marketing, the PR, the finances, dealing with suppliers, with staffing, with front of house. I dealt with the contractors and the team when we did the fit-out. When we were behind schedule for opening night, it was *my* family who came in and worked round the clock to ensure everything was finished. I've poured blood, sweat and tears into Il Paradiso, and no one can take that away from me . . .' He trailed off, and Stephanie noticed how a muscle in his cheek twitched as he glowered into the distance. Then he seemed to catch himself. 'But let's not talk about business today. Let's talk about you. You fascinate me, Stephanie Moon. You're beautiful, talented, intelligent . . .' He tilted his head to look at her, and Stephanie felt herself blush beneath his scrutiny.

'I'm just enjoying the ride, seeing where life takes me, and—'

She was interrupted by the tinny tune from a mobile phone. Paulo pulled it from his pocket and glanced at the screen. 'Sorry, I need to take this.'

He stood up and answered the call, turning away from her and walking swiftly to the back of the boat. The vessel was only small, but from his body language it was clear that he wanted the call to stay private. He spoke in a rapid, low stream of Spanish. Stephanie could pick out the occasional word – '*Palma*', '*noche*' – but understood very little.

She watched him as he spoke, his back broad, his skin tanned, his manner cocky. He was definitely a bad boy, but there was something appealing about him and Stephanie wasn't immune to his charm. She liked the way he flirted so openly, the way his eyes teased when he looked at her. He let out a peel of throaty laughter, followed by a final burst of Spanish before ending his call.

'Sorry about that,' Paulo apologized, as he strolled back to where she was sitting. 'Just a bit of business. Now, where were we?' he asked, as he picked up his beer and clinked it against hers. 'Oh yes, you were going to tell me everything there is to know about the captivating Stephanie Moon. And I mean *everything*.'

Stephanie burst out laughing, unable to help herself. Paulo clearly spelt trouble, but he could certainly make the next couple of weeks a lot more interesting.

Nicolas Martin swore lightly under his breath as the limousine inched forwards, and the air around him was filled with the noise of dozens of car horns, as angry drivers vented their frustration at the New York traffic. Vehicles had ground to a halt on the George Washington Bridge – which at least afforded him a good view of the city – but he was in a hurry to make his flight, and anxiously checked his wristwatch.

Nicolas was heading for Teterboro Airport, just across the Hudson in New Jersey. Whilst he knew his private jet wouldn't leave without him, he was eager to get going, impatient to begin his journey now that he'd decided on a course of action.

He wasn't going to give up on Camille, and he refused to let her simply walk out of his life. They'd known one another for so long now that it was impossible to imagine never seeing her again. It had been hard enough not to be in contact these last few days, which was probably the longest they'd gone without speaking in more than twenty years. Nicolas had lost count of the number of times he'd gone to pick up the phone to call her, before remembering his resolution and hanging up.

Nicolas's heart ached without Camille. He was barely eating, struggling to sleep, and he'd uncharacteristically completely lost interest in his work. He couldn't go on like this – which was why he was heading to Mallorca.

The plan had always been for Nicolas to attend the launch – after all, it was a collaboration between Camille Andre and American Athletics. But more than that, it was a huge occasion for Camille, and Nicolas wanted to be by her side, just as he'd been for every other major event in her life: the launch of her company, her marriage to Andre, the birth of her son. In fact, Nicolas had seen Lucas even before Andre had – Andre had been overseas visiting a supplier and his return flight had been cancelled, so Nicolas reached the hospital before him. And, of course, he'd been the first person Camille had called after the accident, and the one she'd turned to ever since.

Nicolas wanted to fix everything in Camille's world. He instinctively took care of her, determined to resolve every issue and smooth over any trouble. He did it because he loved her – always had, always would.

But now Nicolas was beginning to question how Camille seemed to take his support for granted. Was he destined to always be her fixer, his only role to trouble-shoot her problems? Nicolas wanted to be more than that. He wanted to be her lover again. He wanted to be her husband and for them to grow old together.

The traffic started moving suddenly, the hold-up magically disappearing as they crossed the bridge into New Jersey. Nicolas rubbed his temples, feeling the beginnings of a tension headache.

At least now he had a valid reason to see Camille – the fusion fashion line between their companies had been a long time in the pipeline, a crucial pivot for both brands. But he knew that it wasn't strictly business driving his need to get there. The last few turbulent years had thrown up a lot of questions; now Nicolas was heading to Mallorca, and he wanted answers.

Chapter 8

The pretty little town of Valldemossa was picture-perfect and felt like stepping back in time. It was situated on top of a hill, its honey-coloured stone buildings clustered higgledy-piggledy on the side of the slopes, surrounded by the spectacular Tramuntana mountains. Isobel and Stuart were strolling through the picturesque old town, winding their way through narrow, cobbled streets where bougainvillea ran riot across the walls of the ancient houses, the buildings adorned with wrought-iron balconies and emerald-green shutters.

Isobel was in her element browsing the artisan shops, looking at the trinkets and the jewellery, unable to resist buying some of the beautiful textiles for inspiration. Stuart seemed on edge, showing little interest in the hand-painted vases his wife had fallen in love with.

'Darling, I know shopping isn't your favourite activity in the world, but do try to be a little more enthusiastic. Oh, look at those stunning candles, wouldn't they look perfect in the dining room?'

Meet Me at Sunset

'Mmm,' Stuart replied distractedly. He pulled his mobile phone out of his pocket and glanced at the screen. Isobel watched him and frowned.

'Are you expecting a call?'

'What? Oh no, just checking I haven't missed anything important.'

'We're on holiday. Try to switch off a little. I'm sure your colleagues can cope if anything happens. Ooh, have you seen those batik dresses?'

Isobel raced off, as Stuart lagged behind like a sulky schoolboy. Isobel could feel herself growing increasingly irritated. Why was her husband determined to be in a bad mood? They were on vacation, and there was nothing more taxing to do than laze by the pool, order delicious cocktails, and have the occasional trip out to a nearby village. It felt like heaven to Isobel, but Stuart was acting as though it was torture.

It was as though they'd never left Scotland, Isobel thought in frustration. Stuart was here in body, but his mind was clearly elsewhere. She might as well be on her own – she'd probably have more fun, she thought resentfully. Take last night, for example: they'd both been on a high after their meal at Il Paradiso, where they'd dined with two bona fide movie stars – not to mention Stephanie Moon, who'd been very sweet, and Isobel hoped she'd make good on her promise to let her design a gown for her.

Isobel and Stuart had returned to the hotel, had a nightcap at the bar, then gone back to their room and made love. It was a sultry night, and Isobel had taken a shower afterwards, the water cooling her skin, but when she'd stepped out she'd found Stuart still awake and working on his laptop. It had been the same thing that morning after breakfast – Stuart had jumped straight on his laptop, muttering unhappily about the hotel's Wi-Fi connection. Isobel had practically had to drag him out of their room when their car arrived, and now he was being sulky and distant.

She browsed the rails in the boutique with a practised eye, taking in the styles and shapes. This shop was full of beautiful beach dresses, light and flowing, in bright colours and exquisite prints. Isobel pulled one out admiringly, holding it up against her body.

'Would you like to try?' the saleswoman asked in English.

'Yes please,' Isobel nodded, selecting a couple more items and calling out, 'Stuart, I'll be a few minutes, I'm just going to try these.'

Stuart sighed, looking bored. 'OK.'

Isobel stepped into the cubicle and began to undress, wondering what was going on with her husband. In truth, it felt as though things hadn't been great in their marriage for a while now. When they were at home, it was easy to paper over the cracks, falling back on the excuse that they both led busy lives. They'd become like ships that passed in the night, due to Stuart's high-pressure career and Isobel's boutique, as though justifying why they spent so little time with each other. Now that they were together twenty-four seven, it showed just how far apart they'd drifted, and how little they had in common any more. Conversation was sometimes stilted, and they rarely had fun; Isobel couldn't remember the last time Stuart had made her laugh.

She smoothed the material of a blue-and-white porcelain print dress over her hips then stood back to admire her reflection. She was pleased with what she saw, and she pulled back the curtain, emerging into the shop.

'*¡Qué bonita!*' the saleswoman said, and Isobel smiled. She spoke a little Spanish from the time she'd spent as an intern in Madrid, and her holidays with Stuart to Barcelona, Ibiza and Seville.

Isobel glanced around, eager to show Stuart how good she looked in the dress, but he was no longer in the shop. Her searching gaze found him through the window. He had his back to her, but as he moved slightly from one foot to the other, she saw that he was on his phone once more. Isobel watched him, frustration and annoyance coursing through her. Couldn't he leave work alone for one day?

'I'm sorry, I'm not going to buy it,' Isobel said to the saleswoman, whose face dropped at the prospect of losing a sale. Isobel was too preoccupied to notice, as she went back into the cubicle and quickly changed, ignoring the other dresses she'd selected. She headed outside, fury written across her face, just as Stuart was finishing his call.

'Work?' she asked, raising her eyebrows.

Stuart had the good grace to look ashamed. 'Isobel,' he began, placing his hands on her shoulders, but she shrugged them off.

'What?'

Stuart took a deep breath, and Isobel knew she wasn't going to like what he had to say. 'I'm sorry, but I need to fly to the mainland for a couple of days.'

'What do you mean?' Isobel was aware that her voice was growing louder, that she was causing a scene in the quiet street. Passing tourists glanced at them curiously.

'It's an important client. I can't say no.'

'More important than me?'

'Isobel—'

'Don't you dare roll your eyes at me! Two weeks, Stuart. That's all I asked. Just one holiday where we could spend some time together. Start trying for a baby . . .'

Her husband pressed his hands to his temples in exasperation. 'Isobel, you don't understand the expectations that come with a high-profile career. I'm doing more than running up a few dresses for ladies who lunch.'

Isobel's cheeks coloured. When she spoke, her voice was quiet yet dangerous. 'That's not fair.'

'I know, I'm sorry, I didn't mean it like that. I'm under a lot of stress right now. Look, think of it this way – if we were at home, it'd be a longer flight and I'd probably have to be away an extra night. It's far closer if I fly from here.'

Isobel narrowed her eyes. 'Did you plan this? When you booked this holiday, was it a convenient location to visit an important client?'

He hesitated just a micro-second too long. 'No, of course not. Besides, you're the one who suggested Majorca.'

Isobel stared at him for a long moment. She felt hurt, confused and angry. 'I don't know what to believe any more.'

'Isobel, I've said I'm sorry. I'll make it up to you . . .'

'I wanted you here, Stuart. It's more important to me than you know.'

He stepped towards her, taking her hands in his, and she didn't shake him off. Encouraged, he brought her fingertips to his lips and kissed them. 'I won't be gone for long. Here, take my credit card, buy yourself something nice whilst I'm away. But let's go find a taxi and get back to the hotel. My flight leaves in a few hours.'

As Stuart marched off, Isobel stared bleakly after him.

I don't want to buy myself something nice, she thought sadly. *I want my husband back.*

That afternoon, after Stuart had left for his flight, Isobel decided to explore the hotel. She was still shocked and upset, but had decided to do her best to enjoy her holiday and not let her husband's unexpected absence ruin it. After all, the Palacio del Sol Radiante had an extensive cocktail list, not to mention a small but well-stocked designer boutique, and Stuart's credit card was burning a hole in her pocket.

Isobel strolled past the entrance to the spa, reminding herself to book a full body hot-stone massage before Stuart returned, when a door up ahead swung open and a woman rushed out. Isobel recognized her immediately, instinctively calling her name.

'Camille!'

Camille Fontaine paused, then looked around her distractedly. It seemed to take a moment for her to place Isobel, despite the fact that they'd had dinner together the previous evening. Camille looked as chic as ever, in a printed silk shift dress, and Isobel felt a pang of envy at her easy, French style.

'Isobel,' Camille walked towards her with a smile. 'I'm sorry, there's so much going on, my mind is spinning.'

'Anything I can help with? I find myself at a loose end suddenly . . .' At Camille's frown, Isobel explained, 'My husband, Stuart, has been called away for work. I've been left by myself for a few days.'

'Oh, poor you! But please don't be too hard on him. It was a delight talking to him at dinner, and he does such wonderful work. He did a marvellous job with Lucas's reconstructive surgery: the world needs him.'

'Oh yes – your son's car accident,' Isobel said, feeling momentarily guilty. She saw a trace of confusion flicker across Camille's face, and explained, 'Stuart told me a little about what happened.'

'Yes, that's right. It was four years ago now, though sometimes it feels like it was only yesterday. But let's not dwell on that. If you're not busy, you must come to my launch. That's why I'm here. Your husband said you were a Camille Andre fan.'

'Oh, I am,' Isobel said. 'I'd be honoured!'

Camille hesitated, as though deliberating over something, then seemed to make up her mind. 'We're setting up right now. Would you like to come and see?'

'I'd love to.'

Isobel followed Camille back through the door leading to the Sunset Room, ignoring the No Entry sign. Inside, the room was large and beautiful, with huge west-facing floor-to-ceiling windows, but it was currently in a state of disarray. An elevated catwalk was being constructed in the middle of the room, and all around were stacks of chairs, cardboard boxes with bubble wrap spilling out, half-finished displays and a partially assembled lighting rig. A dozen people were dashing to and fro, and the place was a hive of activity.

Isobel felt the crackle of electricity in the room. The situation looked chaotic now, but she knew that in a couple of days' time it would be completely transformed. She remembered the excitement of fashion shows from when she'd been an intern – months of hard work went into it, and all for barely twenty minutes of showtime. It was exhilarating, and a team effort.

'We're keeping it under wraps for now, but the show is a collaboration between Camille Andre and American Athletics,' Camille explained enthusiastically. 'We're producing a diffusion line, and it will be the first time our brand will be available at affordable prices. Still luxury, but accessible. And this . . .' she continued, as she reached into one of the boxes and carefully opened a dust bag, 'Is the new Camille bag.'

Isobel gasped. 'It's incredible.' Camille bags were known for being chic and classic, a staple for society women who wanted to look polished and elegant. *This* bag was clearly aimed at a much younger, cooler audience, made of soft leather to give it a slouchy look with an adjustable, woven strap that gave it an urban edge.

'I adore it,' Isobel continued. 'It still has that classic Camille feel, but this is far more modern. You know, you should make a crossbody version. For the working woman, or a young mother, who needs to be hands free.'

Camille looked at her thoughtfully. 'You have great instincts, and a real eye for fashion.'

'Thank you,' Isobel breathed, flattered by the compliment. 'I actually design a little myself. I run a small boutique, back in Edinburgh.'

'You do? You clearly have a talent, Isobel, and you must come to the show. I'll put you on the VIP list.'

'I can't wait,' Isobel smiled, her eyes glinting. 'As a matter of fact—'

But whatever she was about to say was lost as a screech and a cry of 'Camille!' came from behind them. Isobel turned to see a tall, leggy blonde strut into the room, wearing a dress that was so short it skimmed her bottom and showed off acres of tanned thigh.

'Oh,' Camille faltered, her face falling. '*Salut*, Elle.'

Elle sashayed over and looked Isobel up and down, as though trying to work out whether or not she was important.

'Elle, this is Isobel MacFarlane,' Camille introduced them. 'She's a guest at the palacio, and her husband was involved in Lucas's surgery. Isobel, this is Elle Mettier, and she's—'

'Camille's future daughter-in-law,' Elle interrupted, with a throaty laugh. 'I'm Lucas's girlfriend, and soon-to-be fiancée,' she explained to Isobel, though it was obvious that the performance was for Camille's benefit. 'And hopefully the future face of Camille Andre,' she added, snatching the bag from Camille's hands and throwing it over her shoulder, striking a series of poses. 'See how good I can make it look?'

'Elle,' Camille began, and Isobel could hear the irritation in her voice. 'You're a very beautiful woman, and I can understand why my son wants to be with you, but I'm sorry, you're not the right fit for Camille Andre. Besides, we've already signed someone, and the announcement is imminent. I know that you're dating Lucas, but I have to do what's right for the brand. Camille Andre always comes first.'

As Elle stood there, open-mouthed, Isobel saw her opportunity to escape the awkward atmosphere. 'I'll leave you two to it. It sounds as though you have business to discuss. It was good to meet you, Elle. See you later, Camille.' Isobel walked away with a smile.

Back in her hotel room, Isobel moved with focus, all thoughts of massages and boutiques and cocktails banished from her mind. Right now, she had something else to think about.

The room felt different without Stuart – no swim shorts drying out on the balcony, or loafers taking up space by the door. His laptop was gone from the desk, his shirts taken from the wardrobe, leaving much more space for Isobel's clothes. Housekeeping had been, so everything was clean and tidy, the air con turned on and the room a delicious temperature. It was cool and quiet, with no one to disturb her.

Isobel lifted down her suitcase, from where it had been stored at the top of the wardrobe. It appeared empty, but she unzipped the hidden inner compartment and slid out a document folder. She carried it over to the king-size bed and took out the papers inside, laying them out across the crisp, white sheets, then stood back to observe the scene.

There was a newspaper article with the headline: **Fashion Mogul Killed in Horror Crash**. Another entitled: **Andre Fontaine Funeral in Paris**, with a photograph of the celebrity mourners supporting a black-clad Camille in the centre. There were other things too, a cutting of Camille in dark glasses taken with a long-lens camera being bundled into a car outside a hospital. Pictures of her with Nicolas. There was a copy of Stuart's notes relating to Lucas Fontaine's reconstructive surgery, beside a cutting from *Vogue* announcing that Camille Andre would be launching its new capsule collection at the Palacio del Sol Radiante in Mallorca. The dates had been circled in red pen, and Isobel had dropped very unsubtle hints to Stuart about where and when she wanted to go on holiday.

She would make sure that Camille didn't forget about her VIP invitation to the upcoming launch. Isobel couldn't wait to be a guest of honour – she would make sure it was an event that no one would ever forget.

Chapter 9

'Lucas, *chéri*, this is very generous of you, but you really didn't have to,' Camille said, as she climbed into his red Porsche Boxster which had pulled up outside the front of the hotel.

'I don't mind,' he shrugged, as the car roared off, stones skittering from beneath its tyres.

'But you get so little free time as it is. I don't want you spending your rare days off ferrying your mother around. I could just as easily have got the hotel to call me a car.'

'True, but I rarely get to see you too, so let's make the most of it whilst you're here.'

'Oh, that's so sweet. And you're sure there's no ulterior motive?' Camille teased. 'No one you want to see at the house?'

'No,' Lucas said gruffly, but Camille knew him too well and detected a slight pink flush on his face. She was pleased.

Today she had another meeting with Catherine Zeta-Jones, and Lucas had offered to drive her up to the estate at S'Estaca. Camille suspected he wanted to see Stephanie again and hoped that was the case – she'd certainly love to be shot of that pushy and trashy model, Elle. The cheek of the girl yesterday, turning up and claiming to be 'just passing', then pitching to be the face of Camille Andre. And all in front of Isobel too. What an embarrassment.

Outside the car window, the Mallorcan scenery flashed by, as Camille's thoughts drifted. It wasn't far to Catherine's villa, just a few miles along a winding coastal road. The land here was bleached by the sun in shades of terracotta and ochre, with pine and olive trees providing welcome greenery, and straggly yellow wildflowers offering a burst of colour. The mountains stretched away inland, whilst the glorious Mediterranean sparkled on the other side, lapping against the rocky shoreline. It was another idyllic day on the island.

'So, what's happening with Nicolas?' Lucas's voice interrupted Camille's reflective mood.

She sighed softly, her gaze fixed straight ahead at the stunning scenery. 'Like I said, nothing for you to worry about.'

'But I *am* worried about it. If you and Nicolas have fallen out, then it must be serious. I've never known the two of you to argue – you always bring him round to your point of view,' Lucas laughed lightly. 'You know I think he's a great guy. Since losing Papa, he's the closest thing I have to a father.'

Camille exhaled shakily, tears pricking at her eyelids. Lucas's words cut deep, bringing up feelings of guilt and confusion that she'd tried to bury. She didn't want to have this conversation with Lucas, but nor did she want to hide the truth from him. 'He asked me to marry him—'

'That's amazing news!' Lucas exclaimed, before Camille had the chance to finish her sentence. 'Congratulations! I'm so happy for the two of you.'

'I said no.'

Lucas seemed confounded by this. '*What? But why?*'

'It's complicated, Lucas.'

'No, it isn't. He adores you, and takes such good care of you. I know you love him too. He makes you happy – you light up around him. And it'd be good for you to be with someone – I'd be more relaxed, knowing you weren't on your own.'

'This is *my* decision to make, not yours.' Camille's tone was sharp, almost snappish. She never spoke to Lucas that way, and he looked at her in shock, the hurt clearly visible on his handsome face.

'Is everything OK, *Maman*?' he asked gently. 'You haven't been yourself recently.'

Camille flapped her hands in her lap. 'I know, I know. I'm sorry. It's just the stress of the show and . . . everything. I have a lot to think about, that's all.'

'I understand,' Lucas said carefully. 'It's just, I love Nicolas. He's been in my life since I was born. I don't want to lose him, the way I lost Papa.'

'I know, *chéri*. I'm sorry. I will think about it all and try to resolve matters with Nicolas. But I don't want to talk about it now. Please, Lucas, leave it alone, for my sake.'

He sighed, 'All right – for now.'

'Thank you. Now tell me what's happening with you, and with the restaurant. The meal was beautiful the other night. Your cooking is better than ever, and my guests were so impressed.'

'I'm glad. It was a great night. We were full to capacity, and there was such a buzz in the air.'

'You'll have your Michelin star in no time,' Camille beamed.

'Perhaps . . .' Lucas forced a smile.

'What is it?'

Now it was Lucas's turn to be evasive, his hands tightening on the steering wheel. 'I don't know exactly. There are a few things that are niggling at me, that don't feel right . . .'

'Like what?'

Lucas hesitated. 'There was an incident the other day. Paulo hadn't paid one of our suppliers – Diego, the seafood guy.'

'Diego? But you've known him for years. Your father and I used to buy from him directly. He always had the freshest sea bass on the island.'

'He still does.'

'Well, I'm sure it was a mistake.'

'I hope so. But there've been a few odd things recently. Paulo's been spending a lot of time in Palma, especially at night – he's rarely around for the evening service. Not that he needs to be – that's not his job. But it just feels like . . . like he's keeping secrets from me.'

Camille stiffened. She knew the importance of trusting your gut, and talk of secrets always put her on edge. 'It's not acceptable, Lucas. He's your business partner, and he needs to be open with you. You must speak to him.'

'I will, *Maman*.' But Lucas looked uncomfortable, and

Camille knew that he instinctively shied away from confrontation.

She was about to press him further when he turned down a slip road and they pulled up at the discreet entrance to S'Estaca. Lucas spoke into the intercom and the gates slid open. Camille forced herself back into professional mode, knowing that her focus needed to be on the meeting with Catherine. Her conversation with Lucas would have to wait until later.

'Camille! Thank you so much for coming. And Lucas – I wasn't expecting to see you too, but I'm thrilled you're here,' Catherine Zeta-Jones purred as she welcomed them into her home. 'Michael and I had such a wonderful time at Il Paradiso. The food was exquisite.'

'You're too kind. It was an honour to have you there. But I'm not staying today, I'm just dropping off my mother.'

'Oh, that's a shame. I was planning a delicious lunch by the pool, and I'd love for you to join us. It won't be as good as your food, of course, but it might be nice to eat something someone else has prepared for once . . .'

'Well, I . . .' Lucas could feel himself weakening.

'We'll eat in half an hour or so, so not long to wait. You're welcome to make yourself at home in the meantime, and I'm sure Stephanie's around here somewhere. Steph?' Catherine called out, and her voice echoed around the expansive villa. 'Besides, you can't make your poor mother take a taxi back,' she teased, as Lucas laughed.

'How could I be so unchivalrous? Of course, I'll stay. Thank you for the invitation.'

'Perfect,' Catherine beamed. 'Now, Camille, I've pulled out some dresses upstairs where I love the shape on me, to give you an idea of silhouette.'

'Wonderful. I've brought some fabric samples, and some initial sketches,' Camille replied, patting her trusty attaché case.

'I can't wait to see them, I'm sure we're going to create something divine. Ah, Stephanie,' Catherine smiled, as she appeared in the doorway, wearing a denim mini skirt and a cropped vest, her long hair hanging loose. Lucas tried to ignore the way his heart rate accelerated when he saw her, the way his mouth felt dry as though he didn't know what to say.

'Did you call?' Stephanie asked Catherine.

'I did. Could you be a sweetheart and entertain Lucas for me until lunch, whilst Camille and I talk gowns upstairs?'

'Sure.' Stephanie turned to him with a grin, her dazzling blue eyes dancing with mischief.

Lucas couldn't help but grin back, thinking how stunning she looked when she smiled; how – even dressed casually and with no make-up – she was one of the most beautiful women he'd ever seen, with her luminous pale skin and tumbling copper hair.

Catherine and Camille headed for the stone staircase, leaving Lucas and Stephanie alone.

'I hope you weren't busy,' he said, berating himself for saying something so banal.

'Nothing that can't wait. I was learning lines,' Stephanie explained, indicating the thick script in her hands.

'Don't let me stop you. I can help, if you like?' Lucas offered.

'OK,' Stephanie agreed. 'Let's go sit outside on the terrace. It's beautiful there.'

Lucas followed her, unable to tear his eyes from her toned, slender legs as she walked, the way her mini skirt barely covered the high, rounded curve of her bottom. He found himself wondering what had happened between her and Paulo on their date – whether she had been attracted to him, and if she had let him take her in his arms and kiss her—

'Isn't it gorgeous?'

'Hmm?' Pulled back to the present, Lucas realized that Stephanie had sat down on one of the wide wicker sofas topped with thick cream cushions, and was indicating the view. They were on a small, terracotta-tiled terrace, with a pergola overhead, interlocking vines and lush purple clematis hanging down and perfectly framing the vista of the Mediterranean, as the cliff fell away sharply below them. 'It's spectacular,' Lucas said, his hazel eyes never leaving her face.

He sat down on the other end of the sofa. Stephanie placed her script down on the table but didn't open it.

'So how did your date with Paulo go?' he asked, unable to restrain himself any longer.

'We had fun,' Stephanie replied, and Lucas felt his heart sink. 'He's a bit of a playboy, I'm not sure I want to get too close to him,' she continued, as jealousy and relief surged through Lucas. He knew it was ridiculous – he was in a relationship with Elle, and Paulo was his best friend, but since he'd met Stephanie two nights ago, he hadn't been able to stop thinking about her. 'Sorry,' she added. 'I know he's your friend and everything, but—'

'No, don't apologize, it's fine. I don't mind,' Lucas

insisted, offering up a silent prayer of gratitude that Stephanie was proving invulnerable to Paulo's charms.

'Thank you, by the way,' Stephanie continued, after a pause. 'For the picnic food . . .'

'Oh, yeah,' Lucas shrugged. 'I just wanted you to have something nice. To make up for the terrible date,' he finished with a grin.

'I didn't say it was terrible,' Stephanie laughed, throwing a cushion at him, which Lucas expertly caught.

'But the food was the best thing about it, right?' Lucas pressed cheekily.

'It was amazing! I'm a terrible cook.'

'I don't believe you.'

'It's true! I can barely boil an egg.'

'Then I'll teach you. How to boil an egg, and a bit more.'

'More?' Stephanie asked, raising an eyebrow as she shifted in her seat. Her skirt slid up her legs, and Lucas had to avert his eyes from the acres of shapely, tanned thigh just inches from him.

'I'll teach you everything I know,' he said, his eyes twinkling.

'Everything? Now there's an offer that's hard to refuse.'

The air between them was crackling with electricity. Lucas found himself staring at her soft, pale pink lips, wondering what it would be like to kiss her, and suddenly he felt a sharp memory pierce his thoughts.

His father revving the engine, in the seat of the car as it sped through the mountains, his lips shaping words . . .

'If he wants to play that game . . .'

What did it mean? He closed his eyes tightly to try and capture more, but then suddenly the memory was gone, slipping away, leaving him grappling for it in his mind, frustrated and confused by what it all meant.

'Are you OK?' Stephanie put her hand on his arm; he found her steady warmth reassuring.

'I just had another memory . . . a sudden flash of something.'

'Yes, I remember you saying something the other night in the restaurant?' Stephanie began. 'Before Paulo came in. You started mentioning the flashbacks, from the accident.'

'Yeah.' Lucas swallowed, his mind pulled from the delights of Stephanie's lips back to that terrible night four years ago. He thought again of the flashbacks he had been getting, out of the blue, which seemed to rise up unbidden. The sensations hit him again: the darkness, the ear-splitting screech of metal, the screaming. Then the silence. 'I could never remember anything about it, but recently . . . There are moments. My father's voice . . . he's telling me to slow down,' Lucas said, closing his eyes and wincing as he recalled the memory. 'I can feel my fingers, gripping onto something, trying to hold on . . . The sensation of being out of control . . .'

He felt someone touch him and flinched. Opening his eyes, Lucas saw Stephanie staring at him in concern. She was sitting forwards, her hands gripping his.

'Are you OK?' she asked again, worriedly, her calm eyes searching his face.

Embarrassed, he pulled his hands away, sitting back. 'I'm fine. I probably just need to . . . I had therapy after the accident, but I haven't been for a couple of years now. Maybe I should start again.'

'You're brave to have worked hard to move on,' Stephanie insisted, as Lucas shook his head.

'I'm really not. But what can I do? It's life. You have to carry on.'

Stephanie nodded, taking in his words.

'You seem like you understand,' Lucas said. A gentle breeze blew in from the sea, ruffling his floppy dark hair, carrying with it the tang of saltwater. 'As though something had happened to you . . .'

'Perhaps I do understand. The circumstances aren't the same, but . . .' Stephanie swallowed. 'I know what it's like to feel the past weighing on you.'

Lucas could sense her hesitance.

'You had a bad thing happen to you too?'

'Oh, no, not like that . . . but I . . . I didn't have the easiest time when I was a kid. I know what it's like to have to do things yourself.'

'You have no family?'

'Yes, I do, but it's complicated.' Her eyes dropped, and Lucas sensed a vulnerability in her.

'Maybe you can tell *me* about it—'

'There you are,' Catherine exclaimed. The two of them jumped apart. 'Well, don't you both look cosy?' she said with a dangerous smile. 'Tell me, Lucas, has Stephanie been looking after you?'

'Yes, she's . . . she's been doing a wonderful job.' His eyes met Stephanie's, and a look of understanding and longing passed between them. Lucas realized his pulse was racing, his heart pounding.

'Excellent,' Catherine declared. 'Now, let's all go and have lunch.'

Chapter 10

'Lucas.'

Lucas was prepping for the evening service, lost in his own world as chopped piles of lush purple aubergines and velvety mushrooms grew on the work surface in front of him. His mind had drifted to thoughts of Stephanie, and everything she'd told him that afternoon, the secrets they'd shared with one another, not to mention how incredible she'd looked in that bikini . . .

'Lucas!'

'Elle,' Lucas exclaimed in surprise, guilt flickering across his face as he turned and saw her. He went to kiss her, but she tossed her head to the side, offering him her cheek instead. *'Chérie*, what's wrong?' he asked, but Elle wouldn't meet his gaze, resolutely avoiding his eyes as she pushed her glossy lips into a pout.

'What is it?' Lucas persisted, beginning to feel frustrated. He was busy with his work and didn't have time for Elle's theatrics today. A sudden pang of worry struck him that she'd somehow discovered that he'd spent time with Stephanie that afternoon, but he quickly dismissed the thought as ridiculous. He hadn't done anything wrong, had he?

Finally, Elle turned her baby blue eyes on him, huge and shining wet with tears.

'I saw your mother yesterday, at the hotel. She was so mean to me, and she said . . .' Elle took a shaky breath, as though fighting back the tears. 'She told me I couldn't model for Camille Andre.'

She collapsed into Lucas's arms, and he had to restrain himself from rolling his eyes.

'Darling, I know you're disappointed, but *Maman* has always said that you're not the right look for the brand. It's nothing personal, it's just . . .' Lucas trailed off, struggling to find the right words. He knew if he said the wrong thing, she could fly off the handle. 'Look,' he continued, pressing little butterfly kisses on her nose, her cheeks, her lips. 'You're beautiful, stunning, everything a man could want. But that's not the Camille Andre look – it's more elegant, and chic.'

'I can do elegant,' Elle screeched, pulling away from Lucas as he inwardly grimaced. 'Are you saying I'm not chic?' she demanded, striking a dramatic pose against the stainless-steel backdrop of the walk-in fridge.

Lucas stared at his girlfriend. She looked like every man's fantasy, with her tumbling blonde hair, enormous kohl-lined eyes and strawberry lips. Not to mention the endless tanned legs emerging from a white, crocheted mini dress, and the full breasts pushing against the criss-cross lace fastening. She looked like Brigitte Bardot in her heyday – but he knew his mother wanted to conjure the image of Audrey Hepburn for her brand.

He'd fallen hard for Elle at first, her fiery temperament and sulky sensuality had driven him crazy with lust. But now her demands and petulance just drove him crazy full stop. She was immature and selfish, and he'd come to realize he wasn't in love with her. But the last few years since the accident had held him in a kind of suspended animation, avoiding big decisions and change. Now he felt like he was finally waking up and wasn't entirely sure he was happy with the way his life looked, and he was as much to blame as Elle for that.

'You're incredible,' he assured Elle, hoping she wouldn't notice that he'd avoided the question.

'It's not fair,' she sulked, stamping her foot in her wedge heels. 'I want that job!'

Lucas's eyebrows shot up to his hairline, and – sensing that she'd gone too far – Elle tottered back across to him and wrapped her body around his. 'It's just a big disappointment for me. A contract like this could catapult me into the big league. I don't want to be doing catalogue shoots for Wonderbra for the rest of my career,' she said bitterly, naming the high-street brand.

At that moment, Paulo strolled into the kitchen. 'You've got a modelling job with Wonderbra?' he asked sarcastically. 'Congratulations, Elle. Your career's really on the up.'

'Shut up, Paulo,' she shot back, her eyes flashing with venom, as Paulo laughed and helped himself to a handful of the fresh red peppers Lucas had been slicing. Elle ignored him, turning back to Lucas. 'Why do you always take your mother's side?' she complained.

'I don't,' Lucas assured her. 'But it's her business. I can't interfere.'

'She interferes in yours all the time,' Elle retorted, as Paulo let out a snort of laughter that inexplicably irritated Lucas. He took his anger out on Elle.

'It's not *my* fault that my mother doesn't think you're good enough,' Lucas snapped. 'She's been running her company for thirty years. You've been a model for two minutes and your biggest job was a print commercial for dandruff shampoo. Why the hell would she want to hire you?'

Elle's mouth fell open in shock. Tears – genuine this time – sprang into her eyes, hurt written plainly on her beautiful face. Then she slapped him hard across the cheek and stormed out of the restaurant.

Lucas exhaled slowly, feeling the sting on his face, aware that his cheek must be glowing red. He knew he'd been an arsehole, that he should run after Elle and apologize, but he'd reached the limits of his patience. He'd meant what he said – he wasn't responsible for his mother's choices, and he didn't appreciate being forced to choose a side.

'You deserved that.'

Lucas glanced up to see Paulo watching him, leaning languidly against the worktop whilst crunching on the crudités. 'Leave some for the customers, hmm?' he snapped.

Paulo's sardonic expression didn't change as he slowly shook his head. 'Lucas, Lucas. Never satisfied, are you?'

'What do you mean?'

'Ever since you were a boy you've been the same. You were given everything – but you never appreciated it. As soon as you got something, it lost its value.'

'Since when did you become such a philosopher?' Lucas replied sarcastically.

'Just sharing my observations . . .' Paulo shrugged, taking a wrap of plastic from the pocket of his shorts and twisting it open.

He tapped out a line of white powder on the shiny steel surface of the countertop, using one of Lucas's best chopping knives to marshal it into a line. Then he bent over, snorting it ostentatiously. Wiping the residue with his forefinger, he rubbed it into his gums.

Now it was Lucas's turn to shake his head. He angrily snatched up the knife, washing it thoroughly before wiping down the counter with a troubled expression. 'You shouldn't do that here.'

'Don't start lecturing me.'

'Well maybe it's *your* turn to hear a few home truths. You're doing too much of that shit. It's not good for you, *or* for the restaurant.'

'Hey, give me a break. We can't all have rich mummies to help us out.' Paulo grinned to imply it was a joke, but Lucas wasn't blind to the deliberate barb. He fell silent as he went back to his prep, slicing deftly and precisely.

'Why are you spending so much time in Palma? You're hardly ever here.'

'I thought you had everything under control,' Paulo replied, a challenge in his tone.

'I have – when it comes to food. You're supposed to take charge of the logistics, and it feels like things are slipping.'

'Don't worry about it,' Paulo said easily, coming up behind him and placing a hand on Lucas's shoulder. 'You need to chill, my friend. Here, take this,' he suggested, offering the rest of his wrap to Lucas.

'Not my scene. And you need to be careful.'

'And *you* need to take the stick out of your ass. Have a good night, man. I'm out of here.'

'You're not staying?' Lucas was frustrated.

'People to see, things to do,' Paulo winked, clapping him on the back. 'Maybe I'll give Stephanie Moon a call, see if she's free tonight.'

'Stephanie?' Lucas's head snapped up so sharply he almost sliced his finger.

'Yeah . . .' Paulo looked at him thoughtfully. 'Hope it's not a late one for you tonight. Remember, all work and no play makes Lucas a dull boy,' he finished, as he strode out of the back door of the restaurant with a swagger in his step.

Lucas cut into an onion with relish, carving it in two in a single, smooth motion. He was frustrated with Elle and irritated by Paulo's hostile jibes. But the thing which annoyed him most of all, he realized, as the glittering blade sliced through the onion's layers with ease, was the thought of Paulo and Stephanie together.

Late afternoon slid into evening and Camille barely noticed. She was so preoccupied with overseeing her small team, making a hundred last-minute decisions and issuing instructions. She was thrilled with how it was all coming together, but still worried it wouldn't all be finished before the show.

Endless boxes were arriving by courier, sample pieces from Italy and Spain, beautiful garments from Morocco and India. Camille said a silent prayer of thanks as each one was ticked off the list. But she knew it wasn't over yet – there'd be alterations to make, and fittings with the models to ensure the clothes hung perfectly as they sash-ayed down the runway.

Camille checked her slender Cartier Tank watch, debating whether to tell the team to take a break and come back in an hour, or whether to order in food and ask them to work straight through, when René strode over with another parcel.

'What's this?' Camille asked, trying to hide her irritation. Her team dealt with the incoming packages – she had more important things to do.

'It just arrived,' René explained quickly, knowing exactly what Camille would be thinking. 'But there's only your name on the front – no import stamp or customs papers. Someone dropped it off at reception, so I thought perhaps it was personal.'

Camille stared at it, a sudden surge of dread balling in her stomach. René was right – it was simply a plain, brown package, a little bigger than a shoe box. Camille's name, and the hotel's, had been handwritten in stark, black letters on the front, but there were no other identifying marks.

'Thank you, René,' Camille said coolly, taking it from him, hoping to conceal how unsettled she felt.

René nodded and moved away, back into the melee. Camille took a deep breath and tore open the package. It contained a box, and inside was a Camille bag – light tan, calfskin leather, gold hardware. She identified it immediately as being from their 1995 autumn/winter collection. But it appeared to be covered in some kind of liquid – something dark and red, with a metallic smell, that had soaked into the leather and stained it . . .

Horrified, Camille felt compelled to continue looking, unable to take her eyes away from the nightmare unfolding in front of her. She realized that there was something inside the bag, something large, with sharp angles.

Summoning her courage, Camille snapped open the clasp. She peered inside, trying to work out what she was looking at. And then she realized, gasping as she almost dropped the box. It was a car wing mirror, its surface shattered and mangled, so that when Camille peered into it she saw her own reflection sliced and broken.

Right now, she was aware of nothing except the contents of the box and her own heartbeat, roaring inside her ears, as she pulled out the items nestled in the silk lining beside the mirror. Two photographs: a grainy one of the crash that had claimed Andre's life, and a second of Camille and Nicolas coming out of the hospital. And beneath them both, a note:

Now it's time to pay, once and for all

Bile rose in Camille's throat. The fight-or-flight instinct kicked in and she was suddenly desperate to get away. She hastily closed the bag, slamming the box lid tightly on top of it, her startled eyes searching the room for René. She found him speaking with one of the team and made a beeline for him, the chatter in the room becoming an alarming buzz in her ears. She realized her body was shaking.

'René,' she interrupted. 'I have a sudden headache. I think it may be a migraine. I'm going back to my room to rest.'

Concern was written across his face, beneath his sweep of white-blond hair. 'Of course. Is there anything you need? Can I get you something?'

'No, I . . . I'll be fine.' Camille went to leave, then stopped. 'Actually, there is one thing. Did reception say who delivered the package?'

René shook his head. 'I can go and ask them . . .'

'No,' Camille replied, more sharply than she'd intended. 'No, don't worry. It's not important. They sent me a vintage bag,' she said, forcing a smile onto her face as she lied, 'I just wanted to thank them properly.'

Then Camille turned and raced to her room as fast as she could without causing alarm. To an onlooker, she would have looked like a busy, professional woman on an urgent mission. But when she got back to her suite and slammed the door shut with shaking hands, her legs gave way and she sank down onto the floor, tossing the box as far away from her as she could.

What do they want from me? she thought desperately. And, more importantly, *How much do they know about what happened that night?*

Camille knew she had been stupid to pay the first time. Remembering the first note she had received months ago, goading her about knowing her 'secret'. She had paid the amount they'd asked for, desperate to keep a lid on the situation, but now it seemed things were spiralling out of control. What did they want this time, and what would happen next? What about her family, and the business she had spent years building up?

The tone of the notes had changed too, more chilling, more insistent: *once and for all* . . .

What the hell did that mean? Camille wished that she could call the police, but that would be impossible without revealing . . . Well, without telling them everything and confessing all her secrets. And that would ruin her. Her reputation, her money, perhaps even her son – all would be gone in the blink of an eye.

There was one person she could call, she realized,

adrenaline propelling her to her feet and across the room. She should never have kept it from him in the first place. It didn't matter what had happened between them – she needed Nicolas right now; he would know what to do.

Camille checked the time: it would be three p.m. in New York. Snatching up her phone, she called his apartment. It rang half a dozen times, eventually clicking through to his answering machine. Camille hesitated, then left a message. 'Nicolas, it's me . . . Camille. Call me as soon as you get this. I really need to speak to you.'

She hung up and dialled Nicolas's mobile number, which went straight to voicemail. Either it was switched off, or he had no signal.

Camille left the same message, hearing the fear in her voice as she said the words. She realized now how badly she needed Nicolas, how desperately she wanted to hear his calm tones offering words of reassurance, telling her that everything would be OK. Camille closed her eyes, trying to ward off the sense of panic that threatened to overwhelm her.

Nicolas, where the hell are you? I need you.

Chapter 11

Stephanie sped down to Cala de la Belleza, a delicious warm breeze on her bare skin as she dared herself to drive even faster on the almost-deserted roads.

At Catherine's suggestion, Stephanie had borrowed a moped. She adored staying with the Douglases – they'd been nothing but gracious hosts, kind and welcoming, opening their home to her.

Stephanie had met Catherine at the party thrown after the last night of her run in *The Tempest*. Catherine loved the theatre and they'd been introduced by the director and had hit it off immediately. Since then, Catherine had taken her under her wing, and when Stephanie ran into her problems on the *Fields of Barley* set, it was Catherine to whom she had turned, and who had offered her the chance to get her thoughts together in the privacy of their villa. Stephanie knew that her time here couldn't last, though. The Douglases were busy people with what seemed like dozens of projects on the go, from movie offers to property deals to business investments, Stephanie knew their time together as a family was precious, and that she was an added complication they didn't need.

When they did take some time to relax, their enthusiasm for golf was a passion Stephanie didn't share, so she decided she'd leave them to it. She had mentioned that she was keen to see more of the island, so Catherine had suggested, in her melodic Welsh accent, 'Why don't you take one of the mopeds from the garage? It's the best way to explore.'

But not before she'd gently nudged Stephanie to do what she knew she should.

'Anthony left me a message this morning. He wants to talk to you, darling – why don't you give him a call? He wants to give you the time to sort your head out . . . but . . .' Catherine's eyes were kind, but also questioning.

Anthony Minghella, the director of *Fields of Barley*. 'You're right, I know I need to talk to him.' Stephanie said, 'I just need a little more time.'

Catherine patted her hand. 'Don't leave it too much longer, my love, will you? Enjoy your whiz around the island!'

Stephanie knew exactly what Catherine meant; films had schedules, budgets, deadlines. She was holding everything up.

I'll think about it later.

After a quick lesson with Catherine's gardener, Stephanie was ready to go, heading along the coastal road wearing Daisy Dukes and a strappy vest top. It was a beautiful day, as ever, with barely a cloud troubling the perfect azure sky, and it wasn't long before Stephanie pulled into the beachside town of Belleza.

The bustling centre was set around a cobbled marketplace, where inviting tables and chairs were set up outside a row of cafés, as couples and families enjoyed their holidays. Cats lazed in the heat, hoping for scraps from the tables, whilst in the centre of the square was a three-tier fountain, bubbling water cascading over the stone basins. Children were paddling in the wonderfully cool shallows, shrieking excitedly as they splashed one another, their fingers sticky with ice cream. Stephanie parked up, locked her helmet in the rear box, and set out to explore the meandering streets.

She knew that Il Paradiso wasn't far from here, and she felt her stomach flip at the prospect of running into Lucas. She *did* like him, she admitted to herself, and there was undeniable chemistry between them. But she had no intention of pursuing him – he had a girlfriend, and she wasn't the kind of person to try and break up a relationship. Besides, her date with Paulo had complicated the situation. She didn't think they had a future together, but she *had* had fun on the boat, and Paulo had messaged her to ask her out again. Stephanie hadn't replied yet, but she knew she should.

She turned down a pretty, tree-lined avenue with whitewashed buildings and cream-coloured awnings outside the shops. It looked very chic, and Stephanie realized that the lane was home to a row of designer boutiques, the skinny mannequins in the windows wearing expensive-looking clothing, and signs for Gucci, Loewe and La Perla hanging above the doors.

She instinctively felt intimidated. Despite Stephanie's newfound fame and wealth, this wasn't the world she came from, and she worried it was obvious that she didn't belong. But she held her head high and told herself that she had every right to be there as she strolled along, taking in the tiny bikinis and the cocktail dresses that cost more than her parents' monthly wage.

'Sorry,' she apologized automatically, almost colliding with a woman who had stepped out of one of the shops, laden with stiff, white cardboard bags.

'No, my fault,' the woman replied in a soft Scottish accent that sounded familiar.

The two women looked at one another for a moment, then burst out laughing.

'Isobel,' Stephanie exclaimed. 'I thought I recognized your voice. Doing a little shopping?' she grinned, nodding at the cluster of bags Isobel was carrying.

Isobel's eyes narrowed. 'Trying to put a serious dent in my husband's credit card. That'll serve him right.'

'Oh no, have you two had an argument?'

'You could say that. He's been called away for work, and has flown to the mainland to see a client. He'll be back in a few days.' Isobel shrugged, though her expression showed how unhappy she was with the situation. 'It's all about work with him. Even now, when we're supposed to be on holiday. I ask him to switch off for two weeks, that's all, and he can't even give me that.' Frustration and sadness were clear in her voice.

'I'm sorry. I'm sure it must have been important,' Stephanie said sympathetically.

'Oh, yes, his work's *always* important.' Isobel couldn't hide the bitterness in her voice.

'Well, you deserve to have fun without him. Listen,' Stephanie said, as she had an idea. 'I have the afternoon free. Why don't we go and find a bar? You, me, a bottle of rosé . . .'

'Sounds perfect,' Isobel grinned.

Five minutes later, the two women were sitting beneath a cream umbrella outside a smart-looking café, two glasses of wine and a dish of olives on the table in front of them.

'You know, I thought your face looked familiar the other night,' Isobel said, as she sat back and examined Stephanie. 'And when I got back to the hotel I realized why. Were you in *Fly Home*?'

'Yes!' Stephanie exclaimed delightedly. 'That was the very first film I did. I loved it, and it got great reviews, but it bombed at the box office.'

'It was fantastic – and you were incredible. I thought it was so moving.' *Fly Home* was a Brit-flick, a coming-of-age drama in which Stephanie had had a small role as the younger sister of the main character, played by Rachel Weisz.

'Thank you. I didn't think anyone else had seen it.'

'I used to love taking myself off to the cinema in the afternoon, and having the whole place practically to myself. I gave up work when I married Stuart, and before I set up the boutique I had a lot of time on my hands.'

Stephanie didn't ask anything further; she didn't want to judge, or pry.

'It must be amazing staying with the Douglases.'

'It is. The villa is beautiful, and they've been so generous towards me, letting me stay for as long as I want to. It's been a . . .' Stephanie didn't want to reveal more to Isobel, they barely knew each other. '. . . busy time over the last few months. I needed time and space to clear my head, to get away from everything, and they've given me that. I'm so grateful to them.'

'I think I read something in one of those gossip magazines that there was trouble on the set of your film, or was that just malicious tittle-tattle?'

Stephanie frowned. 'Did the article say why, or who?'

Isobel cocked her head to the side, trying to remember. 'I don't think so.' Then she laughed. 'Who's the troublemaker? It can't be you, you're too nice.'

Stephanie sighed. 'That's where you're wrong. They do mean me.'

'Really? Something you want to talk about?'

Stephanie wasn't sure she did want to talk about it, but Isobel seemed like someone who wouldn't judge her, so she decided to open up. '*Fields of Barley* is my first big shoot; big budget, big cast, big director.' She looked downcast. 'Little old me.'

'Hey, don't do yourself down!' Isobel said, 'You're an amazing actress – you stole every scene you had in *Fly Home*.'

'Maybe that's because I didn't understand the enormity of what I was getting myself into. It was all new and exciting, most of the cast were unknown, it had a small budget, and the lead actress declined a fee upfront. But this time . . .'

'Did something happen?'

'Yes . . . I was feeling a bit intimidated already, and then one day, nothing was going right, there had been no end of delays due to the Yorkshire rain holding up the shoot. One of the actors had been ill as well, so it was all behind schedule. Anyway, I'm playing the daughter of Richard Harris, and during one of our big dramatic scenes together, I just felt like I was doing everything wrong. All the crew were snappy, and I kept tripping over my lines.' Stephanie cringed, remembering vividly her feelings of inadequacy and failure. 'The director and Richard couldn't have been nicer, but later that day I overheard some of the extras being horrid about my performance while I was crying on the loo.'

'Bitches,' Isobel said, with feeling.

'Maybe, but they were right about my acting that day. I just sat there in the fancy Portaloos crying. Eventually one of the costume girls found me in there.'

'Then what happened?'

'I got through the rest of the day, but the next day I didn't get out of my hotel dressing gown. I told my agent I was wrong for the role, and they should find someone else, someone with more experience. To cut a long story short they said, "Don't be silly, you're wonderful, darling!" They gave me a bit of time to get my head together, and they have shifted some of the filming around, but I should have been back on set last week.' Stephanie sighed, feeling thoroughly defeated. 'My agent and the producers keep trying to get hold of me . . . but I'm avoiding them.'

'Why?'

Stephanie fixed her eyes on her glass, and turned the liquid around in it, deep in thought for a moment. 'If this is how hard I find it to be a successful actress, if this is how unhappy it makes me, then maybe the big career isn't for me? I could do panto, or *Holby City*.' She gave a small, unconvincing laugh.

Isobel reached out and placed a reassuring hand on Stephanie's. 'Look, you're still young. It can be hard to find your voice before you've had much life experience, and it's easy to be taken advantage of.' Isobel's face clouded for a moment and Stephanie wondered if the woman had her own story. 'You just have to fake it until you make it! That's what they do in America, and we Brits could learn a lesson or two from them.'

'That doesn't sound that easy to me.'

'Give it a try! The industry have seen something in your talent that is real, Stephanie. They believe in you, and you just need to learn to believe in yourself too.'

'Perhaps . . .' Stephanie said, unconvinced. 'What about you?'

'Ah, well I have a plan . . . anyway, you *must* go back, I meant what I said – I'd love to design a gown for you, but you need a film before you can attend the premiere in *Camille's* gown.' They both laughed, breaking the tension, though Stephanie still detected an edge in Isobel's comment about Camille. *Fields of Barley* might end up without her in it, which was looking like a real possibility right now.

'Let's drink to that,' Isobel beamed, as they clinked glasses. She took a sip of her rosé and asked casually, 'Do you know Camille well?'

'No, not at all. The other night at the restaurant was only the second time I'd met her, though she came to the house again yesterday to see Catherine. I liked her instantly. She's had a tough time – her husband died in a car accident.'

'I know,' Isobel replied. At Stephanie's quizzical look, she explained, 'I remember reading about it in the papers.'

'I must have been about eighteen when it happened. I wasn't paying a lot of attention to the news back then,' Stephanie smiled. Then she became serious again as she added, 'Her son, Lucas, was badly injured. They didn't know if he'd make it.'

Isobel nodded. 'My husband was consulted on his reconstruction. He was part of the team that performed the surgery.'

'Wow, that's amazing. I mean, it must be hard having him away so much, but it sounds like he's doing incredible work.'

'Mmm,' Isobel responded, her tone noncommittal. 'Speaking of Lucas, it looked as though the two of you were getting on pretty well at Il Paradiso . . .'

Stephanie blushed, unable to hide her attraction to him. 'He's got a girlfriend though, so I don't think anything's going to happen.'

'I met her the other day. She was very demanding and . . . annoying. Stunning, of course, but a real pain in the arse. You're so much nicer,' Isobel whispered, as the two women giggled conspiratorially.

'This is fun,' Stephanie sighed happily. 'We should meet up again, whilst your husband's away.'

'I'd love that,' Isobel replied, then noticed that their glasses were empty. 'Shall we get another bottle?'

'Why not?' Stephanie shrugged, pushing Anthony Minghella and film sets out of her mind. 'We can get a taxi home, and I can't think of a better way to spend the afternoon.'

'And is there anything I need to be concerned about?' Camille asked, looking imperiously at René. She was leafing through the papers on the desk in her suite, wearing a pair of oversized spectacles with thick, black frames, which only served to make her look more chic.

'Everything is on track for the show,' René assured her. 'Gwyneth Paltrow is flying in tomorrow and Kristin

Scott Thomas arrived this afternoon. I believe Nicolas is also on the island,' René continued, his tone neutral, 'if you'd like me to schedule a meeting with him.'

'It's fine, thank you.' Camille swallowed. The information was a surprise to her; she wasn't sure if Nicolas would still attend the launch, and she could feel her pulse begin to race at the news – whether through excitement or anxiety, she couldn't say. 'I'll contact him directly. And tomorrow's trip?'

'Everything's confirmed, and all the details are taken care of. Though I do need to double-check with Torres Charters that they're able to provide the vintage Dom Pérignon you requested.'

A thoughtful look flashed across Camille's face. As part of the pre-show buzz, Camille Andre was taking the invited VIP guests on a yacht cruise, and Paulo's parents' company were providing the vessel. 'Don't worry about that. I'll call directly.'

A flicker of a frown crossed René's brow, but he wasn't going to ask Camille twice. If she gave an instruction, he knew better than to question it. Instead, he nodded. 'Very good.'

'Thank you, René. That'll be all for now.'

Discreetly, René slipped away, leaving Camille alone in her suite. He really was exceptional at his job, she thought admiringly. He'd been with her for many years now, and was hardworking, efficient and – most importantly – loyal. But Camille's mind moved swiftly to other matters, and she sat down at her desk, picking up the phone and dialling a number.

'Paulo? It's Camille.'

'Camille. *Bonjour! Ça va?*'

'I'm well, thank you, Paulo,' Camille said tartly, replying to him in Spanish. 'I wanted to confirm the dozen cases of vintage Dom Pérignon for tomorrow's trip. Have you been able to source it?'

'It's better if you phone the office, speak to my parents—'

'I'm sure you can pass the message on,' Camille replied smoothly. 'And if you could tell them that we have a few extra guests coming. I've invited Catherine and Michael, along with the young actress who's staying with them – Stephanie Moon.'

'Great,' Paulo said, and she could hear the smile in his voice. 'In fact, I'll personally attend to ensure that everything runs smoothly on the day.'

'And two more names for the list,' Camille continued, ignoring his comment. 'Isobel MacFarlane and Elle Mettier,' she finished, grimacing as she said the final name. She hadn't wanted to invite Lucas's girlfriend – in Camille's opinion, she was too much of a loose cannon to be around the high-profile guests. But Lucas had requested that she attend, explaining that she'd felt hurt by the lack of an invitation. And given that Camille had given her such short shrift over her repeated requests to model for Camille Andre, this could be a timely peace offering. After all, Elle might one day be her daughter-in-law – perish the thought.

'Doesn't René take care of this sort of thing for you?' Paulo wondered. 'I thought you'd be too busy to sort out champagne and guest lists.'

Camille hesitated. She and Paulo had long had a tricky relationship. She knew that he was Lucas's *ami* from childhood. Their friendship had been formed whilst Lucas stayed on the island with his grandmother, as Camille and Andre travelled the world. But she knew Lucas considered him one of his best friends, so she had to be content with that. 'For an event this important, I like to oversee the details myself.'

'In which case, everything will be immaculate. I personally guarantee it.'

'Good,' Camille replied crisply. 'Because I hear there are some areas of the restaurant that aren't running so smoothly.'

'I don't know what you're talking about,' Paulo shot back, and Camille could hear the defensive tone in his voice. 'We've had nothing but good reviews for Lucas's cooking, and—'

'I'm not talking about Lucas,' Camille snapped, her patience wearing thin. 'Although he's the one who told me about the little hiccup with the supplier the other day – that Diego had to come chasing for his payment. That's not a good look, Paulo. It's highly unprofessional, and word gets round.'

'That was nothing,' Paulo replied dismissively. 'Why is Lucas running to *Maman* over a misunderstanding?'

'He's keeping me informed, Paulo. I'm an investor.'

'A *silent* investor.'

'That doesn't mean you can waste my money – or run my son's reputation into the ground,' Camille hissed. Then her voice changed, the tone sweet but an undeniable warning in her words. 'But I'm sure it won't happen again, will it?'

'Like I said, it was a misunderstanding. Don't worry, Camille,' Paulo continued smoothly. 'You can trust me.'

Chapter 12

The majestic yacht sliced through the sapphire water, the sun reflecting off its dazzling white hull. It was 160 feet long and three decks high, and right now it was at capacity with glamorous guests. Stephanie readjusted her sunglasses and glanced around: Liv Tyler was standing by the Jacuzzi, speaking to Cate Blanchett; Jane Birkin was smoking a cigarette as she accepted a glass of champagne; and Liz Hurley was laughing loudly with Antonio Banderas. It was a pinch-me moment – proof of how far Stephanie had come, to be mingling with a crowd that most people could only dream of meeting. It was the sort of scene that would once have intimidated her – well, it still did, if she was being honest. Stephanie was finding it hard to shake the sense that she didn't really fit it, of being an outsider.

Everyone was being so nice to her. Treating her as if she was meant to be there, that she was one of *them* – the rich, the privileged, the successful. She was pretty sure she looked the part, in a strapless playsuit with a halter-neck bikini underneath in case they went swimming, her long copper hair pulled back in a low ponytail that served to highlight her flawless skin and high cheekbones. She accepted a cocktail from a passing waiter, and took a moment to enjoy the view, admiring the endless blue of sea and sky that contrasted sharply with the frothy white waves the boat left in its wake.

'Stephanie! I'm so pleased to see you. Oh, and don't you look gorgeous!'

Stephanie turned to see Isobel, and a broad grin lit up her face at the sight of her new friend. She and Isobel had had a lot of fun the other day – one glass of rosé had turned into two shared bottles, and she'd had to call a taxi home, with Catherine's staff retrieving the moped the following day.

'Isobel,' Stephanie beamed. 'You look incredible.'

'A little something new I treated myself to, courtesy of Stuart and his black Amex,' Isobel said, twirling round so that the hand-painted silk of the designer dress flew out in the breeze, showing off her tanned, slender legs beneath.

'I'm almost starting to feel sorry for him,' Stephanie said, then backtracked as she saw Isobel's frown. 'I said *almost*,' she protested, and Isobel laughed.

'Camille's really pulling out all the stops,' Isobel commented, as a waiter passed by with trays of caviar blinis. 'Is that David Guetta on the decks?' she marvelled, peering at the famous DJ as he turned up the volume and the partygoers cheered.

'Looks like it,' Stephanie laughed. 'Camille seems to know what she's doing. I guess she's a pretty shrewd operator.'

'Yeah . . .' Isobel agreed, as she looked around. Stephanie followed her gaze, seeing it land on Camille who was busy schmoozing Penelope Cruz. Then Isobel turned away and grinned. 'Come on, let's go,' she said to Stephanie.

Stephanie was too surprised to protest and followed her, before she realized where they were heading – towards the trio standing near Camille which consisted of Lucas, Elle and Paulo. 'Oh no,' she murmured, knowing that conversation was inevitable.

'*Hola*,' Isobel called out cheerily. 'Lucas, I wanted to say how divine your food was the other night. Stuart and I both agreed it was one of the best meals we've ever had, and he's notoriously difficult to impress.'

'Well, that's because he's a perfectionist. I mean, look at the wonderful job he did on my face. I'm even more handsome than I was before,' Lucas joked, as everyone laughed. 'Is he here?'

'No.' Isobel's face fell. 'He was called away by work. A client on the mainland.'

'Oh, that's too bad, but I'm not surprised he's in demand. You must, of course, enjoy our hospitality. There's no need to be lonely whilst he's away.'

'Thank you, that's sweet of you. Stephanie's been keeping me company,' Isobel said, with a pointed look in her direction.

Lucas's deep hazel eyes slid towards Stephanie, his scarred face creasing into a smile. Stephanie caught her breath. It was as though she'd received an electric shock, a pulsing current racing through her body and setting every nerve ending on fire.

'Stephanie Moon . . .' Lucas began, and hearing him

say her name in that delicious accent almost made her melt into a puddle on the floor. She couldn't fail to notice the way his gaze raked over her body, and said a silent prayer of thanks for all the time she'd been spending in the gym recently. 'It's good to see you again.'

'You too,' Stephanie replied, trying to sound normal, though her mouth suddenly felt dry despite the cocktails she'd been drinking.

'Hey, Stephanie.' Paulo strode over, kissing her on the cheek before wrapping one arm around her waist in a possessive gesture. Stephanie froze beneath his touch, wanting to shake him off, disliking his presumption.

'Hi Paulo,' she said tightly.

'Stephanie, have you met Elle? Lucas's girlfriend?' Paulo continued with a grin.

Stephanie looked up at the leggy blonde model towering over her, dressed in a minuscule bikini covered by a wisp of sheer fabric. There was no doubt that she was beautiful, with blonde hair in a perfectly unkempt, just-got-out-of-bed style, bee-stung lips, and a smudge of black liner around her catlike eyes, which were currently narrowed suspiciously as they looked at Stephanie.

'No, I don't believe so. Nice to meet you,' Stephanie said graciously, hoping that Elle couldn't sense the way the air was vibrating between her and Lucas.

Elle made a Gallic, dismissive-sounding noise and didn't return Stephanie's greeting, clinging tightly to Lucas.

Stephanie felt a flash of rivalry and couldn't resist stirring a little. 'I enjoyed our little conversation when you came with Camille to see Catherine. I must take you up on that offer of a cookery lesson.'

Elle's sharp gaze darted to Lucas. 'You didn't tell me you saw her,' she said, her eyes flashing accusingly.

'Did I need to?' Lucas replied, and Stephanie could hear the irritation in his voice. She didn't blame him. How on earth did he put up with Elle? He seemed like a great guy, and she seemed – as Isobel had so astutely observed – like a pain in the arse.

'Stephanie . . .' Paulo's fingers squeezed her hip, as he moved his lips closer to murmur in her ear. 'Can we talk?'

'Um, sure . . .' she said uncertainly. She met Isobel's eyes, and her friend flashed her a quizzical look, universal girl code for 'is everything OK?' Stephanie gave her a reassuring nod as Paulo steered her away from the group and towards a quieter spot at the back of the boat.

'Did you get my message? I'd love to take you out again. We had a great time, and I think you're hot.'

'Paulo . . .' Stephanie hesitated. She felt bad – she'd avoided replying to him – but she needed to be honest. 'You're a sweet guy, and I had a lot of fun, but I don't think it's going to go anywhere.'

Paulo frowned. She saw disbelief and a flash of ego, and she had the feeling that he wasn't going to take the news well. Then her gaze slid past him, to where Lucas and Elle were standing with an uncomfortable-looking Isobel – Lucas and Elle appeared to be having an argument, judging by their body language.

Paulo followed her eyeline, and a muscle tightened in his jaw. 'I see,' he said coolly, an undertone of malice in his voice, before giving her a forced smile. 'Look, no hard feelings, hey? Have a nice life.'

He stalked off, leaving Stephanie feeling a little guilty, but mostly relieved.

Nicolas felt a kind of sweet agony at being in the same space as Camille. She looked every inch the international success story, in a pair of Camille black cat-eye sunglasses and a white full-length sun dress with a gold thread that shimmered in the sunlight. He could barely look at her, but found it hard to avert his gaze.

He would have to maintain his professionalism, he told himself, and his emotions. He meant what he had said to her in New York that last time, but sticking to his resolution was the hardest thing he had ever had to do. Well, one of the hardest, but it was taking every ounce of self-control not to take her to one side and tell her it was all a mistake, that they could carry on as they had before, no strings, not marriage. Just to be with her; just to take her in his arms again one more time.

He felt like a love-struck teenager, but that wouldn't help either of them.

As the guests mingled, laughter and chatter drifted out across the sea. Nicolas leaned over the stern and his eyes caught sight of a dolphin in the distance, bobbing in and out of the water, until it disappeared into the waves. Mallorca was a beautiful place; if only he and Camille could have given themselves some more time, they could have come here and made new memories, not forever be stuck in the moments of the past.

'A penny for them?'

He was momentarily startled, and turned to see Camille standing next to him, holding a glass of champagne out to him, holding another for herself.

'What are we celebrating?'

'Perhaps this is more for my nerves,' she said ruefully.

'What are you nervous about? You're the queen of cool, aren't you?' he said, not unkindly.

'Don't joke, Nicolas, it's not easy seeing you here. After the way we left things.'

'After the way you left things?'

'That's not fair.'

'Look, now isn't the time or the place. Anyway, we have said everything now, haven't we? Unless you have changed your mind?' He desperately hoped that was the case, but knew in his heart it was a forlorn hope.

Camille hesitated. 'Nicolas, I just want to say . . . that I'm sorry. I know I've hurt you, but can't we be friends . . .? I'm finding things hard without you.'

'Camille, I've never abandoned you, and I won't now, *especially* now, but as a caring colleague, a long-standing associate, that's all I can offer.'

Camille lifted her hands to her glasses and took them off, revealing her amber eyes, which were wet with unspilled tears. Her hand fluttered to her dark lashes, to brush them away before they fell.

'I understand, Nicolas. I'm hurting too.'

Nicolas felt an overwhelming convergence of emotions, Camille seemed so vulnerable, which was unlike her; all he wanted to do was take her in his arms and hold her. He fought the urge, but spoke gently. 'I've been in the background for our whole lives together, Camille, and until recently I thought that was enough, but when you rejected my marriage offer, it opened my eyes.'

Camille turned her face away from him as he spoke, unable to meet his gaze.

'I don't want the bits of you that Andre left behind, the husk of your marriage to him. I want the whole of you, in every way, the good and the bad. I want us to have a future and not just be trapped by our past.' There were tears in his own eyes now, but he ploughed on. 'If you can't love me fully, as my wife and as my life partner, then this way is best.'

He took his champagne glass and touched hers with it. 'Here's to Camille Andre, long may it reign.' He kept his voice steady. 'Today is about that; let's just focus on it and get through the day, OK?'

Camille nodded, took a deep breath and nodded, 'You're right, we have achieved so much together – no one can ever take that away . . . but please, there is something I need to talk to you about, something important. Please come to see me later?'

She met his gaze now, and he nodded. In her eyes Nicolas could see unhappiness, but there was something else in her expression too; something he had never seen in her before.

Fear.

Later, they stopped at a beautiful, deserted island called Isla Blanca. The guests disembarked from the yacht onto a wide crescent of beach fringed by palm trees, the crystal-clear water lapping at the shore, as shoals of fish darted in the shallows. It was as though they'd been marooned in the most picture-perfect location, and by early evening the party was in full swing. Guests were frolicking in the water, and dancing on the soft white sand, as Lucas cooked a giant seafood paella over a roaring bonfire made from driftwood.

Stephanie had tried to put the uncomfortable scene with Paulo out of her mind, which had been made easier by the fact that he'd avoided her since their conversation. She'd spent time with Catherine and Michael, being introduced to their A-list Hollywood friends as an exciting new talent, and now she was reunited with Isobel, the two of them feeling a little tipsy from the delicious cocktails.

Isobel was explaining about the argument she'd overheard between Lucas and Elle.

'She was very jealous of you,' Isobel confided, arching a knowing eyebrow. 'They were arguing in French, but I spent a few months living in Paris so I understood every word. I don't think they realized.'

'You're a dark horse,' Stephanie marvelled. 'Why were you in Paris?'

'In a past life, when I was pursuing a career in fashion – before I ran my own business – I interned for a few big names across Europe. One was in Paris.'

'Oh, which company?' Stephanie asked.

Isobel hesitated, a closed look crossing her face. 'It doesn't matter. Honestly, you should have heard the way Elle spoke to Lucas, it was awful. I don't know how he puts up with—'

Isobel broke off as she heard Camille calling for silence, tapping her champagne glass. The music was turned down to a low background hum, and a hush rippled across the beach as everyone turned to look at Camille, who looked radiant in the white sundress from her latest collection.

'I won't keep you too long – everyone looks to be having so much fun that I hate to disturb you all,' she smiled, as the crowd laughed. 'But I do have two pieces of business that I need to attend to – I promise they're not dull,' she added, as everyone groaned good-naturedly. 'Firstly, I want to thank you all so much for coming here to celebrate with us – a world first for Camille Andre, as it's our debut collaboration with another powerhouse label. I'm thrilled to be working with American Athletics, and I'd like to introduce you all to Nicolas Martin, who's here to represent the brand,' she added, nodding at a man standing nearby. 'He's been a great friend to me over the years, and I'm overjoyed that we're finally bringing our two great companies together.

'Secondly,' she continued, following applause and a smattering of cheers. 'I am beyond excited to announce that we have a new ambassador for Camille Andre. She's going to be the new face of our campaign, and I couldn't think of anyone better. You all know her, of course, but I'm delighted to introduce you to . . . Catherine Zeta-Jones!'

The crowd went wild, applauding and whooping, as Catherine stepped up to stand beside Camille, and Michael watched her proudly. 'Thank you all so much,' she began. 'I'm so honoured to have been invited to be an ambassador for a brand I truly love . . .'

As Catherine began to speak, Stephanie's attention was taken by Paulo. Out of the corner of her eye, she noticed him slip away from the crowd, hugging the edge of the beach along the tree line where the shadows had lengthened as the sun began to set. Glancing around, she noticed a small speedboat approaching the island; it was some distance away, and everyone else had their backs to it. Pushing her sunglasses on top of her head so she could see more clearly, Stephanie squinted and watched as Paulo waded out into the shallows to greet the sole occupant of the boat. Paulo spoke briefly to him, pulling a bag from his shorts and handing it over. It looked as though the man gave him something in return, which Paulo pocketed, before the speedboat pulled away, skimming across the water which had turned golden in the setting sun. Then Paulo strode back towards the crowd and Stephanie quickly turned away, joining in with the applause as Catherine finished speaking and Camille took over once again.

'Now please enjoy the wonderful feast my son has prepared. And if you enjoy it, visit his restaurant, Il Paradiso,' she couldn't resist adding, as the buoyant crowd laughed and cheered.

'Well, I didn't see that coming,' Isobel commented.

'Catherine kept it a secret from me too,' Stephanie laughed. 'But isn't it wonderful? She's the perfect fit for Camille Andre – they're both so chic and glamorous.'

'Yes, aren't they just.'

Stephanie detected something tight in Isobel's tone, but didn't push it any further.

'Let's go and get some of Lucas's paella,' Isobel suggested changing the subject. 'It smells incredible.'

Stephanie hesitated. After what Isobel had just told her about Elle being jealous, she thought it would be best to steer clear. But then she noticed that whilst Lucas was handing out delicious-looking bowls of rice, Elle appeared to be making a beeline for Camille, a furious look on her face as she stalked across the sand.

Stephanie nudged Isobel, nodding in Elle's direction. 'She doesn't look too happy,' she murmured.

'When does she?' Isobel replied with a giggle. The two women watched curiously as Elle stalked over to Camille, who was standing with Catherine and Michael as a gaggle of guests offered their congratulations.

Elle rudely pushed through the middle of them, marching straight up to Camille. 'I can't believe you did that to me,' Elle raged. She was speaking in French, and Isobel hastily translated for Stephanie.

Camille looked utterly shocked at Elle's interruption. She blinked twice, as though trying to work out what was happening. 'Did what? I don't understand.'

'You knew how much I wanted to be the face of Camille Andre,' Elle began, her eyes blazing, her words slurred. Stephanie wondered how much she'd had to drink. 'And then you go and humiliate me like this by giving it to someone else behind my back. She's not even French!' Elle finished, sounding outraged, looking at Catherine as though she were something she'd found on the bottom of her shoe.

Camille's lips tightened into a thin line, her eyes narrowing. Stephanie glanced over at Lucas, but he was too busy dishing up the paella and hadn't noticed what was happening.

'I'm so sorry,' Camille apologized to Catherine and Michael. 'Do excuse me for one moment. I have something I need to deal with.' Camille was clearly livid. Elle had evidently had too much to drink, her voice loud, her actions sloppy. She was a mess, and people were turning to look, a scandalized whisper rippling through the crowd.

Camille went to put a hand on Elle's arm, to lead her away, and Elle reacted as though she'd been burned. 'Don't touch me,' she hissed. 'Get your hands off me.'

'Come with me,' Camille said firmly, a dangerous edge to her voice. 'And don't you dare make a scene.'

Stephanie glanced over and saw that Nicolas had stepped into Camille's place, laughing and chatting with Catherine and Michael, smoothing things over with the other guests.

Meanwhile Lucas's girlfriend was staring at Camille defiantly, arms crossed, her eyebrows raised in a challenge. When they were a suitable distance from the others, but still within Stephanie's earshot, Camille began to speak, this time in English. It seemed she finally had the opportunity to tell Elle exactly what she thought of her, and she didn't hold back. Stephanie wondered if Camille was speaking in English to deliberately chastise Elle in public view; a window into that famous steel she was known for?

'How dare you speak to me and my guests like that! Thinking you could be the face of Camille Andre. Are you deluded? You're only at this party because you're dating my son – certainly not on your own merits. Of course I wouldn't let you represent my business. Camille Andre is synonymous with style and elegance, and Catherine Zeta-Jones is a world-famous, supremely talented, international star. *You . . .*' Camille looked her up and down disparagingly. '. . . are not.'

'Take a day off from being a bitch, Camille,' Elle drawled, rolling her eyes. 'It's getting boring.'

By now, everyone had become aware of the scene taking place further down the beach, and there was seemingly nothing Nicolas could do to stop them watching.

Stephanie saw Lucas look up too, an expression of horror crossing his face as he instantly forgot about the food and ran across the sand. 'What's going on?'

'Lucas, get your girlfriend out of here,' Camille spat.

'She's making a show of herself. This is disgraceful, I should never have invited her in the first place.'

'Elle, come on. Let's go,' Lucas began, reaching for her hand.

'Oh, here we go again. Doing whatever Mummy says. Why don't you care about *me*? Why do you always take *her* side?'

'Elle, stop behaving like this, it's—'

'I don't care,' Elle interrupted, with a yell. Her eyes were wild, and she looked half-crazed. 'That's it, Lucas. I'm done. We're through.' Elle turned her head in Paulo's direction, commanding, 'Paulo!'

Stephanie couldn't take her eyes off the unfolding drama. It was impossible not to stare – all the other guests were doing the same.

'Yeah?'

'I want to leave. Take me home. Now.'

'Sure. I'll call a boat to come and pick us up,' he said easily, following Elle as she stormed off across the island.

Lucas watched angrily as they left. Paulo threw a glance over his shoulder at his friend. 'Someone's got to look after her,' he said coolly.

Lucas went to follow the two of them, but then stopped. He was barely a metre away from Stephanie, and as he looked up and saw her, his face softened. He threw his hands in the air, and shook his head in disbelief, before an undeniable look of attraction flashed in his eyes.

Stephanie held his gaze, her heart racing, the champagne cocktails making her brave. 'Looks like you might be free for that cooking lesson now,' she commented, a slow smile spreading across her face.

Chapter 13

Isobel rose late the following morning and sat out on her balcony, sipping coffee and water, luxuriating in the warmth of the day. She'd had a lot of fun at the yacht party – perhaps a little too much, she thought regretfully, as she popped a couple of paracetamols and felt grateful for her dark sunglasses.

It had been a wonderful event, and she'd enjoyed mingling with the celebrities, drinking what seemed like unlimited amounts of vintage champagne, and eating the delicious food that Lucas had prepared. Everyone had started dancing on the sand, and the night had turned into a lively party, which continued on the boat as it brought them back to Cala de la Belleza, before a fleet of vehicles drove the guests back to their hotels. There'd been gossip about Elle's behaviour and the drama she had caused, a whiff of scandal in the warm, night air, but it didn't seem to have affected the glitz and glamour of the event.

Isobel was trying to decide on her plans for the day

when she heard the phone ring in her room. She strolled back inside to answer it.

'Darling, I'm so sorry I haven't been able to call you until now, I've been so busy.'

'Good morning, Stuart,' Isobel said frostily. She was still annoyed with him, but also secretly rather pleased that he'd called as she wanted to tell him about the party.

'How are you? Did you have a good time last night?'

'It was so much fun! You should have been there, Stuart. There were so many famous faces, it was like the Oscars. And Lucas's girlfriend caused a huge scene because Camille didn't name her as the face of the brand . . .' Isobel chattered on. 'Are you listening?'

'Of course I am. Every word!' he sighed. 'I wish I was there with you instead of working.'

'Well, that was your choice,' she replied tartly. 'Why don't you just jump on the next plane back?'

'I'd love to, but I need to stay for an extra couple of days . . .'

Isobel clenched the receiver so tightly that her knuckles turned white. 'I sincerely hope this is a joke – even if it's not a very funny one.'

'It's not a joke. I'm so sorry. I wish it weren't the case but there's nothing I can do.'

'There *is* something you can do, Stuart. You can say no.'

'I really can't. They're paying me a small fortune and—'

'It's not all about the money,' Isobel burst out and tears sprang to her eyes. 'Why does your work always have to come first? Why am *I* never your priority?'

'I'm doing this for *us*,' Stuart insisted. 'I need to make

sure we're in a really strong financial position and then we can . . . we can think about having a baby.'

A baby was the one thing that she longed for, but she didn't like the way Stuart was using it as a bargaining chip.

'Look,' he continued, his voice softening as he imagined he was winning her over. 'I'll check my diary and move some things around. We can stay an extra night at the hotel when I get back to Majorca. Maybe even two.'

'Don't bother,' she snapped, before hanging up the phone.

Isobel had spent the afternoon wandering through the narrow, winding lanes of the old town, browsing the boutiques. Palma was beautiful. The capital of Mallorca was a lively port town, dominated by the enormous Gothic Santa María Cathedral, which overlooked the shimmering Bay of Palma.

After the argument with Stuart, she had wanted a change of scenery, something to take her mind off her emotions. She longed to feel the bustle of a city. She'd asked the hotel to call her a cab, and after a few hours in the city, she was beginning to realize that she had had a better day on her own than she would have done with Stuart. She imagined him trailing around after her, complaining about the heat and how many shops she was visiting, all the time checking his mobile when he thought she wasn't looking. In summary, in her heart of hearts, she knew she wasn't missing Stuart as much as she should be.

Perhaps because he didn't deserve it.

As twilight fell and the shadows lengthened across the square, Isobel was wondering whether to eat dinner at one of the inviting restaurants down by the harbour, or get a taxi back to the hotel before it grew dark, when she felt someone watching her as she browsed in the window of a ceramics shop. Turning around, she saw a familiar-looking man standing in the street staring at her, as tourists filtered around him. He was dark and olive-skinned, broad-shouldered and stocky, and he stepped towards her, a confident smile on his face.

'You're Camille's friend,' he said to her, in English with a Spanish accent. 'You're staying at the palacio, right?'

'Yes, I am. Staying at the palacio, that is. I'm not Camille's friend . . .'

'Even better,' he grinned. 'I thought I recognized you – I never forget a beautiful woman. I'm Paulo Torres.'

He held out his hand and Isobel shook it. 'Isobel MacFarlane. You were at the boat party yesterday, weren't you?'

'Yes. In fact, it was my boat. I also co-own the restaurant, Il Paradiso.'

'A man of many talents,' Isobel laughed. 'My husband and I dined there a few nights ago, it was wonderful. In fact, I think I remember seeing you as we arrived.'

'And where's your husband now?'

'He's on the mainland. For work.' She rolled her eyes, knowing she shouldn't criticize Stuart to this virtual stranger, but unable to help herself.

'And he's left you here, all alone? He should take better care of you . . .'

Yes, he should, Isobel thought defiantly, though she didn't say so to Paulo. The way her eyes sparkled made it clear she agreed, though. 'I've been having a wonderful time without him. Sightseeing, shopping . . .'

Paulo shook his head and sighed. 'No, this won't do.

A beautiful woman cannot be left alone like this. I was born and raised on the island – I need to show you Mallorcan hospitality.'

'Do you?' Isobel said. There was something about Paulo's easy, flirtatious manner that she liked. After so long feeling neglected and dismissed by Stuart, it was nice to be charmed and flirted with. Besides, it wasn't as though Paulo was a complete stranger – she'd seen him at the restaurant and the boat party, and he knew Camille and Lucas. And he knew Stephanie too, Isobel realized, as the pieces slid into place. They'd been on a date together, but it hadn't worked out and she'd broken it off with him at yesterday's party . . .

'Yes, I do,' Paulo was saying with a grin. 'So how about you meet me back here in an hour's time. I have a little business to take care of first, but I'll be back.'

'And then what?' Isobel asked, tossing her hair coquettishly.

'And then, Isobel MacFarlane, I'm going to take you to dinner.'

Isobel and Paulo were seated outside a restaurant in the marina; the luxurious yachts moored nearby were attracting a lot of attention from passing tourists. The warm night air wrapped itself around them, a candle flickering softly on the table and bathing them in a warm glow. It was an upmarket establishment, catering to an exclusive, international clientele, and Isobel was enjoying herself.

Paulo had ordered a very expensive bottle of wine, and they were discussing the spectacular boats, Paulo clearly trying to impress her with his knowledge of the super-yacht industry.

'And what about the business you had to attend to earlier?' Isobel asked, spearing a forkful of octopus. 'Was that related to your yachts?'

Paulo smirked. '*That* was something else. I can't say too much, but rest assured it's very lucrative for me,' he added, angling his wrist to ensure she noticed the Rolex.

Isobel laughed. Paulo was nothing if not entertaining, and full of bravado, boasting incessantly. But he was young and hot and charming, and right now that was all Isobel wanted.

'And that's in Palma?' she asked, raising her wine glass to indicate the city.

'Yeah. I'll be spending a lot more time here – it's where the action is. Belleza is a backwater. No offence – I know it's pretty for the tourists, but I need more excitement.' He raised his eyebrows suggestively; Paulo certainly wasn't subtle.

'But what will happen to Il Paradiso, if you're spending so much time in Palma?'

Paulo shrugged dismissively. 'It's time to give up on that. Lucas will never get a Michelin star. No one cares about his homemade stews, it's peasant food.' He took a slug of his wine, as Isobel sipped hers thoughtfully.

'How do you know Lucas?'

'I've known him since we were kids. His grandmother lived on the island – she was Mallorcan – and he used to stay with her whilst his parents were travelling. Too busy to have him around,' he said, his eyes narrowed.

'Are you close to the family? I know Andre was in that terrible accident, but you must know Camille well if you've been friends all these years . . .'

'I know she's not as perfect as she pretends to be,'

Paulo said, his tone bitter. The sound of other diners washed over them, the background hum of chatter and laughter, the clink of cutlery against plates, as the water lapped against the marina wall on the other side of the cobbled walkway. Paulo fixed his gaze on Isobel, his dark eyes glittering. 'I know she has secrets. I know things about that family that no one else does, and she should be grateful that I'm keeping my mouth shut.'

'What sort of secrets?' Isobel asked innocently.

But Paulo wasn't falling for her question. He laughed loudly, then shook his head. 'You may be beautiful, Isobel, but I can't give up my secrets so easily.'

'Camille's husband was killed in a car crash, wasn't he?' Isobel said.

Paulo nodded. 'In Switzerland. It was after a party. We were racing too fast on the mountain road, and—'

'We?' Isobel interrupted.

'Hmm?'

'You said "we".' *Was Paulo there too?* she wondered suddenly.

'Did I? It was a . . . How do you say it in English? Slip of the tongue . . . Lucas was in the car with his father. He was badly injured.'

'I know. My husband was one of the team of surgeons who operated on him.'

'Was he indeed?' Paulo glanced across at her, his eyes shrewdly analysing her. 'What a coincidence. The same husband who's not here right now?'

'That's the one.'

'*Descuidado*,' Paulo murmured under his breath, and Isobel laughed.

'*Sí, es muy descuidado*,' she replied casually.

'You speak Spanish?'

'Yes, a little.'

'How come?'

'I trained as a fashion designer. I interned for a few different companies in Europe – in Madrid, and Milan, and Paris . . .'

'Well, Isobel, you're full of surprises,' Paulo breathed huskily.

Isobel took a long swallow of her wine. They were surrounded by strangers, and she was feeling reckless. 'What if I told you *I* had a secret about Camille, too.'

Paulo laughed dismissively. 'Like what? That her favourite colour's blue? That her guilty pleasure is eating chocolate ice cream?'

Isobel felt a shard of ice shoot through her spine. Men made a habit of underestimating her. 'Oh no. Something *much* bigger than that.'

Paulo's eyes narrowed thoughtfully as though trying to figure her out. 'Well in that case, I'd say that we should get out of here. I'm heading back to Belleza; maybe we can carry on this conversation somewhere more private?'

'Sure,' Isobel said casually, though her heart was beating rapidly as she wondered what she was getting herself into.

The two of them sat in silence, sizing each other up, the weight of unspoken secrets between them.

'Thank you for dinner,' Isobel said.

'The pleasure was all mine. I couldn't leave you stranded in a strange city. I'm not the kind of man to leave you on your own.'

Isobel smiled at the thinly veiled dig at Stuart. She was feeling a little drunk, a little reckless.

Meet Me at Sunset

Paulo opened his wallet and threw a pile of notes down ostentatiously on the table, before grabbing Isobel by the hand. She allowed his fingers to close possessively around hers, noticing the way he moved with absolute confidence, his broad shoulders carving a path through the crowd. She didn't know a soul here; no one knew she was with Paulo, and the situation held a frisson of danger.

He turned and winked at her, leading her away from the crowds and towards the darkness. Without giving herself time to think, Isobel followed him. She was intrigued by what Paulo knew about Camille. She didn't want to be alone right now, didn't want the night to end. And she wanted Paulo to tell her his secret, and she would do whatever it took to find out.

Chapter 14

'Lucas,' Catherine Zeta-Jones purred. 'I wasn't expecting to see you here today.'

'And I wasn't expecting you to answer the door,' he chuckled, feeling like a schoolboy as he asked, 'Is Stephanie in?'

'Sure, she's out by the pool. I'll go and get her. By the way, Michael and I are going out for a round of golf shortly, so you'll have the place to yourselves.' She winked as she sashayed off, leaving Lucas blushing.

A few moments later, Stephanie emerged and Lucas's eyes nearly fell out of his head. She was wearing a strapless bikini in a shimmering gold fabric, and her body was incredible. She had a slender, hour-glass figure, with a handspan waist and curvy hips. Her flawless skin was slick with oil, and her long hair was pulled back in a plait that fell all the way down her back.

'Lucas,' she smiled, and her blue eyes sparkled. 'What a nice surprise.'

He held out the bag he was carrying, though now he

felt faintly ridiculous. 'I thought you might like that cooking lesson – if you're not too busy,' he added, his eyes skating over her bikini.

Stephanie grinned. 'No, I wasn't doing anything important. That sounds perfect. Meet you in the kitchen? It's just down the hallway. Maria, the housekeeper, is out running errands so you can make yourself at home. I'll go throw some clothes on.'

'You don't have to,' Lucas replied, before he could stop himself.

Stephanie laughed, turning back to look at him over one shoulder as she walked away, and Lucas felt a wave of longing crash through his body. He'd been worried about making an idiot of himself, driving up to the S'Estaca estate with a bag full of ingredients on the passenger seat beside him. Stephanie might not have been there, or she might have been busy, or – the most galling of all – simply not interested in him. But Lucas could tell from the way that Stephanie looked at him that everything was going to be all right.

Up in her room, Stephanie was giddy with excitement. She was staying in a beautiful guest bedroom, with views out over the garden and the sea beyond, but right now she didn't see any of that as she pulled a stripy sundress from the antique wooden wardrobe and threw it over her bikini. She sat down at the old-fashioned dressing table with its trio of oval mirrors, and added a slick of lip gloss, quickly checking her appearance before heading downstairs again, her heart thumping.

She stopped in the doorway of the kitchen; her feet were bare, and Lucas hadn't heard her approach. She watched as he emptied the contents of the bag into the fridge, pulling out plates and dishes from the cupboards as he familiarized himself with Catherine's large, stylish kitchen.

He looked handsome as hell, and Stephanie's stomach gave a little flip as he reached up to a high shelf and his T-shirt rode up, giving her a glimpse of flat, toned stomach, with rippling muscles and a tantalizing line of dark hair that disappeared beneath the waistband of his shorts . . .

'So, what are we making?' she asked, as she stepped into the kitchen, not wanting him to catch her staring at him.

Lucas turned round, grinning as he saw her. '*Bacalao* – salted cod with vegetables in a traditional sauce. A regional speciality. You like fish, yes?'

'I love it. It sounds delicious.' She took a step closer, standing beside him. He felt so big next to her, tall and strong and capable. She loved the way he moved with confidence; the kitchen was completely his domain.

'Well, the first ingredient,' he began, opening a glass-fronted cabinet and taking out two crystal glasses. 'Is wine.' He effortlessly pulled out the cork from a bottle of white, and poured a glass for Stephanie. 'This is a Sauvignon Blanc that's grown and produced locally, in the foothills of the Tramuntana mountains. I always say that a glass of wine is essential when you're cooking.'

'So are you drinking every night in the restaurant?' she teased.

'Unfortunately not. But when you're cooking at home, for pleasure, it's a necessity.'

'I'll remember that. Cheers.'

'*Santé*,' Lucas replied, as they clinked glasses, not breaking eye contact. 'Or perhaps we should say *salud*, as we're in Spain.'

'How many languages do you speak?' Stephanie wondered, marvelling at how intelligent he was.

'French and Spanish, obviously. A little Italian and German. And English – very badly.'

'Your English is incredible – much better than my Spanish. Or my French, and I studied that in school.'

'Well, perhaps we can teach one another,' Lucas said easily.

'I'd like that. So that's cooking, languages . . . What else can you teach me?' Stephanie said flirtatiously. She was having fun, and the wine was certainly helping her to relax.

'Let's start with cooking and see where it goes,' Lucas replied, raising his eyebrows. 'We need to start by dicing these,' he explained, pulling a pile of tomatoes, onions and garlic across the counter towards them. 'For the sauce.'

Stephanie frowned as he passed her a knife and a chopping board. 'Do you think I'm going to be your sous-chef?' she protested, shaking her head in mock horror. 'You don't get to boss me around.'

'You want to be in control?' Lucas smiled.

'Damn right. Do you have a problem with powerful women?' Stephanie teased.

Lucas shook his head and grinned. 'Not at all. I love them and I'll do whatever you tell me to.'

The laughter and teasing continued as they chopped and diced and simmered, both of them flirting but neither making the first move as the tension in the room ramped up, the chemistry between them hotter than the sizzling pans. There was lots of accidental physical contact as they worked, hands brushing, elbows touching, playfully nudging each other out of the way. While they cooked, Stephanie found herself opening up to him in a way she hadn't for a long time, about being adopted and growing up feeling like she wasn't really wanted.

'My parents couldn't have kids, so they adopted me. I'd already been in foster care since I was a toddler.'

'Oh? What about your real parents?' Lucas asked, stopping what he was doing to look at her.

'My real mum was a drug addict. I was taken into care when I was about three and was with a few different foster carers until I was about six. Everything was great with my new family until I was about eight years old, then my adoptive mother got pregnant, and everything changed.'

'I'm sorry, Stephanie, you've had it rough.'

Stephanie shrugged, but it took her a moment to speak. 'My adoptive mother had always been a bit manic, but when my little sister came along, she went into full Mumzilla mode.'

Lucas raised his eyes in a question.

'The only thing that mattered was my little sis. Phoebe. I was totally pushed out, couldn't do anything right.' Stephanie had worked hard to suppress her feelings, but they sometimes still ambushed her. She ploughed on; for some reason she couldn't explain, it was important to her that Lucas knew this.

'My adoptive dad, he of the chip-shop fame,' she smiled at Lucas, 'he loved me, but the tension between him and my mum got too much and eventually he left her . . .

and me.' She shook her head. 'Then she met someone else, and I spent my life being pushed from one house to another, missing out on family birthdays, holidays, never being allowed to have friends round, treated like a skivvy by my adoptive mum . . .'

Stephanie could still feel the sting of her adoptive mother's words, the criticisms and the slights that peppered her life daily.

'How did you get into acting?' Lucas asked, gently steering her away from darker thoughts.

'I had a great drama teacher, Mr Green. He championed me, encouraged me to go to drama school, helped me get a scholarship. I left home when I was eighteen and I've never been back.'

'And what about your adoptive parents now?'

'My dad's great; he has got a new wife who's lovely.' She paused. 'The thing is, I love my little sister, Phoebe, but she's stuck with mum too, so I have to keep in touch for her sake. I want to make sure she always has someone she can turn to, unlike me.'

Lucas regarded her for a moment. 'You are not what you seem, Stephanie. I'd like to get to know you better, I hope you will let me.'

Stephanie liked the way he said that. God, she fancied him, there was no denying it, and the air between them was electric. She was certain that he liked her too, but prolonging the tension was delicious. And there was always a part of her – the shy, insecure girl she'd once been – that didn't dare to believe that a man as handsome and cultured as Lucas would want to be with her. They were clearly from very different backgrounds; he'd grown up used to wealth and travel, feeling at home in expensive restaurants and high-end hotels, but it was a whole new world for Stephanie. And there was his pouty girlfriend in the picture too.

'Here,' Lucas said, cutting into her thoughts. 'Try this.' He took a teaspoon and scooped it in the lightly bubbling sauce, before blowing gently across the top. They were inches apart from one another as Stephanie leaned forward, her lips parting as she delicately tasted the sauce. The flavours were intense, with pungent aromas of tomatoes and herbs.

'Mmm, it's incredible,' she sighed.

'Close your eyes,' Lucas murmured, and Stephanie obliged. His voice was gravelly and sexy, and it was all she could concentrate on. 'When you lose one sense, your others are heightened,' he explained. 'You can taste the flavours one by one – the bitterness of the olives, the sweetness of the tomatoes, the heat of the pepper . . .'

Slowly, Stephanie opened her eyes to see Lucas standing right in front of her. A strand of hair had come loose from her plait and he reached out to brush it behind her ear, his fingertips grazing the soft skin of her cheek. Stephanie instinctively reached up to take his hand, her palm closing over his as she tilted her face upwards towards him. And suddenly it was inevitable as he reached for her and their lips finally met, bodies locked together as they kissed hungrily. Stephanie pressed herself against him, her small, lithe body moulded to his solid bulk as he pulled her close, his hands exploring her body, setting off delicious explosions wherever he touched.

Kissing Lucas felt even more amazing than she'd imagined – a million times better than Paulo's overconfident embrace, which had left her cold. But all thoughts of Paulo were pushed from her mind as Lucas's lips moved down to her neck and Stephanie threw back her head, arching her back as desire ran through her entire body, a burning point of heat crystallizing between her thighs.

She closed her eyes once again and, like Lucas had said, all her other senses were heightened – the feel of his lips on hers, his tongue exploring her mouth, his powerful body crushed against hers. But then something disturbed the moment; a sizzling noise, followed by the acrid scent of smoke.

'Shit,' Lucas swore, jumping away from her and pulling the pan off the hob. 'We burned the fish.'

Stephanie began to laugh, the situation seemed so ridiculous, and Lucas laughed too.

'I wasn't hungry anyway . . . well, not for food . . .' she murmured, as Lucas came back over, wrapping his arms around her. This time they took it more slowly, kissing softly, without the urgency of earlier. Gently, he lifted her onto the countertop as though she weighed nothing, and Stephanie wrapped her legs around him, pulling him closer as a fresh burst of desire rippled through her. The strap of her sundress slipped from her shoulder and Lucas traced its path, his hands moving down to her breasts, both of them lost in the moment, unable to stop themselves . . .

Then Lucas pulled back, and Stephanie stared at him in confusion as he glanced up at the clock. His hair was dishevelled from where she'd run her hands through it, his breath coming fast.

'What's the matter?' she asked.

Lucas winced. 'I have to go. The restaurant – I need to open up.'

'Can't it wait a little longer?'

Lucas kissed her once again, but she could feel his hesitation. 'Believe me, leaving is the last thing I want to do.'

'Then don't.'

'I have to.'

Stephanie slid down from the counter, pulling up the strap of her dress. 'It's OK. I understand,' she said, trying to hide her disappointment.

'It'll be a late one tonight,' Lucas apologized. 'But are you free tomorrow?'

'Of course. We need to finish what we started.'

Lucas groaned with longing. 'You're incredible, Stephanie Moon. I don't know how I'm going to be able to concentrate tonight.'

'Good,' she giggled. 'I don't want you to forget about me.'

'Never,' Lucas replied, shaking his head. 'Now that I've found you, I'll never forget you.'

They kissed for the final time, a kiss filled with desire and an unspoken promise of what was to come. Then Lucas reluctantly turned to go, leaving Stephanie walking on air, counting the hours until she could see him again.

Lucas could barely remember anything about the drive to Il Paradiso. He was on autopilot for the short journey as his Porsche sped along the coastal road, his head full of thoughts of Stephanie, his body on fire at the memory of her. He was in danger of falling hard for her; she was fun, intelligent and sexy, but they connected on a deeper level too. He instinctively trusted her, and it was as though they understood one another intuitively. He felt as if he could tell her anything . . . but then he thought about Elle and felt a stab of shame and anger dampen his mood. What was he playing at, he asked himself? He'd promised to leave his bad-boy days behind him, and Elle deserved better, but Stephanie was different.

He was in a thoughtful mood as he pulled into the restaurant car park, and was almost at the door of Il Paradiso before he noticed the huge chain and lock across the entrance.

'What the . . .' he began, as two black-clad men approached him. 'What's going on?'

'Are you Lucas Fontaine?' one of them called back.

A bad feeling swept over Lucas, a churning in his gut that told him whatever was happening wasn't good. 'Depends who's asking.'

'We are,' the man retorted coldly. He was tall and well-built, with tattoos on his neck and a menacing expression.

Lucas pulled himself up to his full height and looked him square in the face. 'Yes, I am. Now tell me what's happening with my restaurant.'

The shorter man gave him an unpleasant smile. 'Oh, I think you'll find it's no longer your restaurant.' He reached into his pocket and pulled out a letter. 'Here's the legal notice. This property is being repossessed for non-payment of rent.'

'But that's impossible,' Lucas burst out.

'It's entirely possible. No payments have been received for six months. We've sent multiple warnings and a court order that was ignored. You've had ample opportunity to get in touch, but now we're closing this place down.'

'No! Wait, please – there must be some mistake. Give me one moment.'

Lucas pulled out his phone and scrolled urgently to Paulo's number. Instead of a ringtone, there was a high-pitched beeping noise, followed by an automated voice telling him that the number wasn't recognized.

Lucas felt as though his world was collapsing, utterly powerless as he watched the men affix 'No Entry' signs to the restaurant, heedless of the fact that customers would start arriving in just two hours' time. Everything he'd worked for these past two years, all of his dreams – gone, in an instant.

Frantically, he tried Paulo's number again, but once again it was unrecognized. It seemed to have been disconnected. It was as though Paulo had vanished into thin air.

Where on earth was he? Lucas thought desperately. What the hell was going on?

Chapter 15

It had been another hectic day. Camille was used to it – her life had been lived at breakneck speed for the past thirty years – but she was only human and at times the exhaustion caught up with her.

It was late at night and she was sitting in her suite, sipping hot water with lemon, running through the events of the past few weeks in her mind. She needed to focus on the show and be on top form for the dozens of interviews she'd been asked to do; the press release had gone out that morning revealing Catherine Zeta-Jones as the new face of Camille Andre, and it was making headlines around the world. But Camille couldn't stop thinking about Andre's accident, about the chilling letters she'd been receiving, and the blackmail threats, and about Nicolas . . .

They'd exchanged a few words after Camille's speech, but the conversation had all been focused on business. Camille was so used to being able to tell him anything, and she badly wanted to confide in him about the notes she'd received since arriving on the island. She was starting to realize just how much he was part of her life; how much he was a part of everything she did; how much she had loved him . . .

Her thoughts were interrupted by a gentle knock on the door. Camille glanced at the clock; almost one a.m. Then she smiled. She'd asked Nicolas to come and see her tonight, but when he hadn't shown up, she accepted that he'd turned down her invitation. Now, as she rose from her seat, she imagined him wrestling with himself, debating what the right decision would be, before finally agreeing to grant her request.

Camille opened the door and the sight of Nicolas made her catch her breath. It was almost as though she'd summoned him with her thoughts. He'd clearly been working late, most likely staying on New York time and catching up with his office there. Now he was off duty, he'd undone the top buttons of his shirt and rolled up his sleeves, and Camille felt a sharp stab of desire shoot through her. She'd missed him.

They looked at each other for a long moment. There was a wariness in Nicolas's eyes, as though uncertain how she'd react, and Camille hated to see it, hated the distance that had sprung up between them.

Camille fought to keep her composure, to keep her expression neutral, though if she was being honest with herself, all she wanted to do was embrace Nicolas and sink into his arms, to feel his strong, solid body against hers and fall into bed with him. She longed to lay all her troubles at his door, as she had done for the last three decades, to listen to his words of advice and know he would take care of everything.

But she couldn't do that any more. She'd made her choice and turned him down.

'I thought you'd still be awake,' he replied, and his eyes were soft as he looked at her.

'Would you like to come in?'

Nicolas nodded and Camille stepped aside, closing the door behind him. Her heart was racing. She knew this man so well, yet everything had changed between them and she didn't know how to navigate their new relationship.

'Would you like a brandy?'

Nicolas nodded. 'Yes, please.'

'I'll join you.' Camille distracted herself by fixing the drinks, splashing Courvoisier into two crystal glasses, and handing one to Nicolas. They sat down side by side in the lounge area of the suite, and both began to speak at once. They laughed, easing the tension. 'No, you go first,' Camille insisted.

'The yacht party was a real success,' Nicolas congratulated her.

'Thank you. I think everyone had a lot of fun, and the press have gone crazy since I announced Catherine as the new face of the brand.' Then Camille's face darkened. 'Although Elle made a real show of herself. I knew I should never have invited her. The silver lining is that she and Lucas broke up. Hopefully for good.'

'He's a sensible boy. You raised him well,' Nicolas said quietly. 'He'll make the best decision for him.'

Camille gave him a long, searching look. 'I'm glad you came. I didn't know if you would.'

'Of course. This is business. Like I said yesterday, whatever happened between us doesn't change that.'

Just business. Camille wasn't sure how she felt about

Nicolas's new hardness – relieved that he'd taken a step back? Or devastated that he'd finally given up on her, cutting ties once and for all. Recklessly she asked, 'Is that the only reason you came? The business?'

A muscle flickered in Nicolas's jaw, and he seemed annoyed suddenly. 'What do you want from me, Camille? You made it clear that the only relationship between us was professional so I'm trying to keep it that way. Don't toy with me. It's not fair.' He drained his glass and slammed it down on the table.

Camille was shocked by his outburst – he was usually so contained, so in control of himself – but she knew that what he'd said was true. It *wasn't* fair of her to ask those questions, but the truth was that her feelings were all over the place. 'I'm sorry,' she apologized. 'It's just hard, after all this time.'

'This was your choice, Camille,' Nicolas reminded her. His eyes were firm, but she heard the emotion in his voice again.

Camille stood up. 'I have something to show you. Wait a moment . . .' She went into her bedroom and returned with a letter and a package. She handed both to Nicolas, her face ashen.

'What's this?'

'They've both arrived since I've been here. Someone knows.'

Wordlessly, Nicolas opened the envelope, taking in the photograph, the accident report, the newspaper article, and the note attached to the top: *I know you lied*. He swallowed, placing the pile down on the side table. Then he reached for the package, frowning as he saw the handbag stained by a rust-red liquid.

'Open it,' Camille said.

Nicolas's eyes flickered to hers and he did as she said. *'Putain,'* he swore, with a sharp intake of breath, as he saw the smashed wing mirror and the second, menacing warning:

Now it's time to pay, once and for all

Camille began to tell Nicolas everything: how the letters had started arriving; how she'd been so scared by them that she had just got her accountant to pay the money blindly.

'Why didn't you come to me before?'

'I don't know, I was afraid. I just wanted it to go away.'

'This is serious,' Nicolas said.

Camille shivered, glancing around her as though she expected to see someone hiding in the room. 'I'm scared, Nicolas.'

She felt close to tears. Usually Camille was impenetrable, keeping her fears and emotions tightly bound, but lately she felt under so much pressure that she worried this could break her. She longed for Nicolas to put his arms around her and tell her everything was going to be all right, but neither of them moved an inch.

'I've got contacts in the police,' Nicolas began. 'We must try to find out who is sending these; it's already dangerous.' Nicolas sighed heavily, running his hands through his dark hair. It was late, and he looked tired, Camille realized. In her mind, he was still the youthful 22-year-old he had been when she'd first met him, but she saw now the deep lines around his eyes, the increasing grey in his hair. He'd been at the top of his industry for a long time now, age was catching up with of them . . . and their secrets.

'But what do they know, Nicolas? Who could it be, do you think . . .?' Camille's nerves were in threads. 'Who is it?'

Nicolas's brown eyes were grave. 'What can they know? It is only you and I who . . .' He opened his mouth to speak, but at that moment there was a light knock on the door. The two of them exchanged glances, their faces taut with anxiety, and Camille marched across the suite, her adrenaline racing.

'Camille, wait—'

She wrenched open the door before Nicolas could stop her, almost expecting to find the suspect standing there. Instead, it was a uniformed concierge with an apologetic expression on his face.

'I'm sorry to disturb you so late, Señora Fontaine. This just arrived for you. It was marked as urgent.'

He held the nondescript brown envelope out to her, and Camille recoiled, taking it as gingerly as if it contained a bomb.

'Thank you,' she managed, and her voice sounded faint. She closed the door without another word and Nicolas was instantly at her side. They looked at one another, the tension unbearable.

'Do you want me to open it?'

Camille shook her head. 'I'll do it.'

'Be careful,' Nicolas warned, and Camille knew his head was full of terrible ideas like razor blades secreted in the opening, or a letter laced with anthrax.

Slowly, she opened the envelope, finding nothing more deadly than a single piece of paper. She pulled it out, read the words on there and gasped.

'What is it? Show me.'

Meet Me at Sunset

Camille handed the note to Nicolas, her head spinning, her vision swimming in and out of focus. It was what she knew had been coming all along – a blackmail demand:

I knew what you did. One million dollars is the price of my silence or I'll reveal the truth about Andre's death to the world.

On the back was the same untraceable bank account number.

'Holy shit,' Nicolas breathed. He raced to the door, wrenching it open, but the concierge had gone and right now Camille needed his attention.

'What are we going to do?' she asked, her eyes wide and terrified. Her chest was rising and falling rapidly, and she couldn't seem to catch her breath. It was as though a huge weight was pushing down on her lungs. 'They know, Nicolas. Someone knows! I'm going to lose everything. My business, my reputation . . . And what about Lucas? My God, Nicolas, I can't . . .'

She sank to the floor, her legs refusing to hold her any more. Her breathing was shallow, and she was beginning to hyperventilate. It felt as though someone had punched her hard in the solar plexus, and she doubled over, clutching her stomach.

And then Nicolas was there, his strong arms around her, cradling her against his broad chest, as she collapsed against him gratefully. Camille closed her eyes as he stroked her hair, murmuring words of comfort. She trusted him implicitly. He was the one person that she knew would always be there for her and never let her down, even more than Lucas. He was always so cool and calm, so practical and capable, knowing what to do in every situation and never fazed by the unexpected. In his arms she was safe, and she wanted to stay there for ever.

She could feel his heart beating against hers, the fabric of his shirt soft against her cheek as she inhaled the scent of his Guerlain cologne – the same one he'd worn for over thirty years. He was constant and unchanging, her stalwart in life. It was true that, as a young woman, she'd found his calm and reliable nature rather dull and unsexy. It was why she'd chosen Andre, who was everything Nicolas wasn't – bold, passionate, exciting. But Nicolas had been her stalwart. He'd never stopped loving her, even after everything that had happened . . .

Gradually, Camille's breathing slowed. Her vision cleared and her tears dried up. But she knew that they weren't over the worst. Whoever was threatening her was still out there, and this was just the beginning. The blackmail note had changed everything.

She pulled back and looked up at Nicolas, searching the face that she knew so well. 'God help us, Nicolas . . .'

Part 2

Chapter 16

Paris, September 1968

Camille tiptoed barefoot around the apartment, not wanting to wake Nicolas who was still sleeping. She washed her face and moisturized, adding a slick of mascara and lipstick; her skin was flawless with a youthful glow, and she didn't need to hide beneath layers of make-up.

She pulled on a dress that she'd bought at a flea market the previous weekend. It was an oversized A-line shape, in a garish purple and green pattern. On anyone else, it would have looked like a monstrosity, but somehow on Camille it was the height of chic. She paired it with knee-length socks and Mary Jane shoes, before backcombing her hair at the crown and tying a scarf around her head like a headband, letting the ends flutter loose. Then her look was complete: stylish and gamine, quirky but ultra-fashionable.

She crept over to the bed where Nicolas lay sleeping, the sheets gathered around his waist, exposing his toned stomach and broad chest. Her gaze ran over the curve of his muscular shoulders. With his light brown hair and handsome face, Camille felt a warm glow of happiness as she looked at him. She'd never dated anyone who made her feel like Nicolas did – loved and secure and completely able to be herself.

She stroked him gently on his forearm to rouse him. 'Bye, darling, I'll see you later. Don't forget, you have lectures at ten.'

Nicolas murmured groggily as Camille bent down to kiss him. She smelt of perfume and hairspray, and Nicolas stirred, pulling her down onto the bed with him.

'Do you have to leave?' he grumbled, wrapping his arms around her as she snuggled against him. He was warm and the bed was inviting, and Camille was tempted to peel off her mini dress and slide back between the sheets in the tiny apartment they shared. But she knew she had to go.

'I do. But I'll see you later. Meet me at sunset, the usual place.' she said, giving him a long, lingering kiss before heading out of the door. She ran down the spiral staircase – she and Nicolas rented an attic apartment and it was four floors to the ground – and out through the heavy wooden door into the Parisian morning. It was a warm day, still more summer than autumn, though the leaves were beginning to turn and the boutiques she passed displayed cosy sweaters and woollen cape coats.

Camille bowled down the boulevard towards the Metro, soaking up the energy of the quartier. She lived in Montmartre, in the north of Paris; it was vibrant and cosmopolitan and the apartments were cheap, Camille and Michel always met for a drink at their favourite little café near Sacré Coeur Basilica, watching the sunset from its elevated position was the perfect way to end the day. She headed downhill through the picturesque, winding streets – the eighteenth arrondissement resembled a village perched on top of a hill – before making her way along the Boulevard de Clichy, home to the famous Moulin Rouge nightclub. The city was still reeling from the strikes and student protests that had taken place earlier that year, and the sense of revolution crackled in the air. The world was changing, and Camille was determined to be part of it.

She got on the Metro at Pigalle, hopping on the familiar trains that rushed noisily along the tracks. It was only half a dozen stops to central Paris, and Camille was content to sit and daydream, anonymous amidst the other commuters.

She had grown up in a small town in Normandy, where life was quiet and mundane. Her mother, Béatrice, was a seamstress, and worked in a small shop taking in clothes for mending and tailoring. She'd taught Camille everything there was to know about constructing and fitting garments, and the young Camille became passionate about fabric and design. Her father, Albert, sold electrical goods, like televisions and radios, working long hours to bring in a little more income. They were comfortable, but there was never a lot of money to spare.

Camille had always been a dreamer. She remembered once, when she was around seven or eight years old, the whole family went to Paris on the train. Her father had business there, and Camille and her mother spent the day in the city whilst he attended meetings. For Camille, the French capital was like nothing she'd ever experienced before – glamorous people who all seemed to be rushing along the busy streets, and enormous, beautiful buildings laid out along wide boulevards flanked by horse-chestnut trees. Camille and Béatrice turned onto an avenue where the shops boasted smart iron railings and perfect window boxes and immaculate cream awnings, and Camille couldn't help but be drawn to the wide, brightly lit windows where mannequins displayed exquisite clothes. She remembered feeling that she didn't quite belong as she took in the names on the shopfronts – Chanel, Dior, Givenchy – but knew instantly that this was the world she wanted to inhabit. Not even the uniformed men on the doors who frowned at her, or the imperious saleswomen staring out from behind the windows with a look of distaste, could put her off.

When Camille got home, she devoured everything she could from her local library on clothing and the fashion industry. She learned that Gabrielle 'Coco' Chanel hadn't been born into wealth either. In fact, she'd grown up in an orphanage, being raised by nuns, but her simple, monochrome style had revolutionized the fashion industry. If Coco Chanel had done it, why couldn't Camille?

From that moment on, she devoted herself to her dream, imploring her mother to teach her all she knew about sewing, and dedicating herself to learning everything she could about sketching, designing, and the history of fashion. Her ambition was to leave Normandy and move to Paris to study at the prestigious École de la Chambre Syndicale de la Couture Parisienne. The school admitted only a handful of applicants a year, and was known for its exclusivity. But despite not having wealth or contacts,

Camille had blown the interview panel away with her talent and passion.

Now she was following her dream, taking her first tentative steps into the fashion world by studying haute couture – its history and origins, its rules and regulations and, most importantly, how to create a garment of the highest quality that was like a piece of art.

A few weeks after starting her course, Camille had met Nicolas in a bar one evening when she was out with a group of friends. He was attractive – not classically handsome, but with a certain presence, and a quiet confidence that Camille was drawn to. He spoke intelligently and eloquently, and she discovered that he was also a student, studying for his Masters in Economics.

He invited her for dinner the following night, and it seemed to Camille to be an old-fashioned and romantic invitation, in an era where their contemporaries wanted to get stoned and practise free love. He clearly adored her, and Camille revelled in his devotion. A few weeks later, they moved in together, scandalizing her parents and risking the wrath of the elderly building concierge, who was outraged by the idea of an unmarried couple living together, and shocked by the liberal changes sweeping the nation.

Camille and Nicolas had been together ever since. He was her first serious boyfriend, and they adored one another, swept away by young love in the most romantic city in the world. Nicolas worshipped her like a goddess, but they were best friends too, and Camille felt loved unconditionally, able to be herself entirely around him. Sex was a revelation, and they couldn't get enough of one another. But their relationship was about more than just the physical; Nicolas understood her wants and needs, and supported her in her ambitions, never undermining or belittling her. He knew that she could be headstrong and impulsive sometimes, and didn't try to rein her in, but he wasn't a doormat either. Nicolas exuded a quiet strength; he didn't need to scream and shout to make himself heard, and though they rarely had arguments, he was no pushover. He seemed to know how to handle every situation, and instinctively took control in his calm, assured way. Camille felt so lucky to have found him – they were the perfect fit.

Her train pulled into the station and Camille jumped off, running up the stairs, out into the fresh air. The magnificent buildings loomed above her, the distinctive limestone façades with decorative balconies and mansard roofs looking their best in the sunshine. Outside, people were sitting at pavement cafés drinking their morning coffees, or walking their dogs, or strolling arm-in-arm with their lover; Camille loved being part of the beat of the city.

A short walk along the street was the grand building that housed the École de la Chambre Syndicale. It had been founded by the Fédération de la Haute Couture to train future generations of designers and teach them the strict rules of the industry. Only certain fashion houses were allowed to call themselves haute couture, and they had to follow meticulous regulations covering styles, collections, models, press and taxes.

Today's lecture was on finance. Camille found a seat and pulled her notebook and pen from her bag. She tried to keep her mind from wandering, but she was struggling to concentrate. She knew the subject was important, but it was far from the most interesting aspect of the business; she would have much preferred to be sketching, or sewing, or . . . just about anything else other than learning about VAT and import duty.

Nicolas would have loved it, she thought fondly, watching the lecturer in his cord trousers and polo neck drone on about assets and liabilities. She knew that Nicolas's brain would have made sense of the complicated concepts in seconds; he was a whiz with numbers and had an instinctive flair for business. Camille had no doubt that he'd go far in life; he was focused and determined with a razor-sharp mind.

As her thoughts drifted, she gazed around the lecture hall. A few seats away, she locked eyes with a guy and immediately felt a jolt, as though every atom in her body had jumped to attention. He was incredibly good-looking, with Mediterranean colouring – tanned skin and rich brown eyes and thick black hair, which he wore longer so the ends spilled over his collar. He was wearing a fitted jumper that showed off the shape of his muscular chest, and as he caught her looking, he grinned at her. Camille instinctively looked away, rolling her eyes – who the hell did this guy think he was? But a few moments later, she found herself glancing in his direction once again. This time when he smiled, Camille smiled back.

When the lecture was over, he approached her, as she'd expected he would. Camille knew she looked good, her long, dark hair glossy and loose, her slender body poured into the chic dress.

'I'm Andre,' he introduced himself.

'Camille,' she replied, sizing him up, oblivious to the other students who hurried out of the lecture theatre around them, eager to leave behind the world of balance sheets and corporation tax.

'I'm going to grab a drink, Camille. Would you like to join me?'

Camille hesitated, sure that her desire would be written across her face. She was intrigued by this man who was suave and charismatic, utterly masculine and confident in a completely different way to Nicolas. Nicolas had a quiet assurance; this guy acted as though he knew he had the world at his feet.

'I can't,' she replied eventually. 'I'm meeting my boyfriend.'

Andre threw back his head and laughed. His teeth were white and wolfish, and she could see the shadow of stubble along his jawline. His eyes sparkled roguishly; when he looked at her, it was as though he was imagining her naked.

'Oh Camille, whoever he is, he doesn't deserve you,' Andre smirked. 'And I can promise you, a drink with me will be a hundred times more exciting than *anything* you do with your boyfriend.'

Camille gasped, enraged by his arrogance. But it was impossible to ignore the way her heart was racing, the way her body was already yearning for his touch. There was no way she could say no, and he knew it.

Chapter 17

That first drink was just the beginning. Camille and Andre met almost daily after that. She found him irresistible, unable to stay away from him.

She was aware that she couldn't stop talking about him to Nicolas. It was as though she wanted to share how extraordinary Andre was with the most important person in her life: Nicolas. She knew it made no sense, but she couldn't seem to help herself.

The two men met one evening, unexpectedly, in a bar.

'That's Andre,' Camille said, gripping Nicolas's arm as his rival walked in the door. Nicolas couldn't fail to notice the way she lit up when she saw him, excitement written across her face as her almond eyes followed him across the room.

Andre spotted her within seconds, coming over to introduce himself to Nicolas. Camille felt giddy, as though her parents were meeting her new date for the first time. It was a completely messed-up situation, and Camille knew it. She was undoubtedly in love with Nicolas, but falling hard for Andre at the same time, and she had no idea what to do about it. She was barely eating, hardly sleeping, unable to focus on her studies for the first time. Her head was all over the place. She was young, beautiful and in love – with two men simultaneously.

Nicolas was as polite as ever. He shook Andre's hand and said warmly, 'Good to meet you. I've heard a lot about you.'

'You too. You're a very lucky man,' Andre replied.

'I know,' Nicolas said evenly. Camille could see that he was determined not to fall into the trap that Andre had set. Nicolas wouldn't try to compete with Andre, or one-up him, or indulge in over-the-top displays of affection towards Camille that hinted at hidden insecurities. He was dignified and honourable, and Camille loved him for that.

But the chemistry between her and Andre was sizzling. She could feel how every eye in the room turned to him, how every woman gravitated to him, and it roused Camille's competitive instincts. She longed to be the one he desired, the one he took home at the end of the night. Andre outshone Nicolas in every way – he was taller, broader, more handsome, and immaculately dressed – and Camille was dazzled by him, yet at the same time she felt horribly guilty. She loved Nicolas, but the sparks between her and Andre were impossible to ignore.

'I'll go get some more drinks. What are you having?' Nicolas asked Andre pleasantly.

'I'd love a beer,' Andre smiled. Nicolas nodded and left, and Andre turned to Camille. *'That's* the famous Nicolas? I don't get the attraction. You might as well be dating your accountant.' He slid his arm around Camille, one hand splayed across her bottom as he leaned in to nuzzle her neck.

'Andre, stop,' Camille protested weakly, but his touch sent electricity through her body, sparks intensifying in her stomach and moving lower.

She pulled away when Nicolas came back through the crowd, though she knew her cheeks must be flushed, her face betraying her desire.

'So, Andre, I hear you know everything there is to know about the fashion world,' Nicolas began, and Andre smiled in response. Camille watched their conversation, each gently testing the other, but she could see that Nicolas was winning Andre over, the latter forming a grudging respect for his rival.

A few evenings later, Camille came home late from the part-time waitressing job that helped fund her studies to find Andre in her apartment, the two men sharing a bottle of brandy and discussing investment strategies.

The sight threw her – the two of them together, and her attraction to both. There was Andre with his good looks and easy charm, then Nicolas with a quiet determination, and the inexplicable, unbreakable connection between him and Camille. She felt her stomach flip with excitement and confusion. How French! She knew this situation couldn't continue indefinitely. It was as though she was walking a tightrope and would inevitably fall, but she didn't know who would catch her.

'Camille.' Nicolas noticed her, and she walked over to kiss him, aware of Andre's eyes on them.

'*Bonsoir*,' he smirked, his wolfish eyes flashing over her, though he didn't alter his relaxed pose. 'I was having a little trouble with our latest essay from Professor Henry

– the finer points of finance are not my strong point. I have to say, Nicolas is a genius.'

'Isn't he?' Camille beamed, stroking his hair affectionately.

'Between the three of us we could take over the world. Maybe we should all go into business together after we graduate.'

Camille laughed, but the idea was appealing and lodged in her brain. This was why she adored Andre – he was bold and driven, his ambition unstoppable.

She knew that Nicolas loved her unconditionally, that he would always support her and never let her down. When she envisaged their future, she saw them as comfortable and secure, with Nicolas working in a steady job, the two of them living in a nice apartment, hosting dinner parties at the weekend and spending their summers in Provence or on the Île de Ré. With Andre, however, the possibilities felt limitless. He promised her the earth, and she believed he'd deliver it.

One day after lectures, Andre approached her in the corridor. 'You've been avoiding me, Camille.'

It was true. Being around him weakened her resolve, and she'd vowed to stay true to Nicolas. But the physical pull between her and Andre was impossible to ignore. She looked up at him and knew she was lost. 'Andre, please, it's not fair . . .'

Andre pulled her into his arms and kissed her deeply. Electricity went racing through her body, and thoughts of Andre consumed her. It was as though she couldn't think straight, couldn't behave rationally, didn't care about anything else when she was with him. Her judgement was clouded by lust, pure and simple.

Meet Me at Sunset

'I want you, Camille. Leave him for me. You said you'd do it before. Promise me. We can be so good together. We'll have an amazing life, and you'll have everything you ever wanted, I promise you.'

Camille stared back into his dark eyes and felt as though she was falling. 'All right,' she promised, feeling that she would have agreed to anything in that moment. 'I'll do it.'

Telling Nicolas was the hardest thing she'd ever done. She couldn't shake the feeling, deep in the pit of her stomach, that she was making a huge mistake. She'd been determined not to cry, but she broke down in floods of tears. Nicolas was stoic, and she hated to be the one who was crying when she was the one who was breaking them up.

She wanted Nicolas to fight for her – she might even have changed her mind if he had – but Nicolas had too much dignity for that. He wasn't going to plead and beg.

Camille tried to justify her behaviour by telling herself that she had finally found her *grand amour*, her true love, and she was helpless in the face of fate. Yes, she loved Nicolas, and felt overwhelming guilt at what she was doing, torn between the two men. But ultimately, Camille knew that what she had with Andre was different. Andre himself was like no one she'd ever met before.

Nicolas took the news with good grace, as though he'd never expected that Camille would stay with him, always knowing that one day she would leave.

'I love you, Camille, and I always will. If you ever need anything at all, come to me. I'll be here for you, I promise.'

'Thank you, Nicolas.' There were tears in Camille's eyes as she hugged him goodbye, preparing to leave him alone in the apartment they'd once shared. Andre was waiting downstairs in the car, which was filled with Camille's things. 'You're a good man. You'll find someone better than me.'

'No,' he shook his head. 'I won't.' As Camille turned to go, Nicolas said, 'I hope he makes you happy. That's all I want for you.'

Camille stayed silent, unable to reply. Then she walked out without looking back.

It was harder to move on from Nicolas than she'd imagined. They had friends in common, they hung out in the same bars and cafés, and she found herself grabbing coffee with him from time to time. A platonic friendship grew between them, as Camille discovered that she valued his advice and appreciated his calm, rational way of thinking when Andre was being hot-headed. The three of them had grown close over the past few months. Andre had come to like and respect Nicolas, learning that beneath his sensible exterior, he had a wry sense of humour, and offered a balanced approach to Andre's volatility.

Nicolas dated occasionally, but there never seemed to be anyone serious or permanent, no one he moved into his apartment within weeks in a giddy flush of romance, the way he had with Camille.

On New Year's Eve, the last day of 1969, the trio found themselves at the same party, in an elegant, expansive apartment in the eighth arrondissement, with a stunning view across the Seine to the Eiffel Tower. It belonged to a mutual friend whose wealthy parents were ringing in the new year at their chalet in Val d'Isère, and right now there was dancing on the parquet floors, the remains of joints stubbed out in the pot plants, and the drinks cabinet had been raided and depleted.

Camille made her way out onto the balcony, in search of fresh air and a break from the mass of bodies and thumping music inside. The night was freezing, the pavements twinkling with frost, as boats packed with revellers ploughed up and down the river. In the distance, near the Tour Montparnasse, someone had let off fireworks early, and the inky sky was lit up with explosions of red and green stars.

'Cigarette?'

Camille turned to see Nicolas. He was wearing a moss-green sweater paired with tan-coloured trousers, and looked somewhat out of place amidst the bright colours and crazy patterns sported by the rest of the partygoers.

'I didn't realize you were out here. It's crazy in there,' Camille smiled, gratefully accepting a Gauloise. She leaned in close as he lit it and saw his eyes skim over her.

'You look beautiful, by the way,' he told her. She was wearing a flared jumpsuit in crushed red velvet, and she grinned at him.

'Thanks. Designed and made it myself.'

'Naturally. Was that at work?'

Camille pulled a face. Since graduating from university, she'd found a job with a small atelier catering to the bourgeois set. There was little creative freedom, and it was a long way from the design career she'd dreamed of. 'Of course not. All I get to do there is make dreary dresses for society girls or twin sets for old ladies.'

'It's a start.'

Camille raised her eyebrows, unconvinced. 'How about you? How's your new job?'

'Long hours, lots of detail. It's . . . fine,' Nicolas shrugged. 'Uninspiring.'

Camille took a drag on her cigarette, watching the smoke curl into the night sky. 'Not quite where we thought we'd be, hmm?'

'Hey, there's still time to take over the world,' Nicolas grinned.

'There you both are!' Andre emerged onto the balcony, bringing a blast of noise and warmth from the inside as he opened the door. He was carrying an unopened bottle of Dom Pérignon, and was clearly in a jovial mood, full of energy. It appeared he'd partaken of more than just alcohol.

He looked devastatingly handsome in a fitted floral print shirt that was unbuttoned to the waist, and yellow flared trousers that fitted snugly round the crotch, leaving little to the imagination. He kissed Camille and slid his arms around her waist, pulling her close. 'What are you two talking about?'

'How life hasn't turned out the way we expected.' Nicolas didn't take his eyes off Camille and she felt a shot of regret, suspecting that he was referring to more than just his career.

'Tell me about it,' Andre sighed dramatically, as Camille held her cigarette to his lips and he took a drag. He'd been working in a men's clothing store since graduating, an upmarket boutique at the smart end of the Rue de

Rivoli, but – like the rest of them – he was hungry for more. 'But it's a new year. A new decade. 1970,' he exhaled, gazing out over the city. 'We can be anything we want to be.'

Camille smiled wanly, while Nicolas said nothing.

'I mean, screw it,' Andre exclaimed, letting go of Camille to gesture with his hands, waving the bottle of champagne wildly. 'Why not start our own company? Our own fashion house? Camille designing, Nicolas the numbers guy, me . . . everything else.'

'You always were a dreamer, Andre,' Nicolas said ruefully.

Andre looked indignant. 'I'm serious! Why not?'

Nicolas frowned, glancing across at Camille. A slow smile spread across her face. 'Maybe we *could* . . .' she began, her excitement rising. *This* was why she loved Andre – he was so passionate and ambitious, and it felt as though they could do anything together. But there was one more person she needed to consider. 'What do you say, Nicolas?'

Uncertainty and indecision flickered across his face, and Camille knew that Nicolas would be wrestling with himself. He liked certainty and security, to consider every angle before making a decision.

Camille leaned into him, squeezing his arm. 'Come on, Nicolas. What do you say? You know we can't do it without you.' She gazed up at him through long lashes, pouting gently as he hesitated.

'All right, I'm in,' he declared recklessly. 'Let's do it.'

Camille began to laugh as Andre whooped, picking her up and spinning her around. 'The Three Musketeers,' he roared joyfully, shaking the bottle of champagne with abandon and releasing the cork, letting the spray fly off the balcony, falling like rain onto the street below. He took a swig from the bottle then passed it round to the others, as they drank to seal the deal.

Inside, they could hear cheers of excitement, and Camille heard someone cry, 'One minute!' She checked her wristwatch and saw that it was almost midnight.

'There's one more thing we have to celebrate tonight,' Andre announced, holding the champagne bottle out to Nicolas.

'What's that?' he asked.

Camille's gut twisted, and she found that she couldn't meet his eyes. 'I haven't had a chance to tell him yet,' she murmured to Andre.

'No time like the present,' Andre insisted. 'Nicolas, Camille has made me the happiest man alive. She's agreed to marry me.'

'*Trois . . . deux . . . un . . .*'

The noise of the countdown came from inside. Across Paris fireworks exploded, revellers cheered and church clocks chimed, in a nationwide celebration. Andre swept Camille into his arms and kissed her passionately. She didn't see how the colour drained from Nicolas's face, as he made no attempt to hide the utter shock written across his features. All around him, people joyfully embraced, but Nicolas stood alone, drinking champagne from the bottle to welcome the new decade.

Chapter 18

Mallorca, May 1971

Camille looked radiant. It was the evening before her wedding, and her hair hung loose and glossy, her skin glowing as though she was lit from within. She was wearing a golden slip dress that draped over her body like flowing water, rippling lightly in the evening breeze.

Nicolas watched her, feeling like an outsider. He'd known this woman so well, and tomorrow she would become Andre's wife. Nicolas had loved her – he still loved her – but now he was about to lose her and there was nothing he could do about it.

The three of them now worked together every day. They'd founded their own atelier, just like Andre had suggested, though it was still a fledgling company, and trying to get a foothold in the fashion industry felt like climbing Mont Blanc. For Nicolas, being around Camille every day was torture. Seeing her, talking to her, laughing with her – but not being able to be with her. He'd grown almost numb to it, closing himself off as a form of self-preservation, but the recent flurry of activity in the run-up to the wedding seemed to have heightened every emotion. His heart felt like it was breaking all over again.

So much had changed for them since that New Year's Eve party. They'd founded their business in 1970, which they'd christened Camille Andre – Nicolas was content to take a back seat – but after their initial rush of optimism and energy, the reality was hard.

Nicolas had succeeded in raising some initial investment, but they were all living on a shoestring and margins were tight. Camille adored being able to design and create all day long – it was what she'd always dreamed of – but Andre and Nicolas were less idealistic and often clashed over the practicalities. Andre always wanted the best, regardless of the cost, and Nicolas would encourage him to make a realistic decision – not compromising on quality, but not blowing their budgets either. Nicolas also highlighted environmental and ethical concerns when choosing their suppliers; Andre disparagingly called him a hippy, arguing that the world was unjust, and a fashion label could do little to change that. The two men had developed a grudging mutual respect, but there were always underlying tensions – not helped by the fact that Nicolas was in love with Andre's fiancée.

Tonight, he was unable to take his eyes off Camille as she mingled with the guests at the pre-wedding party, laughing, smiling, perfection. Andre was never far behind, their eyes and hands instinctively finding one another, always a touch or a glance that kept them connected. Each one was like a dagger blow for Nicolas. As Camille leaned up to kiss her future husband, Nicolas averted his eyes.

Meet Me at Sunset

'Here, try some of this dessert, it's delicious.'

Nicolas turned to see Juliette holding a forkful of *cardenal de Lloseta* out to him enticingly. She looked at him teasingly, her eyes full of hope. Not wanting to embarrass her, Nicolas went along with the moment, feeling ridiculous as she fed him the dessert as though he were a child. There was nothing sexy in it at all, and he turned away before she could see his distaste, not wanting to see the disappointment written across her face. Nicolas wished he wasn't here, wished he hadn't brought Juliette.

No, that wasn't fair. Juliette was beautiful, vibrant and charming – but she wasn't Camille. Nicolas and Juliette had been dating casually for months, but he knew he was going to have to end it soon. He always did. He would start feeling guilty, unconsciously stepping back, and they would put pressure on him to commit. To onlookers, he was the eternal bachelor, a smooth-talking playboy with a different girl on his arm every week, his rented apartment a rotating carousel of attractive, intelligent women. The truth was different: none of his girlfriends ever measured up to Camille, and so he swiftly moved onto the next before he had time to break their heart. Each assuaged his loneliness for a short time, filling a space in his bed if not his heart, and ensuring he was never without a partner for parties and events.

Juliette was the latest in a long line, and she'd drawn the short straw to be his date for Camille and Andre's wedding, held at Andre's mother's spectacular villa in Mallorca. Tonight the soon-to-be-wed couple were hosting a dinner for their family and friends, who'd flown in from all over the world ahead of tomorrow's nuptials.

Camille had said that the wedding was going to be a relaxed, casual affair, celebrating love with everyone *they* loved, but if tonight was anything to go by, then the wedding itself would be spectacular.

A long table, seating around sixty people, had been set up in the garden beneath an archway draped with roses. Fairy lights twinkled in the oleander trees, and candles flickered softly in hurricane lamps, casting the scene in a warm glow. The table itself was dressed in white linen with a profusion of flowers running down the centre, hydrangeas and peonies giving off a heady scent beneath the starlight. The wine was flowing, the food was delicious, and everyone looked relaxed and happy against a background of music and laughter. Camille was the most stunning of all.

As Nicolas swallowed the creamy dessert, feeling nauseous at the way it slipped down his throat, he glanced over at Camille. Andre moved across to her, wrapping his arms around her waist, the gesture completely natural between two lovers. Camille gazed up at him adoringly, and Andre leaned down to plant a kiss on her lips.

Nicolas looked away, feeling like a voyeur, as though he'd been spying on an intimate moment. But that look between the two of them – complete and utter adoration from Camille – was killing him inside.

Nicolas noticed that Juliette had put her fork down and sat back in her seat. 'Have you finished?' he asked, the words coming out more gruffly than he'd intended. Juliette nodded, the whisper of a frown crossing her pretty face. 'Then let's go.' Nicolas pushed back his chair and rose to his feet.

'Back to the hotel? Already?' Juliette looked at him

in confusion with those luminous green eyes, and Nicolas felt a stab of guilt. It wasn't her fault, but once more he regretted having invited her.

'Yeah, I'm sure things will be wrapping up soon. It's a big day tomorrow. Let's get some sleep.'

'Goodnight, darling. Sleep well. We'll see you in the morning – we can't wait.'

Camille kissed her parents on both cheeks then let herself into her suite. Béatrice and Albert were staying in the next room at the Palacio del Sol Radiante, and she'd shared a taxi back with them. Camille could have stayed at the Fontaine family villa, but she preferred her own space in which to get ready. Besides, all their friends and relatives were staying at the hotel, and it felt like one big party. Andre would come and collect her in the morning – it was French tradition that the groom presented the bride with her bouquet, which he'd chosen himself – then he would drive her to the venue in a classic cream Mercedes.

It had been so generous of Andre's parents to offer to host the wedding at their villa. In fact, they'd been incredibly generous when it came to the entire day. Camille had designed and created her own dress, and her parents had given her a small amount of money towards the wedding, but with Andre's extravagant tastes it barely covered the wine budget. She knew that was all they could afford and was incredibly grateful for it, but Andre's parents were swallowing the bulk of the costs. His family were considerably wealthier than hers, and she knew they wanted the occasion to be spectacular. Camille appreciated the gesture, but she also felt rather uncomfortable with such generosity, and didn't want to start off married life feeling indebted to her in-laws.

She was about to undress and sink down onto the bed, but found that she couldn't settle. Her mind was racing, adrenaline rushing through her body after the excitement of the party, and she needed to wind down.

It wasn't even that late, and it was still warm – it had been unseasonably hot for the last week, Andre's mother had told her. Acting on a whim, Camille turned and walked out of the door, heading down the back stairs and outside into the gardens.

She followed the winding pathways, small lights along the flower borders offering just enough illumination to guide her steps. The waves crashed in the distance, and in front of her lay a dazzling sky, a riot of purples and dark oranges, a glorious twilight, which sparked with thousands of pinpricks of light from a descending blanket of stars. Camille stared up at the sky above. Looking at it brought everything back into perspective; even though Camille was about to embark on the biggest day of her life, she was a tiny part of the universe, her decisions and actions insignificant.

She heard a stone skitter on the path nearby and caught the scent of cigarette smoke. She wasn't concerned – just surprised. She'd thought she was alone out here.

Then he took a step forwards and she saw him: Nicolas, alone in the darkness, staring out at the black sea. His features were silhouetted against the moonlight, but Camille could read the sadness on his face. She hesitated, wondering whether to turn and slip silently away, but before she had a chance, Nicolas looked up and saw her.

'Camille,' he said softly.

Camille smiled cautiously and moved closer. This was Nicolas, she reassured herself. Her long-time friend, her former lover, her colleague that she saw every day at the Camille Andre offices. *So why does tonight feel different?*

'I thought you'd be asleep by now,' Nicolas said. 'Big day tomorrow.'

'I think it's the adrenaline. I thought I'd take a final walk before bed.'

They looked at one another, the weight of unspoken words hanging in the air between them. Nicolas was still in love with Camille, and she knew it. But it was as though they had an unspoken pact between them never to discuss it.

'Meet me at sunset,' he said. 'Remember we always used to say that to each other.'

'Of course. How could I forget?'

Nicolas didn't reply. He stubbed out his cigarette, and she came to stand next to him, both staring out into the night. The night air was infused with the scent of jasmine and the incessant hum of cicadas.

'No second thoughts?'

Camille smiled sadly and shook her head. 'I love him, Nicolas.'

Nicolas nodded slowly, digesting her words. 'I know. And if you're happy, then that's all I want for you.'

'Damn it, Nicolas, I want you to be happy too! What about Juliette? Do you think she might be the one? She's very beautiful.'

'No, I don't think she's the one. But I didn't want to come alone.' Nicolas cleared his throat. 'I just want you to know that if you ever need anything – and I mean *anything* – I'll be there for you, OK? I'll *always* be there for you, Camille.'

'Oh, Nicolas . . .' Camille linked her arm through his and leaned into him, resting her head on his shoulder, feeling safe and secure and protected. Being with Nicolas was different to being with Andre. With Andre, she could shout and scream and throw plates at his head, then the next moment they were in bed, passionately making up, the cause of their argument forgotten. That had never been her relationship with Nicolas; it ran deeper and defied explanation. He wasn't showy, in the way Andre was, but his every action showed he adored her, always putting her feelings before his. Camille was certain that if they'd stayed together, he would never have cheated on her.

Andre, on the other hand, was a force of nature, and she strongly suspected he'd been unfaithful to her before. Women were drawn to his magnetic presence, arousing Camille's jealousy, and bringing out her competitive instincts. Andre wouldn't have dreamed of demeaning himself by cooking a meal for her, but he had no hesitation in taking her out to a Michelin-star restaurant. Camille loved the glamour and grand gestures that accompanied her life with Andre, but Nicolas was always there, strong and steadfast, and Camille was grateful for that. Perhaps that sounded cruel or selfish, but she couldn't help how she felt.

Right now, with his solid presence next to her, she could sense how much she meant to him. They'd once been as close as two people could be, and they would never lose that connection. He was as familiar to her as her own heartbeat, and she clung to him for a moment, closing her eyes and letting the scent of cigarettes, Guerlain aftershave and Marseille soap wash over her. Her head slotted perfectly against his shoulder, and everything felt so easy.

'I love you, Camille,' Nicolas said simply. 'Since the first moment we met. And I always will.'

Camille lifted her head and met his eyes. 'I know. And I love you too, I always will, but—'

Nicolas placed a finger over her lips, cutting her off. 'I know I'm not enough.'

Camille nodded, sadness and guilt washing over her as she realized how unhappy she was making him. 'I have to go,' she whispered.

Nicolas unclasped her. 'Yes. You've made your choice.'

'Nicolas . . .' Camille wanted to tell him that he wasn't being fair, that he was making her feel bad the night before her wedding. But she didn't say a word. Ultimately, *she* was the one who wasn't being fair, keeping his heart captive when she should have let him go. 'Are you coming in?' she asked, wrapping her arms around herself. It had grown cooler now, away from Nicolas's embrace, and the bare skin on her forearms had puckered into goosebumps.

Nicolas shook his head and turned back towards the sea. 'No, I . . . I'll stay out here a little longer. Clear my head.'

Camille hesitated. She longed to hear him tell her once again how much he loved her. But she was marrying Andre in the morning, and *he* was the love of her life, she told herself firmly. He was the future, and Nicolas was her past.

Camille turned away and slipped silently into the shadowy gardens. Tomorrow she would become Camille Fontaine, and her new life would begin.

Chapter 19

Paris, November 1973

'Oh, Camille. No!'

'What? What is it?' Camille looked up from her desk in surprise as Andre loomed over her.

'This,' he snapped, jabbing his finger towards the tunic that hung on a mannequin behind her. 'Is this the finished design? But this is not good, Camille, you must see that?'

Camille looked up from the sketch she was drawing, a long-sleeved maxi dress in a printed fabric that reflected the new bohemian style. It was late, and she was tired, but right now Andre was looking at the sample they'd received as though it was something he'd stepped in. It had arrived earlier in the day, and Camille had hung it on the dummy in their small atelier so that she could view it through the day and work on it later.

'What's wrong with it?' she shot back, her voice sharper than she'd intended.

Andre picked up the hem between his thumb and

forefinger, as though he didn't want to be contaminated by touching it. Then he let it go dismissively, letting it drop back down.

'You don't see the problem? You have eyes, yes? I thought you were a fashion designer, Camille, but perhaps you still think you're producing shapeless sacks for old ladies.'

Anger rose in Camille's chest, stung by Andre's words. They'd always enjoyed a free and frank exchange of views, but lately all Andre seemed to do was criticize, without offering any ideas of his own.

A chair scraped and they both spun round, surprised by the interruption. It was Mathilde, the intern. She pulled on her jacket and grabbed her bag, looking awkward as their eyes swivelled to her.

'Goodnight, Camille. Goodnight, Andre,' she stammered. It was clear that she wanted to get away before the arguing began, to avoid being caught in the crossfire. Camille and Andre's fights were legendary.

'Goodnight, Mathilde,' Camille said calmly. 'See you tomorrow, and thank you for your work today.'

The young intern scampered out of the door, leaving Camille and Andre alone. It was dark outside – the nights drew in early now – and it was chilly too, with the small, three-bar heater in the corner doing little to raise the temperature. The space was tiny, with half a dozen mismatching desks crammed in at all angles, all littered with sketches and fabric samples, partially constructed garments and rolls of fabric. A sewing machine was set up in one corner, along with half a dozen mannequins. If they'd rented an office in the outskirts of the city, they could have afforded something double, or even triple, the size. But Andre wanted the prestigious address in the seventh arrondissement, so they were crammed into this second-floor space above an antiques shop.

There was a pause after Mathilde left, which could have led to a ceasefire, but then Andre spoke.

'I need to leave. I'll see you at home later.'

'You're going home?'

'No, of course not. I have drinks with Carine Roitfeld, and then the *Elle* magazine event.'

'But I thought I was coming to *Elle* with you?'

'You were. But now you're going to stay here and fix that heap of shit,' Andre snapped, with a dismissive glance at the maligned tunic. 'We need something decent to show the buyers at Samaritaine next week. As it stands, they'll laugh us out of the building.'

Camille's mouth tightened into a thin line. 'Will Héloïse Beauvais be at the *Elle* party?' she asked pointedly.

A flicker of something crossed Andre's face, then he laughed cruelly. 'Just concentrate on the clothes, Camille. Jealousy doesn't suit you.'

'I'm sick of you making a fool of me, Andre. Always running round with other women, not caring who sees you.'

'I've told you before, darling, you're so *petite bourgeoise*. No one in our circle bats an eyelid at a little *aventure*. Don't wait up,' he added with a smirk, before shrugging on his smart woollen jacket and walking out of the door.

Camille let out a scream of frustration. She picked up a pair of fabric scissors and hurled them after him with a cry of rage. They hit the door and fell to the floor. It didn't make her feel any better. Glancing down at the sketch she'd been drawing, Camille immediately saw all its faults, imagining how Andre would react if he'd seen it. She screwed it into a ball, threw it in the bin and slumped down in her chair, overwhelmed by frustration and exhaustion. She let her head drop forwards into her hands as her hair fell around her face, feeling the solid gold of her wedding ring press into her temples.

Life was not working out the way that Camille had imagined. The business was taking an age to build up. She wasn't naïve – she hadn't imagined that they'd become Chanel overnight – but it was such a long, hard, thankless slog and it was beginning to wear her down.

Camille spent day after day, night after night, working away with their small team, designing garments, selecting fabrics, running up samples. All Andre seemed to do was swan around town, attending parties and galas, wining and dining journalists at expensive restaurants, always charging the costs to the company. Networking, he called it.

When Camille, Andre and Nicolas had first sat down in the early days of 1970, buoyed by the wave of optimism that had swept them up on New Year's Eve 1969, they had drawn up their roles in the new business. Camille would, naturally, be creative director, responsible for all design decisions and the aesthetic vision of the brand. Nicolas, with his head for numbers, was chief financial officer, whilst Andre designated himself CEO. All major decisions had to be signed off by him although, Camille thought uncharitably, he seemed to avoid most of the hard work, instead throwing his weight around and enjoying the perks of the job.

Sometimes it was stifling being together twenty-four/seven. There was no part of their lives that didn't revolve around the business; it was like a third person in their marriage, constantly coming between them. They were still as passionate as ever, but often that found an outlet in a different way – instead of wild lovemaking in the bedroom, they had vicious rows in the boardroom, often in front of the whole team.

Despite everything, Camille still loved Andre desperately. There was no doubt that his ego was enormous, but he was charismatic and undoubtedly the driving force behind the business. Sometimes she would watch him from across the room at a dinner party or event, see him laughing, flirting, being so goddamn dominant, and it was sexy and enraging as hell. She loved knowing he was hers, but it came at a price.

Dimly, Camille heard footsteps, then someone cleared their throat close by. She glanced up, startled out of her reverie. 'Nicolas! I'd forgotten you were here.'

The small office off the main atelier was shared by Nicolas and Andre. Nicolas had obviously been working quietly inside, and Camille's cheeks reddened as she realized he must have heard every word of her argument with Andre. She swiped at her eyes which had filled with tears.

'Are you OK, Camille?'

There was something in the gentleness of his tone, the kind look on his face, that made Camille crumple inside. 'No.' She shook her head, in an unexpected show of vulnerability. 'No, I'm not.'

Nicolas stepped forward, taking her in his arms, and Camille fell into them willingly. It felt so good just to be held, as she snuggled into the softness of his shirt, the steady fall and rise of his chest instantly calming her. She and Andre made love almost every day, but tender moments between them were rare; Andre wasn't one to snuggle up on the sofa, or laze in bed on a weekend doing nothing but cuddle. He offered passion, but seldom affection.

Camille sighed, not wanting to move, feeling loved and adored in Nicolas's arms, his chin resting on the top of her head. Memories came flooding back of when they'd first got together. He'd been her first love, but they'd been little more than kids, in the first flush of youth.

Camille wondered how different things would have been if she'd stayed with Nicolas. Andre was handsome and exciting, but as a result, Camille was often jealous or anxious. Life with Nicolas would have been a smooth boat ride on calm seas, not an out-of-control rollercoaster like her current existence. And Nicolas would have adored her unconditionally. She remembered the sweet little gestures he had made when they were together – impulsively buying a bunch of freesias from the flower seller by the Metro, or running her a bubble bath after a long day of classes. Andre would never do anything like that. His actions were always grand and public – what was the point in being extravagant if there were no witnesses?

Camille exhaled slowly, louder than she'd intended. Nicolas's strong hands caressed her body, and she could feel his warmth through the thin cashmere sweater she was wearing, setting off unexpected sparks. She remembered their slow, unhurried lovemaking, the deep sense of connection she had always had with him, the sense he was her soulmate, that he knew and revered every inch of her.

'I should have come out sooner,' he apologized. 'I wasn't sure whether to intervene.'

'It's fine,' Camille insisted.

'I hate the way he treats you. He doesn't deserve you.'

Camille looked up at him. 'You're a good man, Nicolas.'

'I told you. I'm here for you, Camille. If you ever need anything.'

'I know you are,' Camille murmured gratefully. He'd never stopped loving her, it was plain to see on his face. And she loved him too, she realized; there was a deep and unbreakable bond between them.

Camille stroked his cheek, her fingers tracing his clean-shaven jawline. Nicolas closed his eyes and whispered her name, the word full of longing. And then somehow her lips found his and it felt like coming home, the taste of him bringing back long-buried memories. Camille could feel how much he wanted her, years of pent-up desire in that one kiss, and she needed him too. Nicolas had put her on a pedestal and he made her feel like a goddess; it felt so good to be adored after Andre's cruel words and casual dismissal.

Nicolas's hands slid beneath her sweater, roaming over her bare skin and awakening her body as though she'd been sleeping, every inch of her bursting into life. With fumbling fingers, she began to undo the buttons on his shirt before moving down to his belt.

'Wait, Camille . . .' Nicolas panted, his voice thick with wanting. 'Are you sure . . . I don't want you to regret this . . .' He trailed off, undisguised lust in his eyes.

Camille didn't want to think about anything right now. She wanted to push everything from her mind and act on instinct, to block out all the horrible things Andre had said and concentrate purely on the physical. She knew that Andre had cheated on her over the years whilst she'd stayed resolutely faithful, but now that was about to change and, perhaps selfishly, she relished the thought of revenge.

Camille pulled her sweater over her head, revealing her breasts encased in just a wisp of lace, gratified to see the desire flare in Nicolas's eyes. Her breath was coming fast, determination in her eyes. 'Yes,' she said boldly. 'I'm sure.'

Chapter 20

Paris, July 1974

'Are you OK, Camille? Can I get you anything? A cushion? A cold drink?'

'I'm fine, thank you,' Camille said, trying to hide her irritation as she waved Mathilde away. She was eight and a half months pregnant, and had had pains in her abdomen all morning, but she was telling herself it was far too early. Besides, she needed to finish their latest collection – the baby couldn't come before that.

Camille exhaled slowly, trying to gather her energy. Paris was currently gripped by a heatwave, and the second-floor room was stifling. The windows were flung wide open, and the fan in the corner was whirring, but it barely made a dent in the thick, humid air. Camille had been wearing voluminous smocks in the lightest cotton, which she'd run up herself, but she couldn't take much more of this. She was sleeping badly, needing to pee every five minutes, and it felt as though the baby was practising karate inside her.

Camille sat down heavily at her desk, pushing tendrils of her dark hair away from where they'd escaped her topknot and were clinging to her forehead. Her skin felt clammy, beads of perspiration dotting her face.

'Actually, a glass of water sounds good,' she said, getting to her feet once again, stopping dead as another deep pain gave her cause to pause. Mathilde was by her side in an instant.

'I'll get it. You stay there.'

'Thank you.' Camille smiled appreciatively, secretly rather pleased that Mathilde was looking out for her. Movement now was cumbersome, and she felt permanently exhausted, yet Camille's days were as full as ever and there was no let-up in her schedule.

The label was growing, little by little – though not fast enough for Andre's liking – and they'd been able to offer Mathilde a full-time design position after her internship. Camille Andre was gradually making a name for itself, and Camille felt under pressure to keep up the same pace, despite her pregnancy. She had no plans to slow down when the baby arrived either. They had already engaged a nanny, and she intended to take a very short maternity leave, hoping to be back at her desk in a couple of weeks. She wasn't sure how realistic that would be when the time came, but for now she was telling herself everything would be fine and keeping focused on her plan. Andre was encouraging her to take more time off, to bond with the baby. That was fine for him to say, Camille thought in frustration. He wasn't the one in danger of having his position usurped, and besides—

Camille gasped, as she felt a gentle gush of warm water trickle down her legs. Her first, mortified thought was that she'd wet herself; that the pressure of the baby on her bladder had caused an unexpected leak. Mathilde raced back over with the glass of water, in time to catch Camille staring down at the floor, wetness pooling around her sandals.

'Your waters have broken,' Mathilde stated, and Camille almost laughed in relief. Of course, how had she not realized what had happened? Her mind had been so foggy recently. And then, a few seconds later, she was hit by the reality of what that meant.

'The baby's coming,' Mathilde said, panic crossing her usually unflappable face. The other employees turned to stare, whispers of excitement and uncertainty buzzing through the office. 'We need to call an ambulance.'

'Don't worry, there's plenty of t—' Camille broke off as her face twisted in pain, the shock of the contraction taking her breath away. 'Call the hospital,' she managed. 'And call Andre.'

'Shit,' Mathilde swore, her eyes widening.

'The details of his hotel are in the big diary on his desk,' Camille explained, a sense of unreality sweeping over her. This couldn't be happening. Not now. She had too much to do, and Andre was hundreds of miles away.

She had told him it wasn't a good idea to take a business trip so close to her due date, but he'd insisted that first babies were always late. 'Besides, I'm only going to Italy. I'll catch the next plane and be back in a couple of hours,' he'd insisted. 'First babies take forever to come anyway.'

'How do you know so much about first babies?' Camille had grumbled, knowing that Andre wasn't going to change his mind. Now she found herself wishing she'd pushed harder to make him stay.

'Can you do me a favour?' she asked Mathilde, who was already on the phone.

'Anything.'

'Here's my key. Go to my apartment and grab my hospital bag, it's next to my bed. Can you get it and bring it to me.'

'Of course. Where are you going?' she asked, fresh alarm written on her face as Camille stood up and moved slowly towards the door.

'To catch a taxi. I'll meet you at Saint Joseph's.'

'You're doing so well, Camille. Breathe, deep breaths, don't push yet, it's too early . . .'

Camille reached for the gas and air, and took another deep lungful, exhaling in relief as the pain lessened temporarily, her thoughts fuzzy and incoherent. She was dimly aware that the effects of the drugs were wearing off more quickly and were no longer as effective against the surging contractions.

Camille felt that she was becoming primal, going deep inside herself as it became impossible to focus on anything except the next contraction and the brief moments of peace between each one. It was like waves pummelling the shore, and right now a storm was raging. One thought pushed through the fog: Andre wasn't here yet. She didn't know how much time had passed since she'd left the office – it felt like days, but she knew it could only be a matter of hours – and she sensed it was too early for him to arrive from Italy. Assuming Mathilde had even been able to get hold of him.

Distantly, Camille realized that this was not the way she wanted the birth of her child to unfold. She had never dreamed that she would be alone, save for the patient, encouraging midwife – who'd introduced herself as Édith – by her side. She'd sent Mathilde away. It had been tempting to ask her to stay, but Camille hadn't wanted a junior staff member to see her during possibly the most intimate and private moment of her life.

Another powerful contraction surged, pushing all thoughts from Camille's mind. When it subsided, she became aware of raised voices outside her door – a man and a woman – and saw a shadowy outline through the small, opaque window. Both the voice and the silhouette looked familiar . . .

'Nicolas,' Camille called out weakly, feeling a rush of relief.

The midwife followed her gaze towards the door. 'Is that your husband?'

Camille avoided the question, unsure whether they would allow him into the room. But all she knew was that she wanted Nicolas with her. She didn't want to be alone, and God only knew where Andre was. 'Please,' she begged. 'Let him in.'

Édith opened the door and Nicolas rushed to her bedside. Camille realized how she must look from his shocked expression; far from her usual poised and immaculate self, clothed in a hospital gown, her hair wild, her face clammy. But right now she didn't care.

'I'm so glad you're here,' she gasped, grabbing his hand.

'Mathilde called me at my meeting. I came straight here.'

'Have you heard from Andre?'

'Not yet. Mathilde is trying . . .' Nicolas began, but trailed off as Camille gripped his hand more tightly, another contraction bearing down on her.

'You're doing brilliantly, Camille,' Nicolas said, awed by how strong and powerful she was in this moment, literally about to bring life into the world. 'Not long now.'

'He's right,' said Édith. 'I can see the baby's head. So when I tell you to, you're going to push down as hard as you can. OK?'

Camille looked up at Nicolas, fear and pain etched on her face. Nicolas didn't let go of her hands. 'You can do this, Camille. You can do anything.'

Then Camille's expression changed as the next contraction began to build and all she could do was follow her instincts, her body urging her to push, knowing that she was just moments away from meeting her baby.

The taxi pulled up outside Saint Joseph's hospital and Andre threw some money at the driver then leapt out.

'*Bonne chance!*' the driver called after him, but Andre was already sprinting across the pavement and through the front door. He looked around him, wild-eyed, trying to make sense of all the signs directing him to different departments, before yelling at a passing doctor, 'Maternity ward?'

The doctor indicated a corridor to his left, and Andre

was off again. He was furious with himself for travelling to Italy; Camille had told him not to go, but he hadn't listened. If he was being honest, perhaps he'd been in denial. He didn't want to think about how a baby would change their lives, or how *he* might have to step up with the responsibility of being a father. He'd blithely carried on as though everything would remain the same.

When Mathilde's call had been put through to him at the hotel, he'd been in the middle of a steamy liaison with an eighteen-year-old aspiring model, whose youthful flexibility allowed her to contort herself in ways that took Andre's breath away. He'd ignored the telephone at first, but it had been insistent and off-putting, and he snatched it up irritably. On the other end was a breathless Mathilde, and he had been given the news that his wife was in labour with his first child. Andre figured he was already late, so he might as well finish what he'd started – a final fling before fatherhood.

Andre had kicked the girl out straight afterwards, showered quickly, then raced to Linate Airport and paid a small fortune for a seat on the next flight back. When he finally landed at Charles de Gaulle, he hailed a taxi straight to the hospital, cursing the Parisian traffic. The long queues gave him time to think, his conscience gnawing at him as he thought of his wife, alone without him. Even in this day and age, he knew childbirth could be risky; he'd heard stories of emergency c-sections, of blood transfusions, of being rushed into surgery for unexpected complications . . . If anything had happened to Camille or the baby, he'd never forgive himself.

Andre burst through the doors onto the maternity ward and ran up to the young woman on the front desk.

'My wife is having a baby! Camille Fontaine. Where is she?'

A frown crossed the woman's face. *'You're* her husband?' She looked him up and down, as though trying to make her mind up about something. 'Follow me.'

She led him along the corridor, stopping outside one of the many identical doors and knocking on it gently. Andre heard Camille's voice say, 'Come in.'

Without needing to be told twice, Andre rushed inside. It took a moment for him to take in everything he was seeing. Camille was sitting up on the hospital bed, looking exhausted but elated. In her arms, she was holding a tiny baby, swaddled and apparently sleeping soundly. Perched on the bed beside her, gazing at the newborn, was Nicolas. The tableau took Andre aback; they looked for all the world like an idyllic family, as though the three of them were a unit and he was the interloper.

Nicolas looked up as he heard the door; was that guilt flashing across his face, or did Andre imagine it?

Andre's gaze slid from Nicolas to Camille, and then to the perfect baby she was holding in her arms. Tentatively, he took a step forwards. Nicolas leapt to his feet, relinquishing his place beside Camille, but Andre was focused on the baby.

'Are you . . .?' He began. 'Is it . . .?'

Camille beamed, and the smile lit up her face. She looked tired but radiant. 'It's a boy. Darling, we have a son.'

Chapter 21

Paris, April 1975

Warm spring sunlight spilled in through the tall French windows, casting pools of gold on the parquet flooring. Baby Lucas, now almost ten months old, played happily on the rug with a wooden shaker. He was a bundle of energy and had already mastered crawling, so now he was trying to pull himself up on the furniture, determined to learn to walk as soon as possible. Camille had had to move all of her ornaments and breakables to higher shelves, as Lucas's curiosity was insatiable, and she couldn't turn her back for a moment.

Andre came through with a steaming cup of coffee and handed it to Camille, who was sitting in an armchair watching Lucas play.

'Thank you,' she said, looking up at her husband. He looked especially attractive today in a fitted shirt and flared trousers that emphasized his great body. The whole scene was idyllic, and Camille felt a burst of happiness at the sight of her little family. It was constant hard work, but once Lucas had started sleeping through the night and she'd emerged from the fog of those early weeks, Camille found motherhood to be a creatively inspirational time. The new designs she was sketching were better than ever, and she was sure that this latest collection was going to be their best yet. She felt very positive about the future.

'Should we take a stroll to the park this morning?' she suggested, as she sipped her coffee. The weather was bright after a week of grey skies and rain, and it was shaping up to be a perfect Saturday morning. They had moved from the one-bedroom apartment they had rented in central Paris out to the sixteenth arrondissement, where they could get a larger property with space for a nursery. Whilst they didn't have a garden, they were close to the Bois de Boulogne, which was ideal for pushing Lucas in his pram.

Their new place was further from the office, but Camille didn't mind the longer commute. Besides, she often stayed at home designing now and only went into the atelier once or twice a week. They'd employed a nanny to look after Lucas whilst she shut herself away to sketch, but she could see him whenever she took a break. Camille, somewhat to her surprise, thoroughly enjoyed being a mother. She had bonded quickly with Lucas and loved discovering the world through his eyes. He was always excited to see her, and the adoration was mutual; to her, he was perfect.

'Sure,' Andre agreed, planting a kiss on the top of her head. 'Sounds great. I'll run down to the bakery, get us all some breakfast.'

'Thanks, darling.'

Andre grabbed his wallet from the sideboard when the doorbell rang. They looked at one another in confusion.

'Expecting anyone?'

Camille shook her head.

Andre spoke into the entry phone, and Camille heard Nicolas's voice crackle over the intercom. Camille felt something shift in her stomach. She saw him less often now that she was no longer in the office every day, and she wasn't entirely sure what her feelings were towards him. He'd been present for the most momentous events in her life, and she was grateful he'd been with her when Lucas was born, but her mind often drifted back to that night in the atelier. She'd been feeling low, and frustrated with Andre, and Nicolas had been there for her. Not that he'd taken advantage – if anything, he'd been the one asking if she was sure, and she was the one who'd pushed ahead. Camille felt a guilty twist of desire at the memory, Nicolas's lovemaking had matured in their time apart, and he'd seemed to understand all those secret parts of her instinctively.

Andre strode down the corridor, as Camille stayed with Lucas. He was sitting up, bright and alert, trying to work out where Andre had gone. Lucas's hazel eyes, which were so like hers, lit up at the sound of voices. He was a sociable baby and loved it when they had visitors.

Nicolas walked in and Camille stood up to greet him, kissing him on both cheeks. Her feet were bare, and she wore wide-legged trousers with a paisley-print blouse. Nicolas was dressed formally, even though it was the weekend, his clothes a neutral palette of greys and browns. He certainly didn't look as though he represented a fashion house, she thought affectionately, though the plain clothes couldn't hide his toned physique and handsome face.

He held out a bottle of Moët & Chandon and a large paper bag. 'I stopped off at the bakery and bought pastries,' he explained. 'I know it's early – I didn't know if you'd have eaten breakfast yet.'

'You saved me a trip,' Andre grinned, taking the bag from him and heading over to the small, open-plan kitchen.

'Hello, Lucas,' Nicolas grinned. He bent down to him, and Lucas burbled and giggled, reaching for the champagne. 'That's not for you, I'm afraid,' Nicolas laughed.

'Is that for breakfast too?' Camille wondered.

'Yes, if you think it's appropriate.'

Camille caught the excitement in his voice, as Andre came back through, placing the plate of pastries on the coffee table. They both looked at Nicolas curiously.

'I only had it confirmed last night,' he began. 'We were on a late call, trying to finalize the details. But the good news is . . . Galeries Lafayette have agreed to stock Camille Andre.'

Camille's hand flew to her mouth as she let out a cry of delight. Andre punched the air, with a 'Yes!', and even Lucas clapped his hands, making excited squawking noises.

'That's amazing. Incredible job, Nicolas,' Andre said, pulling him in for a bear hug and clapping him on the back.

'I can't believe it,' Camille gasped. 'Nicolas, you're a genius. This could be the break we've been waiting for.'

Galeries Lafayette was an enormous, historic department store on the Boulevard Haussmann, set in a grand Art Nouveau building. Its stocked everything from fashion to homeware, toiletries to furniture, and in recent years it had developed a reputation for working with up-and-coming designers. Sonia Rykiel's career had taken off a decade earlier, after being stocked in Galeries Lafayette. She was an idol of Camille's, and now it looked as though Camille Andre would follow in her footsteps.

Until now, the label had been solely stocked by independent boutiques, which placed small, infrequent orders. The dream was to have their own store, but Andre wanted a prestigious Parisian address and wouldn't settle for anything less. Now, the income from Galeries Lafayette might allow that to become a reality, and Camille felt both excited and relieved. At times, she'd questioned whether she'd chosen the right career path, and Andre's criticism weighed heavily on her. But this deal felt like a vindication of her choices and her talent, and she was so grateful to Nicolas for making it happen.

Andre popped the cork on the Moët and poured it into three coupes, handing them round.

'It's only ten a.m.,' Camille laughed.

'Who cares – you don't get news like this every day! Seriously though, Nicolas. This wouldn't have happened without all your hard work.'

'Or your talents, congratulations to both of you,' Nicolas replied, as they clinked glasses. 'Here's to the continued success of Camille Andre.'

Camille felt a warm glow inside her that wasn't just

from the champagne bubbles. Her business was a success, they were climbing the ladder, and the two men she cared about most in the world were getting along, professionally and personally. But when she turned to Nicolas, she noticed something in his expression that didn't tally with her own happiness. 'What is it?' she asked, noticing that he wouldn't meet her gaze.

Nicolas smiled ruefully. 'I could never hide anything from you, could I? I have some news. Possibly not as welcome as my last announcement . . . I've had a job offer, from American Athletics. And I've decided to accept it.'

'Son of a bitch,' Andre swore, and Camille glanced at him sharply. 'What do you mean?' he demanded. 'You're leaving us?'

Nicolas nodded slowly. 'I don't start until the end of next month, and it'll be a gradual transition, so I'll have time to help you find someone else. I thought perhaps—'

'American Athletics?' Camille interrupted. 'Isn't that based in—'

'New York, yes,' Nicolas finished. 'I'm being brought on to assist with their European expansion, so I'll be back and forth, but I'll be based out of New York. They'll pay me a relocation fee, rent an apartment for me, and sort all the visa paperwork.'

'Sounds like you've got it all figured out,' Andre said coldly.

'This was never the plan,' Nicolas insisted, putting down his champagne glass; the mood dying quicker than the bubbles. 'But they approached me, it was too good to refuse, and it feels like the right time . . .'

'It was supposed to be the three of us. It was always

the three of us,' Camille whispered. The colour had drained from her face, and she looked stunned.

'It's called Camille Andre,' Nicolas said softly, but with steel in his eyes. 'I'm not sure there was ever room for me.'

'We can change the name if that's what you want,' Camille suggested desperately. 'Give you a salary rise, a higher percentage split, whatever you want . . .'

'I've made up my mind. Look, you're well established now, turnover and revenue are increasing year on year – you don't need me. I was thinking of Charles Cazeneuve over at Pierrot. He could be a great replacement, and I know he's looking to jump ship.'

'I don't want Charles Cazeneuve, I want *you*,' Camille exploded, her voice shaking. The two men stared at her, astonished by her outburst. Lucas began to cry, and Camille closed her eyes, as though it was all too much to deal with. 'He's tired,' she said quietly, as Andre scooped up Lucas. 'Can you put him down for his nap?'

Andre looked from Camille to Nicolas and back again, but didn't protest. He understood that the two of them needed to talk. 'Sure,' he said evenly. He walked out of the room and closed the door behind him.

There was a long moment of silence, until Camille couldn't hold her feelings in any longer. 'I can't believe you're doing this. I can't believe you're leaving me.'

Nicolas moved towards her, reaching out for her, but she jumped back as though she'd been electrocuted. The memories were still fresh of the last time he'd comforted her, the way she'd allowed herself to fall into his arms, and everything that had happened afterwards. She needed to stay strong. She folded her arms across her chest and turned on him, eyes blazing. Being angry with him was easier than confronting the tangled emotions she was feeling right now.

'I can't live this lie any more,' Nicolas whispered, keeping his voice low, conscious of Andre in the room along the hall.

'What do you mean?'

'Be around *you*. And Andre, and Lucas. The three of you playing happy families and pretending it doesn't tear me apart.' His voice sounded strangled. 'It's breaking my heart every single day, knowing that I'll never be a part of your world again, or be able to have that for myself.'

'Of course you will. You'll meet someone and fall in love,' Camille assured him, as tears filled her eyes.

There was a pause. Nicolas looked down at the floor, avoiding Camille's eyes, and then the penny finally dropped.

'Lisa,' Camille said, inhaling sharply. Nicolas nodded, and Camille felt a wave of panic and fury and jealousy wash over her. Lisa Schwartz was American and worked as a data analyst for Goldman Sachs. She was on secondment in Paris, and she and Nicolas had been dating for just over three months. Camille had met her only once, and her overriding impression was of an intimidatingly self-confident, whip-smart and flawlessly groomed young woman who was clearly destined for great things. Camille had hated her instantly.

'She's decided to return to New York,' Nicolas explained. 'And I'm going with her. I want to try and make things work between us.'

Camille nodded slowly, fighting unsuccessfully to hold

back the tears. She knew she had no right to be upset – she should be happy for Nicolas that he'd finally found someone he cared about – but selfishly all Camille could think was that she didn't want him to leave.

'Are you in love with her?' she whispered, knowing that she didn't want to hear the answer, knowing that his words would be like a knife wound.

'Yes,' he said simply.

'You barely even know her.'

'Goddamn it, I want to give this a chance.' There was desperation in Nicolas's voice now. 'I compare every single woman I meet to you, Camille, and they can't live up to it. It's driving me to despair. This is the best way for everyone. A clean break. A fresh start. An ocean between us.'

Camille searched his face. 'Does it have to be so final? You've been in my life for so long now. Barely a day has gone by where I haven't seen or spoken to you, and now you want to move to another continent? How am I going to live without you?'

'You have Andre,' Nicolas said, and the unspoken accusation hung in the air between them: *You chose him over me.* 'If you ever need me for anything – anything at all – I'll always be there at the end of the phone.'

'What about Lucas?' Camille asked, her eyes searching his.

'What about him?'

'He's going to miss you. He . . .' Camille faltered. 'You won't be around to see him grow up. He's your godson, Nicolas.'

Nicolas considered her words, the air between them thick with tension. 'I'll always do right by Lucas,' he said finally, a desperation in his voice. 'But I *must* move on with my life, Camille. You're keeping me prisoner.'

Camille was about to protest, but deep down, she knew he was right. She would miss him desperately, but she had to let him be free. What was the phrase? *If you love someone, let them go.* She loved him, and he loved her, but she had chosen Andre and now he had found Lisa. It was time to let Nicolas go.

Chapter 22

Mallorca, August 1982

Camille stretched languorously in the morning sunshine, enjoying the taste of freshly brewed coffee and *ensaïmadas* that lingered in her mouth. It was so peaceful in the Tramuntana mountains, only the call of birds and the drone of insects to disturb the silence. Right now, the temperature was perfect. It would be almost unbearably hot later in the day, but by then Camille would be gone.

'I wish we could stay a little longer,' she sighed.

'No rest for the wicked,' Andre laughed, his gaze running over her. Camille knew she looked good, in pale pink shorts and a sleeveless T-shirt, her dark hair cut into a fashionable crop that emphasized her fine bone structure and gamine frame. At the age of thirty-two, she felt as though she was in her prime, both personally and professionally. She'd found her signature style as a designer, and Camille Andre was now well established, not to mention her little family.

'*Can* you stay a bit longer, *Maman*?' asked Lucas. He was sitting across from her on the terrace, outside Andre's mother's villa.

'I'm afraid not, darling,' she sighed, feeling guilty as she saw his face fall. He had just turned eight years old, was tall for his age and slender, with a shock of dark curly hair and a freckled face, his eyes the same enchanting hazel as Camille's.

'When will you be back?' he asked solemnly.

'In a couple of weeks. Perhaps three.'

'And then it'll be school again,' he said glumly.

'Yes, but in the meantime you'll have lots of fun with *Abuela*,' his grandmother assured him, wrapping her arms around him and cuddling him to her. Andre's mother Margarita was glamorous and flamboyant, in a brightly coloured kaftan and white-rimmed sunglasses, and she doted on her son and grandson.

'I guess,' Lucas replied, not looking convinced.

'Cheer up, Lucas, we'll be back before you know it,' Andre said briskly. 'And we'll bring you a fantastic present. What would you like, hmm? A BMX? Sony Walkman? A new Lego set?'

Lucas thought for a moment. 'All three,' he said eventually, as Andre roared with laughter.

'Just like his father,' he chuckled. 'Knows what he wants, and he wants it all!'

Camille watched the scene play out, feeling uneasy. Sometimes she thought that Andre spoilt Lucas. He seemed to be creating a boy in his own image at times, often treating him as though he was older than his years and Andre would often give into his son's urges and Lucas had grown used to having whatever he wanted.

Perhaps it was guilt, Camille thought. They both worked long hours, and although they told themselves it was for Lucas's future too, it was ultimately for selfish reasons – they both wanted to be successful.

All three of them had spent a long weekend together at the villa, but now Camille and Andre would spend the rest of the summer working. It wouldn't be too much of a hardship; most of Europe took August off, and so instead of formal meetings, there'd be networking on yachts in the Greek islands, long, boozy dinners in the south of France, and raucous parties in Spanish villas. It was no life for a child; they didn't want to be dragging Lucas round with them, and he'd have been bored out of his mind anyway, so Margarita had helpfully stepped in.

Business was slowly building. The Camille Andre label was now stocked in high-profile outlets all over France, and they had their own boutique on the prestigious Avenue Montaigne. Their designs were a favourite of the sophisticated, monied French women who were their target demographic, and they were beginning to make inroads into the fashion capitals of Europe – London, Milan, Madrid and Stockholm. But like any high-end, high-priced product, it was hard to sell in volume, and Andre insisted on such high quality that their margins were squeezed.

Their next target was America, and that meant leveraging Nicolas's connections. He and Lisa had married three months after he'd moved to the US. It had been a spontaneous decision – they'd got their licence and married the following day, in the presence of a witness who they'd invited in off the street. Camille had been utterly shocked, and their relationship had come under strain. But when Nicolas filed for divorce less than six months later, they'd gradually started to rebuild their friendship. They were both busy, but there were long, late-night transatlantic calls, where they would pick one another's brains about business issues, or simply catch up and chat about what was happening in their lives.

There were periods when they spoke almost every day, yet at other times Nicolas pulled back from her, his calls becoming infrequent, and the messages Camille left on his machine going unanswered. At those times, she respected his decision and left him alone, though it would eat her up inside, wondering if he'd met someone new, if it was serious, if he'd marry within weeks like he had with Lisa. Camille knew she had no claim on him, and didn't have any right to think so possessively about him, but in truth she considered him one of her best friends and missed him terribly when—

'Lucas!'

A young boy came running up the path towards them, seemingly right at home on her mother-in-law's property. Camille was astonished when Lucas's face split into a broad grin and he called back happily, 'Paulo!'

Paulo came up to the patio with a swagger, beaming at Lucas. He reminded Camille of the Artful Dodger in an old movie she'd once seen; he had jet-black hair and was dressed scruffily, dirty marks across his face like an urchin who'd been left to fend for himself. His expression was full of mischief, his dark eyes alight as he and Lucas conversed in rapid Spanish which Camille struggled to follow.

'Darling, why don't you introduce me to your friend?' she suggested sweetly.

'Mama, this is Paulo. He lives on the farm over there.' Lucas waved his hand vaguely in the distance. 'They have a dog, and chickens, and a pig called Chancho,' he added excitedly. 'We played together the last time I came to stay with *Abuela*.'

'How nice,' Camille said, but the sentiment didn't reach her eyes, as she looked critically at Paulo from behind her dark glasses. She didn't want to be a snob, but equally, she didn't want Lucas to come home with lice at the end of the holiday, and this boy looked as though he was infested.

Camille glanced at Margarita, but she was beaming at the two boys, clearly not sharing her daughter-in-law's misgivings.

'Would you like something to eat, Paulo?' she asked, indicating the spread of bread and pastries and fruit on the table.

He took an apricot *coca* in one hand and a croissant in the other, biting into them ravenously, as Lucas jumped up from the table. 'Can I go and play now, Mama?'

'Your father and I will be leaving shortly. Don't you want to wait and say goodbye?'

'I can say goodbye now,' said Lucas, hurling himself into Camille's arms, then formally shaking hands with Andre. 'I'll see you in a few weeks,' he called, as he ran off down the path with Paulo, the two of them laughing and calling to one another.

'He'll come back when he's hungry,' Margarita smiled.

'Will they be safe?' Camille asked in alarm. Perhaps she should insist to Andre that they needed to stay here, or at least take Lucas with them.

'This isn't Paris,' Margarita said easily. 'He'll come to

no harm around here; everyone looks out for one another. It's nice for him to have a friend, and not have to spend all his time with his grandmother.'

'Hmm,' Camille said, pursing her lips. Lucas and Paulo were little more than specks in the distance, and she couldn't hide her concern. She'd bet her last *sou* that that boy was trouble.

Lucas hadn't returned before they left, and – as they said goodbye to Margarita – Camille couldn't shake the uncomfortable feeling she'd got from his friend. In the taxi, heading for the airport, the relaxed atmosphere of the morning was slowly drifting away, to be replaced by an unmistakeable sense of tension. Camille was powerless to stop her thoughts turning to work, and it seemed as though Andre was feeling the same as he turned to her and said, 'I don't want to waste this summer. We have so many opportunities, and we're on the cusp of something big, I can feel it. I want to push us to the next level.'

Camille bristled. 'You don't have to tell me. It's my business too. I want us to be as successful as you do.'

'We should be doing better than we are by now. Look at Diane von Furstenberg or Vivienne Westwood. Their labels have exploded over the past few years.'

'I know.'

'Which makes me want to figure out what the problem is with Camille Andre . . .' Andre trailed off and stared pointedly at his wife.

'*Me?*' Camille asked incredulously.

'Not you. Your designs. I know they're elegant and tasteful, blah blah blah, but they're plain. Unadventurous.

Look at Diane – she designed one incredible dress that every woman fell in love with and now she's a multi-millionaire. Vivienne's doing punk – it's fresh, it's innovative, it's *sexy*. No man wants to be with a woman in a Camille Andre dress.'

Camille was too stunned to reply, her mouth falling open. When she recovered, she said, 'I'm not doing *punk*,' she pronounced the word disdainfully, 'because we agreed our aesthetic right at the beginning – French, chic, classic. Neutral colours, clean lines. And if *I* were to think about the problem with Camille Andre, I'd say it's not the designs – it's that they're not reaching the buyers. And that's *your* job, darling,' Camille said sweetly, a dangerous edge to her voice. 'You're supposed to be overseeing the marketing, making contacts, schmoozing the journalists. You're out every night spending a small fortune on *networking*. Most of our profit goes on dinners and drinks that you deem necessary, and for what? Something's not adding up, Andre.'

'None of that's going to work if the designs aren't good enough! How can I do my job with one hand tied behind my back?'

Camille was stung, but she wasn't backing down from this fight. 'Did you ever consider that *you're* the problem?'

'*Me?*' Andre laughed dismissively.

'Yes, you. You have this bullish attitude which alienates people. You're so convinced that you're right about everything, but you're patronizing and arrogant. And the truth is that you're not talented enough to design, and you don't have the business acumen of . . .' Camille trailed off. A pulse twitched in Andre's jaw, and she knew that he was furious.

'Of Nicolas? Is that what you were going to say?' Andre turned to her, eyes blazing.

Camille stood her ground. 'Yes, actually. We should never have let him go. Look at all the incredible things he's achieved at American Athletics. They have a presence in every country in Europe, with flagship stores in all the major cities. They're one of the biggest names in the world, they've just signed Farrah Fawcett as the face of their new campaign, and they had the highest opening share price of any fashion retailer when they floated on the stock exchange last year.'

Andre gave a slow, sarcastic handclap. 'Bravo, Nicolas. He did all this single-handedly, did he?'

'You know damn well what I mean. He's been instrumental in their success, whilst all you ever do is criticize other people to hide the fact you're not good enough.'

The tension in the air was thick enough to cut with a knife. Outside the windows, the motorway flashed past at speed, and the driver kept his eyes firmly fixed on the road ahead. Camille doubted he spoke much French, but it didn't take a linguist to work out that they'd just had an epic fight.

Camille was livid, but relieved to have got some home truths off her chest. Everything she'd said was true. In just a few short years, American Athletics had become one of the most recognizable brands in the world, specializing in high-end leisurewear. Nicolas had pioneered the use of ethical labour, and favoured short supply chains that were better for the environment. His views were revolutionary. Whilst he'd been painted as a crank by his detractors, the tide of opinion was now moving in his direction, and American Athletics were leading the way.

Nicolas had been rewarded with all the trappings of success. He had a stunning penthouse flat in New York, a chauffeured limousine at his disposal and access to a private jet – everything that his rivals aspired to. Yet although Nicolas enjoyed the perks that came with his position, he remained resolutely unimpressed by them all. His response was always to put his head down and work harder, always looking for the next deal, the next innovation. And he had never remarried after the disastrous, short-lived union with Lisa, despite regularly appearing on Page Six of the *New York Post* with an ever-rotating carousel of models on his arm.

Camille found herself wondering – more often than she would have liked – about what her life would have been like if she'd stayed with Nicolas. She could be wealthy and successful, instead of exhausting herself by trying to build up a business and constantly fighting with Andre. And she would feel loved and secure, instead of belittled and neglected.

'Well,' said Andre, as though he could read her thoughts, 'perhaps you should have turned me down all those years ago. Stuck with Mr Dull.'

Camille didn't reply. He was being sarcastic, but perhaps Andre was right. Maybe she *had* made the wrong choice.

Chapter 23

Paris, October 1992

The new Camille Andre headquarters on Avenue Marceau were enormous. Situated on the third floor, the offices ran the length of three buildings, and were decorated in neutral, muted tones to ensure the backdrop didn't influence the design work. The ever-growing team worked busily, sketching and sewing, earnestly debating new ideas and trends, and there was a constant buzz in the air. Working for Camille Andre felt exciting, inspiring and creative.

Over the last decade, the brand had continued to grow steadily but surely, finding a loyal customer base amongst an elegant, upmarket clientele who wanted to ensure they looked stylish and polished, with a classic French twist. Camille Andre remained somewhat niche, a label for those in the know rather than a household name. That suited Andre, who didn't see the appeal of mass market; in his opinion, having every other person on the high street wearing a design cheapened its value. But Camille – spurred on by Nicolas's advice – recognized the opportunities it could bring. Whilst only the wealthiest fashionistas could splurge on Chanel couture, almost everyone could afford a lipstick, or perfume, or pair of sunglasses, and in recent years these had provided the big fashion houses with a valuable additional revenue stream.

Andre and Camille continued to hotly debate the future of their business, but there was no doubt that they were well established on the French fashion landscape and were making strong progress across Europe and the US.

'Could you run out and get me a coffee?' Andre said, as he passed by the desk of the newest intern. He glanced at her briefly but found he couldn't remember her name. She was pretty – they inevitably were if they wanted to work in fashion, and were always well-groomed and sophisticated if they'd applied to Camille Andre. This girl had thick, dark blonde hair, and her frame was larger than the stick-thin French fashionista silhouette, but Andre didn't mind a little meat on a woman's bones. His eyes ran unashamedly over her curves.

'Of course,' she stammered, her French laced with an accent Andre couldn't identify, Irish or Scottish. 'You prefer a *café serré*, yes?' she continued, naming the extra-strong shot of coffee.

Andre nodded, pleased that she'd remembered. Then his gaze fell on the sketch she'd been drawing. 'What's this?'

The young woman flushed. 'Oh, nothing. Just something I was working on.' Embarrassed, she attempted to hide it, but Andre persisted. 'Let me see.'

Reluctantly, she handed it over and he examined it with a practised eye. 'It's good. Very good.'

'Thank you.'

'But it's a handbag. We don't make bags.'

'Perhaps you should,' she replied, before catching herself and blushing even harder. 'I'm sorry, I didn't mean—'

'That's OK.' Andre smiled charmingly.

'It's just a sketch – nothing really, which is why I didn't want you to see it. I know you don't make bags, but I was thinking about what would go perfectly with the Brigitte dress over there,' she ran on, indicating the part-finished garment hanging from a mannequin. It was made from a black tweed fabric, reminiscent of Chanel, but was far sexier and edgier, with a strapless bustier top and flared skirt with layers of tulle underneath. 'It was so inspiring, and I just found myself drawing,' she finished.

'I love it,' Andre beamed. 'Mind if I borrow it?'

He held it out admiringly and the intern looked thrilled. 'No, of course not. I'm so happy you like it. Now, let me go and get that coffee for you.'

Camille had her own office in the new atelier. It was light and airy, the perfect mix of the modern and the traditional, with its stark glass walls and angular furniture contrasting with the building's period features. It echoed what Camille was trying to do with her design work – to seamlessly blend the classic with the innovative.

Right now, Camille was taking advantage of a brief window between meetings to immerse herself in design. She'd discovered that the more successful she became, the less time she had for doing what she really loved. She longed to spend all day sketching and designing, tinkering with ideas as though she had all the time in the world. Now, her days were taken up with phone calls, meetings and interviews, not to mention being asked to sign off on endless decisions about marketing and suppliers and finance and recruitment.

What she wanted more than anything was to spend time on the new collection. Camille had rediscovered the fire she'd felt in the early days of her career, inspiration flowing through her, and now she was pushing herself – and the brand – out of her comfort zone. Camille saw now that she'd been too reliant on the classic French style, heavily influenced by Chanel, Dior, Yves Saint Laurent and Givenchy. Now she was determined to push the boundaries, and her new ideas were sexy, like the Italians, and cool, like the British. Camille herself was now in her early forties, but she had a renewed sense of confidence in herself, an attractiveness that went beyond youth. She'd reached the age where women were supposed to disappear, but Camille had no intention of being invisible.

Her new attitude was even reflected in the way she was dressing. Today she wore an oversized shirt teamed with a figure-hugging pencil skirt of her own creation and a pair of Ferragamo heels – bold and sexy, just like her new designs.

The door to Camille's office swung open and she looked up, although she knew exactly who it was – no one else would enter without knocking. Excitement was written across Andre's face, his expression triumphant.

'What do you think of this?' he asked, spinning round

the piece of paper he was holding and slamming it down on her desk.

'It's a handbag,' Camille stated, wondering what he meant.

Andre nodded, as though she was an idiot. 'There's no getting past you, darling. But what do you think of it?'

Camille looked at it, examining the shape and the detailing, imagining the construction and the stitching. Her heart began to beat a little faster. 'It's wonderful. Although perhaps if we add a zip here, and a concealed pocket there . . . And it would look better in plum or anthracite, rather than black . . .' Instinctively, Camille picked up a pencil and began sketching.

'It was inspired by the Brigitte dress,' Andre explained.

Camille frowned. 'Where did you get this?'

'One of the interns.' Andre waved his hand dismissively. 'But it's good. Better than good, in fact. I think we should make it – a mock-up, at least. Our very first handbag. We could call it the "Camille",' he grinned.

'I like that idea,' Camille smiled, hiding her amusement. Over the past few months, she'd been having an ongoing conversation with Nicolas about the direction of Camille Andre. He'd insisted that the future was in accessories, explaining how American Athletics were making a fortune from gym bags, baseball caps, scarves and so on. Camille had raised the subject with Andre, but he'd remained stubbornly disinterested, insisting it would dilute their brand. Now *he* was the one suggesting it. Sometimes, all Andre needed was to believe that he'd come up with the idea himself, Camille thought with a grin. 'But it's a big change, and a whole new style of working. I know clothes – I don't know handbags.'

Andre shrugged, seemingly unfazed. 'I'll ask Louis to take a look at the pattern and pull together the technical sketches. We can use our manufacturers in Cadiz.'

Camille nodded. They often used leather buttons or trim on their garments, and worked with artisans in Spain.

'I'll explain to José that we need something special for this. No need to go into production just yet. We'll run up a couple of samples and send them down the runway for the autumn/winter '93 show, see how they're received.

'Sounds perfect,' Camille breathed. She was genuinely excited by this new challenge, fired up by the prospect of adding a new string to the Camille Andre bow. She turned back to the sketch lying on her desk, quietly absorbed in making subtle changes, visualizing how the soft leather would fold, imagining the solid gold hardware. She didn't notice as Andre slipped from the room, yelling at some poor intern that his coffee had gone cold.

Chapter 24

March 1993

Camille had been running on adrenaline and black coffee for weeks now, and it had all been leading up to this – the spring show at which they displayed their designs for the following season. They were just about to showcase the Camille Andre autumn/winter 1993 collection, and, backstage, Camille was on tenterhooks. Fashion Week was always insane. There was chaos, drama, arguments and bitchiness, all fuelled by alcohol and caffeine. It was both the highlight of the year and the most stressful time in a designer's calendar, and it could make or break careers.

This season, the Camille Andre show was taking place in the renowned Petit Palais, a beautiful Beaux-Arts building just off the famous Champs-Élysées. In the domed exhibition space, with its marble walls and mosaic floors, the great and good of the fashion world waited expectantly. There were journalists and celebrities, alongside the industry's movers and shakers; Anna Wintour was seated beside Carine Roitfeld, whilst Charlotte Gainsbourg looked immaculate in a vintage Camille Andre cream shift dress decorated with pearls. Kristin Scott Thomas looked as elegant as ever, seated beside Naomi Campbell, who had all eyes on her in a black tuxedo jacket with nothing underneath, paired with leather trousers.

Behind the scenes, Camille barely had time to breathe. In between answering questions from the reporters who'd been invited backstage, she ensured that each model looked perfect before they hit the runway, whispering words of encouragement to every girl. Some of them looked so young, full of youthful enthusiasm, and Camille couldn't help but think back on how far she'd come over the years. But right now she didn't have time for reflection.

The last six months of her life had been leading up to this crazily busy, stressful time. The fashion world was like a treadmill, with shows twice a year, and the need to design and produce an entirely new collection for each one. Not to mention the cruise shows in between, and new accessories drops every quarter.

For Camille, there was more riding on this show than ever before. She'd gone out on a limb, taking a radical new direction, and she wasn't sure how it would be received. Andre had been pressing for change, and Camille had delivered – it seemed to blend the new grunge style that had been showcased in New York, with the overt sexiness of Versace and Gucci at Milan Fashion Week, in addition to the quirkiness from the Brits. Camille had focused on metallics and leather, with figure-hugging silhouettes and low-cut necklines to display decolletage.

She was dimly aware of the music and lights in the main auditorium, of the cheers and applause, then suddenly it was all over. Fashion shows were surprisingly short – six months of hard work for just ten minutes of showtime – then the models and journalists would pack up and race across town to the next presentation. But before that happened, it was time for Camille to take her bows, knowing that she'd earned the adulation.

Andre appeared at her side. 'Time to go,' he said, taking her hand, looking incredibly handsome in a black polo shirt and relaxed-fit trousers.

Camille was glad to have him beside her as she stepped out onto the runway, feeling uncomfortable in the full glare of the spotlight – she wasn't a model or a celebrity, and this wasn't her natural arena. Andre adored the limelight, enjoying it far more than Camille. Even though she was the head designer, together they were Camille Andre, and they always presented a united front after each show as they smiled and waved for the cameras, flashbulbs popping like fireworks.

With a final bow they turned and returned backstage, as Camille fought off a sense of anticlimax. It was over, and all she could do now was wait for the reviews, then start work all over again on the next collection. It was in the hands of the critics now, and there was nothing more to be done. A few friends and admirers were still milling about, but most had to dash off to the next shows, the most popular models and make-up artists jumping on the back of motorbikes to speed them through the traffic. The Camille Andre employees quickly packed up the space – Comme des Garçons would be showing in the Petit Palais later that day – then someone thrust a glass of champagne into Camille's hand. She took it, grateful for a moment of calm amidst the chaos.

'I don't know why you're celebrating,' Andre's voice hissed beside her. 'That was a goddamn disaster.'

Camille turned in alarm. 'What?'

Fury was written across Andre's face. 'Anna Wintour left before the end – didn't you notice?'

Camille's blood ran cold. 'No, I didn't see. Maybe she—'

'Do you know what Carine Roitfeld just said to me? "It wasn't one of your best." That's what they were all saying out there, Camille. Confused. Chaotic. Shambolic. You took a gamble and it backfired.'

Each word was like a dagger in Camille's heart. 'Let's wait for the reviews,' she managed, with a calmness she didn't feel. She'd been so proud of this new direction, so certain that she was doing the right thing.

'Let's not,' Andre shot back. 'I won't put myself through the humiliation of reading them, and I suggest you do the same. Unless you can pull off the biggest coup of your life, we're finished.'

Then he stalked off, leaving Camille alone and in shock, her face flaming. She couldn't believe he'd been so cruel. Regardless of success or failure, they were supposed to be a team.

The champagne glass in her hand felt totally inappropriate now, and she set it down on the side then looked around for her assistant – she would call a taxi and get out of here as soon as possible.

'I *love* that bag,' a voice beside her said in English. 'Mind if I have it?'

Camille looked up to see Naomi Campbell standing beside her and almost gasped. She looked incredible, her skin glowing, her cheekbones razor-sharp, as she towered over Camille in skyscraper heels. It took Camille a moment to process what she'd said, and she looked across to see the 'Camille' bag still sitting on the accessories table as an assistant hastily packed everything away.

'Sure. Of course,' Camille replied in surprise. She didn't care if she never saw the damn thing again. Right now, she hated everything about this collection. 'Please, take it,' she smiled, picking up the bag and handing it to the supermodel. 'And thank you so much for coming to the show.'

Naomi didn't reply, simply taking the bag from Camille and swinging her long, glossy hair over one shoulder before sashaying out of the door.

Camille stared after her, trying to take in what had just happened. The space was almost empty now, and there was no sign that the show had ever taken place – all traces were gone, vanished. She just hoped the same wouldn't happen to her career.

'*Mon Dieu*,' Camille gasped, leafing through the Saturday papers the weekend after the show. She'd risen late, after attending a number of Fashion Week parties the night before, flitting around the city from one to the next. Andre had insisted they keep up appearances, and Camille had been surprised how much she'd enjoyed herself, catching up with old friends and hearing the latest industry gossip.

'What is it?' Andre asked. He was seated opposite her at the breakfast table, the radio playing softly in the background. Lucas was already up and had headed out with his friends.

Excitement and disbelief were written across Camille's face. Pale spring light spilled in from the long windows, bathing her in a warm glow, as she slowly turned the copy of *Madame Figaro* round to face Andre. An enormous picture showed Naomi Campbell stepping onto a yacht in the Caribbean. She looked stunning, her long legs spilling out of a white mini dress, her glossy hair flowing almost down to her waist. In her right hand, displayed prominently, she carried the 'Camille' bag. It was the epitome of chic, complementing her outfit perfectly.

Andre inhaled sharply, looking up and locking eyes with Camille, who let out a cry of jubilation. They'd had celebrities, socialites and even minor royals wearing their clothes before, but this felt different. It was a breakthrough to the mainstream; an A-list, international supermodel – and one of the most famous women in the world – endorsing their brand. And it was for a handbag, something completely new to them. This could create an explosion of interest in the company outside their native France – *if* it was handled correctly. Andre stood up abruptly.

'Where are you going?'

'To make some calls.'

He strode over to the telephone, punching in a number. 'Get me Marie,' he said, naming the head of their PR company. 'I don't care if it's the weekend, God knows I pay her enough to be available when I need her.' There was a short pause, then she obviously came on the line. 'Have you seen the newspapers? Good. I want a press release out within the next hour – "Naomi Campbell, pictured in Jamaica, carries the Camille Andre 'Camille' bag. Made from the finest lambskin and crafted by artisans in Spain, the 'Camille' is the first handbag from the chic French label. Adding a timeless elegance to your wardrobe, the bag is a powerful statement piece that blends artistry with innovation, and will be the most sought-after piece in your autumn/winter wardrobe . . ." Etc., etc. Add the rest as you see fit. Call the picture agency and have them send over the best shot. I need it done asap, OK?'

Camille watched him as he worked, hanging up and dialling another number. Emotions raced through her – excitement, vindication, relief. The French critics had not been kind to her last show. They'd called it confused, a mess, and in one particularly vicious case 'a garish jumble of clashing ideas that shows the once-elegant label is having a midlife identity crisis'. The words had stung, undoubtedly, but Camille had stuck to her guns. The coverage in the US and UK had been kinder; they'd appreciated the new direction, the fresh and innovative style. And now it seemed that Naomi Campbell agreed . . .

'We'll start with five thousand,' Andre was saying. 'Well, I don't care if you can't fulfil it – do it, or I'll terminate your contract and find someone else who can. Don't skimp on quality either. There'll be a bonus if you deliver on time. Employ extra staff if you need to, but just get it done!'

Andre hung up the phone, looking exhilarated. 'I've placed an order for five thousand bags with the Spanish factory. They're going to struggle to fulfil it, so I'll look at other options – there's that place in Italy we've used. I can fly down tomorrow with the patterns and brief them.'

'Five thousand,' Camille breathed. 'Andre, that's—'

'It's happening,' he told her firmly, fixing her with his penetrating gaze. 'The moment we've been waiting for is finally here, and we need to seize it.'

Camille looked at him in wonder and excitement. She could feel it too – the anticipation and optimism, as though they were on the edge of a precipice, ready to fly. Andre had always dreamed big, unafraid and unashamed, and now, finally, it seemed that their faith in themselves had been justified.

Chapter 25

Indian Ocean, October 1993

From the window of the private plane, the ocean was the most dazzling blue. It was made up of myriad shades – turquoise, aqua, sapphire and cerulean – and lush, green islands were scattered like emeralds across the water.

Seated opposite Camille was Andre, and across the aisle was Lucas, now a strapping young man of nineteen. His long legs were stretched out in front of him, his brown hair flopping over his forehead, and there was a moody expression on his face as he looked out at the view.

It was the first time Camille had taken a holiday for over a year. After Naomi Campbell had been pictured with the 'Camille' bag, life had gone crazy. They couldn't produce stock fast enough to keep up with demand, and nor did they want to – Andre said exclusivity was the key to success. The scarcity made great headlines, with women clamouring to get the 'Camille', dubbed the first 'It' bag. Their clothing collection – which had been panned by the

French critics – slowly won over their fashion-conscious clientele. The British and Americans loved its cool, urban, sexy take, and slowly the French were captivated too. It felt wonderful to be celebrated on their home turf.

Camille and Andre had had offers right, left and centre for loans, for investment, or for an outright buyout. Whilst the sums of money on offer were eyewatering, neither of them wanted to give up the company at this stage. Nicolas's advice had been invaluable – although Camille hadn't let Andre know just how much influence he'd had – and eventually they'd agreed to sell a minority stake to LVMH, the huge conglomerate that owned Louis Vuitton, Celine and Givenchy amongst others. It meant they could retain creative control, whilst still having the investment, supplier contacts and distribution channels of a multinational corporation.

Last week, Camille Andre had shown their spring/summer '94 collection, and it had been their most successful to date, with gushing reviews and record-breaking pre-orders. Their label was widely recognized, and they were now a household name. Camille and Andre were riding the crest of a wave, hitting the heights of their career – and they were both utterly exhausted, close to burnout. They'd decided to take a private jet to an island in the Maldives, where they could completely switch off and do nothing apart from sleep, swim, and eat delicious fresh food prepared by a personal chef.

Camille had seen pictures of their accommodation, and it wasn't simply an overwater bungalow – it was more like an overwater mansion, set in a perfectly calm, clear sea, close to a pristine white sand beach fringed by palm trees. She hoped it would be a relaxing family holiday – memorable for all the right reasons – and that none of the cracks that were beginning to show between them would split open.

Camille glanced across at Lucas, who was still staring sulkily out of the window. He'd been reluctant to even come on this trip, preferring to spend time with his friends – including the ever-present Paulo – and the stream of beautiful young women who seemed to permanently surround her son. Camille had pulled the guilt card, telling Lucas how much it meant to her for him to accompany them, and had managed to persuade him. She knew he'd enjoy it once they were there – he and Andre were adrenaline junkies, and had a packed itinerary of scuba diving, jet skiing, even swimming with reef sharks – whilst Camille looked forward to sunbathing and getting stuck into a good book.

'We'll be landing soon, darling,' she called across to Lucas, as the stewardess came to clear his plate. They'd had a delicious meal of filet mignon with fondant potatoes, followed by tarte tatin, then a cheeseboard, all washed down with a fine Burgundy. Flying private was even more luxurious than Camille had imagined, and she realized she could get used to this; Andre had already been making noises about them buying their own plane.

Lucas's eyes followed the stewardess as she walked away, and Camille raised her eyebrows. She understood that her son was becoming quite the player. He was rich and good-looking, and she knew the possibilities open to him would be endless – certainly far more than she'd had as a young woman from rural Normandy, with no money and no connections.

Lucas grunted in reply, barely responding. He'd been like this since they left Paris, and she was frustrated by his behaviour. She wasn't the only one.

'Come on, Lucas, answer your mother properly,' Andre said sharply. 'You're behaving like a spoilt child.'

'I didn't want to come anyway,' Lucas shot back resentfully.

Camille sighed, a sinking feeling in the pit of her stomach. 'I wanted us all to do something together – something special and fun. We're all so busy these days, especially now you're away at university. This is a chance to spend some quality time together.'

Lucas snorted. 'It's a bit late for that. You shipped me off to boarding school the first chance you got, and I spent practically every holiday with *Abuela* so you could pursue your business. *Now* you want to spend time together?'

Camille was stung by the barb – all the more so because she knew it was true. She was trying to make up for lost time with her son, but feared it was too late. Andre rolled his eyes irritably.

'Stop being so stroppy, Lucas. Your mother's planned this amazing trip and I don't want you to spoil it for her. What will it take to cheer you up, hmm? A new Rolex when we land at the airport? Or how about a car? Your Audi's a year old now, maybe it's time we upgraded to a Ferrari?'

Lucas brightened, but Camille frowned. Andre had always spoilt Lucas materially, and now that money was no object, Andre was throwing it around recklessly. She understood that he also felt guilty for the years they'd put Lucas second to their own needs, but she didn't think lavishing gifts on him was the best way to make up for that.

'Come on, let's toast,' Andre was saying, as he waved for the stewardess to refill his champagne glass with vintage Krug. 'We have everything we've ever dreamed of, so let's enjoy ourselves. To success!'

Camille raised her coupe, the bubbles fizzing on her tongue as she took a sip. Andre was right – they'd achieved everything they'd ever wanted, and all because of a leather bag, named after her, which was nestled on Camille's lap right now.

But despite the private jet and vintage champagne and stunning view outside her window as the plane descended, something didn't feel right. Camille couldn't put her finger on why, but it troubled her that, if she had the world at her feet, why did she feel so unhappy?

They landed at Malé Airport and were whisked through the terminal by the hotel concierge, who was taking them to a private seaplane that would transport them directly to their island. This was the hub every traveller passed through when arriving in the Maldives; the airport was busy but no one was in a rush, there was just a relaxed holiday vibe in the air.

Camille was walking out of the terminal towards the jetty, feeling the welcome tropical warmth of the sun on her skin, and she pulled down her sunglasses against the bright light. She saw the white seaplane glistening in the sunshine, the crystal-clear water gently lapping at the wooden jetty, when she heard Andre greet someone. She turned in curiosity and Nicolas was standing there.

Camille's heart leapt. She saw Nicolas whenever he

was in Paris, or when she was in New York, and they spoke on the phone regularly. But right now she was heading for a family vacation and he was the last person she expected to see. The unexpectedness of the encounter caught her off guard, and she inhaled sharply in surprise.

Nicolas looked more handsome than ever, a relaxed confidence radiating from him. He was wearing shorts and a white polo shirt, which contrasted with his light tan. His hair was starting to show a few flecks of grey, but they only served to make him look more distinguished. Camille had known this man for twenty years now, and the connection between them only grew deeper.

She tore her eyes from him to take in the woman holding his hand. She was slim, blonde, immaculately presented – and age appropriate. Nicolas had never been interested in trophy girlfriends or vacuous arm candy, and this woman was chic and elegant, wearing a pale blue Ralph Lauren sundress and tan leather sandals.

'Camille,' Nicolas smiled, and his eyes crinkled at the corners. 'Fancy running into you here.'

'Nicolas . . .' For a moment Camille couldn't speak. 'Are you on your way home?'

'Yes, unfortunately. We flew out as soon as New York Fashion Week was over for some much-needed R&R, and now we're heading back to the city – via a brief stopover in Rome for some meetings. Duty calls. This is Jennifer, by the way,' he said, indicating the woman beside him, as she smiled broadly and stepped forward to air-kiss Camille. 'Jennifer, this is Camille and Andre Fontaine, the geniuses behind the Camille Andre label, and my long-time friends. And this is their son, Lucas.'

'Oh, *the* Camille Fontaine! I adore your new bag,' Jennifer gushed, in a nasal, New York accent.

'Thank you,' Camille said, trying to regain her composure. She couldn't work out why she was so thrown by the unexpected meeting. After divorcing Lisa, Nicolas had fallen back into the same pattern of dating successful women, rotating them every few months before either side got too attached. Camille hadn't expected that he'd live like a monk, pining for her in his penthouse apartment. But there was something about being confronted with him and Jennifer like this – proof that he was leading a fulfilling life without Camille. She realized that the two of them had probably just had an incredibly romantic vacation, falling in and out of a rose-petal-strewn bed, falling in love . . . The notion pained her.

The concierge approached, interrupting the moment, and Camille was grateful. 'Mr and Mrs Fontaine, your plane is now ready.'

'Thank you,' Andre replied. 'Good to see you, Nicolas. Let's catch up soon.'

'Of course,' Nicolas smiled, shaking hands with Andre, before giving Lucas a backslapping hug. Lucas had cheered up immensely at the sight of Nicolas, who he liked and respected.

Nicolas leaned in to kiss Camille on both cheeks, and the physical proximity was almost too much. It was a sensory overload – the familiar scent of him, the feel of his stubble lightly grazing her skin. Images came rushing back – the two of them, around the same age that Lucas was now, making love with a youthful urgency, unable to get enough of one another. Then another memory – in the old Camille Andre offices, Nicolas's hands on her body, the taste of his lips, the feel of him inside her . . .

Camille closed her eyes for a second, grateful that she was wearing dark glasses. 'Goodbye, Nicolas. It was nice to meet you, Jennifer,' she said, fighting to control her emotions as she watched them walk away hand-in-hand. She realized her heart was pounding, her pulse racing.

'Camille?' Andre asked, touching her lightly on the arm. It was enough to break the spell, but she was still distracted as they boarded the seaplane and took off once again over the stunning Indian Ocean.

Yes, she'd lived an exciting life with Andre, and they'd built something incredible together. But their marriage had been plagued with arguments and infidelity, and Andre had never let her forget her humble origins. They'd never had the same connection, the same deep, unbreakable bond or unconditional love that she shared with Nicolas.

Before, Camille had always wondered, but now she had her answer – Nicolas was her soulmate, and she should never have let him go. She'd chosen Andre because she'd been young and foolish, blinded by lust. She'd let Nicolas get away, and he'd gone on to forge his own path without her. Now it was too late, and Camille would have to live with the consequences of her choices for the rest of her life.

Part 3

Chapter 26

Mallorca, June 2001

For the next couple of days after she had received the letter, Camille had tried to bury herself in her work, but it had felt like there was a black cloud hanging over her. Every time there was knock at her hotel room door, or someone was walking behind her in the corridor; every time she caught someone's eyes at dinner, or passed someone in the lobby, she wondered, *is it you?*

Camille felt like she was cracking into a million tiny pieces.

Then Nicolas came to her with news late at night.

'I think I know who is sending the letters,' he told her, over a drink in her suite. 'Amongst other leads, I've been able to gain access to the guest list.'

'How?'

'By telling them a partial truth – that you'd had a threat, and we needed to look at the list for security purposes. I've had my team run a few checks on the guests, and we've turned up a person from your past.'

'Please, Nicolas,' Camille begged. 'Just tell me.'

Nicolas paused, his face serious as he looked at her, a furrow forming between his eyebrows. 'We believe her name is Isobel MacFarlane – or at least it is now. She was Isobel Murdoch when she interned for Camille Andre about a decade ago.'

It took Camille a moment to place the name, but then her jaw dropped. 'Isobel? But I . . .'

'She's staying here, at the hotel, this week. She befriended you, yes? She was at the yacht party, and her name is on the VIP list for the show.'

'How do you know all of this?' Camille stared at him with shock and wonder and open admiration.

'I have my sources, mainly a big company legal department who are good at digging.'

Camille was in a state of shock. It felt incredibly sinister that this woman knew who she was and had targeted her deliberately when Camille had been nothing but welcoming this week. She'd even invited Isobel to dine with them at Il Paradiso, not to mention extending invitations to the yacht party and the fashion show.

What was Isobel's reason for sending those threats? Had she taken a dislike to her for some reason, all those years ago? But why pursue this vendetta a decade later? Perhaps it related to Andre in some way – oh God, she hoped her late husband hadn't slept with this young intern, promised her the world, maybe even got her pregnant . . . Camille's mind was racing.

'Do we know anything about her? About her motives? I just don't understand why . . .'

Nicolas shook his head. 'It seems too much of a coincidence that she's here this week. Right now. The week of our big show.'

'She's never mentioned that she used to intern for us. She runs her own boutique now, she said. Oh, I even told her the other day that she has a real eye for fashion.'

'Perhaps it's professional jealousy?' Nicolas wondered, but they both knew the suggestion was too weak to warrant the extreme lengths that Isobel appeared to have gone to.

Camille stood up, her almond eyes blazing. 'Let's go and confront her. I don't care what time it is, I want answers. I'm going to hammer on her door and ask her what the hell she's doing.'

She moved to go, but Nicolas caught her wrist lightly. A flame flickered through her at his touch, and the two of them locked eyes.

'We can't,' he said softly. 'This is not the way to handle this. We're not vigilantes. We have to be one hundred per cent certain. Look,' he continued, as Camille acquiesced and sat back down. 'The investigators said she was there in late 1992. Can you think of anything significant that happened around then? Can you remember her at all?'

Camille's forehead creased in concentration. Her mind was jumping all over the place; this was a lot to take in. 'It was the year before we went big.' She tried hard to cast her mind back, thinking of the interns she had in the office, and then her mind alighted on the young Irish or Scottish girl. 'It's hard to recall . . . There was so much going on. Unless . . .' A thought struck her, and her blood ran cold.

'What is it?' Nicolas was looking at her intently.

Camille felt sick as the memory came flooding back. She took a fortifying sip of brandy and noticed her hands were shaking. 'The "Camille" handbag. Our most famous product, and the one that launched the company into a different league. The design was sketched by an intern, the one Andre thought was very talented. It changed significantly from the original version, but . . .'

'Camille . . .' Michael winced, letting out a groan.

'The interns weren't there to design,' Camille protested. 'Their role was to run errands and make coffee and learn about the industry and pick up skills. It was a complete fluke that Andre picked up that sketch that day. Once we'd decided to make a sample and use it in the show, I wanted to speak to her, to give her credit. But she'd left abruptly – I can't remember the reasons.' Camille screwed up her face, trying to remember, but it was so long ago now and she'd paid little attention at the time. 'And then events overtook us. If I'm being honest, I'd completely forgotten how the bag started life. Like I said, I'd made countless changes, chosen the leather, selected the hardware and the lining . . . As far as I was concerned – am concerned – it was *and is* my bag. She worked for us; any designs done inhouse were our intellectual property.'

'But perhaps not as far as Isobel was concerned,' Nicolas said sagely.

Camille sighed, imagining how Isobel must have felt as a young woman, seeing the bag she'd had a hand in creating take off worldwide. It had gained international press coverage, universal praise from some of the most influential people in the industry, and it had catapulted

Camille Andre to becoming a household name. 'I should go and speak to her. Explain.'

'Please, Camille. It's late, and whether your theory is correct or not, she's been threatening you. Blackmailing you. A criminal. We have to proceed carefully.'

Camille nodded ruefully. 'You're right, as always.' They sat quietly, finishing their drinks, unsure what to do next. Despite the late hour, Camille felt energized by the adrenaline racing through her body. She knew she should tell Nicolas to leave so that they could both get some sleep before the show tomorrow, but she didn't want him to go. Besides, something was niggling at her. She glanced across at Nicolas, who was swirling the last drops of brandy in his glass, deep in thought.

'There's just one thing that doesn't make sense,' he said slowly. 'All the notes refer to the crash. She's not blackmailing you about the origins of the bag. How could she know about Andre's accident?'

'It was in the newspapers. It's public knowledge.'

Nicolas looked uncomfortable. 'I mean, how could she know that there was . . . more to it? This latest note refers to the "truth" about the accident and Andre. She couldn't know . . .' He trailed off.

Camille shifted in her seat before standing and walking to the balcony. She opened the sliding doors and stepped out into the night, breathing in the air, with its fragrant notes of sea salt and jasmine. Camille put her fingers to her temples, thinking for a moment; she knew she was missing something, a piece of the puzzle. The silence briefly enveloped her, before a flash of realization: 'Of course! She's Stuart MacFarlane's wife. He was one of the consultants for Lucas's facial reconstruction.'

'After the accident?' Nicolas was by her side.

'Not immediately, but he'll have had Lucas's medical records, and all the details of what happened. What if Isobel somehow got hold of them?'

'Perhaps . . .' Nicolas looked unconvinced. Camille could almost see his sharp mind working, examining all the angles, dissecting all the arguments.

'We have to go and speak to her,' Camille insisted once again.

'No, we don't. Not without proof. You invited her to the show tomorrow, haven't you? If she has the audacity to attend, then we'll keep a close eye on her. If we need to, we'll call the police.'

'All right,' Camille agreed. She felt exhausted and had to put on the show of her life tomorrow. She must get up in four hours' time, and desperately needed to sleep, but she wasn't sure if she could. She had a terrible feeling that she'd simply lie awake all night, tossing and turning until the sun rose.

'Nicolas,' she asked in a quiet voice. 'Will you stay with me? I don't want to be alone tonight.'

Nicolas hesitated. 'I'll take the sofa.'

'No, I meant . . . I want you,' she said simply.

A look Camille couldn't interpret crossed his face, then he closed his eyes and shook his head. 'I think the sofa would be best. You need to get some sleep, Camille. I'll see you in the morning.'

'Goodnight, Nicolas,' Camille said softly, and leaned her head into his chest for a moment. He brushed the top of her head with his lips, before she straightened and turned to cross the suite to the bedroom.

* * *

A few miles away, across the island, Lucas was also still awake. He was in his apartment in the town, part of an exclusive complex with its own pool and gym facilities, a concierge and a maid service. It was within striking distance of Il Paradiso, and right now the restaurant dominated his thoughts.

Lucas was utterly confused by the events of that evening, feeling completely clueless as to why his restaurant had been closed down, beyond what those two goons had told him. They'd said the rent hadn't been paid, but that was impossible – it was Paulo's responsibility, and Lucas knew they were making enough money to cover it. Sure, the cashflow could be tight, but if there had been a major problem, Paulo would have spoken to him about it. Lucas had seen large payments going out of the account, and Paulo had assured him he had everything under control.

Lucas had been calling his number repeatedly, before eventually giving up. Now, he rolled over on the Egyptian cotton sheets, reaching for his phone from the bedside table. The screen illuminated the darkness as Lucas tried again. Nothing. The number was no longer in service.

What did it mean? Anxiety prickled across Lucas's skin, his racing mind refusing to let him rest. His childhood friend had swindled him? But for what reason? So that he could steal a few months' rent money from the company bank account? It didn't make sense. They'd known one another for twenty years; Lucas would have trusted him with his life. He wasn't naïve – he knew that once they were older, and his mother's company had gone stratospheric, money had become a source of tension between them. The difference in their situations inevitably drove a wedge between them, no matter how generous Lucas tried to be.

But Paulo's family had done well for themselves, too; their boat hire business had been hugely successful, boosted by the massive influx of monied tourists that had transformed their lives from the poor farming family Lucas had first known. And Paulo had his fingers in all sorts of pies, never one to pass up a potential business opportunity. He was a hustler, and Lucas respected that. Paulo loved dressing in designer labels, living the high life. It was true that he'd been acting strangely recently, but Lucas couldn't tie all the pieces together. He had to be missing something . . .

In truth, their relationship had fundamentally changed after the accident. When Lucas had first woken from his coma, he couldn't remember a thing, but snatches of memory had returned to him over time. His therapist had warned him that might happen. Lately, Lucas had been having terrifying flashbacks that he didn't dare to share with anyone. He remembered the feel of the cold steering wheel beneath his hands, the blackness of the night through the misty windscreen. But there was no way he could have been driving, Lucas assured himself. Besides, he distinctly remembered Andre taking the keys from the valet before climbing into the driver's seat. He knew now that his father should never have got behind the wheel either – the cocaine levels in his system shown by the autopsy results proved that beyond doubt.

As Lucas tossed and turned in his king-size bed, his mind drifted to Stephanie, and he felt an overwhelming urge to talk to her about the way he was feeling. Memories of her invaded his thoughts as he remembered their passionate kiss. It was more than just the physical for him; they shared a connection, and he wanted to confess his fears about the accident to her. He couldn't shake the memory – real or invented – that he'd been driving, and that Paulo had somehow been there too . . . Perhaps Paulo could help solve the mystery. If only he could find him.

Outside the window, the sun was coming up. It was his mother's important show today, and he was supposed to attend. Lucas sighed and tried Paulo's number again: still disconnected. Then, in a moment of inspiration, dialled a different number. It rang for a long time, but just as he was expecting it to go to voicemail, someone picked up.

'Lucas?' Elle sounded sleepy, and he suspected he'd woken her up. 'What is it?'

'Have you seen Paulo?'

There was a noise in the background and – Lucas couldn't be sure – was that another voice? 'Paulo?' Elle replied languidly. 'Not since the party. Why?'

Lucas frowned. 'Is there someone there with you?'

'Of course not, and why do you care anyway?'

'Look, I haven't seen him for a couple of days,' Lucas said carefully. 'He's not picking up my calls.'

'Really,' said Elle, sounding completely uninterested.

'If you do hear from him, tell him to call me.'

'Sure. Wait . . . Before you hang up. I'm glad you called. There's something you need to know.'

Lucas sighed inwardly. He'd known it was a bad idea calling Elle, but he'd been desperate. Now he was beginning to regret his decision, imagining she'd want a favour of some kind. 'What is it?'

Elle paused for a fraction of a second. 'I'm pregnant.'

'What?' Lucas felt as though the breath had been punched violently out of him. 'Is it mine?'

'Screw you, Lucas.'

'I didn't mean . . . I just meant . . . Christ, Elle. How long have you known?'

'Not long.'

Lucas's mind was racing. 'What are you going to do?'

'I don't know . . .' She sniffed, tearfully, 'Can we talk?'

'Sure, of course.' His tone was gentler now. 'Look, whatever happens, I'll stand by you and the baby and—'

'OK, Lucas, we can talk about it all later,' Elle said, sniffling.

'Where's good for you?'

'Get me on the guest list for the show. We can talk afterwards.'

Lucas shook his head in disbelief. 'After what happened at the yacht party? There's no way my mother will—'

'Oh grow up, Lucas.' Her voice was flinty now, the tearful Elle of a moment ago now gone. 'You're about to be a father, and all you care about is what Mummy says? Be a man.'

Lucas bristled, but hated that Elle had a point. 'OK, OK, I'll smooth things over. Then we can talk afterwards.'

'Good,' Elle said, and hung up.

Lucas lay in bed, watching as the sun came up, mind racing. His business partner had gone AWOL, he suspected he'd been involved in the death of his father, and now his ex-girlfriend was pregnant with his baby. At least there was no way the day could get any worse.

* * *

Elle rolled over in bed, smiling to herself, as Paulo strode into the room wearing nothing but his boxer shorts. He had a great body, Elle thought lazily as she watched him walk towards her. It was tight and muscular, like a boxer's, with tribal art tattoos covering his arms and a snake curling its way across his chest. He climbed into bed and kissed her hungrily.

'Did you tell him?' he asked, biting her neck playfully.

'Yeah,' Elle said, giggling. 'He reacted exactly like you said he would.'

'I guess it's a big day for you tomorrow,' he said, as he moved his attention lower, his tongue trailing a path down to her cleavage.

'Once that model calls in sick, I'll be waiting to step in. Thanks for helping me with that,' Elle murmured, gasping as his hand slid inside her bra.

'It was easy – I just sprinkled laxative in her drink. Lucky that you knew which bar they were going to in Palma.'

'My friend, Anouk, is walking in the show, so she called me yesterday. We shared an apartment in Milan when we were both starting out . . .'

'Tell me more,' Paulo grinned. 'I want to hear about everything you and your model friends did together.'

'Paulo!' Elle squealed, playfully slapping his firm backside. She knew that this was a form of revenge for both of them, but there was nothing to say it couldn't be fun, too. 'So what about you? What's your big plan?'

'You'll see.'

'I thought you were Lucas's best friend?'

Paulo snorted dismissively. 'Goes both ways, right? Once upon a time, maybe. When we were kids. But things change. Life isn't a fairytale, and Lucas needs to learn that. But let's not talk about him now. I can think of something else I'd much rather be doing,' he grinned, as his hands slid down her body. His fingertips trailed over her flat stomach, stirring heat between her thighs, and Elle moaned loudly, all thoughts of Lucas firmly pushed from her mind.

Chapter 27

When Camille's alarm went off at six a.m., she was instantly awake. She was surprised to find that she'd managed to doze, but the events of the previous night came rushing back. She still felt just as confused and disturbed by everything as she had a few hours ago.

She pulled on her robe and quickly checked her appearance in the mirror. She looked exhausted, with dark bags under her eyes, and felt grateful she had a team of skilled make-up artists on hand for the show. She would ask them to work their magic on her.

Camille went through to the living room where Nicolas was getting up from the sofa, his face as crumpled as his clothes. It lifted her heart to see him there; just his presence reassured her.

'How are you doing?' he asked her, his tousled hair and stubble making him look younger, and painfully reminding her of their early lives together.

'Truthfully, I'm not sure yet. Still trying to take everything in.'

'Just concentrate on the show – the most important thing is launching the new collection and the show being everything it should be. Clear your mind, focus, and I'll take care of everything else.'

'Thank you, Nicolas.' Camille wanted to throw her arms around him, but neither of them moved.

'I'd better go back to my room, take a shower. I'll be back in around an hour, OK? And Camille?'

'Yes?' She looked up hopefully.

'Be careful. There's someone out there making threats against you, and we don't know what they're capable of.'

A chill ran through her as she realized Nicolas was right. 'I will. But Nicolas . . . Hurry back.'

After Nicolas had left, Camille took a shower, then dressed in a pair of wide-legged beige slacks and a loose-fit white silk shirt. She would change before the show, but this morning she needed to be comfortable and casual – by her standards at least. She called room service to order a light breakfast of tea and fruit. She wasn't sure whether she'd be able to eat anything – her stomach was churning, and she didn't know whether it was the usual pre-show nerves, or if Nicolas's dark warning had affected her more than she'd realized.

Camille had just finished blow-drying her hair when a room service attendant arrived with her order, knocking on the door and entering with a tray. It was a different staff member to the one who'd brought the note last night, and she was glad. He left the tray on the coffee table as directed, then wished her a good morning and left. As Camille poured a cup of green tea, she noticed a small, white piece of paper folded on the tray beside the fruit plate. A bolt of fear shot through her, her gut clenching as she picked it up and opened it, noticing that her hands were shaking.

One million dollars before the show starts, or I tell the world the truth about Andre's death.

Beneath were the bank account numbers again. Camille let out a cry of fear, before clamping her hand over her mouth. She couldn't lose control, not now. She had an incredibly important day ahead of her, and thanks to Nicolas they were so close to exposing the blackmailer.

She pictured Isobel rising early and creeping around the hotel, hanging around in the corridor by Camille's room, slipping the waiter fifty euros to deliver the note along with the breakfast tray . . .

Camille's face hardened. She wouldn't let her get away with it. Isobel MacFarlane wasn't going to destroy everything Camille had built and worked for, for almost three decades.

She strode over to the phone and dialled the extension for Nicolas's room.

'No more playing nice,' she told him, her eyes narrowing, her pulse racing. 'I'm not taking the risk. Let's call the police. Now.'

It was early afternoon when Isobel returned to her room to get ready for the Camille Andre show. She'd had a relaxing morning, going for a leisurely swim followed by lunch on the terrace, but it was impossible not to be caught up in the buzz that was sweeping through the hotel. Many of the celebrities who'd been at the yacht party were staying at the palacio, and Isobel felt a surge of excitement whenever she spotted a famous face – Vanessa Paradis in the lobby, or Thandie Newton by the pool.

There were plenty of comings and goings, with cars arriving and couriers leaving, and the area by the Sunset Room was a hub of activity. Isobel felt excited to be part of it, thrilled that she would be attending the Camille Andre show as though she were a VIP too. It felt like justice. If life had worked out the way it should have, she would have been there anyway, Isobel thought bitterly, a tingle of anticipation running through her at the thought of what was to come.

She dressed with care, knowing that today was important, and wanting to look her best. She'd selected a navy-and-white wide-legged jumpsuit from her own collection, accessorized with her tan Camille bag. There would be press and cameras, and Isobel wanted to ensure that she blended in with the glamorous guests; she didn't want to stand out and draw attention to herself.

Now, she was sitting in front of the vanity mirror, Gwen Stefani playing on MTV in the background, and a glass of sparkling Asti in her hand as she finished getting ready.

She took a sip of wine as she reflected on the evening she'd spent with Paulo. Now *that* had been interesting, and a slow, secret smile played across her lips as she regarded herself in the mirror . . . They'd both been a little drunk, and not a little indiscreet. Paulo had turned out to be a lot more useful than she'd originally given him credit for. Being a long-time friend of the Fontaines meant he was privy to all kinds of secrets. Ones which Isobel was sure the family wouldn't want to be revealed.

Isobel had used every drop of her charm on Paulo,

coaxing him to share what he knew. She could see that he was desperate to reveal all, to brag about his closeness with the family. They'd traded stories of how Camille and Andre's marriage wasn't as perfect as they'd led the public to assume. Isobel wasn't shocked by that – when she'd interned for them all those years ago, it was obvious that Andre was a philanderer. The atelier had been rife with rumours of his cheating, and Isobel had been warned that he had an eye for pretty young interns. By all accounts, women fell at his feet and he could take his pick, whilst Camille slaved away in the office, working to make the business a success.

No, Andre's infidelity was hardly a surprise. What Paulo *had* found surprising was the rumour that *Camille* hadn't been faithful, and it was even possible that . . . Oh, it was too delicious! Yes, it seemed that – over the years – Camille had accumulated a significant amount of dirty laundry, and now it was time for it to be aired in public.

Isobel jumped in fright as she heard the door click and realized someone was in the room with her. She leapt to her feet, letting out a cry as she spun around.

'Stuart!' she burst out, as she saw her husband standing there. 'What are you—?'

'Isobel, I'm back,' he said, dropping his suitcase by the door, they stared at each other for a moment. Isobel was confused by his sudden appearance, and surprised to find she wasn't overjoyed to see him – she was getting used to being on her own and had been quite enjoying herself.

He came towards her and kissed her on her cheek, and Isobel felt a flash of anger. He had swanned off with barely an explanation, and now here he was, as cool as anything.

Stuart stood back, his hands on her waist, taking her in. His eyes ran over her. 'Christ, you look amazing.'

'Thank you. I'm attending the fashion show this afternoon. Camille Andre – the handbags,' she added. 'We dined with Camille the other night – Lucas's mother.'

'Oh yes, of course,' Stuart nodded, and Isobel thought he looked stressed for once.

'But why are you here? I thought you were in Spain for a few more days?'

'I . . . I needed to get back here . . . to see you.' Stuart reached out to embrace her.

'Careful,' Isobel wriggled in his grasp. 'I've spent ages doing my hair.'

'It's so good to see you again,' he sighed.

'So . . . no more work, this holiday?'

Stuart shook his head. 'No. No more work.'

Isobel felt a wave of relief wash over her as she allowed herself to sink into Stuart's arms. Perhaps she was glad to have him back. No more dining alone, no more filling up the time aimlessly. Sure, she had his credit card, but it wasn't the same as having him to treat her. She felt a wave of guilt over the evening with Paulo, memories of the time they'd spent together troubling her conscience . . . She would get this show out of the way, then she and Stuart could go back to enjoying their holiday.

'What time do you have to leave?' Stuart asked.

'In about half an hour.'

'I'll jump in the shower quickly, then we can talk.'

'Sure, darling,' Isobel beamed.

Stuart strode off towards the bathroom. Moments later, she heard the water running. Isobel had almost finished her make-up and was adding the finishing touches when

Meet Me at Sunset

she noticed Stuart's suitcase lying where he'd left it. She tutted inwardly, setting down her bronzer and wheeling the case out of the way. Then she paused for a moment – Stuart *had* come back; she'd do something nice for him and unpack, one less job for him to do.

She lifted the case onto the bed, unclipped it and began sorting through, making a pile to send to the hotel laundry. His clothes were all casual, which seemed strange, but then he hadn't brought work clothes on holiday, Isobel reasoned. She picked up his washbag and shaver, and was about to take them through to him in the bathroom, when something caught her eye.

Isobel frowned and hesitated, wondering if her eyes were playing tricks on her. There was something bright red peeking through the clothes, something caught up in a pair of his boxer shorts. She knew Stuart didn't own anything in that colour. With her thumb and forefinger, she took hold of the corner and pulled. A lurid red lace thong that she'd never seen before in her life emerged from the depths of Stuart's case as fury surged through Isobel.

She stormed into the bathroom, which was cloudy with steam, and wrenched open the door to the shower.

'What the hell is this?'

Stuart jumped in alarm as he turned round. He took in the red thong, which she held out to him, holding it at arm's length as though it might explode into flames.

One look at Stuart's face told her everything she needed to know – panic, guilt and terror flitted across it, plainly signalling his transgression.

For a moment, Isobel thought he looked so ridiculous standing there, naked, half covered in soap bubbles, that she almost wanted to laugh hysterically. But then anger, sadness, betrayal welled up inside her, and it was all she could do not to scream.

Stuart stepped towards her, and she jumped backwards.

'Don't you dare touch me,' she hissed. 'Who was she? One of your wealthy divorcee sluts, who are happy to be underneath *you* as well as under your knife?'

Stuart swallowed. 'We need to talk. And you're not going to like what I have to say.'

'You bastard,' she shot back, turning to march out of the room.

Stuart turned off the shower, grabbing a towel and hastily wrapping it round his waist, before following her through to the bedroom.

Isobel threw the underwear in his face. 'You're pathetic, disgusting—'

'Isobel, sit down,' Stuart said firmly.

'Don't you dare tell me what to—'

'I've been having an affair.'

Isobel's mouth dropped open. She knew things between her and Stuart hadn't been perfect, but she'd never imagined he'd cheat on her like this. A one-night stand she could perhaps have forgiven, but an affair . . . To her horror, she felt tears welling up. Then the pieces slid into place. 'There was no client on the mainland . . . You were with her.'

Stuart nodded slowly. He sank down onto the chair in front of the vanity table, where moments ago Isobel had been polishing her look.

'Her name is Valeria Perez – the actress. It's been going on for months now . . .'

Isobel couldn't take it in. Valeria Perez was known as

the Goddess from Girona, the bombshell model-turned-actress who had been linked with everyone from Tom Cruise to Antonio Banderas. What the hell was she doing with Stuart, with his slight paunch and receding hairline? She felt dizzy, as though the bottom had fallen out of her world; adrenaline was coursing through her system.

'Is it serious?' she whispered.

Stuart shrugged. 'There's something I need to tell you. The . . . um . . . the newspapers have found out about it. They're going to publish this weekend. I've been speaking to my lawyers, trying to get an injunction, but they say there's nothing they can do in Europe.'

Isobel put her fingertips to her forehead, her eyes wide with disbelief. So she was going to be humiliated, on top of everything else? Her private life splashed across the tabloids for all to see. Everyone would know that her husband had betrayed her, that she was a fool. 'How the hell did you meet her? Was she one of your clients? Did you throw in a free facelift with every lay? I hope you're struck off for that,' she raged.

'That's how we met, but I never operated on her. She came to me, asking for work done. She *wanted* a facelift. I said no, she was too young – only twenty-eight. It was unethical and I wouldn't do it.'

'Oh, *now* you have morals! You wouldn't operate on her, but you'd happily screw her behind your wife's back.'

Stuart had the good grace to look ashamed. 'I never meant to hurt you. It just . . . happened. She asked me out for a drink after the consultation. I was flattered, I suppose. I never expected . . .'

'Never expected what?' Isobel held his gaze, her eyes like chips of ice.

'To fall in love with her.'

Isobel gasped. All her dreams lay shattered in front of her – her future, a baby, growing old together. She'd put her needs second, all these years, for Stuart, and this was how he'd repaid her. She couldn't think straight. All she knew was she wanted to get out of there. She grabbed her bag.

'I'm going now. Going to the show. I'll be back in an hour. When I return, I want you gone. Pack up your things, and get out. I never want to see you again.'

Chapter 28

At the S'Estaca estate, perched high above the sea on a rocky cliffside, Stephanie Moon was preparing for the show. She was dressed in vintage Camille Andre, which Camille had arranged to be couriered over especially from the archives in Paris. It was the flowing white tuxedo suit, which a teenage Stephanie had seen Kate Moss wearing on the runway, and she'd confided in Camille how much she'd adored it. It fitted her like a glove and, as Stephanie stared at her reflection, her copper hair pulled back in a sleek low ponytail so it didn't detract from the outfit, she couldn't believe how incredible she felt to be wearing something so iconic.

Stephanie was beyond grateful to Camille for such a wonderful gesture, and was eager to thank her in person. She wanted to support Catherine too, who was the star attraction at today's show. Having been named as the face of the brand, she would also be walking the runway, and the two of them would head over to the palacio together just as soon as their driver arrived.

More than anything, Stephanie couldn't deny that she was looking forward to seeing Lucas. She was hoping that after the show they could pick up where they'd left off yesterday, before he'd had to run off to open the restaurant. The chemistry between them was electric. He was gorgeous and charming, and Stephanie was incredibly attracted to him; she was pretty sure the feeling was mutual. And now that Elle was out of the picture, there was nothing to stand in their way.

Lucas had been so supportive these past few days; he hadn't judged her, or patronized her, when she'd revealed her turbulent background and the childhood insecurities that had led her to almost sabotage her career. Instead, he'd listened and seemed to understand – his upbringing as a spoiled only child had been very different from hers, but he too had suffered more than his fair share of trauma and knew what it was like to feel unwanted by your family.

With both his and Catherine's support, Stephanie had blossomed over the past couple of weeks. She was almost ready to go back to work, though she knew she would have a lot of apologizing to do, and would have to go above and beyond to get her career back on track. Just as soon as this show was done, she'd bite the bullet and call Victoria, her agent, to put the wheels in motion for her return. Though the worst part about returning to the UK would be leaving Lucas behind . . .

She broke off from applying a final coat of mascara as her phone began to ring, Lucas's name showing on the caller display.

'Hey,' she grinned as she picked it up, her smile evident in her voice. 'I was just thinking about you.'

'Oh really? What were you thinking?'

'I'll show you later,' she teased. 'I hope you had a good night at the restaurant, and it was worth running out on me like that . . .'

'What? Oh, not exactly . . .'

'Is everything OK? You sound distracted.'

'Yeah, you could say that. There's a lot going on.'

'I can imagine. Are you at the venue yet?'

'No, not yet. I have some other things to take care of first.'

'Anything I can help with?' Stephanie zipped up her make-up bag and sat down on the stool at the vanity table, looking out of the window at the terraced gardens stretching down to the dazzling blue of the Balearic Sea, the colour deepening as it approached the horizon. Boats bobbed up and down on the white-tipped waves, as the sun reflected off the water like diamonds. 'You do sound really stressed.'

Lucas hesitated. 'You're definitely coming to the show, right?'

'Of course. I want to support Catherine, and your mother. They've both been so good to me – Camille's sent me the most gorgeous outfit; I can't wait for you to see it.'

But Lucas didn't acknowledge her words. 'Stephanie, there's something I have to tell you and I don't want you to change your mind about coming. But you need to know before you get there – it's not fair for you to walk in unprepared.'

Stephanie frowned. Lucas sounded serious. 'You're worrying me. What is it? Have you changed your mind about us?'

'No, of course not, but . . .' He took a deep breath. 'I spoke to Elle this morning.'

'OK,' Stephanie said, trying to keep her tone neutral. She told herself that there was nothing to be jealous of – they had recently ended a long-term relationship and the split was still raw, of course they would speak from time to time.

'She . . . she's pregnant.'

Stephanie almost dropped the phone in shock. 'Oh my God! But what . . . what does this mean for us, Lucas? What are you going to do?'

There was a long pause and Stephanie's stomach tightened with anxiety, 'What do you *want* to do?'

When Lucas spoke, she could hear the uncertainty in his voice 'I don't know yet. I need to figure it out. But if she's pregnant with my child then . . . I can't just abandon her.'

'Of course not, but . . .' Stephanie trailed off. This was too much to take in right now. Her world had been turned upside down in an instant. A few moments ago, she been hopeful and excited for the future, with barely a care in the world. Now, the man she'd hoped might play a part in that bright future was having a baby with his ex-girlfriend. It felt messy and problematic, an added complication that Stephanie didn't need right now.

'Look,' she began. 'Maybe . . . this isn't the right time for us. You need to sort things out with Elle, take some space, decide what you want to do . . . I need to go back to England anyway, see if I can rescue what remains of my career.' She laughed humourlessly.

'Stephanie, I don't want it to end like this. Hell, I don't want it to end, full stop.'

'Neither do I, Lucas. But what choice do we have?'

They fell silent, knowing there was no easy solution, but neither wanting to say the words and make it final.

'I'll see you at the show, OK? We can talk . . .'

'Lucas, I'm not sure what's left to say . . .' Stephanie's voice was quiet, and she bit back the tears that threatened to fall. 'Goodbye.'

She heard him swallow, his throat thick with emotion. 'Please, Stephanie . . .' But she didn't wait to hear the rest.

Isobel was in shock. She had fled from her room, and she'd meant it when she'd told Stuart that she never wanted to see him again. He'd better have packed his things – including that trashy thong – and got the hell out of there by the time she got back, or she wouldn't be responsible for her actions . . .

Then again, it sounded as if he'd be glad to be gone, and Isobel had given him an easy way out. He was probably on his way to the airport already, to fly out to his lover . . .

He'd said he *loved* this woman, Isobel recalled in disbelief. Valeria Perez, the Goddess from Girona, with *Stuart*? Isobel let out an incredulous laugh as she walked quickly along the corridors of the palacio, wanting to put as much distance as possible between her and Stuart.

He would want a divorce, obviously, and although Isobel could take him to the cleaners, she didn't want a penny of his money right now. She was devastated that the future she had planned had been snatched away from her, that the baby she had longed for was now little more than a distant dream.

Tears sprang to her eyes and she blinked them away. She could break down later, but right now she had to be strong. Nothing was going to stop her from going to the Camille Andre show. That had been the whole point of coming to Mallorca, and to the palacio – not that Stuart had known that.

Isobel stepped into the lift and checked her appearance in the mirror. She still looked immaculate, only the merest hint of red around her pupils indicating that she'd been upset. Her thick blonde hair was swept up elegantly, and delicate diamond earrings dangled from her earlobes, following every slight movement of her head. Isobel lifted her chin and smoothed down her jumpsuit as though she was putting on armour.

The lift door opened onto a lobby filled with people, chatter and laughter, as famous faces greeted one another, waving across the space and air-kissing ostentatiously. Isobel looked around for Stephanie but couldn't see her, so she headed towards the Sunset Room and joined the queue which was beginning to form. It moved quickly, and as Isobel reached the front, she gave her name to the security guard who checked his list. He was wearing dark glasses, so she couldn't see his eyes, and he had a radio in one hand and a thin wire snaked round his head attached to an earpiece. He found her name and paused.

'Isobel MacFarlane? This way.'

'Thank you.' Isobel gave him a broad smile and fell into step behind him. She was so distracted by thoughts of Stuart that she failed to notice no one else was getting a personal accompaniment to their seat. She'd experienced a pang of sadness as she'd given her name to the security guard, wondering if she should revert back to her maiden name. She'd built up her boutique and was known in the business as MacFarlane, but she no longer wanted to be associated with Stuart . . .

It was only when the security guard opened the door to a banqueting room, that alarm bells began ringing.

'Where are we—?'

'Could you wait in here for a moment, please?'

'But why? What's happening?'

'Someone will be along shortly to explain everything. But I've been asked if you'll wait here for now.'

Isobel frowned, uncertainty flashing through her mind. Surely Camille couldn't have discovered . . . Either way, it seemed she had no choice but to comply. The security guard was tall and wide, his shoulders almost the width of her arm span. Isobel wondered what he'd do if she resisted. Slowly, obediently, she sat down on one of the banquet chairs, looking up at him questioningly.

'Thank you,' the man said curtly. It was only when he left the room and locked the door that Isobel started to panic.

'Francesca, darling, thank you so much for coming.' Camille air-kissed the journalist from *Elle España* magazine, one of the select few who'd been invited backstage to capture the atmosphere. 'Now, are we looking after you? René, take Francesca and make sure she has everything she needs. I'll catch up with you later, darling, it's nonstop here. Now, has anyone heard from Katerina?'

Backstage was a hive of activity, as everyone raced around frantically and Camille did her best to remain cool and calm, like the eye in the centre of the hurricane. She had coordinated dozens of these shows over the years, but they were always challenging, with problems arising that no one could have anticipated and everyone working flat out right up until the last second.

In the main room outside, the invited guests and the press pack were gathering, the hum of conversation and anticipation filtering backstage over the incessant beat of the music. René turned back to her, holding out his phone, pulling a face.

'Katerina's sick. She can't make it.'

'Why the hell didn't anyone tell us before?' Camille fumed, striding over to the rails where Katerina's opening outfit was still hanging, unclaimed.

'She was sleeping.' René rolled his eyes. 'She'd been up half the night with a bad stomach. Her agent's furious. They've been trying to get hold of her for the last two hours.'

'Tell them to send a replacement.'

'There's no one on the island. Half of their roster seems to be in Ibiza right now, but they wouldn't get here in time.'

'Make a note never to use that girl again,' Camille ordered. 'I understand that people get sick, but you don't wait until fifteen minutes before a show to tell someone. *Merde*,' she swore. 'Get me the schedule. Is there anyone spare? Perhaps we can change the running order so the girls get more time and fit in the extra looks? I don't see how else we can do it . . .'

She snatched René's clipboard from him, eyeing the schedule critically. Around them, the backstage area was crammed with models, clothes, make-up artists, hairdressers and reporters, everyone wanting something from her.

'Camille, more flowers have arrived. Where do you want them?'

'Alejandro Simón from *El País* wants to interview you after the show. Can you give him five minutes?'

'Camille, how is this belt supposed to be styled?'

It was hot, noisy and chaotic. Camille usually revelled in the pre-show atmosphere, but today she couldn't stop thinking about the blackmail notes, and the fact that Isobel was threatening to expose Camille's darkest secrets.

Then one voice cut through the mayhem:

'Camille.'

She turned around to see Nicolas. He looked handsome and composed, in a crisp white shirt and stylish suit trousers, unflappable amidst the chaos. Once again, she realized how lucky she was to have him on her side, always looking out for her.

Nicolas ensured Camille's attention was on him before he spoke, saying discreetly, 'She's here.'

A burst of adrenaline surged through Camille, then her face hardened, and she turned to René. 'Keep everything under control here. I need ten minutes.'

Camille looked at Nicolas, their eyes meeting in silent understanding. 'Let's go.'

It was time for the showdown.

Chapter 29

'Morning, Emilia,' Paulo said, as he approached the hotel's reception desk. 'You're looking beautiful today.' He'd parked his car a short walk from the hotel, leaving it on a deserted track far from the main road. Today was all about flying under the radar – he wanted to keep a low profile for now.

Panic jolted across her face as she saw him, and she quickly stood up, coming out from behind the reception desk and ushering him to one side. 'Paulo—'

'Hey, it's all cool, just relax,' he grinned, putting his hands on her shoulders and exerting a gentle pressure. Emilia was dressed in the hotel's uniform of a navy suit and crisp white shirt, her dark hair neatly pulled back in a chignon, her make-up discreet. 'You won't get into any trouble, I promise.'

She looked up at him, big dark eyes, and nodded.

'Did you manage to arrange everything this morning, with the note?'

Meet Me at Sunset

She nodded once again. 'Yes. On the breakfast tray, as you said.'

'You're more than just a pretty face,' he grinned. 'I knew I could rely on you.'

'But Paulo, I . . . I don't know if I can let you in today. There's so much security, and I'm under strict instructions not to let anyone enter unless they're on the guest list.'

'C'mon, Emilia,' he smiled flirtatiously, reaching out to brush a stray hair away from her face. 'You know me. You know I'm friends with Lucas and the whole Fontaine family. Where's the harm?'

'So why can't *they* let you in?' she frowned.

'Maybe my invite got lost in the post,' he grinned. 'Look, I'll tell you the truth. Lucas and I had a stupid argument. I feel really bad about it and I want to make things up to him. If you let me in, you'd be helping two guys repair a twenty-year friendship. That'd be your good deed for the day,' he laughed charmingly.

'I could lose my job,' she said, firmly.

'That's OK, Emilia, you don't have to . . . But then I don't have to keep those photos of you to myself either. I'll could just walk out of here right now and give them straight to your boyfriend.'

Panic crossed her face. 'No, please don't, if he ever finds out about you—'

'I don't know why you're so worried – you look great in them, that body underneath your uniform. He's a lucky guy, I hope he knows that?'

'Paulo . . . how could you?' She gazed up at him, with tears in her eyes, only to meet his pitiless ones. 'OK, I'll take you.'

She quickly ran behind the desk to remove a key from the drawer. 'We'll have to go the back way,' she said tearfully, pointing him towards a deserted corridor that led past the kitchen. 'Follow me.'

'With pleasure,' Paulo replied, falling into step behind her.

The door flew open, and Isobel looked up as Camille and Nicolas walked in.

'What the hell is going on?' she demanded, as she jumped to her feet. 'Did you seriously tell someone to lock me in here?'

Camille's gaze was like ice. 'Yes, I did. I didn't want you to have the chance to cause any more damage.'

'What are you talking about?'

'You can drop the innocent act, Isobel. We know why you're here, what you're planning. We know that you interned for Camille Andre.'

Shock registered on Isobel's face, then she regained her composure. 'Yes, I did. I'm surprised you remembered. You barely paid any attention to me at the time.' Camille's eyes flickered briefly to Nicolas, and Isobel had a flash of realization. 'You didn't remember, did you?'

'Do you know how many interns we had come through the offices over the years?' Camille defended herself. 'I was running a business, not a crèche. Of course I can't remember them all.'

'Perhaps not. But you would think you'd have remembered the one who designed the bag that revolutionized your company.' Isobel's breath was coming fast, her blue eyes blazing. She felt triumphant. She'd dreamed endlessly of confronting Camille over the years, and now she finally had the chance to say everything she wanted.

'So it *was* you,' Camille declared, turning to Nicolas. 'You admit it!'

Isobel followed Camille's gaze, taking in Nicolas Martin. She knew who he was, of course. She'd seen him at the yacht party, and she knew that he and Camille were old friends; that he'd been one of the founders of the business, and that he now worked for American Athletics, who would be launching their collaboration with Camille Andre any moment now.

'Of course I admit it,' Isobel laughed. '*You're* the one who's been keeping it a secret all these years, taking credit for my work. I designed that bag, Camille, and you know it. You made a fortune from it and took the credit. You're a liar and a fraud!'

'Please, Isobel, you sound pathetic,' Camille scoffed. 'I took what was little more than a scribble on a piece of paper and turned it into one of the bestselling bags of all time. Do you think you'd have done that on your own? Your sketch would have ended up in the bin if Andre hadn't picked it up. Besides, I think you're forgetting about the contract you signed – everything produced remained the property of the studio. Even our head designers don't get name checks – they design for the company, for Camille Andre.'

'But . . . but it's wrong!' Isobel exploded, suddenly feeling uncertain. This conversation was not going the way she'd planned, and after being hit with the shocking news of Stuart's affair, Isobel wasn't sure that she could take much more.

Nicolas stepped forward, placing a hand on Camille's

shoulder. 'The most important thing is that we've found out the truth and the show can go ahead. Everything else can be dealt with afterwards.'

But Camille wasn't easily pacified. 'No, Nicolas. I won't be accused of something I didn't do. We tried to find you, Isobel. I asked Andre how he got the sketch. He spoke with Personnel, and we were told that you'd left, gone back home. You hadn't even given us any warning – you simply didn't come back.'

'My father was dying!' Isobel burst out, her voice breaking at the memory. The day after I drew that sketch, I went back to my apartment on cloud nine. I knew Andre had taken it to show you, and I was ecstatic, thinking that my career was about to take off. But when I got in there was a message on my answering machine from my mum, telling me my dad had had a heart attack and I needed to come home right away. I didn't even hesitate, just threw a few things into an overnight bag and got a taxi to the airport. He died the following week.'

Camille softened, just a little, at this. 'I'm sorry,' she said gently.

'I wanted to come back, but I couldn't. I had to stay and look after my mum. There was no way I could leave her, alone and grieving, while I went gallivanting round Europe, following some frivolous dream. It was over,' Isobel said distantly. 'Can you imagine how I felt when I saw that photograph of Naomi Campbell carrying *my* bag? The one *I'd* designed. I had to watch your career, your company, go stratospheric, whilst I was stuck in Edinburgh, mourning my father, caring for my mother. That bag was in every magazine, carried by every celebrity, and all my friends bought high-street rip-offs. You were out there, living the life that should have been mine.'

Camille shifted uncomfortably, and Isobel knew her words were hitting home. Camille had had the backing of Andre and Nicolas and the juggernaut that was Camille Andre.

'*You* had the money to make it happen, but *I* had the vision. The bag's success proved that I was talented, that I should have had a wonderful future ahead of me, snapped up by one of the big fashion houses. Instead, I've been little better than a trophy wife, running a boutique financed by my husband, who – it turns out – is a lying, cheating piece of shit.'

Camille frowned, and Isobel went on, 'Yes, the wonderful surgeon who treated your precious son has been having an affair, and you can read all about it in the papers next week. Maybe I'll tell my side of the story – I'm sure the press would be very interested in what I have to say.'

Camille and Nicolas exchanged glances. 'Isobel, I don't know exactly what's going on, but it seems like you've been through a lot and perhaps I can understand why you've behaved the way you have, even if I can't forgive it. We're not going to pay you the money, but perhaps we can find a way to avoid getting the police involved.'

Isobel's mind was spinning, but she slowly registered Camille's words. 'Police? What are you talking about?'

'The threats, Isobel. The blackmail. The smashed wing mirror, the bag covered in blood . . .'

Isobel's mouth fell open, and she looked stunned. 'I don't know what you're talking about.'

'Oh, come off it, Isobel. It all fits. You said it yourself

– I had the life you should have had. So you talked yourself into believing that it was justified? That you *deserved* my money, and would stop at nothing to get it?'

'No, I—'

'Was it really a coincidence that you were here this week, when I was launching the new range? Your husband told me that you have a whole collection of "Camille" bags.'

Isobel looked ashamed, seemingly caught out. 'No, it wasn't a coincidence,' she admitted. 'I knew you were going to be here. I . . . I don't know what I thought exactly. I wanted to know if you'd recognize me. Maybe I thought about confronting you. But I don't know *anything* about threats or blackmail or anything, I swear to you.'

Nicolas looked at his watch anxiously. 'Camille, they'll be waiting for you. It's time to start. Let's just call the police and let them deal with her.'

'You can't keep me locked in here,' Isobel insisted, raising her voice. 'I didn't do anything!'

'So you're going to deny this, are you?' Camille hissed, pulling that morning's note from her pocket and brandishing it in front of Isobel's face. She was shaking with adrenaline, as Isobel took in the words:

One million dollars before the show starts, or I tell the world the truth about Andre's death.

'I've never seen that before in my life,' Isobel insisted, knowing how clichéd that sounded, and terrified that her denial made her sound guilty. 'Camille, I promise you, I'm not lying, you have to believe me!'

'Come on, Camille,' Nicolas said firmly. 'We can't wait any longer. Let the police deal with her. It's out of our hands now. Don't let her leave this room.' He told the security guard.

Camille was staring at Isobel intently, her forehead creasing in thought as Nicolas guided her out of the room. As they headed back towards the show, she couldn't shake the feeling that Isobel was telling her the truth.

'Nicolas . . . what if we are wrong?'

Chapter 30

Stephanie and Catherine arrived at the palacio, stepping out of the limo Camille had arranged for them. The sun was high overhead, reflecting off the dazzling white walls of the building, and the palm trees either side of the entrance rippled gently in the light breeze.

'Ready?' Catherine asked with a smile.

'As I'll ever be,' Stephanie responded. She hadn't told Catherine about the situation with Lucas – she'd already burdened her with enough of her problems, and besides, today Catherine would be the star of the show and Stephanie didn't want anything to detract from that. She pasted on a smile and the two women walked up the steps and through the arched doorway, into the lobby where a bank of photographers and journalists were waiting to greet the new arrivals.

Stephanie felt wretched inside, though she looked a million dollars, and she turned and posed, trying her best not to react to the intrusive questions from the press.

'Stephanie, is it true you walked off the set of *Fields of Barley*?'

'Have you been hiding in Mallorca this whole time?'

'Steph, what would you say to the rumours that you're difficult to work with?'

'Ignore them,' Catherine murmured, not letting her dazzling smile slip for a moment as she reassured Stephanie. 'Thanks, guys, that's enough for today,' she purred, putting a hand on the small of Stephanie's back and steering her away from the press pack.

'Thank you,' Stephanie said gratefully.

'Hold your head high and keep smiling,' Catherine told her. 'They're looking for a reaction – don't give them one. Now, duty calls. I'll see you later, darling.' Catherine squeezed her arm reassuringly, then melted away into the crowd, heading backstage to prepare for the show.

Left alone, Stephanie felt a moment's uncertainty, but then she remembered Catherine's advice, lifting her chin and marching boldly towards the Sunset Room. There was a real buzz in the atmosphere, a sense of excitement now that a gaggle of A-listers had descended on the sleepy town of Belleza. Stephanie almost felt resentful that the place which had become her sanctuary had been invaded in this way. Catherine had given her a place to rest and recuperate, to take stock of all the crazy things that had happened to her over the past couple of years, but Stephanie knew that soon it would be time to head back to real life.

She heard another round of yelling from the photographers, and turned to see who had arrived. Her heart lurched, and she almost tripped in the vertiginous heels she was wearing. It was Lucas, hand-in-hand with Elle, who was practically wrapped around him and beaming from ear to ear as the camera bulbs flashed. Stephanie wanted to flee but she couldn't seem to move, her feet glued to the floor, unable to take her eyes off the unfolding scene.

Lucas looked so handsome, his dark hair artfully tousled, his scar only serving to highlight how attractive he was. Stephanie thought how unfair it was that just yesterday they'd been in one another's arms without a care in the world, excited to see what the future held. Now he was having a baby with his ex-girlfriend, and Stephanie didn't know if he wanted to see her again – or, indeed, if she wanted to be with him and be part of his complicated situation.

Her gaze flickered to Elle beside him, tall and leggy and beautiful, her incredible figure showing no trace of a baby bump yet, but she was undoubtedly glowing as she held onto Lucas's hand tightly, gazing up at him adoringly. Life wasn't fair, Stephanie thought bitterly. Even if she and Lucas somehow worked it out and decided to give their fledgling relationship a chance, Elle and the baby would always be part of their lives.

As if sensing her eyes on him, Lucas looked around, his gaze finding her immediately in the crush of people. His expression was full of warmth and regret and sadness, but then Elle tugged on his hand, leaning across to whisper something in his ear and Lucas turned to her, giving her his undivided attention.

Stephanie swallowed, exhaling deeply, before remembering Catherine's words once again. She smiled brightly, enthusiastically greeting the famous faces she'd met earlier that week at the yacht party, as she made her way to her front-row seat.

Elle's fingers were laced through Lucas's, and she was holding his hand so tightly that it was almost painful as she sashayed through to the Sunset Room, throwing a smug look to the security guard.

Outwardly, Lucas was smiling and pleasant to everyone he saw, but inwardly he was in turmoil. It felt as though his life had been turned upside down, as though everything had been put in a bag and shaken up and he had no control any more.

When he'd arrived at the palacio, Elle was already there, waiting for him. It looked like she'd been one of the first to arrive. Camille had been furious at Lucas's request to put her on the guest list, and had outright refused at first. He'd had to beg, insisting that there was a good reason, and that he'd explain everything later. Fortunately, his mother seemed too distracted – presumably by all the preparations – to put up too much of a fight.

Lucas wanted to talk to Elle, but they hadn't had a moment alone so far. Instead, she'd paraded him round like a prize-winning racehorse, unwilling to let him out of her sight. She looked drop-dead gorgeous, Lucas had to give her that, in a Camille Andre pink tweed mini dress with oversized gold buttons, which had been a present from Camille last Christmas. But he realized now that he no longer loved her. Their relationship should have been over a long time ago, and she'd been right to end it.

Lucas was determined not to run from his responsibilities, though, and if he'd fathered a child, he wanted to be there for them, to play a positive role in their life. The prospect of fatherhood brought up all kinds of emotions linked to the death of his own father, and the way Andre had been alternately distant then spoiling him materially. Lucas vowed to do better.

He didn't know how this situation would play out, but he would stand by Elle and be the best father he could. But he hoped – perhaps selfishly – that he could work things out with Stephanie. He was really falling for her, and had dared to think of a future with her, but she'd looked so disappointed and regretful when he'd seen her moments ago, he couldn't imagine how they could make it work now. He'd try to convey his feelings in that one quick glance, but he knew exactly what the scene must looked like to Stephanie, with Elle hanging off him, showing him off like a trophy.

'Elle, can we talk?' he suggested, as they moved from the chaos of the Sunset Room, where the show was about to take place, to the mayhem of backstage. 'We must be able to find a quiet spot somewhere around here.'

'Not now, Lucas,' Elle admonished him, as she looked around to see who else was there, her wide blue eyes lighting up as she spotted famous models and influential journalists.

'Just five minutes. I really think we need to discuss . . .' He broke off as he saw his mother and Nicolas coming towards them through the crowd. His gut lurched. Whilst Camille had agreed to let Elle attend, it was wisest to keep the two of them apart. And he knew that at some point he needed to speak to his mother about what had happened at the restaurant – the fact that it had been closed down and Paulo seemed to have disappeared off the face of the earth.

She was an investor, so he needed to tell her, but he wanted to wait until after the show. Plus, he was hoping that by then he'd have located Paulo and everything would be resolved. He didn't want to bother her with that right now. It wasn't unusual for Camille to be anxious before a show, but right now she seemed more stressed than he'd ever seen her.

'Everything OK?' he asked, trying to keep his tone light, as he air-kissed her on both cheeks and shook hands with Nicolas.

'Not exactly,' Camille said tightly. She and Nicolas exchanged glances as Lucas wondered what was going on. His mother stepped closer, keeping her voice as low as she could with all the noise in the background. 'It's been a challenging morning. We can catch up tomorrow, but everything's going wrong right now. Katerina has called in sick, the one who was supposed to be wearing the skintight bodice, so we're having to change the entire running order.'

'I can do it,' Elle suggested.

Camille turned to her as though noticing her for the first time. She exhaled sharply and shook her head. 'No, Elle. I've had quite enough drama for today without you getting involved.'

'No drama, I promise,' Elle said, as Lucas stared at her in surprise. It was as though she was a different person, polite and demure, standing tall and elegant. 'Camille, you know that I've always wanted to model for Camille Andre. Why would I do anything to jeopardize that?'

To Lucas's surprise, his mother seemed to be genuinely considering it.

'You know that I can do this, Camille. I'm a professional model – it's my job – and that bodice will fit me perfectly. I understand that you may not like me, but surely you can put that aside for the sake of the show. What choice do you have?'

'She's right,' Nicolas said to Camille. 'Why not give her a chance?'

Camille hesitated for a moment, before agreeing to the inevitable. 'All right,' she said quietly. 'But any more histrionics . . .'

'None, I promise!' Elle was gleeful. 'Thank you, Camille,' she managed to say without a hint of sulkiness.

Lucas looked on in disbelief, wondering what he'd just witnessed. He was astonished that Elle had put herself forward, and even more astonished that his mother had agreed. As Elle was about to rush off towards the make-up chair, he placed a hand lightly on her arm.

'But what about . . .?' he trailed off.

'What about what, Lucas?' she said, a dangerous edge to her voice.

'Your . . . condition, that tight bodice,' he murmured, aware of his mother and Nicolas watching the conversation.

'It's fine,' Elle replied dismissively, shaking off his hand. 'Don't worry about it.'

'What do you mean?' Camille asked, turning to her son. 'Her *condition*?'

'It doesn't matter,' Elle was almost pleading. 'Forget about it, Lucas.'

'Forget about it?' Lucas was stunned. 'What do you . . .? *Maman*, Elle's pregnant.'

Camille's mouth fell open in shock. She looked from Lucas to Elle in disbelief.

'Yes, I am.' Elle's demeanour changed, as she smiled manically and wrapped her arms around Lucas. 'We're both ecstatic. So, given that you're going to be my baby's grandmother, I think you should point me in the direction of the runway, because we're just wasting time here.'

It took Camille a moment to recover, then she shook her head. 'No. Absolutely not. That bodice is like an extra skin, I don't know what's going on here, but this is one surprise too many today. We'll talk about this later. Nicolas, let's go back to our original plan. Anouk can double up on the first look, Livia on the second then—'

As they began to walk off together, a look of panic crossed Elle's face. 'Wait!' she called out. 'I didn't mean it . . . Please let me do it, I'm not pregnant, I promise.'

Lucas and Camille looked at her in horror and confusion. 'What?'

'I'm not pregnant, OK? I lied. Now please just let me walk in the show, you can't do it without me!'

Camille laughed in disbelief, as Lucas's face was a mask of disbelief, betrayal and confusion flashing across his features.

'Are you OK?' Nicolas asked softly, coming across to him.

'I can't believe it. I can't believe she would . . . What are you saying, Elle?'

'I'm sorry, OK, Lucas. I didn't want to hurt you, but I must do the show today . . .'

'You told me I was going to be a father.' Lucas laughed

hollowly. I took it seriously, I took *you* seriously. I'd even told . . .' His head snapped up as he realized who he needed to speak to. 'I need to find Stephanie.'

'Stephanie? That's a brilliant idea,' Camille exclaimed. 'Why didn't I think of her before? She'd be perfect, Lucas. Where is she? Is she here?'

'I didn't mean . . . but yes, she'd be perfect. I'll go find her,' he said, suddenly desperate to see her. 'I'll be as quick as I can.'

'Stephanie?' Elle shrieked. 'You're going to put that *troll* in the show instead of me? She's short and ugly and . . . You can't! It should be me!'

She was raising her voice now and people were starting to stare. It felt to Lucas horribly like they were right back at the beach after the yacht party.

'Call security,' Camille said under her breath, as Nicolas signalled for two burly guards to come over and escort her away. Elle was determined not to go quietly, but right now they all had other things on their mind.

'Lucas, find Stephanie, I need to get her into hair and make-up as quickly as possible,' Camille instructed.

'Camille, we need to start the show,' Nicolas said urgently. 'We're fifteen minutes over, and people are getting restless.'

Camille nodded, searching the crowd for René, who was at her side in moments. 'Tell everyone we'll start in ten minutes, then get the models lined up for a final inspection.'

As René nodded and got to work, Camille exhaled and turned to Nicolas.

'It's all right,' he assured her. 'We're almost there. Everything's under control.'

Meet Me at Sunset

Camille looked up at him, her almond eyes wide and uncertain. 'But what if Isobel's telling the truth?' she asked him. 'What if she didn't send the notes, and the real threat is still out there?'

Chapter 31

Lucas could sense the restlessness in the air as he stormed back through to the Sunset Room. Mutters of disquiet were increasing in volume, annoyed expressions on famous faces. Some of the guests had grown tired of sitting and had got to their feet, hands on hips, immaculately painted lips pouting. These people were used to the world revolving around them, and didn't expect to have to wait around. Lucas knew he had to act fast.

He scanned the room and quickly located Stephanie, chatting with Emmanuelle Alt beside her. She looked so elegant and poised, so chic in a white suit that showed off her incredible figure. To him, she stood out even amongst the renowned beauties in the room. A wave of anxiety washed over him as he realized how close he'd come to losing her – he couldn't believe what Elle had done, or that he'd fallen for it. What an idiot. But there was no time to think about all of that now . . .

When Stephanie saw him approach, her face lit up and Lucas felt a jolt of hope.

'Stephanie, I know this sounds crazy, and there's no time to explain properly, but we're a model short and my mother would be honoured if you'd step in today. Regardless of what you think of me right now, you'd be doing her the biggest favour.'

Panic flashed across Stephanie's face. 'Me? But I'm not a model, Lucas. I can't do it, I . . . In front of all these people?' She glanced around the packed room, her eyes wide with fear. 'I'm sorry, Lucas, I can't.'

Lucas crouched down beside her. 'Look, I understand why you're nervous, and why you wouldn't want everyone's eyes on you right now. But I hate to see you not believe in yourself. The girl I fell for is strong and confident and beautiful, and I believe in you, Stephanie. Life is all about taking risks – so why not take a chance on this one?'

'The girl you fell for?' Stephanie repeated, her expression soft as she took in his words.

'Yes,' Lucas nodded. 'And I'll explain everything properly later, but I'm really hoping we can give things – give *us* – the chance we deserve.' Tentatively, Lucas reached for her hands, taking them in his. 'There's something you need to know – Elle isn't pregnant.'

Stephanie's forehead creased into a frown as she struggled to take in what he was saying. 'What? But this morning—'

'She lied,' Lucas said simply. 'She's not pregnant. It was a way to get an invite to the show today. I don't know what she was planning, but when she heard one of the models was sick, she pushed herself forward and confessed she wasn't pregnant.'

Stephanie's mouth fell open in shock. 'But that's crazy. *She's* crazy. Why would anyone lie about . . .?' She trailed off in disbelief.

'I know,' Lucas agreed grimly. 'It's . . . unbelievable. But I hope that we can put all this behind us and carry on where we left off. I think we could have something special . . .'

Stephanie smiled hesitantly. 'I'd like that too, I really would. But it's a lot to take in.'

'I understand.' His eyes sparkled, 'But *right now* we're a model short and the only person my mother wants on the Camille Andre runway is you. You'd be amazing up there. I wish you'd believe in yourself, Stephanie Moon, half as much as I believe in you.'

Lucas was still kneeling beside her, oblivious to the rest of the room. Stephanie reached down to stroke the stubble on his cheek, and Lucas smiled, suddenly feeling that everything was going to be OK.

'All right,' Stephanie agreed, her blue eyes sparkling. 'I'll do it.'

'That's amazing! *You're* amazing,' Lucas grinned, leaping up and reaching out a hand to help her to her feet. 'And I cannot wait to make up for lost time. But this fashion show is starting in about thirty seconds, and my mother is going to have a heart attack if we don't get you into your outfit right now. Follow me.'

He set off backstage, pulling Stephanie along behind him, and she giggled with excitement and happiness. 'Let's do this.'

Isobel paced up and down inside the banqueting room. The door was locked, and outside she knew that the security guard was still there standing sentry; she could hear him on his walkie-talkie speaking in Spanish.

Isobel kept thinking back to what Camille had said

about being blackmailed. What were the words she had used? *The smashed wing mirror, the blood . . .*

She thought of Nicolas and Camille standing together, then she thought of Lucas . . .

There was something that was gnawing away at Isobel's consciousness, a memory . . .

Then something clicked.

She realized instantly that she needed to get out of this room as quickly as possible. If the police arrived and she was taken away for questioning, it would be too late.

She looked around her. The windows in the room looked out over the extensive gardens, but they were all locked when she tried them. She looked around her once more at the large room. It appeared to be the type of space where a wedding might be held. At the end of the room there was a set of large double doors. Without much hope, she walked towards them. They were room-height, perhaps hiding a big storage area for furniture. She turned the handle and the door opened towards her but, instead of another storage area, she found another big room. It appeared to be an overspill area overlooking one of the hotel's pretty patios.

She walked through into the second room and towards a set of large French doors. She tried one of the door handles and to her delight they opened silently, and she stepped out onto the terrace, free at last.

So much for security.

The show was starting, and time was running out . . .

Camille was on autopilot, checking over the models' looks, making final tweaks before they stepped out onto the runway. The atmosphere was as exhilarating as ever, a maelstrom of make-up artists and stylists and dressers, enormous spotlights looming above them and whirring fans to try to combat the heat. There were rails of garments with photographs of every look taped to the wall above, and thousands of dollars' worth of clothes were slipped off and hastily discarded as the models raced to make their quick changes.

But finally, it seemed as though everything was coming together. The show was running smoothly, and the audience were enjoying themselves, seemingly forgetting the earlier delays.

Camille was thankful for that, but her mind was racing. Nicolas had convinced her that Isobel was the one responsible for the notes, and they'd left her in the banqueting suite to be watched by security. As soon as the show was over and the VIPs had departed, the police would be called. Camille didn't want them arriving mid-show, interrupting the spectacle with sirens and flashing lights. Camille Andre's first collaboration would make headlines for all the wrong reasons.

But something still felt wrong to Camille. How could Isobel have known the details of Andre's death? How could she have learned the secret Camille had been keeping for all these years? It didn't make sense. Camille was terrified that they'd accused the wrong person, and the real blackmailer was still out there, biding their time . . .

'Camille, thank you so much. This is the most beautiful dress I've ever worn – and I've worn a few!'

Camille looked up to see Catherine Zeta-Jones beside her, the image of a bombshell in a silver silk gown which clung to her curves. It was overlaid with sheer lace panels and decorated with hundreds of hand-sewn beaded flowers.

Camille was almost speechless. Despite all of her anxieties, this was a moment to be savoured, the purpose that gave her so much joy; beautiful clothes that made women feel beautiful. 'It's I who should thank you, Catherine. You look divine; it's exactly how this dress should be worn. I couldn't have chosen anyone better for Camille Andre.'

The two women hugged, with Camille taking care not to disturb an inch of Catherine's look, before the Welsh siren stepped out onto the runway, receiving a deafening cheer from the crowd, sashaying down the catwalk like she belonged there. It was almost over, Camille realized with relief, and the show had gone without a hitch. But there was still something . . .

She turned around and saw Nicolas. As ever, he was standing at a discreet distance, but close enough that he could be there in moments if she needed him. He was always there for her. She caught his eye, and he moved towards her.

'Everything OK?'

'I just can't shake the feeling that Isobel was telling the truth, Nicolas. I'm terrified something's going to happen. She could be the key to solving the riddle.'

'You could be making a mistake,' Nicolas said.

'I need to be sure, and the only way I can do that is by speaking to her.'

'We can do that after the show,' he told her, before Camille's attention was taken by Catherine, returning backstage followed by a wave of applause. She was glowing, a beaming smile across her face, and Camille could see that she'd had a ball out there.

'Your turn,' Catherine winked, holding her hand out to Camille. 'It's time for you to take your bow.'

Camille took her hand with a smile. 'I want Stephanie too. Has anyone seen her?'

'I'm here,' Stephanie said shyly, stepping forward with Lucas just behind her. 'Are you sure?'

'Of course,' Camille insisted. 'You saved the day.'

The three women held hands and stepped out onto the runway. The cheers and applause and whistles rose in volume as Camille took in the crowd, dazzled by the bright lights and the popping of the camera flashes. She felt grateful that she had Catherine and Stephanie with her. Ever since Andre's death, it had felt odd going out there on her own, as though a piece of her was missing. She always thought of him in these moments, wondering what he'd think of the show, if he'd approve of the collection she'd given her all to pull together.

The guests had risen to their feet in a standing ovation, and Camille saw so many faces she recognized, feeling the warmth and goodwill in the room. She glanced up as she always did, in a silent tribute to Andre, pushing down the guilt that inevitably assailed her when she thought about the accident and its aftermath. She hoped Andre's spirit was with her today, that he was looking over her when she needed protection. And she hoped Nicolas was right – that Isobel *was* the blackmailer and they were safe from the threats that had been made in the notes. But a shiver ran through her as her eyes sought out the darkest corners of the room, wondering if someone was out there, watching. Someone who meant her harm and would stop at nothing to expose her . . .

Backstage, Lucas watched as Stephanie walked out onto the runway beside Camille. Pride and happiness bubbled up inside him, along with hope and anticipation for what was to come. He felt like an idiot for believing Elle's lies, and for not ending things with her months ago, but he told himself he'd been trying to do the right thing.

'Hello, Lucas.'

Lucas whipped round as he heard a familiar voice behind him.

'Paulo! Where the hell have you been? I've been trying to call you.' Memories of last night's humiliation came rushing back – the locked restaurant, and those goons telling him the rent hadn't been paid. Now that Paulo was here, he could finally explain. Surely it was all a mistake?

A sardonic smile crept across Paulo's face. 'Didn't Elle fill you in? I'm surprised as I've spent the past twenty-four hours in her bed . . .'

Rage flared briefly within Lucas, before he remembered what Elle had done to him, and he reminded himself that they were no longer together. It hurt, he couldn't deny that – his best friend had betrayed him. He didn't understand why Paulo was behaving like this, but he wasn't going to give him the satisfaction of showing how much his words had affected him.

'I hope you'll both be very happy.'

Paulo shook his head. 'I don't want your sloppy seconds. I can do better.'

Lucas stared at him, his anger rising as he took in the

coldness in Paulo's eyes, the unmistakeable tension in the air between them. It seemed clear that Paulo had taken something, from his dilated pupils and the telltale clenching of his jaw, but drugs alone didn't explain his behaviour.

'What the hell are you doing?' Lucas asked. 'What happened to the money for the restaurant? You know I'd have helped you out if you were in trouble.'

Paulo laughed mirthlessly. 'Always the last to figure out what's going on, aren't you? So many secrets, and poor Lucas is too stupid to see the truth.'

'You little—' Lucas broke off as Camille, Catherine and Stephanie emerged triumphantly from the runway. René was immediately on hand to offer glasses of champagne, and Catherine was swallowed up by the excited crowd, everyone eager to speak to the star of the show. Stephanie came straight to Lucas's side, a questioning expression on her face as she looked at Paulo.

'Hello, Stephanie,' he said, with an unpleasant smile, flagrantly ogling her revealing dress.

'Hey,' she replied neutrally.

'By the way, Lucas,' Paulo continued, jerking his chin in Stephanie's direction. 'You're welcome to *my* sloppy seconds.'

Lucas lunged at him, his fist raised and ready to strike.

'Lucas, no!' Camille screamed.

'What the hell's going on?' Nicolas yelled, darting across to put himself between the two men and pulling Lucas away, his hands on his shoulders to calm him down. People were turning to stare, and Lucas was breathing heavily, looking murderously at Paulo.

'You're so angry, Lucas,' Paulo taunted him. 'I bet your

therapist would have a field day with that. What did she diagnose, hmm? *Daddy issues . . .?'*

'Screw you, Paulo,' Lucas shot back, exhaling deeply as he ran his hands through his hair.

Stephanie placed a calming hand on his arm, and there was a moment's silence before the onlookers gradually went back to what they were doing, conversations resuming, and fresh champagne being poured. Only Lucas, and those standing near him, heard a voice say, 'It was you.'

Lucas turned and recognized the woman who'd spoken. It was Isobel, the wife of his surgeon, Stuart. She'd been at his restaurant the other night, and she was friends with Stephanie. Right now, she was as white as a sheet as she pointed at Paulo.

'Nice to see you again, Isobel,' he smirked. 'We had a lot of fun the other night, didn't we?'

'*You* were there that night,' she said, her voice shaking, pointing to Paulo. 'You said, "*We* were driving too fast on the mountain road, racing" . . . you must have been there . . . the way you asked all those questions about Camille when we were together.'

Lucas blinked, a sudden pressure in his skull like a migraine, his father's voice ringing in his head.

'*Lucas, slow down, huh?*'

Then his mother's sharp voice jolted him back to the present.

'Get everyone out of here now. Call the police . . .' Camille stared at Paulo, slowly shaking her head in shock and anger and disbelief. 'I should have known . . . I should have realized all along . . . It was *you.*'

Chapter 32

Within minutes, the backstage area was cleared. Acting under Camille's instructions, René expertly shepherded everyone through to the bar and terrace area where a drinks reception had been set up, and the VIP guests were none the wiser that anything out of the ordinary was taking place. A couple of journalists attempted to linger, having heard raised voices and sensing something was amiss, but the burly security guards soon dealt with them.

'I've called the police. They'll be here shortly,' Nicolas said discreetly to Camille, who nodded in thanks.

Paulo was pacing the room like a caged animal, fury and self-righteousness emanating from him.

'You could have just paid me the money, Camille,' he said, rounding on her, his eyes wild and his face contorted. 'And all this would have gone away. But now everyone will know, and your reputation will be ruined.'

'What is he talking about?' Lucas frowned. 'What money?'

'It would have been a drop in the ocean to you, Camille. But you were as tight-fisted as ever and couldn't bear to part with it. Maybe you thought I was bluffing, but you underestimated me. I'll tell the world!'

'What's going on?' Lucas demanded, looking as though he might explode in frustration.

'So it was you, Paulo. I should have guessed as much, you were always spiteful and jealous of my family,' Camille said, turning to her son. 'It appears Paulo has been blackmailing me for some time, until he got greedy.'

'Blackmailed?' Lucas burst out. 'About what? Wait, is this to do with the restaurant?'

Paulo laughed loudly. 'Lucas, you really are pathetic. You think this was all about your little restaurant? No one cares about that. Just go back to being a spoilt little rich boy, it's what you do best. You don't need to pretend to earn a living, Mummy will bail you out, just like she always has.'

Lucas looked shocked by the venom in Paulo's voice. 'But what was the blackmail about?'

Paulo, seething with rage, stared straight at Camille. 'Why don't you tell him?'

Everyone turned to her, and Nicolas put a steadying hand on her arm.

'It's about the accident,' Camille said carefully. 'Andre's accident.'

'Tell him the truth,' Paulo heckled. 'Tell him what really happened that night.'

'Stop it . . . I already know . . .' Lucas began, his voice coming out as a whisper. 'At least I think I know. It was me, wasn't it?' He looked up at Camille, his hazel eyes – which were so like her own – filled with anguish, and she felt as though her heart would break for him. She'd tried to protect him from the truth for so long, and now she'd failed.

'It was an accident, darling,' she insisted. 'It wasn't your fault.'

'I've been having flashbacks. I . . .' He trailed off, piecing together what had happened that fateful night.

'Happy birthday, Papa,' Lucas grinned, pulling him into a hug, as he toasted Andre with a glass of champagne.

'Thanks, Lucas,' Andre grinned, taking a slug from his own glass, before Lucas topped it up.

'Paulo?' Lucas offered, holding out the vintage magnum of Dom Pérignon. It had cost the equivalent of most people's monthly salary, but Andre had wanted to push the boat out on his birthday, with no expense spared.

'Don't mind if I do,' Paulo said, as he stared round the room at the wealthy-looking patrons, the beautiful women, the low-key décor that screamed old money. 'You Fontaines certainly know how to throw a party.'

'You fit right in,' Lucas laughed. 'Even if you are wearing one of my tuxedos.'

'I never needed my own. There's not much call for formal wear in Cala de la Belleza,' Paulo replied, before draining his coupe.

They were celebrating Andre's forty-ninth birthday at Badrutt's Palace in St Moritz. It was a legendary five-star hotel, beloved by celebrities and socialites, a stunning building in the centre of Saint Moritz that looked like an ancient castle. It overlooked Lake Sankt Moritz, and offered stunning views of the snowy Swiss Alps surrounding it. The Fontaines loved mountain sports and ski season was one of their favourite times of year.

Meet Me at Sunset

Camille hadn't been able to attend Andre's birthday weekend – she was being honoured with a prestigious design award at an event in Paris – so for Andre, this expensive lunch party was a culmination of a boys' weekend of skiing at a luxurious rented villa, and three days of après-ski hedonism with a dozen of his friends and his beloved son, and with Paulo invited along to keep Lucas company.

Everyone downed their glasses and cheered. Lucas was starting to feel drunk, his vision blurring, as Andre clapped his arms around Lucas and Paulo.

'Are you having a good time, boys?'

'Yes, Papa,' Lucas laughed at his father's exuberance.

'How about you, Paulo? Have you ever seen anything like this before?'

'No, I haven't.' Paulo smiled tightly, and Andre didn't seem to notice the acid touch to his tone. 'I wouldn't mind spending a lot more time in places like this. I feel right at home.'

Andre roared with laughter. 'Nice to see a guy with ambition. Right, I think it's time to take this party back to the chalet. Shall we head off, Lucas? Everyone can follow.'

'Sure,' Lucas grinned. 'You coming, Paulo?'

'Of course. You go on ahead. I'll be there shortly.'

Andre helped Lucas into his jacket and the two of them walked outside, feet crunching in the snow, the bright sun giving the late afternoon a residual warmth. Lucas carried an open bottle of champagne, taking swigs from it as they waited for the valet to bring the car round. He handed the keys to Andre and the two men climbed in.

'Top down, don't you think?' Andre said as he touched the control on the dashboard and the roof of the Ferrari convertible roof rolled back. Then he gunned the engine and the Ferrari roared to life.

Andre set off at speed, heading down the mountain on the narrow, winding roads towards their chalet, Lucas finding the air bracing, and shaking off a little of his alcoholic stupor. Before long, another car appeared in the rear-view mirror, which then shot past them at speed, overtaking on a blind bend.

'What the hell . . .' Andre began, then he burst out laughing. 'That was Paulo! Well, if he wants to play that game . . .' Andre expertly revved the engine, the car roaring as it raced after the car in front.

They quickly caught up – Paulo's GTI was no match for Andre's powerful Ferrari – and swung out to overtake, the two vehicles side by side on the narrow mountain road. Lucas was laughing uncontrollably, waving and gesticulating as they overtook Paulo.

The road was silvery with a sheen of ice forming as the sun fell, the pinpricks of fading sunlight flickering on the mountainside.

'Hey, Dad, let me drive,' Lucas grinned. 'I want to beat Paulo.'

'Lucas . . .' Andre smiled indulgently. 'I'm not sure that's such a good idea. How much have you had to drink?'

'Just a couple of glasses, I'm fine. Come on, I want to have some fun too,' Lucas pleaded. 'We're almost back at the chalet. Look,' He pointed at a passing place on the roadside. 'Pull in there and we can quickly swap over.'

Andre hesitated, then pushed his foot down on the accelerator, speeding to the spot next to the metal barrier at the side of the road and hastily pulling in. 'Quick,' he cried, as he jumped out of the car, flying high on a combination of adrenaline and cocaine. Father and son were laughing hysterically as they ran around and swapped places, Lucas taking his father's place in the left-hand driver's seat, and quickly clicking his seatbelt in place. 'I can see him!'

Meet Me at Sunset

Paulo's car breezily overtook them, and Lucas rammed his foot on the accelerator and pulled out so fast that his head slammed back against the seat, as Andre continued to fumble with his seatbelt. Lucas was laughing harder than ever as the Ferrari ate up the distance between the two cars. Paulo was going to flip when he realized it was Lucas who was cutting him up this time. Lucas knew the road, but had never driven it at this speed, the champagne was fizzing in his system. Lucas felt the coolness of the leather steering wheel in his palms, the smooth curve of the gearstick as he drove instinctively.

And then they were catching up with Paulo, and Lucas pulled out into the empty road, giving him a triumphant finger as they shot past, Andre banging on the dashboard in triumph.

'Lucas, slow down, son, be careful, huh!'

Lucas was giddy with testosterone. He turned to look at his father, relishing the feeling of excitement, how connected he felt to his father at that moment. But then he was struck with a moment of clarity, realizing his father was worried, and Lucas could see he was still struggling with his seatbelt, so he took his foot off the accelerator, and put pressure on the brake, as he approached the next bend. As he did so, he caught sight of Paulo's car coming up behind him fast in the wing mirror. Lucas barely had time to register that the gap ahead was too sharp for them both to take it at speed, and as he slammed hard on the brake, Paulo rammed into their bumper and instantly the Ferrari was lifted sideways towards the barrier, breaking through it and hitting the tree on the other side before nestling precariously close to the steep incline.

Then everything fragmented for Lucas. A scream of agony. A crunch of metal. And then blackness.

Paulo had taken the corner too sharply to see what had happened to the Ferrari as they rounded the bend. Maybe he had mistimed his overtake, he told himself, but Andre was driving like a lunatic, and it served him right if that penis-extension sports car of his had taken a dent.

He pulled over to wait for Andre and Lucas to come around the bend. Where were they? His eyes shot nervously over the side of the mountain. The drop here had no trees to break the fall, and it was a long way down . . . still no sign of them.

'Shit.'

Paulo reversed out of the verge and turned his car around, it was twilight now, and he switched his car headlights on. As he rounded the bend, he felt the air knocked out of him as his headlights picked up the mangled Ferrari, upended, and dangerously close to the mountain verge. He pulled over, his hands and legs shaking as he quickly climbed out of the vehicle, and walked in a horrified daze towards the wreck.

'No, no, no.' He dragged his hands across his scalp, willing the sight to be just a bad dream.

As he approached, he could see Andre had been thrown from the car, and was lying unconscious in the road, his limbs and neck nauseatingly contorted, blood pouring from his head. His eyes darted to the vehicle . . . Was that Lucas in the driving seat? He'd been driving? Of course . . . it was Lucas who had flipped him the bird, Lucas who always thought he was better at everything than Paulo.

Not this time.

'Help me . . .'

Paulo saw Lucas struggling in his seat, dangling upside down, as blood poured from a gash across his face, his arms flailing as he tried to release himself, caught in the snare of his seatbelt, which had saved his life, but which now threatened to kill him by strangulation.

Suddenly released from his inertia, Paulo raced over to the car. He pulled uselessly at the driver's door, which was too crushed to open properly, but with the top down, Paulo was able to stretch himself over and release the belt, groaning as Lucas dropped out of the seat with a tortured cry, partially falling into his arms.

Paulo hauled him out, then stumbled for a couple of steps before collapsing to the ground with Lucas, who was now groaning in agony.

'My dad . . .' Lucas gasped. 'Where is he . . . my dad?'

Paulo shook his head, not able to say the truth, that Andre looked like he was about meet his maker. Lucas grabbed Paulo's tuxedo jacket with his bloody hands, his words ragged.

'You . . . you did this.'

'No,' Paulo shook his head, and Lucas gripped him harder, his eyes wide and wild.

'It was you . . .' The effort seemed to drain every last effort from Lucas whose head fell back, seemingly slipping into unconsciousness as his head crashed onto the road surface.

Paulo rose to his feet, staggering back. 'You can't blame me, it was you, you idiot, if you die it's your own fault, not mine.'

Paulo scrabbled back to his car, threw himself into his seat, fumbling to get his key in the ignition. Casting one more glance in the wing mirror at the prone bodies lying in the road, his car tyres screeched as he spun the wheel around and slammed his foot on the accelerator, speeding as quickly as he could away from the scene, driving like all the demons in Hell were on his tail.

'So it was me driving . . .' Lucas said slowly, his throat thick with emotion as the memories came flooding back and the realization dawned. 'Paulo was right.'

Camille turned to Paulo, a stunned expression on her face, her tone accusing. 'I didn't know you were there. I thought Andre and Lucas were alone. I didn't know—'

'That's how I knew,' Isobel said to Camille, 'when Paulo talked about the accident, that night, he said "we were racing too fast on the mountain road." Though there was never any mention of that in the reports, which just mentioned the icy conditions.'

'I saved his life,' Paulo yelled, looking at Lucas. 'He would have choked to death if I had left him hanging there. When I realized Lucas had crashed his dad's car, I was less than a mile from Günther's Bar. It was still open. I drove straight there to use their phone and called an ambulance.'

'And then you fled,' Camille spat.

'I was in shock!' Paulo shot back. 'I didn't know what to do!'

'You saved your own skin, as usual,' Camille yelled.

'Well, you wouldn't have saved me! I'd already spent the evening being treated like the poor friend, having to borrow Lucas's clothes just to fit in and paraded around Andre's rich buddies like some kind of pet monkey. It was made clear to me exactly what my place was that night, so can you imagine what would have happened if I'd told the authorities that I'd been there when the accident happened? That we were racing? That *Lucas* was the one who was driving that night? Andre shouldn't have been driving – he'd been drinking and taking cocaine – but he was in a better state than Lucas. It's a miracle they weren't *both* killed.'

'I killed my father . . .' Lucas murmured, as everyone turned to look at him. Stephanie moved across to comfort him – whatever the truth of everything, it was clear that her heart went out to him at that moment – but Lucas barely noticed. 'I'm a murderer . . . I killed him . . . I killed my father . . .'

'No, you didn't kill your *father*.' Paulo shook his head, a triumphant expression on his face. 'It was only when Isobel told me about the rumours of an affair that were circling around before Lucas's birth that it suddenly all made sense to me. You only have to look at the two of them closely and it's obvious. Why don't you tell him, Camille?'

Lucas's head jerked up. 'Tell me what?'

Paulo stared at Camille, his dark eyes boring into hers. 'Tell him everything.'

Chapter 33

Every pair of eyes in the room turned to look at Camille. She felt sick suddenly, her pulse racing, her palms sweating. It was as though she had been plunged into the middle of a nightmare, but she knew she wouldn't wake up from this. Everything she'd fought so hard to keep buried for so long was tumbling out, and there seemed to be no way to stop it. How did Paulo know all of this? How long had he been keeping secrets, harbouring resentments, concocting his plan?

Camille glanced across at Lucas, then at Nicolas. They were both looking at her intently, waiting to see what she would do next. She opened her mouth to speak, not knowing what she was going to say, but then she was transported back to the night of the accident, the night her whole life had been turned upside down . . .

It was almost one a.m. and Camille was preparing for bed, slipping off her high heels and her gown, removing her make-up and brushing her teeth. She was exhausted. As the guest of honour at a dinner held by the Fédération de la Haute Couture de la

Mode, at which she'd been presented with an award, it wasn't the done thing to slip away early. Camille had stayed to mingle and socialize, declining invitations to the after-parties and leaving just after midnight. She was sad to miss Andre's birthday party in St Moritz, she just hoped he had behaved himself, she knew anything could happen when he was on one of his hedonistic trips.

Camille climbed in between the cool, crisp, Egyptian cotton sheets and had just turned off the lamp when the telephone by the bed began to ring. She groaned, flicking the light back on. Who was it, and what did they want at this hour?

'Madame Fontaine? I'm afraid there's been an accident . . .'

Camille went into shock. She didn't scream or cry, just calmly listened to what she was being told before replacing the receiver. Her priority was to get to Switzerland as quickly as possible to be with her son and her husband. Hysteria could wait.

Camille picked up the phone once again and instinctively found herself calling Nicolas. It felt entirely natural to reach out to him at this terrible moment. She heard the click as the call was redirected, and he sounded groggy when he came on the line.

Briefly, Camille relayed what had happened, and Nicolas was composed and focused, just as she'd hoped.

'I'm in Milan,' he told her. 'I'll go by chopper – I can be there in less than an hour. Call a taxi to Le Bourget then pack an overnight bag. I'll have a jet there waiting for you.'

'Thank you, Nicolas,' Camille said, hanging up and following his instructions. If she allowed herself to think for even a moment, she would shatter like crystal.

It was shortly after four a.m. when Camille arrived at the hospital in St Moritz. Nicolas was waiting for her as she exited the taxi and ran through the main door.

'What's happening?' she demanded, her pale face etched with fear.

Nicolas looked grave as he reached out for her. *'I'm so sorry, Camille. Andre isn't going to make it. He's on life support, but . . . they're waiting for you.'*

Camille gasped, her hands flying to her face in shock. *'No,'* she murmured, shaking her head. Her husband of more than twenty-five years, her partner in everything . . . Her stomach was churning as she asked the question, *'And Lucas?'*

'He's in a bad way. They're operating on him right now.'

'My God . . .'

Nicolas steered Camille to a seat as her legs threatened to buckle.

'What happened?' she asked. *'The officer on the phone said there'd been a car accident, but I don't know the details . . .'*

'It was a couple of miles from the chalet . . . Andre and Lucas were driving back from a lunch. I don't know exactly what happened either – the police are still investigating. The car spun out of control apparently. Perhaps there were icy conditions . . .'

The news propelled Camille to her feet. *'Show me where Lucas is. Andre too. I need to see them, I want to speak to the doctors.'*

Nicolas led her along a corridor that was perfectly white and clean. At this time in the morning, there were few people around and the hospital was eerily silent, save for the occasional nurse or doctor, their expressions formal and serious.

'Lucas is in here. But we have to wait outside,' Nicolas told her.

Hysteria was starting to build inside Camille, as she looked at the closed door separating her from her Lucas. *'I want to see him, Nicolas. I want to see my son. And Andre too. Where is he? Oh God, I need to put out a statement before the story hits the press, I need to make some calls, I don't think I can cope right now, I . . .'

She broke off as a surgeon in scrubs stepped out of the room, pulling down his mask. He was dark haired and dark skinned, and his manner was calm and reassuring.

'I'm Camille Fontaine, Lucas's mother,' she said urgently, stepping towards him.

'Madame Fontaine, I'm glad you're here. I'm Dr Bachmann. I'm so sorry for everything that's happened.'

'Thank you,' Camille managed. 'But tell me about Lucas. Can I see him?'

The surgeon looked from Camille to Nicolas. 'Just for a moment.'

He led them through into the hospital room, where Lucas lay, surrounded by machines that were bleeping and flashing, his arms hooked up to fluid and plasma. His head was a mass of bandages. A dark stain of bruising ran down the upper left side of his body from his neck right across his sternum.

Dr Bachmann saw her looking at it. 'That's a stress fracture, from his seat belt, but he's a fighter, and he is young and fit,' Dr Bachmann said gravely. 'We're expecting him to pull through, but his injuries may be life-changing. He's sustained considerable damage to his cranium, he has multiple breaks in his upper body including his collarbone, and his facial wounds are extensive, he'll need reconstructive surgery.'

'But he's alive,' Camille whispered. 'That's all that matters.'

'He is,' Dr Bachmann nodded. Camille touched her son's hand and whispered, 'I love you.' Nicolas led her from the scene, and the surgeon pointed them to a small annex room off the corridor.

'There's something else I need to discuss with you.' He told them as Camille sat, shellshocked. 'The injuries your husband sustained were catastrophic. He won't regain consciousness, you're aware of this?'

Camille glanced at Nicolas, her eyes wet and shining. 'Yes, I've been told.'

'I'm very sorry, I know this is hard. Currently, he's being kept alive artificially, but his brain is no longer functioning.'

'I understand. Are you asking for my consent to switch off the machine, is that it? I need to see him . . .'

'Yes, of course, but that's not what I'm asking right now. Your son has lost a lot of blood and needs a transfusion. His blood type is rather rare – AB negative. We are running low on stocks of that and it may not be sufficient for Lucas's immediate needs. One of his parents could have been a donor for his son, but we now know his father is not a match, perhaps you . . . perhaps we should talk privately,' he added, glancing at Nicolas.

But Camille didn't hear anything further. There was a roaring sound in her ears, as though a tsunami was heading her way, ready to destroy everything in its path, and there was nothing she could do to escape it. She had to tell Nicolas the truth.

Camille swallowed. 'Dr Bachmann, could you give us a moment alone?'

'Of course. I'll be back in a few minutes,' he said, looking from one to the other, before heading back into the operating room.

The door swung shut and the corridor was silent.

But before she could speak, Nicolas lowered his voice to a whisper. 'Lucas was driving.'

'What? How do you know?'

'The stress fracture on his collarbone. It runs from left to right across his body, he must have been sitting in the driver's seat when the car crashed.'

Camille's eyes widened and she inhaled sharply as she realized the implications of what he was saying. Andre was in a coma, on life support, and was not expected to live. Lucas was responsible for that. 'Nicolas, this will destroy him, it—'

'It's OK.' Nicolas took Camille's hands in his, trying to calm her down. He didn't want her to become hysterical in the hospital, or draw attention to them. 'I'll take care of it.'

Camille's forehead creased as she searched his face for answers. 'What will you do?'

'It doesn't matter. I'll do whatever it takes for Lucas.'

Her hands were still nestled in his. They felt small and protected, Nicolas's hands large and warm and strong. 'Thank you,' she said sincerely, but she felt dread in the pit of her stomach at what she was about to tell him.

'Nicolas, the blood transfusion . . . Andre isn't a match for his blood group and . . . neither am I.'

Camille hardly dared to meet Nicolas's eyes, and when she finally looked up, the expression on his face was a mixture of heartbreak and anguish.

'Camille,' he said, his voice ragged with emotion. 'What are you telling me?'

'I should never have kept it from you,' Camille whispered. 'You're the only one who can give him blood, Nicolas . . . but I always thought you knew, deep down . . .'

'Yes,' Nicolas whispered. 'Lucas is my son.'

In the backstage area of the palacio, Lucas had turned pale. 'You knew,' he said, turning to Nicolas, shock and betrayal written across his scarred features.

Nicolas swallowed. 'I'd suspected it long before it was confirmed, but it wasn't my place to—'

'You two had an affair?' Lucas's voice was growing louder. 'Behind my father – behind Andre's back?'

'It was one night,' Nicolas said gently. 'It should never have happened. Though I've loved your mother as long as I've known her. Andre didn't always treat Camille well, and—'

'So you thought you'd step in?' Lucas shot back. His eyes were blazing with indignation and confusion, uncertain where his loyalties lay.

'That's enough, Lucas,' Camille interjected. 'Nicolas saved your life. He donated his blood for you.'

It was possible to hear a pin drop in the silence that followed Camille's announcement; the sense of astonishment in the room was palpable.

'Let's talk about this later. In *private*,' she added pointedly, looking around at everyone else. 'There's a lot to discuss.'

Lucas set his jaw, but didn't argue. He felt as though he'd been hit by a bulldozer, and knew it would take time to process everything he'd been told today.

'There's one thing I don't understand,' Camille frowned, addressing Paulo. 'How did you know? That Nicolas was Andre's father?'

There was a long pause, and Paulo merely smirked, saying nothing. Then an unexpected voice spoke up.

'It was me,' Isobel said quietly, as everyone's head whipped round to look at her. 'I'm so sorry, Camille. I bumped into Paulo the other night in Palma. We were drinking, and indiscreet and . . .' Isobel lowered her gaze, a blush suffusing her cheeks, as the others filled in the blanks of what had likely happened between them.

'I was furious with you for . . . well, the reasons we discussed earlier,' Isobel went on. 'There were always rumours, you know, when I worked at Camille Andre. Andre's indiscretions were well known, but there was office gossip that *you* had been unfaithful too, a couple of months before you announced your pregnancy. It was all based on hearsay – some unnamed employee had seen or heard something years ago – but the whispers had never quite gone away, recirculating on nights out and passed down to new staff members.

'A couple of years ago now, I went through Stuart's medical records,' Isobel admitted, looking ashamed. 'I found Lucas's file. It was stupid, and I never should have done it, but at the time I felt so powerless and I . . . I was curious, really, but I found something I hadn't been expecting.'

'About the transfusion?' Camille asked, as Isobel nodded.

'All of the notes from the accident were there. They outlined that Lucas's blood group was rare, and that an M. Martin had been found who was able to donate. It didn't take a maths genius to add two and two together . . .'

'And then *I* had everything I needed,' Paulo said gleefully.

Camille regarded him for a long moment, narrowing her eyes. 'Why do you hate me and my family so much? We've been nothing but welcoming to you. We took you on family holidays, Lucas gave you a role in his business . . .'

'Can't you hear how patronizing you sound, Camille? That's all you've done for years – treated me like the poor kid, made me feel I should be grateful for the crumbs from your table. You made it clear from the start that I was never good enough to be friends with your precious son. And you wanted to control everything – Lucas, the restaurant . . . Why should I bow down to you and do everything you tell me? Because you have more money than me? I worked my ass off trying to keep up and then I thought, why the hell should I? You owe me, Camille. And you can afford it. I've been keeping your secrets all these years – that Lucas was the one driving, that he killed Andre – and you never appreciated it. Not to mention saving your son's life by calling the ambulance after the crash.

'So now it's time for me to get what I'm due. It's your choice, Camille – pay me the money and you'll never see me again. If not, there are a dozen journalists out there who'd be very interested in the conversation we've just had.'

'Wait!' Lucas said sharply. 'There is something else that I remember, just before the crash.' He rounded on Paulo. 'You pushed us off the road.'

Paulo's eyes flashed with anger, 'Liar!'

'It's not a lie, I remember very well now, you pushed us off the road and then you left us there to die.'

'You deserved it!' Paulo seethed. 'You and that precious father of yours thought that you were better than everyone else, you were a spoilt little rich boy then and you are a spoilt little rich boy now. I'm not sorry I drove you off the road, I'm just sorry you pulled through.'

The two men squared up to each other, but before their fists could meet, there was a sharp bang on the door, and everyone turned as it flew open and half a dozen police officers surged in.

'Paulo Torres,' one of them said, as they spotted him.

'We've had our eye on you for some time now. Dealing, fraud, embezzlement . . . I reckon we've got enough to put you away for a very long time.'

Two of the policemen grabbed his arms to restrain him, pinning them behind his back as they handcuffed him. Paulo kicked and yelled as he was dragged from the room, and Camille had the distant thought that she hoped no VIPs or journalists would witness the commotion.

Lucas looked broken as he sank down onto a chair, and Stephanie put her arms around him. Camille glanced across at Nicolas. She longed to do the same – to fall into his embrace and be comforted by him, to have him fix everything as he always did. But she feared that, this time, the situation might be broken beyond repair.

Camille's shoulders sagged and she felt utterly drained. She wanted to go back to her room and sleep for a week, hoping that when she woke up again, today would all have been some terrible dream. But as she turned to look for Nicolas, a female police officer approached her.

'Señora Fontaine? I'm afraid we're going to need to ask you some questions.'

Camille nodded wearily. 'Yes, I understand. I'll make a full statement.'

Chapter 34

Yorkshire, July 2001

In the back of the chauffeur-driven Range Rover, Lucas turned to Stephanie and smiled, reaching across to take her hand. They had just left the cosy little cottage which the production company had rented for Stephanie, and now they were being driven across the North York Moors to the set where she would resume filming *Fields of Barley*.

Lucas stifled a yawn. It was shortly after five a.m. and the sun had just risen, bright golden light spilling over the landscape. It was going to be a perfect day. Despite the early start, Lucas was mesmerized by the view – miles of desolate, craggy moorland stretching as far as the eye could see, with gently rolling hills and freshly shorn sheep cropping at the long grass.

Lucas's eyes fell on Stephanie beside him. She looked youthful and fresh, with no make-up, and her long copper hair hanging loose, but Lucas could tell that she was nervous.

After Catherine had given her the time and space she needed in Mallorca, Stephanie's confidence had gradually been rebuilt, her ambition reignited. She had finally called her agent, and Victoria had managed to smooth things over with the director, who was only too happy to have her back and resume their schedule.

Lucas liked to think that he, too, had played a role in Stephanie's renewed self-assurance. If recent events had taught him anything, it was that life was too short, and you had to seize every opportunity that came your way.

Both he and Stephanie had been through so much in the past couple of months. The revelations about Paulo had been shocking. He'd been Lucas's friend for so many years, and though Lucas had sensed in recent months that something was amiss, he could never have imagined the truth. He'd been devastated to realize how much Paulo hated him, the jealousy and resentment he'd been secretly harbouring over the years that had finally reached boiling point. But to have been blackmailing Camille, terrifying her with notes and threats when she'd welcomed him into the heart of the family . . . It was almost beyond Lucas's comprehension.

The Spanish police had arrested Paulo after the show. It turned out that they had been watching him for months, trying to gather enough evidence to compile a case against him. He had developed a lucrative sideline as one of the biggest drug dealers on their island, using the boats from his parents' hire company to receive drop-offs, which were then distributed amongst his network in Palma. As well as local contacts, their targets were the groups of young tourists who came to the island looking to party.

It explained why Paulo had been spending so much time in the capital, as well as where his recent influx of cash had come from, which he'd been spending liberally on designer labels and renting flash cars.

In recent months, Paulo had overextended himself, finding himself in debt to some extremely shady characters, who didn't like to wait for their money. It was then that he'd started siphoning funds from Il Paradiso, embezzling the restaurant's income and hiding debt letters from Lucas. Paulo's trial date was approaching and, unless his lawyer could work miracles, he was looking at a considerable stint behind bars.

The blackmail matter was more complicated. Whilst Camille had initially wanted to press charges, she knew that the truth about the accident would be revealed. It seemed that the police had put the accident down to poor driving in icy conditions and drink and drugs found in Andre's system. There were no suspicious circumstances as far as they were concerned, and no one had ever made the connection between Lucas's injuries and his position in the driving seat.

The knowledge that Lucas had been at the wheel during the accident that had killed Andre still tormented him. His judgement was undoubtedly impaired, but Andre should never have let his son drive in the first place.

Paulo had clearly rammed the Ferrari off the road either by accident or on purpose, which ultimately caused Andre's death. Taking Nicolas's advice, Camille had decided not to take it further. Paulo would likely be going to prison for a long time anyway, and by the time of his release, Camille hoped they would all have come to terms with what had happened.

It had been a lot to process, along with the discovery that Andre wasn't his father, and Nicolas was. On some level, Lucas wondered if he'd always suspected it. He and Andre were very different people, and his mother had always been close to Nicolas, though Lucas didn't know the extent of their history. As far as he was concerned, he would always think of Andre – the man who had raised him and loved him as his own – as his father. But Lucas was close to his godfather Nicolas, who had always been in their lives, and always as a force for good. He loved and respected him, and now that the truth was out there, both men were keen to build on their existing relationship.

Lucas had wrestled with the revelations over the past few weeks, but the one thing that had stopped him from losing his mind was Stephanie. They'd been inseparable in the days that followed the Camille Andre show, getting to know each other, taking walks in the old town, on the beach, swimming in the sea, and making love at night, sleeping wrapped in one another's arms. They'd fallen hard for one another, each day a step towards healing and repairing their wounds, cushioned by the bubble of happiness they'd created. Both had been damaged, in different ways, by their upbringings, each battling feelings of not being good enough or deserving of love, but together, they were slowly overcoming their insecurities and moving forwards.

The Range Rover slowed down as it approached the filming location. From his window, Lucas could see an entire set springing up out of the barren moors, with a veritable fleet of trailers and Winnebagos parked up on the scrubland, dozens of crew members scurrying around, with camera equipment, lights and reflectors all set up. Stephanie reached for the car door, then hesitated.

'Everything OK?' Lucas asked.

She looked up at him and nodded, but he could see the clear tension on her face, and the fear clouding her dazzling blue eyes.

'Stephanie, you are the most incredible woman, you know that? You've overcome so much in life, and now you're back here with the courage to face your fears. You should be so proud of yourself. *I'm* proud of you. You've been here for me these past few weeks whilst I dealt with everything I needed to, and now I'm here for you. I love you, Stephanie Moon.'

Stephanie's expression had transformed during Lucas's speech, and she gazed at him, her anxiety draining away and a look of steely determination flashing across her features. 'I love you too,' she murmured, leaning across to kiss him, and Lucas felt the familiar stirring in his body. He couldn't get enough of her. If it was up to him, they would turn the car around and head straight back to the cottage with its inviting double bed, but he knew that this was where Stephanie needed to be right now.

'I'm so glad you're with me today,' she told him. 'I wouldn't have wanted anyone else beside me on my first day back.'

'I'll be with you, whenever you need me,' Lucas promised, as the driver opened the car door and the two of them stepped out. The fresh, early morning breeze whipped across the moorland, waking them up, stinging their eyes and making their faces glow.

Lucas hung back, letting Stephanie go ahead, as the cast and crew turned to greet her. He could almost see her confidence returning, blossoming beneath their warm welcome. She looked so beautiful and natural, completely in her element. This was where she was meant to be. She was a star, and Lucas felt almost overwhelmed by the strength of his feelings for her.

Stephanie turned around and smiled at him, catching his eye, and Lucas grinned back. Whatever had happened to them in the past was over. He and Stephanie had their whole futures ahead of them, and he couldn't wait to see where life would take them.

Isobel put the finishing touches to her outfit and checked her reflection in the hallway mirror. She'd lost weight – partly due to the stress of the ongoing divorce with Stuart, but also due to her new Parisian lifestyle. She was living on coffee and niçoise salad, and walking everywhere, eager to reacquaint herself with the iconic city.

Isobel had rented a small apartment in the seventh arrondissement on a short-term let, until she determined what her future would look like. From there, it was a short stroll across the Pont d'Alma to the Camille Andre offices, and she'd made the trip every day for the past month.

Today was a scorcher, and Isobel luxuriated in the heat, enjoying the feel of the sun on her bare arms, aware of the glances she was attracting from the French men as she passed by. It was a welcome boost to her ego, but Isobel wasn't looking for love right now. The experience with Stuart had bruised her. More than that, in fact, it had devastated her, making her question everything about their marriage. She found herself tossing and turning at night, unable to sleep, wondering if she'd somehow driven her husband into the arms of another woman. Deep down, Isobel knew that was ridiculous – nothing could excuse Stuart's behaviour, and blaming herself was ludicrous – but it played on her insecurities.

The story coming out in the national newspapers had been one of the worst times of her life. She'd been utterly humiliated, and for a few days had been a virtual prisoner in her own home whilst journalists knocked on the door, offering big-money deals to tell her side of the story. She'd be lying if she said she wasn't tempted.

Ironically, Stuart and the Goddess from Girona had broken up a couple of weeks later, and he'd been begging Isobel to come back, but she had steadfastly refused. Thanks to Camille, she had other options.

'Bonjour,' Isobel smiled brightly as she entered the Camille Andre building on Avenue Marceau, calling hello to Françoise on reception.

Isobel passed through the light, airy offices, which hummed with activity, looking at the sketches being drawn by the design team, and exclaiming over some material samples which had just arrived. She sat down at her desk, putting down her handbag – a 'Camille', naturally – and firing up her computer. Whilst she waited for her emails to come through, she pulled a sketch pad towards her and began doodling. She had an idea for a bridal gown that would be perfect for closing the next runway show . . .

'Isobel?'

René appeared beside her desk, and she smiled at him. 'Yes?'

'Camille would like to see you in her office, whenever you're free.'

'Of course,' Isobel replied. 'I'll be right there.' She

quickly added a few pencil lines to the sketch then stood up, smoothing down her dress. It was her own design, a light sundress in a bold, lemon-print fabric, which was part of her final collection for the boutique in Edinburgh. For now, Isobel had left it in the capable hands of the manager, Freya, giving her a substantial pay rise and free rein over which designers to stock.

Isobel made her way over to Camille's glass-fronted office, at the far end of the atelier. She couldn't help but think how different the company was from when she'd first interned there, almost a decade ago. Back then, Camille Andre had occupied one floor and were still relatively unknown outside the industry. Now, the company had taken over the entire building and was a household name, thanks to the 'Camille' bag. A lot had changed for both women over the past ten years.

'You wanted to see me?' Isobel asked, as Camille saw her coming and beckoned her in.

'Yes. Take a seat.' Camille smiled, gesturing to the Eames chair opposite her own. 'I wanted to catch up and see how everything's going. You're doing a wonderful job, and I hope you're enjoying being here.'

'Yes, I am. Every minute. I can't thank you enough for giving me a second chance.'

'It was the least I could do after . . . well, you know.'

Isobel smiled, smoothing over any awkwardness. Shortly after the show at the palacio, and its chaotic aftermath, Camille had got in touch with Isobel. The two women had had a heart-to-heart during a long telephone conversation, and Camille had offered Isobel a trial in a senior design position at Camille Andre. It meant a new start and a new city – exactly what Isobel needed.

She hadn't hesitated to say yes. Her house was being staked out by journalists, and Isobel simply packed a bag and took a taxi to the airport, eager to leave her old life with its memories of Stuart behind.

Paris was exactly what she needed. Who wouldn't adore living and working in the City of Light? Isobel had enjoyed brushing up on her French once more, and had made a lot of friends in the office, who invited her for after-work drinks and to the hottest parties in the capital. She couldn't deny that she was loving the glamour. But mostly she wanted to design and create. She was overflowing with new ideas and inspiration, and she was often the first to arrive in the office and the last to leave at night.

'In fact,' Camille continued, 'I was wondering how you'd feel about stepping in for me for a while . . . Possibly permanently . . . Taking charge of the atelier and leading the creative side for the new collection. You'd be fully credited of course,' Camille added hastily. 'We'd put out a press release. How does "interim creative director" sound?'

Isobel gasped. Her head was spinning as she tried to take in everything Camille had said. It was an incredible opportunity, but a huge responsibility at the same time. 'I don't understand . . . You're not retiring, surely – you're far too young.'

Camille sat back in her seat, looking levelly at Isobel, as Isobel tried to read her. Camille was fifty-one years old and had been in the business almost as long as Isobel had been alive. She was poised and elegant, driven and ambitious, and, knowing everything she had been through, Isobel had nothing but respect for her. Camille was a formidable force who had reached the very top of the fashion world. She had seen and done it all.

'It's time for me to take a step back – for now at least,' Camille said thoughtfully. 'Take life a little easier and make time for what matters. You're hungry and passionate, I can see it in your eyes. And you're incredibly talented. That's exactly what the company needs – new input; someone fresh to shake it up.'

'I mean . . .' Isobel blew out the air in her cheeks. 'It's a yes, of course. I'm honoured. But how long for?'

'I'm not sure yet.'

'But where are you going?'

Camille paused, a smile spreading across her face as she spoke. 'New York.'

Chapter 35

New York, August 2001

Nicolas was standing at the window of his corner office at American Athletics. It was on the thirty-seventh floor of the skyscraper on Madison Avenue, and the city was spread out beneath him. From here he could see Bryant Park and the Empire State Building, all the way from the East River to the World Trade Center towers in Lower Manhattan. He felt like a master of the universe up here, indisputable proof that he'd made it to the very top of his profession.

He'd been in this role for more than twenty years now and it still fired him up, giving him a reason to get out of bed in the morning. The collaboration with Camille Andre had been a smash hit, both critically and commercially. There had been rumours in the press of some backstage drama, but the details were scant and the speculation only served to fuel the public's interest. The old saying seemed to be true – there was no such thing as bad publicity – and the collection had sold out as soon as it hit the shelves.

Yet, despite his professional triumphs, Nicolas had been plagued by a feeling of restlessness in recent weeks. A sense that he'd achieved everything he could in the corporate world, and perhaps it was time to find fulfilment elsewhere. The confirmation that Lucas was his son had changed things for Nicolas. He'd always had a sense of being alone; relationships came and went, with no one staying permanently in his life. Now he had someone he could call family, a blood tie that could never be severed. Nicolas was finally realizing that there was more to life than work, and he was eager to make up for lost time.

Turning away from the panoramic view, Nicolas tried to shake himself out of his introspective mood. He had a meeting to chair in ten minutes, and it wouldn't do to be melancholy.

There was a knock at his door and his assistant, Erin, entered. Erin was a New Yorker born and bred. She didn't stand for bullshit, and she guarded Nicolas's diary like a pit bull. She'd worked for him for over a decade now, and he knew that her husband's name was Robert, that she had two teenage sons, that she lived in Brooklyn and liked to watch the Yankees play at the weekend. Sometimes Nicolas envied her that simple life.

'You have a message from Camille Fontaine,' she said, holding out a piece of paper. 'I wrote it down – she was very specific.'

Nicolas took the note and read it:

Meet me at sunset. I'll be at Bow Bridge.

Nicolas stared at the words for a moment. 'Erin, do I have any meetings this evening?'

'You have dinner at Nobu with a journalist from *Forbes* magazine.'

Nicolas looked thoughtful. 'Cancel it.'

The shadows were lengthening across Central Park. It had been a scorching summer's day, but the heat was finally fading, and New Yorkers were making the most of it. There were groups of friends relaxing on the grass with picnics, teenagers listening to music, virtuous joggers panting their way around the edge of the lake, dog walkers, roller bladers, and people from all walks of life enjoying this oasis in the heart of the city.

Camille was nervous. She had dressed carefully in a chambray shirt dress, with a cream belt that accentuated her slender waist, and had added a spritz of the latest Camille Andre fragrance. The whole effect was chic and feminine, the style she knew Nicolas loved.

Right now, she was standing in the centre of Bow Bridge, an elegant cast-iron structure dating back to the Victorian era, which spanned the lake from Cherry Hill to the Ramble. Rowing boats drifted on the water, which was bordered by sprawling trees, the skyscrapers of Fifth Avenue soaring beyond. The sky was streaked with colour as the sun began to set, deep hues of pink and purple blending into fiery orange and dazzling yellow. It was going to be a spectacular one tonight.

Camille had got there early, wanting to take a moment and calm her nerves, ensuring she was there before Nicolas arrived. *If* he arrived.

But she needn't have worried. A few minutes later, she saw him striding across the bridge towards her and her heart soared, her stomach doing somersaults. She felt like a teenager meeting her crush for a first date. He was wearing navy suit trousers with a tan belt, and a crisp white shirt with the sleeves rolled up in a concession to the heat. His look was formal, for the fashion industry, but Nicolas had always done things his own way, and Camille adored him for that.

After all these years she still loved him, more than she ever had. She realized now that he had always been the one. She should never have left him for Andre. They had gone their separate ways but always found their way back to one another, like two rivers flowing to the same sea. She just had to hope that he still felt the same. That it wasn't too late.

'Camille.' Nicolas smiled as he approached, a warmth in his eyes as they crinkled at the corners. He stepped forwards to embrace her, and for a moment his sudden proximity took her breath away. She wanted to hold him and never let go. But it was too soon for that. Her pulse was racing, and she forced herself to calm down and behave normally.

'I didn't know you were in town,' Nicolas said, and she could detect the faint frown denoting his confusion. She knew his features so well, understanding every fleeting expression, every slight nuance.

'Walk with me,' Camille said softly, taking his hand as they strolled southwards across the bridge. She wondered briefly what they must look like to onlookers. Was it obvious that she was madly in love, that something big was about to happen and she was moments away from taking the biggest risk of her life? Or did they simply look like an unremarkable, middle-aged couple, taking time out to catch up at the end of the working day?

They made small talk for a while about their mutual connections, about business, and the success of the collaboration. Camille filled him in on Isobel's progress at Camille Andre, adding, 'I want to take some time out. I'm thinking of naming a successor.'

'That's a big step. You are the brand – hell, it's literally your name above the door. And you've always been so hungry for success.'

'Things have changed. I'm not twenty-five, I don't need to prove myself. I'm starting to think there's more to life,' Camille said, unknowingly echoing Nicolas's thoughts from earlier.

'I feel that too,' Nicolas nodded. 'You can't take it with you, isn't that what they say? I want to travel to distant places, see the world, have new experiences . . . fall in love all over again.'

He looked intently at Camille, and her stomach flipped as she tried to read what he was saying. Did he mean he was ready for solo adventures, to make a fresh start and get away from the life he knew? To meet someone new? Or were they on the same page, finally contemplating a future together with nothing to stand in their way?

'How's Lucas?' Nicolas asked, before Camille had the chance to question him.

'Madly in love with Stephanie,' she beamed. 'They've been through a lot, but they're good for one another.'

'He talks about her often. It sounds serious.' Camille looked surprised, and Nicolas explained, 'We speak on the phone – most days, in fact. It was a little strange at first, but I think we're both enjoying building the connection. We're getting to know one another again and figuring out how to navigate the future.'

'I'm glad,' Camille said, with genuine feeling.

'The past is in the past,' Nicolas said gently. 'Whatever mistakes were made, we can't change them. We can only move forward.'

'You've always been the best thing that ever happened to me,' Camille said, emotion in her voice now. 'I was just too selfish to see it.'

'Camille—'

'No, let me finish. I need to say this. I could never have got through these past few months without you. I couldn't have got through the past thirty years without you. I shouldn't have reacted as I did when you proposed, and I've been haunted by what you said to me on the yacht in Mallorca, about you not wanting just a small part of me.'

'I told you a long time ago – too long ago to even think about, when we were both young and foolish and didn't have lines on our faces or any grey hairs – that I would always be there for you. I meant it. I still do.'

'Nicolas, I've been a fool. All those years with Andre, I should never have . . . You were always there for me. My guiding star. The love of my life.' Camille paused, hearing the weight of those words, giving Nicolas time to take them in. 'I want you to have all of me, my heart, *and* my soul. Nicolas. I love you, more than I ever realized.'

'I love you too, Camille. But you know that already. Always have, always will.'

The sun had dipped below the horizon, but its influence could still be seen as it lit up the sky in spectacular colours, from thick velvety blue to blushing rose to burnished gold. The skyscrapers were silhouetted dramatically against the brilliant display, shadows of the grand sycamore trees reflected on the water, as a waxing moon rose in the heavens. Memories flooded back to Camille of the sunsets they'd seen together over the years – from Montmartre in Paris when they were both penniless students, to the ones over the paradise island off the Mallorcan coast that they'd visited on the yacht just a few months ago. But none had been as perfect as this one.

Camille stopped walking and turned to Nicolas. They had reached Bethesda Terrace, with its magnificent fountain. People were sitting on the low stone wall, dipping their hands in the cooling water, enjoying the light spray of mist as the water spilled over the stone basins. It was an idyllic clash of the ordinary and the extraordinary.

'Marry me, Nicolas,' Camille said. 'You said you'd never ask me again, so now I'm asking you. I want to spend the rest of my life with you. Marry me.'

Nicolas swept her up in his arms, kissing her softly at first but growing in passion, neither of them caring who might be watching. There was a fizzing in her belly, sparks shooting through her veins, and a deep pulse of desire that she couldn't hold back. Nicolas slowly pulled away and gazed deep into her eyes, and she saw the love reflected there.

Then he lifted her into the air and swung her around joyfully and Camille threw her head back, laughing, her head spinning as the heavens whirled above her, before he gently brought her feet back to earth.

'Yes, Camille,' he whispered. 'Yes. There could only be one answer.'

Meet Me at Sunset

The sky was growing dark, the myriad colours fading into blackness as pinprick stars emerged scattered across the inky night sky. Tomorrow was a new day, but right now they had their glorious sunset, one which seemed to stretch into forever.

Acknowledgements

Firstly, I would like to thank each and every one of you who has read and reviewed my books – in any of its forms. Without you, none of this would be happening. I never take this for granted and I'm so grateful to you all.

Steve, my husband (getting used to calling you that now!), for having total confidence in my capabilities – even when I doubt myself. Your love and support mean everything to me. And as I always say, your patience knows no bounds!

To my wonderful family and friends – your encouragement, support and enthusiasm for each new book is humbling. Thank you.

To Kerr MacRae, for approaching me initially about writing the book – and for all your support along the way.

Kate Bradley, Editor extraordinaire! Please do not edit that out Kate as it is meant sincerely. You are one in a million. Your talent is second to none. You truly 'get' what I am trying to achieve. I love working with you.

Elizabeth Dawson and Maddy Marshall for their publicity and marketing expertise, and Claire Ward for designing the fabulous covers of all my books.

Finally, my grateful thanks to the whole team at HarperCollins for all you do for me and for publishing my books.

Love Carol xxx

Follow Carol Kirkwood

Join Carol online to hear the latest news about her upcoming books as well as exclusive access to content and competitions!

- @OfficialCarolKirkwood
- @carolkirkwood
- smarturl.it/CarolKirkwood-newsletter